TICKET TO OREGON

TICKET TO OREGON

A THREE GENERATIONAL SAGA

Edward T. Frye

ARPress
45 Dan Road Suite 5
Canton MA 02021

Hotline: 1(888) 821-0229
Fax: 1(508) 545-7580

Ordering Information:
Quantity sales. Special discounts are available on quantity purchases by corporations, associations, and others. For details, contact the publisher at the address above.

Printed in the United States of America.

ISBN-13:   Paperback   979-8-89330-303-2

Library of Congress Control Number: 2024900552

TABLE OF CONTENTS

Acknowledgements

Ino longer watch those Hollywood award shows. Just cannot abide the sappy, obligatory acceptance speeches. Often in or near tears the humbled recipient rattles off the legions of heretofore unknowns who made the whole thing possible. Year after year, gala after gala, winner after winner, it is always the same thing. Sure such creative people could find a better way.

But I can't, and now I find myself in a similar situation.

The words and stories in Ticket To Oregon are my own. A few seminal ideas came from others. Those who believe that a writer simply sits at a computer and grinds out a novel are unaware of the dependence on quality research and the uses of friends and family.

Herewith I thank profusely those who helped make this book possible. I am aware that most readers will not know these folks, or, in all candor, care very much. But I do, and I do.

I required some boots-on-the-ground information from some people, whom I had never met before this undertaking. I needed help with the role of timbering in Oregon, the lifestyles of a hundred years of western settlers, details on Vietnam firefights, the history and geography of north central Oregon, the smaller details of saloon-keeping, and so forth. I acquired this information from folks I now call friends. Please review them through this lens: no friends, no Ticket To Oregon.

I start with Oregonians, Pete and Darlene Barber served dinner for my wife and me – complete and utter strangers. Our chatter resulted in several story ideas and topics found throughout this book. Pete is a retired executive of Mt. Fir Lumber Company; he provided the "wood" background. Rod Woodside, a Maupin businessman willingly walked away from his business to offer hours of deep background on the both the Oregon landscape and old stories from the past. In my mind, Rod is the quintessential characterization of the New West.

Diane Barber, of a local chamber of commerce, added more information and then steered me to others. That included Sarah Hennessey, a local librarian, who traded a copy of Fools and Children for one of Chaff In The Wind, a wonderful and personalized history of the setting of this book.

Ah, but for friends! John Barnowski served up the details for the chapter on Vietnam. John, amalgamated into two roles, is an American hero. Beverly Connors, a family friend, read and edited an early cut of the text. So did Stuart Gansell, a hawk-eyed reviewer of both Fools and Children.

Scott Hohe, bartender of The Subway Café in Harrisburg, allowed me to design Ticket's Bar according to the specs in his own establishment. A fellow racquetball player, Pat McLane, was interested enough in my work to give me at least two story ideas.

My wife, Doris, was extraordinary in her support and idea provision for character development. Her creative edge is revealed throughout the book.

"Oh, dear, I know I've missed someone." That's how the celebrities cover their inadvertent omissions. Guess I'll use that line here.

PROLOGUE

Just The Ticket
2008

From my fourth-story hotel window, the squat, flat-roofed cube seemed to have sprouted up out of the gravel and weeds surrounding it. The reflection of its own neon sign and the ambient glow of a single streetlight washed its front to an eerie pink and green. The red and green fluorescent sign vertically spelled out BAR, its bottom forming a lighted arrow pointing to the solid door. The sign sputtered spastically, as if gasping for enough breath to continue.

Decidedly, this blanched wooden box was on the wrong side of the tracks, which in fact, ran past its front door, separated only by a wide concrete apron. It featured that worn door and one small window on the right. The hesitating neon did its job though; it announced just what I was seeking. I assured myself that it wasn't a mirage.

I was tired and road-beaten, so the rugged bar looked good enough, if not pretty. It would have beer, and I needed a beer. It also had convenience going for it.

At the time, I was traveling and speaking across most of the United States. This day I was in Cordell, Oregon, to do a morning-only gig. I live in Pennsylvania, so I had spent most of the day in two airplanes and a rental car. I had flown to Portland, then driven back east, through the Cascade Gorge of The Columbia River, and down the state road to the small town. I had left the Keystone State in the dark, and I arrived in Cordell in the dark – the life of a mole.

Five minutes later I entered the bar. It wasn't busy. I was the only patron, though the hour was not particularly late or the weather discouraging. Just I and the barkeep. A little creepy for a second or so.

The man was mopping a shiny birds eye maple floor. The long, wide planking ran from front to back, tying the room to a distinctive, but darker, wooden bar. The fellow had his back to me as he swung the mop back and forth at the rear of the barroom.

"Am I too late for a beer?" I asked. "Are you still open?"

"I sell beer. I'm open as long as anyone is buying beer. There're some bottles there," he said, motioning to a glass-fronted cooler on the right wall. "If you want a draft, just go behind the bar and draw yourself one. The glasses are right under the taps. Just give me a second here, and I'll be finished with this mop." He bent back to his task.

I looked at the cooler and saw nothing special. Not being shy, I stepped behind the bar, found a glass, and drew myself some cold relaxant.

I sat down at a round table centered in the little room. While the gray-haired gent deposited his bucket and mop in a closet marked "Private," I took account of my surroundings.

Stark, to say the least. The room was no more than twenty feet wide and thirty feet deep. The walls and wood-slat ceiling were mental institution green, faded, and thin, with another shade of green showing through. Three translucent glass globes hung from the ceiling on short metal rods, their low-wattage bulbs producing yellowish light. The place had the bedraggled look and stale beer odor of a long-time watering hole.

The five red-vinyl-topped chrome-legged stools nestling up against the bar bled horsehair stuffing. Maybe they were from the fifties, but they were the newest pieces in the place. Five scarred tables of different sizes dotted the floor; two obviously intended to accommodate card games. Mostly though, there was open floor space.

The freshly mopped floor looked strangely luxurious and out of place with everything except the bar itself, an ornately two-stained wooden creation running fifteen or more feet down the left side of the room. All that wood was broken only by a polished brass foot rail. A mirror, framed by filigreed wood, ran almost as far as the bar, reflecting the requisite liquor bottles and a dozen fancy glasses. It was a place of striking contrast, the wood belittling its surrounding dinginess, like artwork stored in an attic.

A hand-painted sign announcing "Draughts – 15 Cents" hung near the mirror. The only other art in the place was on the right wall: side-by-side sepia photos of two men I assumed were former proprietors. At the far end of the mirror was a kitchenette-type arrangement with a metal stovetop and smallish refrigerator. Then a door that probably led to the basement.

The six-pack cooler hugged the right wall. The men's room, with limited clearance, was tucked under the upper half of a broken stairway. The ladies' room was an obvious later addition on the back wall, along with an exterior door topped with an exit sign.

On the corner stairway an old mongrel-imitating-a-retriever was plopped on the landing. That dog had noted my arrival by raising his head, but he quickly returned to his original position. No tail-wagging, no bark, no sniffing out a stranger.

And then there was the barkeep, tall and somewhat emaciated. His gray hair was buzz-cut short, but full. Where the gray ended, the man's face and wattled neck were about the color of the bar's exterior. I was sure the thin, wiry guy was older than I, but putting an age on him was difficult. Probably seventy or so I decided.

Certainly not feeble. He was pushing that mop around with the rhythm and efficiency of a Seabee. He wore a checkered, long-sleeved, collared sport shirt, Sears Roebuck style, with green Dickies. He appeared tidy enough, clean-shaven, shirttail tucked in, and fresh-looking, especially for the hour of the day.

He slid past me on his way to the bar and asked if I wanted another beer.

"I do."

"Want company, or do you want to be left alone?" he asked.

"Oh, I'll take company. I've been alone all day." Those with whom one shares a pressurized aluminum tube at 36,000 feet do not qualify as company.

I chose a not-too-creative start to the conversation. "Is it going to snow tomorrow? The lady at the hotel said it was going to snow or ice by noon."

"Not goin' to snow or ice tomorrow," an assertion made with extreme confidence.

"I hope you're right. I'm supposed to fly in the afternoon."

"Don' worry about it," he assured me. "My ribs say no water, frozen or otherwise. Seldom wrong. If they ache or go numb, then some bad weather. Better than the weather gal on TV. Nothing tonight.

"Your ribs?" I inquired.

"Yeah, I have an old injury here in my chest," he said, pointing to somewhere just opposite his heart.

"Well, I hope your ribs are right, because I want to get back to PA tomorrow."

"I'll get you a beer, and some tea for myself."

"No beer?" I asked when he returned.

"Barkeeps have to watch the beer. Occupational hazard. I usually have tea before I go upstairs. Besides, I snore after a beer or two, and Grover hates that."

"Grover?"

"That mutt snoozing over there. He sleeps with me. Wakes me up if I snore. Never could decide if it bothers him or scares him."

Grover, up there on the landing, heard his name, opened his top eye, determined this was not important, and went back to sleep.

"So, you own this bar?" I asked.

"Yep, for thirty-six years now. Took it over from my father in 1972. He took it over from his father in 1937. This bar has been here since 1903. Never closed in all that time. Ticket's has been here through two world wars and those after them, Prohibition, the Depression, the recession, the booms, the bubbles, and the heartaches. Ticket's was one of the first establishments in Cordell.

"Ticket's?" I repeated. "That's the name of this place?"

"Always has been. Lots of people don't know that anymore 'cause the sign outside doesn't say so. Most call it 'the bar.' Used to have a sign though. Said 'Tickets.' My grandpa tore it down – well, actually, a chinook blew it down, and he didn't replace it."

"So this bar has been in your family for, what – a hundred years?"

"Uh-huh," he nodded. "I'm the last, though. When I'm gone, so is Ticket's. I have no kids –never married – but it doesn't matter. No one can make a living off this bar anymore. I live upstairs, but when I die, that's it. If a thing can't go on, it stops. No real loss, I guess."

For a moment, the barkeep looked at himself in the mirror behind the bar; then re-focused. "My name is Owen Ticket. Who are you, and what brings you to Cordell?"

"Ed Frye. Pennsylvania. I speak for a living, and tomorrow I'm speaking to some school people from around the area. South of here, in Blaspher."

"Yeah, just up the river. What do you talk about?"

"Well," I said, "I talk about lots of things, mostly about school leadership. What works, and what doesn't. But, honestly, I tell stories more than anything. I tell tales and examples about my experiences, and try to promote discussion about running organizations. I'm just a story-teller in a three-piece suit."

Owen's eyes brightened. "You tell stories for a living? Are you telling me that you're a professional story-teller? People pay you to tell stories?"

"Yep," I chuckled. "Funny way to make a living, huh? But, people keep asking for them. I like to think they learn something from my tales, maybe apply that stuff to their own situations. It's a living."

"Always a way, I guess," Owen said, shaking his head. "In the bar business you get paid to hear stories, not tell them."

Silence again. Then Owen said, "Do you have time to tell me one of your stories? You know, I live in this place. I don't go anywhere. This is my world. Life comes to me, I don't go to life. I enjoy stories from anyone, but especially someone on the other side of Cordell."

"Owen, barkeeps accumulate stories, I know that. Aren't you bartenders really just priests without collars? Now you want more?"

"Oh, yeah, lots of stories," he acknowledged. "Bars are great places for stories. Stuff gets told in a bar. Some people like stories, some don't -- probably depends on the story, and more likely, the storyteller. Now my grandfather especially, but my dad, too, were both storytellers. I'd like to think I tell them the way those two could; probably can't. Sometimes, too, you can't enjoy a good story if you don't know something about the people in them. Makes storytelling dicey."

I nodded. "No kidding. There's a real trick to that. I've been practicing it all my life."

"Well," Owen said, "let's see if you're any good at it. Let me get you another beer – no charge – and you tell me a story."

I was struck with a sudden inspiration. In my line of work, one is always looking for another story. "Owen, I'll make you a deal. We'll trade stories. Let's see who can top the other."

"Deal." Owen walked around the bar to draw me another draft and pour himself some hot water.

"Owen, here's what we do," I continued. "Our stories have to be about real people and real events – about you, your family, this bar, this town, that sort of thing. No jokes, no 'Three guys walk into a bar' stuff.' Every story has to be somehow connected to the one just told. If I tell a story about girls, you have to, get it?"

"Sure."

"We'll flip a coin. Loser goes first."

I won the flip.

CHAPTER ONE

Gus Had A Hand In It

Owen scratched his chin and gazed about, rummaging around in his mind for a few seconds. "I'm guessing you want something a bit raucous —something from an old Wild West bar."

"Raucous?" I blurted, immediately sorry I said it.

"What's wrong? You think I don't know any big words? You're not thinking I'm just some old, ignorant saloonkeeper, are you? He paused for a long second, and then he smiled. "I can read, too.

How about I tell you about the only gunfire we ever had in all the years here, from 1903 'till now? You're not going to shoot me tonight, are you?"

"No."

"Nor I you. So the streak remains intact. Still the only gunplay Ticket's has ever hosted."

"Sounds like just the ticket." Oh, man, I thought, I did it again. I hadn't intended any pun when I said it, but we both rolled our eyes. Owen waved that off and started our first tale.

"Been a lot of cards played in this bar," he began. "Poker, mainly, but blackjack and rummy were popular for a spell. In the old days Ticket's was a popular place – steady business every night, shoulder-to-shoulder on some. Now these poker games could become pretty hotly contested. Typically, they were penny ante games as our regular customers didn't arrive with very deep pockets. No violence though; people knew each other, and arguments were mostly in good sport.

But that all changed on one February night, 1936. A flare-up at that table over there brought out Drew Gephart's little .22 revolver. My grandfather, Noah Ticket, still owned the place, but Brush was behind the bar that evening.

Many a man carried a weapon in those days — a remnant of the Old West, so there was nothing strange about Drew toting one. On any given night probably four or five customers would have pistols in their pockets. But nobody was foolish enough to go waving a gun around in here.

Anyway, Gus Driver and Drew Gephart were two of five friends playing poker. Now, Gus was a cheater, always was, and everyone knew it. He cheated mostly because he could. It was more about the scam and less about the money with him. He just enjoyed trickery. He had an arsenal of strategies, some better than others.

Catching him at it was difficult and had become a challenge to other players. Usually people just joked or complained about it. If confronted, Gus would laugh off the accusations and declare himself just lucky. Or, he'd claim it was his first time ever and gamely push the little pot over to the plaintiff. Gus was one of those guys who got along with a little charm and a lot of deceit.

This night, however, the pot got a little bigger than normal, and the game a bit more intense than usual. Drew Gebhart hadn't been doing well all night. He'd been studying Gus Driver very closely. When he finally caught him, the evidence was pretty overwhelming.

What happened was Gus took this particularly large pot, flopping four jacks. Immediately, Drew laid down two pairs, with a jack in the middle. Now there were five jacks on the table, two of them diamonds.

Everyone just stared for a moment. Drew catapulted out of his chair, screaming obscenities at Gus, who, by all accounts, was already looking sheepish. Just that quick, Drew pulled out his Smith and Wesson snub nose, waved it at Gus, and searched for the trigger. Gus started out of his chair, throwing one arm in front of his chest and the other out to slow Drew down. 'Wait! Wait!'

Drew fired off two rounds. The first one missed everything but the wall behind Gus. Before the second shot hit the wall, it tore right through the palm of Gus' extended hand.

Of course, the other three players scattered. At the first shot at least four other pistols appeared around the room. Our 'associates' were getting ready to drop Drew if he turned on them. He didn't though; his argument was with Gus.

Brush was a large black man who'd come into the bar one day for a beer and never really left. He tended bar for all three of us Tickets. Everyone knew and respected Brush for the no-nonsense guy he was. They knew he said what he meant and meant what he said. Brush was a gentle giant, but no one chose to challenge his command of the bar.

At the first shot Brush swept his arm under the bar and snatched the shotgun racked there. Noah had bought our Browning Auto-Five for just such moments. That old twelve-gauge is still over there. My grandfather had sawed off the barrel some and shaved down the stock a bit, so it was a nimble and dangerous thing.

Brush held it aloft and chambered the first of three shells in its magazine. That sound is sobering. The pump action makes an altogether distinctive, mechanical 'ka-shnnk' as well-oiled metal moves on metal, first the parts sliding back against themselves and then forward to engage the shell. There's no sound like it, and no way to convey it accurately. But anyone at all familiar with guns recognizes it. If you are at its front end, your focus of attention narrows decidedly. Total silence in an instant.

"I know the sound," I interjected.

"Well, anyway," Owen continued, "everyone in Tickets looked at the scattergun. Time stopped. 'Now,' Brush said in his deep, steady voice, 'let's slow this down. Drew, holster that weapon. See to Gus,' he instructed the onlookers. Other poker players moved back to the table and began to minister to Gus' bloody hand.

Gus was yelping in pain and hollering at Drew. 'Why'd you shoot me, you durned fool? It's only a card game! You could've had the pot!'

Drew, meanwhile, had shoved the gun back in his jacket and was looking guilty and righteous at the same time. 'I wasn't really aiming at ya! I just wanted to get close with a round or two, 'cause of your damn cheating. If I had wanted to hit you, I wouldn't have missed that big belly or ugly face from less than five feet. But you had to stick out your hand! Actually, you hit my bullet with your hand. This is all your fault.'

"That little speech actually made some sense to our beer drinkers. Probably kept Drew from disgrace.

Drew spun about the room, unable to look at Gus, beseeching others for good news in a bad situation. 'Is he okay? How bad is it? Is he goin' to live?'

"Gus was holding his bleeding hand up above his heart. He was hurting, and he was getting a little dizzy. He needed medical attention.

Lucky for everyone – Gus, Drew, Noah – Doc Rider was a Ticket's regular. According to some folks, too much of a regular. I say, 'lucky' because nobody wanted the authorities involved. Calling in the county sheriff was going to make problems for everyone. Drew would go to jail for attempted homicide or something, Gus would be publicly humiliated, and Ticket's might lose our license. The reliable and discreet Doc Rider could squelch any such firestorms.

Doc wasn't in the house that night, so two muleskinners loaded Gus into Skinny Sam's Plymouth and delivered him to Doc's office, the front rooms of his old Victorian. Doc rolled out of bed and tended to Gus. He, of course, had seen lots of gun injuries as a physician in the Big War.

Doc stopped the bleeding, cleaned the wound, sewed and bandaged Gus, and gave him some sulfa drugs. Only then did he ask the others for the story. He got out the appropriate medical folder and listed the incident as an 'industrial accident.' That was Doc's sense of humor.

And so it was. Few of those present talked about the shooting. Their wives already had serious reservations about their husbands and barrooms. It never became a big story across town. Just a little altercation between friends.

Gus healed. But his hand was never the same. Three of his fingers were mostly numb and stiff, just about unusable. He could slide things about with that hand, and he could hold a fork. He'd resume playing poker again, but his new disability discouraged any attempt at cheating. Just not agile enough with that hand. From then on, he lost any real zest for the game. He and Drew remained friends. They played lots of cards after that incident. I guess Gus knew who was to blame for what.

Ever after, we Tickets have used Gus' misfortune as a cautionary tale for card sharks. 'A Smith and Wesson beats five jacks every time.'

"Now, look over there behind that table. You see the two bullet holes there, behind the table? The one on the left still holds the first shot. The second shot didn't stick. Lost to the world it is. We never patched those holes. Add character to the place, don't you think?"

"Oh, yeah, they certainly do, I agreed. "Great story, Owen! The Wild West days, huh? Only later."

"This town was the Wild West well into the 1900s, he answered. "Well into the forties Cordell was a man's town – guns, women, rustling, horses, cattle, sheep, water rights, all of it."

"I'll want more on that later," I said, making myself a mental note to revisit such topics. "You're a real storyteller. I don't think I can match that."

"Well, you're gonna try," Owen retorted. "I'm ready."

"Okay, but first, a few questions." I asked a few; Owen answered them. We discussed guns for a few minutes.

"Let's get to it," he said when all that tapered off.

According to the rules I'd set, my story needed to be somehow related to his. So I figured I ought to do one involving a gun, or violence of some kind.

I chose the night I looked down the barrel of a shotgun being waved about by a nut-case I knew would not hesitate to use it. Being only about nineteen years old at the time, it was a rather vivid moment, one I have never forgotten. Owen was certainly correct about how one's reality is suddenly changed by being on the wrong side of that "ka-shnnk." It is a good story, especially since I wasn't shot that night, and I told it pretty well, having had some practice with it.

"It's almost eleven o'clock, Owen. Do we have time for another round?"

"I got nowhere else to be. When you leave, Grover and I just go up to bed. Eleven o'clock, twelve o'clock, what's the difference to us? I open in the morning anytime I choose. Your choice."

"Let's do it. I'm leaving tomorrow afternoon. If I want another story, I need to get it now."

"Okay," Owen agreed. "Since we're talking about guns, how about I tell you about the other time they made an appearance in this bar?"

"Whoa, you said in the other story that it was the only gunfire in Ticket's."

"Yep, so I did," Owen said, looking at me as if I were somehow missing the point. "I told of the only shooting we ever had in here. I didn't say it was the only time a gun ever presented itself."

"So, guns, but no shooting?" I finally got Owen's drift here.

"Here's the story." Owen launched into the tale.

"You certainly know that the early railroads were prime targets for train robbers and thieves.

Originally, the preferred method was to blow a breach in the tracks or destroy a bridge to stop the train. You've seen that in the movies. Later on, thieves found it was easier to attack trains in the rail yards at night. Later still, especially after automobiles arrived, the scalawags would board a slow-moving train, climb into a box-car, and throw goods onto an adjacent road so an accomplice in a truck could retrieve them.

Of course the railroads fought such crime in any way they could. In the late 1800s they hired Pinkertons to guard the trains and patrol the yards. Later on, they created their own police force. Here in the west they were called 'special agents,' and they carried the full authority of regular lawmen.

Neither the Pinkertons nor these agents enjoyed popularity or respect from the citizenry. Some of these special agents were really full of themselves. They were arrogant, bullish. In fact, they were called railroad bulls. Self-righteous little men with big guns and impervious discretion about when to use them.

Westerners never cottoned to rules, rule makers, or rule enforcers, so lawmen were not held in particularly high regard. In truth, there was a certain contempt for authority. Rather, folks admired the pluck of outlaws. Guys like Butch Cassidy and the Sundance Kid were heroes, even while they were forcibly stopping trains and submitting men, women, and children to utter terror. The same held through at least the 1940s -- Bonnie and Clyde, John Dillinger, Baby Face Nelson, Al Capone. People were more interested in them than the lawmen they were outwitting.

Train cops were usually seen as annoyances to the 'common guy' just trying to get by, the Box-car Willies who couldn't afford a ticket, the underprivileged, and certainly the con men and robbers."

Owen stopped, seemingly to reflect on what he just said.

"Of course, over time, this low respect for police began to change. I believe the tide may have turned in 1921 after Special Agent J. 'Buck' Phillips was shot and killed in Portland while attempting to arrest several boxcar pirates. When Agent Phillips and his partner accosted the thieves, Phillips was mortally wounded in the ensuing gunfight. The suspects were later arrested and the shooter hanged.

In the lurid press that followed, the public learned that Agent Phillips had a wife and child. His brother had also been shot and killed in the line of duty four years previously. Buck was portrayed as a decent man, 'one of us regular folk' who died just doing his job. A peacekeeper, just like those sons and fathers who'd fought in the big war. Now there was this human face on a badge. Maybe he was a hero after all.

I mention all this so that you recognize the ambivalent attitude many had toward the railroad police in the twenties. It figures into my story, and explains why no one in Ticket's at the time just naturally jumped to help the arrest of two boxcar thieves.

Sometime in 1920, two special agents strutted into Ticket's. One had a coach gun hanging from the end of his arm, and the other had a big lump under his open coat."

Owen paused and asked me, "You know what a coach gun is, right?"

"Yes I do," I said proudly. "It's a short, double-barreled shotgun. It was the stagecoach driver's weapon of choice. Still available today."

Owen couldn't improve on that. "Correct. So, this agent is swinging a coach gun against his leg, and that pretty much defined him, his pal, and his intent. He loudly announced that they were here to arrest two suspects in a recent boxcar theft.

There were perhaps a dozen patrons, all locals. Two of them were from a small ranch, a few miles upstream. These brothers were just human wreckage. Actually, the whole family was. Lazy, thieving liars and sloths, they all were. But we serve all kinds here.

Noah's quick scan of the room led him immediately to these two. All chatter and two card games suspended. Coach Gun honed in on the two brothers and headed over to their card game. The brothers stood up. Whatever their plans, flight or fight, no one ever knew, because Paws got involved.

Ticket's has always had a dog, sometimes two at a time. Noah owned the first, Paws, who set the standard for every other Ticket dog. He was good company. He was a one-man, fiercely loyal mix of shepherd and something else that was large. He slept on that staircase landing all day, mingling with customers for attention and snacks.

But he could be ferocious, a junkyard dog. If things were out of whack somehow, like loud arguments, pushing or shoving, or sounds of malice, he'd growl and bare his teeth. If he stood up, someone was headed for trouble. 'Let sleeping dogs lie,' as they say. All the regulars knew this, and Paws' presence kept things in check around the bar.

No growling or baring of teeth this night, however. Paws saw those two agents, saw the scattergun, and sensed the tension, the brewing of something bad. He bounded off that landing and was on that agent in a heartbeat. Closed his big teeth on that agent's gun arm and whipped him sideways.

Man, mongrel, and gun all hit the floor. Paws was the only one to get up, snarling and hovering over the agent's prone body. The other agent started over, reaching for his weapon. Someone stopped him before he could do either. 'That dog will kill you,' someone said. 'If he doesn't, Noah will.'

'Stop, Paws!' Noah commanded. Paws backed off a step or two and, by choice or by chance, straddled the coach gun with all four legs. (There was a great deal of later discussion about his intent there.) He stood still and glared, teeth bared, but no growl, as the agent struggled up, analyzing his arm.

'He bit me! I'm bleeding!' the agent cried. 'He's on my gun. Get him out of here!'

Now four men were squared off, with the dog in the middle, waiting for direction. Like it or not, Noah knew the next move was his. In the few seconds he used to think it through, the two brothers started telling everyone that they weren't any train robbers. The agents had the wrong suspects. They were pleading their case, but guardedly; there was no value in getting Paws going again."

"Sounds like a Mexican standoff," I said.

"That's exactly what it was. Noah looked around the room again and weighed the dangers to his customers, himself, and his bar. He decided there wasn't going to be any shooting in his bar.

No arrests either. The railroad had no business in his business. If they wanted to capture someone, fine and dandy, but not in Ticket's.

Noah strode over to the standoff. 'Everyone stop! Now, let's get sure no one gets hurt. What are you fools thinking, coming in here, waving a weapon? Paws, stay.' He did, right over that shotgun.

'We aim to arrest these two,' offered the second agent. 'We're going to do our duty.'

'Be that as it may, it won't be in here,' Noah seethed.

The brothers started up again, thinking they might have just found Jesus. 'Throw 'em out, Noah,' they urged. 'They got the wrong guys. We ain't robbed no train. No one is going to arrest us for something we didn't do.'

'Well, that isn't for me to decide,' said Noah. 'But I'll tell you what is. There won't be any gunfire or handcuffs in Ticket's tonight.'

Noah took the route of Solomon. He would split the baby in half. 'Here's what is going to happen.' He nodded at the brothers. 'You two walk slowly out that back door – if you run, Paws will eat you alive. 'Once out, you run, drive off, or give up.

You bulls wait with Paws for a minute or so. Then you get your shotgun back, and you go out the same door you came in. If you want these two, go find them. Anyone have a problem with that? If so, just tell Paws there. Take your chances and go for that gun.'

And that is exactly how it went – brothers out the back, agents out the front."

"So, were these two the robbers?" I asked.

"Oh, sure. Cops got them the next day and convicted them. But, that isn't the point of the story, is it?"

"Nope. Just wanted the ending."

"Well, the real ending is the fact that Noah wasn't going to allow his bar to become either a haven for thieves or a trap for the suspected."

"Yeah, yeah, I get it," I conceded the point. "Good story. Dogs, huh? Paws the Wonder Dog!"

I looked up to the landing where Grover camped. He had slept through the whole story. "How does this guy live up to the Paws tradition?"

"Old Grover? Now there's a dog. I've had him here for sixteen years. Long time for a big dog. I'll tell you a quick dog story, about Grover and his mother."

"Well, son of a bitch!" I said. This time, catching the intended pun, Owen rewarded me with a slight smile.

"My dad and I counted up six Ticket dogs from over the years; he didn't know Grover, who makes seven. Most of them are buried out back. My mother had one cremated, placed in an urn and put on her mantle. I've had three dogs here myself. Every one of them -- I mean all seven -- has claimed that landing. Grover is just like every dog before him, better than some."

"I thought dogs weren't allowed in restaurants and bars," I said, "except the seeing-eye ones."

"Yeah, that's pretty much true here in Oregon; law's a little iffy on it. But we never worried about it. We always reasoned that the dog isn't actually in the bar. The dog is between floors, halfway between the beer and the bedroom. Who's to say? Actually, no inspector ever challenged us on it.

Anyway, a beautiful black-and-brindle mixed breed named Chloe was Grover's mother. I found her one winter day in ninety-two. Well, found her or rescued her."

A bemused look crossed Owen's face as he remembered the meeting of a man and his dog. "I left to bar one Monday morning to take the weekend receipts to the bank. I looked up the tracks and there I see just a pitiful sight. This scraggy, dirty, worn-out, hungry, thirsty, dead-on-her-feet dog is wobbling down toward town. She was just about ready to fall over. She was just skin and bones, except for a swollen tummy. I figured at first that was because of starvation. Turns out she was pregnant.

She was soon going to be a goner, she was in such bad shape. I didn't know if she came in on a train, was a stray from over in town, or was dumped by some disappointed hunter. I did know that she had been pretty once."

Owen stopped again, reflecting again. "She was stumbling down toward me. She stopped for a moment and looked at me. I could see in her eyes that she gave up at that moment. She decided she could run nowhere else, she'd go no further. She was going to let me decide what was going to happen next. I know that might sound silly, but I tell you, I could see all of that in those big, sad, bewildered eyes. She just sat down on a railroad tie and waited for me to do what I was going to do.

I walked up to her, hands spread open-palmed, and said gentle things to her. I let her smell my hands and then gently petted her head. She whimpered. I scooped her up with both arms. She stank terribly.

I gave her some water. She refused food. In the cellar sink I gave her a bath, well, two baths, actually, to get the smell off her. She sat there quietly, not moving a muscle. I wrapped her in towels and laid her on the landing to dry. She looked at me; I looked at her. That was it. She fell deeply asleep; I went to the bank. She was now my dog, and we both knew it. I named her Chloe, after a girl I knew from school.

Well, to make a long story short, Chloe never really ever left that landing. She was like Brush in that regard. She eventually ate; she got stronger, she had her litter a few weeks later. I gave three pups to good homes and kept Grover. Now I had two dogs, mother and son. And my regulars took right to them, offering up pats and treats.

We really didn't need a watchdog, but Chloe was certainly that. Just as Paws, Chloe could be nasty. She wouldn't abide loud arguments. If folks became strident, Chloe would start growling. She'd stand up and stare hard at the growing turmoil. If it seemed to be getting worse, she would take a step or two down the stairs, giving everyone fair warning. That stopped many a confrontation. If she had to complete her trip down the stairway, everyone knew she would not be progressing kindly across the barroom."

"So, whatever happened to Chloe?" I asked.

"She had a cataract problem," replied Owen. "Chloe was a healthy dog, once I got her back to speed. But, after I first brought her in, I took her to see a vet. He confirmed that she was mostly healthy, about four years old, certainly pregnant, and, unfortunately, had the beginnings of cataracts in both eyes. About two years later Chloe began losing her sight. I could tell because she started walking into things, especially those I just moved. She didn't stray as far from the building when I put her out back to do her business.

She finally went totally blind. Some said I should put her down. But you should have seen that dog. Blind or not, she could negotiate her way around this place without incident. She knew where the steps and landing were, she knew where Grover was, and she could migrate over to the bar for water, food, or attention.

She knew when someone entered the bar. Uncanny. She had this way of ambling about so that she didn't seem to hit her nose or body into anything very hard. She'd sort of brush off the chairs or table legs and actually used such occasions to reorient herself to her destination. We had a guy come in here for more than a year before he realized Chloe was blind."

"What about Grover? They were together, right?"

"That's another part of it. Chloe was the boss, and Grover never challenged that. They'd lie together, side by side, but with Grover facing her rear end, on that landing. Chloe was queen; Grover did exactly what she did. So, pet her, pet him. She growls, he growls. She marches through the barroom, he's right behind her. Chloe was the alpha dog, no question.

After she passed, Grover took on every one of her traits. Everything I told you about Chloe became the way Grover acted. Things he never did before, he started doing immediately after she died. Except a bit more viciously.

Grover is a male. He's more expressive than his mother. She was tough, a force, a fear to those who meant no good. Grover is worse, well, was worse. He's old now, and you don't see that anymore. But in his day there was no one in Cordell who would think of messing with Grover. Nicest dog you'd ever see; toughest dog you ever faced. Like mother, like son."

"Do you think he'd like me?" I asked.

"Go see for yourself,"

I walked over to the steps. Grover opened his eyes. He didn't look all that interested. I said his name and moved up toward him. He raised his head, studied me, and then looked over at Owen. Not a sound. I reached forward and petted his head. He looked me straight in the eyes, made a small guttural sound, and lay back down.

"He likes you," Owen said from across the room.

"Why'd you name him 'Grover', Owen?"

"I guess I thought 'Rover' had been a bit overused."

For my part, I was starting to like this place.

"Your turn." Owen couldn't have been more clear.

I told a short story about my beagle. By the time I was finished with a story of Cleo's run-in with a groundhog, Owen seemed satisfied that he had gotten what he had given.

It was obviously time to go.

"Owen, it's been a pleasure. Thanks for the beer. Loved your stories. If I ever get another trip to this part of the country, I'll make some time for Cordell, so we can do this again. What do you think?"

"I'd look forward to that." I think he meant it, even though I had sort of forced an affirmative.

"Deal."

I left. By the time I looked out my hotel window, the fluttering fluorescent was dark and so was the window by the front door.

CHAPTER TWO

Noah's Arc

It snowed the next day. Snow mixed with icy rain, nasty sleet. Everything falling was sticking to something. Roads and walkways, rooftops and trees, power lines and parked cars were all encased in a quarter inch of cloudy glaze.

Fortunately for me this storm didn't start until almost noon, so I was able to make my living in the morning. Pre-storm, I drove my rental up to Blaspher and gave my presentation. At lunch, the bosses sent everyone home, given the impending doom.

I had planned to drive from Blaspher directly back to Portland and fly home. I called the airport to confirm my flight.

Nope. Worse weather on the western side of the Cascades had everything on the ground. Clearly, I would be in Oregon for another twenty-four hours, perhaps more.

This isn't all bad, I thought to myself. I'll go back to Cordell and spend some time with Owen.

After a tricky drive down a skating rink of a highway, and a re-up at the hotel, I was in Ticket's by 1:00.

"Hey, Owen, I thought your ribs said it wasn't going to snow or ice," I sneered, on entering the otherwise empty bar.

"Sometimes they're wrong," Owen responded, matter-of-factly. "I was wondering if you got out."

"Portland's shut down. I'm here until tomorrow; new flight plan. I thought I'd just come back here, have you make me lunch, and spend the afternoon telling stories. How does that sound?"

Owen shrugged. "I'm not otherwise engaged. Goin' to be quiet here, what with this weather. Now lunch is a crapshoot. My menu is so small I don't have a menu. Here's what I make: grilled hot dog, hamburger /cheeseburger, grilled cheese, and fried bologna sandwiches. Add a bag of chips, a beer, and those are your lunch options, right there."

"No prices?" I mocked concern. "How do I know I can afford this establishment?"

"If you have to ask, you can't afford it. Now a big-time speaker like yourself shouldn't even have to ask."

"Yeah, okay. I'll gamble on the fried bologna. I'll take the chips and a beer. Is that considered a platter?"

"That's a platter," Owen sighed. "Maybe I'll put up a Food sign, list some prices, and add Platters." Owen flipped his bar rag into the sink and headed to the yellowed refrigerator to start my meal.

"How'd the speech go?" he asked over his shoulder.

"As always. Dazzled 'em. Some of them danced in the aisles and spoke in tongues, some of them cried. Moments for all time."

"Uh-huh," some skepticism in his reply. "Must have been something for the ages. Wish I could've been there."

"Here's the good news. I was so good that they want me back for another group. See, Owen, one talk turns into another. So here is my idea: Today we drink beer, tell some stories, and wait out this ice. Then, next month, we do it again. What do you think?"

"Better than dying alone. I'll finish your gourmet lunch, then we'll sit over there."

At the table near the bullet holes, I with my 'platter,' Owen with his tea, he asked, "Got a topic in mind, or do I just select something?"

"I'd like to know how this bar got dropped in the middle of a gravel bed like one of those little Monopoly game pieces. It's odd, you know. Must be a story in there somewhere."

"There is," he acknowledged, "but it is a big story; takes a while to tell if you want to make sense out of it. It's all tied to how the entire town got started and grew. But I guess I'm not going anywhere, as long as you're buying 'platters' and beer."

I started to eat; Owen started to talk.

"Hmm," he pondered. I'm going to tell this story inside-out. I'm going to talk about the bar first and how it came to this pitiful end.

I 'spect you look at this place, all by its lonesome, as just a run-down watering hole, a half mile from downtown, on the wrong side of the tracks -- a throwback. You would be correct, but only partially.

Actually, Ticket's started out at the original center of Cordell, the most popular bar in town. Ticket's has been part of most things that ever transpired in Cordell. It's only been the last twenty-five years that this bar has become a bastard child. All that gravel out there? That used to be building after building, all snuggled up against the rail tracks.

Of course the centerpiece was Franklin Cordell's train station next door to us, on the left. Franklin and John Witherspoon built a line of buildings here that everyone called The Strip. Once the railroad came through, from The Dalles, Bend, Portland, and Salem, travelers got off the train and needed something. Some needed horses and carriages, out-fittings, canned goods, supplies, and sundries. And, a place to eat, a place to sleep, perhaps a drink.

Well, all that was right here, on The Strip. At the end were the hotel, then Prinder's Café, the post office, the train station, then us, a mercantile, a combination butcher and produce shop, an apparel store, and Stuart's Restaurant.

At the end was another bar, making three bars, if you count the small one in the hotel. My grandfather, Noah Ticket, leased this place from John Witherspoon in 1905. That's Noah, there on the left, in his middle years." Owen nodded to the portraits. "The story of Ticket's starts with Noah Ticket."

"He was here from the earliest days of the town?" I asked.

"Pretty much." Owen took a big breath and continued.

"In 1897, Frigyes Csizmadia, a Hungarian of seventeen years, boarded a steamship to America and headed off to the land of opportunity with his widowed mother's blessing and encouragement. She had four other children to feed and was already living in poverty. Still, Frigyes had a small stake, garnered from friends and family. He guarded the money belt he wore like an eagle with one egg.

What he didn't have was any knowledge of the English language. Dirty and tired, he stood for hours in a long line of immigrants waiting to be processed in the old wooden building that was Ellis Island. He was scared and hungry, he had to urinate, and he was cold. He was utterly alone. Right there are his memories of the experience.

Finally, he stepped up to the wooden table facing a drunk, fat-bellied, red-faced Irishman, who barely looked at him and whose voice dripped disdain.

'Papers,' the uniformed drunk announced, waving his hand toward himself.

'No,' Frigyes replied. During the voyage he had been given to understand that officials would ask for 'papers,' whatever they were. Frigyes had nothing to show that he was Hungarian, nothing to show that this new country was expecting him, nothing to indicate that he was here legally or illegally, whatever that meant. He had been instructed by others in steerage to say 'no' to about every question. 'Don't worry,' he was told, 'they won't send you back.'

'Passport?'

'No.'

'Country?' Hunched shoulders, Frigyes stared at the agent. He finally figured out the question.

'Hungary.'

'Proof of citizenship?' Another blank stare; no answer.

'Personal I.D?'

'No.'

'Name?' Frigyes knew that word.

''Frigyes Csizmadia.'

'What?'

'Frigyes Csizmadia.'

'Spell it.' Red Face put a pencil over his form.

'Frigyes Cs.., the Hungarian started.

'What the hell is that? Start again.'

'F-r-i-g-y-e-s.'

'You have a ticket from the ship?' Red Face demanded.

'Ship?'

'The boat, you silly bastard. Do you have a ticket from the boat?' Red Face waved a paper at Frigyes.

'No. No teekeet. Boat is teekeet.'

'Screw this. That's it. 'No teekeet,' Red Face imitated the boy's pronunciation. 'You know what? We're going to give you a new name. Name you Noah Ticket. How's that?' Without waiting for a response, not even looking up at Frigyes, Red Face completed a form.

'Here you are, Noah Ticket. Welcome to America. Get on with you. Go over there,' he demanded, pointing to the medical area.

"Hours later Noah was on the boat to the mainland."

"So, the newly-minted Noah Ticket is in New York City. How did he get to Oregon?" I asked.

"Do you have a date?" Owen snapped. "Don't rush me. I'm getting there.

Noah spent two nights in a flophouse in the old Five Points. On the third day, two things occurred. First, that old wooden building at Ellis Island burned to the ground. Noah always wondered what became of Red Face.

Second, he followed a small group of Irishmen to a hiring hall and signed with a railroad company which was getting started in Chicago to lay western track, connected to the Transcontinental. Noah was shipped off to the Windy City, throwing a sledgehammer the next week. He did this for five years, slowly heading west all the time. Slowly learning English and hating railroad life and labor.

Noah worked on different railroads – there were hundreds then – saving as much money as he could. He earned meager wages, but he had food and a cot at the company Hell on Wheels tent towns."

Owen stood up. "Let's get some fresh product," he said decidedly. We took that short break, and then he returned to his story.

"While the labor was arduous, Noah always said the loneliness was worse. Railway workers were slow to make friends, knowing that their co-workers were often misfits, scoundrels, boozers, or gamblers. They also were a diverse lot, mostly Irish though; the Chinese and Japanese started out of Portland and worked eastward. Most of the American-born seemed cliquish and disdainful of foreigners like Noah.

Until Noah met George Fagan, he was simply isolated. George became Noah's first real friend. As he and Noah went from one railroad to another for the next four years, they became inseparable. George helped Noah with his English. Taught him to stay out of the nightly card games, to avoid the always-present alcohol, and to avoid the seamier laborers. Taught him how to avoid fights with the quicksilver Irish.

Until George's accident. One day a chain broke as the crew was lowering a batch of ties ahead of the tracking. George was under that load, pinned by head and shoulders, bleeding from everywhere above his waist. The first workers on the scene knew he was a goner, so no attempt was made to free him. They hailed Noah, who was already running down the tracks. The others left the friends alone for the last moments.

Words were said by both. George then told Noah to dig into his inside pocket and to retrieve the money he was carrying, his life savings, if you will.

'Take it, Noah. Do something with it, Get off the railroad.'

Noah took the purse. When he counted the money later, Noah realized George's saving almost equaled his own meager stash. A bittersweet experience for Noah, without doubt.

He had to work to protect it, though. Certainly other trackmen figured Noah had obtained George's money. The body was penniless, the two were friends, or, maybe Noah had just taken the money.

A few attempted to get that cash. Some offered this or that deal, some threatened Noah, some attempted to befriend him. Noah had no truck with any of this. The one or two who tried to strong-arm him left badly bruised. Once Noah had to stab a fellow with the other man's knife, something about which he felt oddly guilty for most of his life. Mostly though, he just went back to the life of personal loneliness.

When the railway reached the confluence of the Deschutes and the Columbia, Noah got off. No more railroading for him. He was going to pick a place and settle in for the first time since he left Hungary.

A month later he landed in Cordell. There, are you happy now, Ed? We have gotten Noah to town." Owen's little smile took the sting out of his reference to my rudeness.

"Indeed I am. Please continue, Owen."

"Noah saw an empty storefront on The Strip and made an appointment with John Witherspoon. Noah rented the building and opened Ticket's. The rest, as they say, is history. It was 1905."

"So, more than a hundred years for Ticket's, eh? Noah found a home in Cordell," I guessed out loud.

Owen grunted thinly. "Yeah. Noah Ticket became a respected and honest barkeep. People took to him immediately. He was genuine and personable, if somewhat stubborn and sparing of words.

The customer base he built was a cross-section of town, the rich and the poor, the downtrodden meek and uppity shopkeepers. This place reflected his heart and soul, and Cordell liked Noah's heart and soul. He gave, and he received. Noah could have been the poster boy for the American Dream."

"So, Ticket's was part of this strip, then? Whatever happened to the rest of that?"

"I'll give you the simple answer to that: they were torn down." Owen smiled at his statement of the obvious. "But how they got here and what happened is really all part of the town's history, meaning there are several stories in there. You want to hear about that, or go back to your room and watch soap operas?"

"The stories, for sure." We paused for a bathroom break and some bartending for two thirsty locals. Owen brought over some beverages, and started in again.

"This turn-of-the-century town was created for two reasons: one, to make money for its founders, and two, to feed on western expansion, made possible by the Homestead Act and the railway system.

The Oregon Territory became a U.S. acquisition in the 1840s, and the government was helping everyone get into western development. That meant wagon trains, of course, and then the Transcontinental Railroad. On both sides of the Cascades, places like Portland and The Dalles were growing fast. Homesteaders gobbled up acres on this side, starting ranches and farms, raising beef, sheep, hops, and wheat. Most of them were poor, and they worked alone.

Franklin Cordell and John Witherspoon were not poor, nor did they work alone. These two men were exemplars of the western entrepreneurial spirit. Cordell had made a small fortune in real estate near and about Portland. A sharp, shrewd businessman, he was loud, strong, confident, chest-to-the-wind, nobody's fool. Cordell saw unlimited economic growth and financial opportunities in the new, raw, and underdeveloped prairies of central Oregon.

Franklin and John Witherspoon were men of different visions. Cordell always had his eyes on the stars. He was a dreamer – big dreams, big plans, big investment, big reward. Why not? His earlier dreams hadn't yet cost him anything but shiny shoes and a big smile. He was a relentless advocate of the future. He sensed the west was going to grow, grow, grow, given both the good and the bad from the gold rush days and the expansion of the rail system. He saw eastern Oregon as a vast resource, waiting to be developed. Who better to capitalize on that than the Cordell Real Estate Agency?

John Witherspoon was not quite so well-heeled as Cordell, but Witherspoon Lumber Company had profited in Oregon City. John had but one passion: wood, simple as that. John spoke not of possibilities, but of assurances – things he knew for sure. And he knew wood. He was tight with a dollar while Cordell used money as grease.

A small, wiry, soft-spoken fellow, John's appearance and mannerisms could be off-putting. He could be abrupt. He spoke with his eyes on the floor, he dressed like a lumberjack, he lacked social grace. I think he was always fearful of being cheated or being made a fool. He approached every transaction, big or small, with a certain distrust of mankind, an attitude that permeated all his interactions. John's eccentric distrust of most people eventually sank into paranoia. Add to that his temper and you have a recipe for restraint when dealing with him. Thankfully, if it wasn't about wood, it likely didn't interest him.

By the end of his life, he was a mad-man. But all that came later.

So, while Cordell looked at eastern Oregon as a golden goose, Witherspoon looked at the eastern mountainsides as places to reap wood.

These two had done mutually fruitful business before, when Cordell was developing parcels of Oregon City, and Witherspoon was providing the wood. They were not really friends, though. Cordell had a social circle; Witherspoon did not. But the creation of the town of Cordell ultimately intertwined them and their families for a hundred years, to this very day.

It must have been about 1898. Over whiskey in the newly-renovated Hotel Portland, Cordell shared his latest idea with Witherspoon. He reminded John of the Homestead Act and the free land it offered throughout the country, including Oregon. He flopped out a map of the high country on the eastern side of the Cascades. He pointed to some surveyed but yet undeveloped tracts less than a day's ride south of the Columbia River and Deschutes River convergence.

'Free land, John! If we put small grazing ranches on our land to prove it up, we can each claim 640 acres.' He pointed to a circle he'd drawn on the map. 'That's two square miles, John. For pennies per acre we can buy some additional parcels next to all that. If we have the gut for it, we get the land and build anything we want on it – an entire town along the banks of the Deschutes. Think about that! Think about the wood we'll need!'

Cordell knew the tender chord to strike Witherspoon's interest. It worked. John sat up a bit in his chair.

And guess what, John? The wood that you, and only you, will provide is virtually free also. See those foothills, John? Wood, less than ten miles from our town. And then there's all that old growth up the eastern side. Just need a permit from the government, and pennies on the thousand feet. You put up a sawmill around here,' his finger traced the White River, 'and we haul the "dress" right into town.'

You'll have precious little competition, John. There are only a few mills over there, spread out some, and most of them are well to the south, near Bend, all small. Some only do this or that, nothing of the scale you'll be doing. You'll have exclusive rights to all the wood sold in our town.

You know what else, John?' Cordell continued. 'Our timing is perfect! The railroad is coming right down the Deschutes. I know this; my guy in the A&O told me so. He says they are already preparing to lay track. Hiring labor, planning which side of the Deschutes to follow, and gathering up the necessities. They'll tie into the TCR and head down to Bend. The railroad party out here is just getting started. Railroads are not just in the east anymore. Track is going down this valley to serve these tiny hamlets and ranches. In fact, my friend says two railroad men are racing each other to be the first to build it. One is going down one side of the Deschutes and the other on the other. Oh yes, there will be railroads in there, and they will open up all of north central Oregon. And we'll be sitting on the railway right-of-way. We want to be part of that.

John, in less than ten years you'll be shipping wood throughout Oregon. The eastern side is where to be, That's the future for your business and mine.'

Cordell made no effort to sound philanthropic. His huge ego was considering the legacy that he, Franklin Cordell, would leave. This new town, his from the ground up, would be a monument to himself. Historic undertaking, this, and the Cordells would be forever known for it.

For his part, Witherspoon was mostly sold when Cordell first said 'wood.' His fixation on wood had made him plenty of money. He knew how to select it, how to cut it, how to sell it, and how to make something from it. Unknown to Cordell, Witherspoon also knew that the leases on two of his three biggest tracts of forest in the western Cascades would soon expire. Now might be the right time to move his entire setup. He already knew the eastern Cascades, their foothills, and the smaller forests. He knew there was Ponderosa pine, western larch, various firs, cedars, and lodge-pole pine on both sides of the Cascades. Timbering permits would be no problem.

He accepted that people would be building ranches, towns, and businesses. They were going to need wood. And carpenters to build it all. And houses for the carpenters. This was a good idea, and doing it with Cordell was a plus – less investment, greater return possibilities. Cordell might be overbearing, but he was astute. He'd be a good part-ner, Witherspoon thought, probably better than he.

Still, it would be a huge gamble for the already-weathered lum-berman. He was skeptical of any scheme that included risk. 'A bird in the hand' and all that. There was appeal in the notion, however. He was feeling crowded in Oregon City. Too many easterners moving in, and while they were buying wood, competitive sawmills were starting up everywhere around him. All the 'free' parts of Cordell's proposition counted, too. But to a conservative, one-pony life like his, it would require some caution.

Yet he was intrigued.

John Witherspoon put on his studious look. 'I'd have to see it first' he responded – all of it – the woods, the valley, the White River, the land, the Deschutes.'

'Of course, of course,' Cordell agreed. 'We'll go right over the mountain. This whole thing, you know, is right up the Oregon Trail, from here to there.'

The next week they took a wagon up the trail. As they descended into the eastern valley, Franklin pointed out all the wood waiting to be cut. He and John identified a perfect spot on the White River for a sawmill. While they crossed the valley, John noticed several ranches, a few horses and cows, even some sheep, grazing in the tall grass, and small wheat fields nestled up against rough wood cabins. John spotted only two sawmills on the trek, both very small operations. No problem there. They passed several hop fields and two large hop yards. They progressed through one or two tiny settlements of several houses and a store or two. 'Well, at least there will be beer here,' John observed.

'For sure, John. And enough people to drink it. See all these spread-out settlements? They need a center – a town that offers everything – central post office, supplies, materials, homes for woodmen and railroaders, the whole thing. This is going to be a boom area, John, and you and I are going to develop that center. We're on the new frontier, my friend.'

They followed a stagecoach route to the Deschutes and Cordell's suggested site. John's every question simply evaporated. A long bluff buffered and contained the Deschutes. Except for a homesteader or two, well up from the site, and a ferry operation, the place looked just perfect for growing a town. Cordell was right. John turned and looked back at Mt. Hood. A beautiful view. He'd move his sawmill on down the White, a tad closer to town. 'Just get us the railroad, Franklin,' he said.

One week later each filed the necessary government paperwork. Soon they were homesteaders.

Cordell also purchased twenty-one parcels of land that ran contiguously to his homestead, including several just across the Deschutes -- a big triangle, actually. Witherspoon purchased fifteen parcels, mostly mountain acreage in the foothills and a tract across the river, thick with old growth.

Together, Franklin Cordell and John Witherspoon now owned the entire area that was to become Cordell, Oregon. Taken together, the land mass totaled almost three miles of Deschutes frontage, stretching back toward the mountains. Cordell's piece here was larger, but Witherspoon's purchase included that mountain land.

Three months later, over drinks at the same hotel, the two easily reached some gentlemen's agreements:

1. The price of each lot within one mile of the river would be the same, regardless of investor.

2. The town would be named Cordell. (Witherspoon couldn't care less.)

3. Franklin would represent the two in all railroad negotiations. Whatever financial or easement deals he crafted with a railroad would be binding on Witherspoon.

4. Witherspoon held rights for all forest product procurement and provision. All processed lumber provided to this new town, the railroad entering it, and any area within the borders of either man's property would be milled by Witherspoon Lumber Company.

5. The train terminal would sit on Cordell property, on the line separating the two purchases.

6. Development of real estate on either side was the choice of the property owner. Each was free to do whatever he wished with his land.

Owen stopped, then clarified: "This was a handshake agreement. No lawyer ever wrote them into a contract. Just two Oregon men planning how to turn their investments into gold.

When they were ready, Cordell and Witherspoon steamed up the Columbia to The Dalles. They freighted some beginning materials and were accompanied this time with a small group of surveyors and engineers. They followed the Deschutes to their new holdings.

Cordell viewed this occasion as an historical tour de force. With pomp and jubilance, Franklin stretched his arms out to encircle the broad, flat land and the rock cliffs down to the river. Witherspoon looked off at his new timberland, at the horizon behind him, and at his tract to the east. Both were happy.

'The Cordell train station will sit just about here,' Cordell announced, as if he were addressing a group of news reporters. He reminded those gathered that he had already convinced the railway of the need to connect central Oregon to points both east and west. After showing several of the railroad builders the location, demographics, and possibilities of the Deschutes River basin, Cordell had already struck a deal with the A&O to run a southerly track down the basin, intersecting with the Transcontinental Railway further east.

'Our town will push out in all directions,' Cordell continued. 'At the river edge, factories, supply houses, warehouses, and brothels, housing for laborers and shopkeepers. Residences will grow behind them, back from this industrial zone to our terminal, and then from here back to the foothills. Folks will follow that track right to us, and Cordell will prosper.

John, my man, you are standing on Witherspoon Avenue, the main artery into Cordell. Up there a couple hundred feet, intersecting with the Avenue, will be a tree-lined boulevard extending to the river's edge. That, and streets that cross it, will be house-to-house thick and will boast shops and enterprises. And you and I, Mr. Witherspoon, will supply every need – the lots, the trade services, and the wood. We will dedicate space for churches and schools, and municipal government. And we shall build them, too, with one eye on our noble undertaking and one eye on our fatter and fatter purses.' Cordell rattled on for several more minutes. It was a speech worthy of a mayor on Independence Day.

Witherspoon tolerated this flourish with distracted casualness. 'Good,' he grunted, 'just get them to come.' Witherspoon was no real estate developer, no salesman. He was gambling – a flight of fancy for the conservative woodman – on the notion that Cordell knew how to create a town from nothing at all. If that actually occurred, Witherspoon knew that he would be rich. All he needed was a buyers' market, more lumbermen, and some cabinet-makers.

They strolled down the dividing property line to the river and back. Surveyors drove a marker pole into the flat ground, flanked by the bluffs on each side, almost 1500 yards west of a big, gentle bend in the Deschutes. They walked another 1500 yards west and drove another marker. When moved only slightly by the official survey, these markers delineated the property line and the spine for the new town.

"Witherspoon looked about again. He was coming to accept Cordell's promise. Five hundred yards up the road was an old, deserted shack, once a stagecoach stop. The big watering trough remained and most of the wooden corral. Further out were a few tiny homes and a ranch or two. Some of these had to be 'squatters,' maybe a homesteader or two. Cordell would work something out with the former. Witherspoon wished Cordell all the luck in the world."

Owen shrugged emphatically. "And that's how it all played out. The town of Cordell, Oregon, was born, just as Franklin Cordell had envisioned it. The A&O Railroad laid track right down the Deschutes basin, to the door of Franklin's train station. A small town started almost immediately, and Cordell and Witherspoon were soon selling land and building houses. Before the A&O sold out to Union Pacific, it forged on south toward Bend and west to Portland. The two entrepreneurs reaped right-of-way fees for some of that.

Franklin advertised the railroad presence in the Portland and Boise newspapers, along with the farming and ranching opportunities associated with a town that already had a new post office and all the businesses located on a central strip. That seemed to work.

Settlers arrived. During the first decade of the new century, the cooperative venture of Franklin Cordell and John Witherspoon went just as cool and smooth as the whiskey over which they had created it.

This strip, Franklin's planned center of town, was naturally developed first, and became a bustling place. Franklin and John built at least a dozen buildings along here with the station in the very center. Witherspoon lumber, from a water-powered sawmill over on White River, was in such demand that John's crew kept growing and growing. Cordell, incidentally, built his office right on The Boulevard, with a big sign, 'Cordell Real Estate Agency, Franklin Cordell, Agent.'

Most of the new establishments were prosperous. The one exception was Clyde Horner's harness shop. This building right here. Clyde, by all accounts, was a strange, peculiar sort. For whatever reason, he closed the shop one day at lunch hour and never came back. This is the space Noah rented.

Obviously, the place was in rough shape with a rough plank floor, a forge in the center, and big hooks hanging on the bare walls, holding up pieces of leather and steel. Oh, yeah, an old pot-bellied stove over there in the corner. Used to provide all the heat this place needed until my dad put a furnace in the basement.

Anyway, there was living space upstairs. Noah lived here until he got married. Changing it from a harness shop to a barroom kept Noah hopping for a couple of weeks. He cleared the clutter and laid three wide planks to serve as the bar. Noah had a new sign made, 'Ticket's, and nailed it over top of the false front that Clyde had erected on the flat roof. Two kegs of beer and a case of whiskey later he was in business.

It was a glorious time. By 1910, slews of people were coming through, with loads of money changing hands. Ticket's took off, like everything else. Noah used to say that every night the place would start out smelling like Bay Rum, the shaving soap and fragrance of choice. By closing time, it smelled of beer and cigar smoke. Standing room only, three deep at the bar, on many a night. Well, that's deceiving. Everyone except card players stood in bars in those days. No bar stools, that's for sure. My dad put them in much later on.

Cordell was in high cotton. The Strip was buzzing, and Ticket's was at the center of it all.

Your turn."

Chapter Three

The Great Falling Out

I wrapped up my story about the Musser family with drama and flourish, but quickly, as my interest in Owen, Ticket's, and Cordell was growing. In summary, Owen commented, "Goes to show you. You can pick your friends, but not your family. Aren't you glad that wasn't your lot?"

We stretched and repositioned ourselves. Owen obviously knew where he was going with his next story.

"I have more to tell about the Cordell and Witherspoon families. An extension, as it were, of the town's history, and why my bar sits here like a bread truck in a deserted parking lot.

As I said, lots of people were passing through in that first decade. Many were staying. Some were descendants of the early French trappers, putting down roots. There were woodsmen, ranchers, muleskinners, and gandy dancers. By the way, you know what a gandy dancer is, right?"

"A strip-tease artist?" I gambled.

"I figured that's where you'd go," Owen laughed. "No, a gandy dancer is a track-layer, or a guy who inspects the tracks laid. Railroad term, not a sexual one. The guys who laid the track were gandy dancers. The women who laid the men were whores." Another smile from the wry devil.

"Anyway, lots of people. Some were leftovers from meager missionary efforts out of Portland. Asians, too, of course. First Chinese, then Japanese, who'd laid track. A few Indians, although most of them ended up on the Warm Springs Reservation. The easterners, our 'pioneers,' mostly European, rumbled in the aftermath of Manifest Destiny and all that.

And, of course, there were the ranchers. They were grazing cattle and sheep up and down the foothills. They were raising larger herds, and they needed more cowboys.

Now that there was a railroad, better supplies, electricity, and modern equipment were arriving. Ranchers could now ship cows and sheep to Chicago. Farmers were plowing over the grasslands, replacing them with wheat fields. Wheat did so well that the town needed a few grain mills and storage silos. But fruits and onions, alfalfa and hay, too. And hops. Hops became a big market. Of course, the railroad itself was generating jobs and business. Lots of woodsmen, of course, tradesmen and shopkeepers. As these men wandered in, so did the families and hookers who followed them.

Several trains a day were coming through, so commerce was brisk. A bank moved in; later on the Cattlemen's Association opened an office.

Ticket's was enjoying this influx of people, even though it was within two hundred feet of two other bars. Noah did have the advantage and convenience of being next door to the train station. He also profited from his name. He had that Tickets sign up top, Some travelers would see the sign and, needing new train tickets, would step into the bar. Realizing their mistake, some would just turn and leave. Many, however, decided, 'What the heck, we're here, might as well have a drink.'

Watching this confusion, Noah considered changing his outside sign because of the annoyance and wasted traffic. Then he realized that the mistake was working in his favor. The sign stayed.

Such confused visitors often included women, escorted or otherwise, so Ticket's was really the first Cordell bar frequented by women. For his part, Noah simply turned on the charm, offered them one of the card tables, and served them up. He even put a handmade sign in the window that said, 'Tables for Ladies.' Ticket's has been forever known as 'female friendly.' It all started then."

Owen was beginning to warm up to his topic. He re-adjusted his seat and resumed his narrative.

"Certainly the early 1900s were a boom time for Franklin Cordell and John Witherspoon. But nothing gold can stay – from green buds to golden leaves to naked branches.

Things often turn on a dime. Franklin Cordell made two decisions which affected this town forever.

Remember, Franklin originally planned for The Strip to be the center of town. The town was to grow from it down to the river, not develop from the river back. The riverfront was to be for industry. Residences and shops were to start right out my front door and then out my back one, from the intersection of Witherspoon Avenue and The Boulevard.

But Franklin encountered a curious situation. Newcomers wanted to build homes in Cordell, but they seemed taken by the land closer to, or at, the river edge. In fact, when they learned that Cordell also owned that property across the river, that triangle quickly known as The Wedge. The wealthier wanted that ground.

Figuring that a sale was better than no sale, Franklin started selling more of The Wedge, and the lots just on this side of the river for residences, rather than for commerce or industry. All that land was his, not Witherspoon's.

That personal profitable decision was the first of two unilateral moves Franklin made. He didn't think Witherspoon would care all that much.

Well, he did. John could see that the original plan was being sullied. Cordell was selling his own land for the wrong purposes.

Witherspoon grew increasingly angry. He wanted to sell his land as quickly as possible, all of it from the river to the foothills. Particularly galling to John was that he was supplying the wood for these new, expensive houses. Good news, bad news there. He'd say later that he was tying the noose for his own hanging.

Franklin's second decision was devastating for Witherspoon. The railroad, as it continued its southerly expansion, needed to house its labor force. As with an army, the railroad traveled on its stomach. Workers needed to be fed and bedded.

The railway had attended to this with the Hell on Wheels encampments, tents, awnings, and supply booths set in muddy fields just ahead of the progressing tracks. But increasingly, laborers – especially the gandy dancers -- wanted better living conditions. A stew cook and an old white tent are no one's idea of comfort. Some wanted to own something. Some had families. They couldn't put them beside the whores, renegades, and scam artists who followed the railway.

The railroad also wanted a small rail yard between The Dalles and Bend for train and track repair, engine and coach maintenance, and homes for the railroaders who would provide it. The railroad needed low-cost housing. Some migrants had already begun slapping together old slabs of scavenged wood or tin, building a 'temporary shanty town' just out of sight from and behind, this bar. Asians, black, poor, un-skilled laborers, penniless, end-of-the-trail immigrants, worn-out French trappers and pelters, scofflaws, and hookers – all looking for cheap housing.

Franklin Cordell watched this happening. He had anticipated the need for low-cost housing years earlier, planning on the tract along the Deschutes for it. Heretofore, the poor always got the water bottoms or bluff land, like in San Francisco and Portland. But now that new buyers were choosing that land for quality homes, the riverfront was going residential, not industrial. So, without consulting Witherspoon, Franklin dedicated the corner of his holdings behind the hotel to low-cost housing. It was as far from the river as he could build or develop, and there were many makeshift dwellings already in place.

Somewhere around 1910 this all came to a head. When the two met to discuss this major change of development, John was already irate. Cordell attempted to soften the blow. 'It's only an acre or so,' he reasoned. We have to put them somewhere, and this is as far from town as we can.'

'It wouldn't be if the town was growing in the direction we planned,' spat Witherspoon. 'That acre will ruin the value of all the land west of the tracks. How am I ever goin' to sell my piece? You sold me out. You'll still make money off your land, and I'm still holding mine, you rat bastard!'

Franklin shrugged. 'Sell them some wood, John. Get them out of those tents.'

'Like they could pay for wood!' John Witherspoon rose and stomped out of the last meeting the two ever had. The creation of The Acre – that's what it has always been called – caused a rift between the Cordells and the Witherspoons that has lasted for three generations. Along the way, it put Ticket's, and every other business on The Strip, on the wrong side of the tracks."

"It is said, Owen, that life is a set of unintended consequences," I observed.

"True here, for sure.

The shanty town grew to more than an acre, of course. There are always the poor. When you leave, look back toward the mountain. You'll see The Acre. Franklin let that acre expand as necessary, with all kinds of make-do homes. The railway and the sawmills made large parts of The Acre a company town. They built little places up there and rented them to laborers for money deducted right from their pay-checks. Franklin made money there; John's nearby land went unsold, and lost value.

For their part, town folk were in the middle. Some believed the Cordell decision to be reasonable, while others thought Witherspoon had been sold out. Those who bought property from the smooth-talking Franklin Cordell, in his pressed shirt, portraying all the aspects of a high-country gentleman, tended to side with him. Those who owned properties on Witherspoon's side of the fence, had purchased lumber for their homes from him, and believed that he had been mis-led, sided with John. Just so you know, that included Noah Ticket. But it was a minority view.

Part of the problem, though, was John Witherspoon himself. Un-fortunately, he lacked the savvy to deliver any kind of counterpunch. He couldn't marshal any organized response to this unanticipated pat-tern of Cordell's growth.

John was no canny land developer; Franklin was the lead pony in the entire endeavor. Franklin held sway over almost everything. John allowed that from the beginning, so he shouldered some of the consequences. John needed a new deal. But Franklin held the good cards. No man with four aces ever asks for a new deal."

I shook my head sadly. "Cordell had the power, the authority, and the stones for it, eh?"

Owen nodded. Silence for five seconds.

"Basically, Franklin was a decent, mostly honest fellow, and certainly a good businessman. He was the first mayor. He formed, and then presided over, the first Rotary Club. He helped raise the funds for the first church's building project. He lobbied hard against the mostly-Protestant population to allow a Catholic church to come to town on land he donated. But he also hand-picked fawning cronies for seats on the town council and all the related committees. So, unchallenged, he was the undisputed boss of Cordell, John Witherspoon notwithstanding.

Still, Franklin was pompous, arrogant, and cunning. He constantly reminded everyone that Cordell was Cordell's. He had planned the town, brought in the railroad, developed the land, and so on. Franklin seldom needed to threaten, cajole, or trick anyone. Imperious in his dealings, he simply told folks the way it would be, and it was. For sure, all the Cordells, for that matter, were full of themselves. Figured themselves to be town royalty, ruling their fiefdom.

Cordell Real Estate's rocketing business was selling and reselling lots and houses all the time. Well into the 1930s, his was the only real estate agency in this stretch of the Deschutes. He steered the black, Asian, and Irish laborers to The Acre, the white families to his lots in town, and the big shots to The Wedge. He was developing this town just the way he had hoped, with the exception of the where the poor would live. Life was good for Franklin.

Anyway, that's how Cordell still looks today. You come into town on Witherspoon Avenue, what should have been the town center. Instead, it consists of my bar and some weeds. Your motel across the avenue was built in the 1980s, across the tracks, you notice. Could have gone another way."

And John Witherspoon watched while Cordell land was being sold at a five-to-one ratio to his. The falling out changed both men, neither for the better.

Franklin was living in luxury. He made money and found time to marry and to father an heir to the family throne, Charles, and twin daughters, Merrilee and Naomi. He built himself a fine house in The Wedge, but he began buying wood from another lumberman upriver. Miffed at John's tirade, Franklin recommended that all his clients obtain their building materials, cheaper and better, he said, from any of John's competitors.

Franklin had simply tossed the gentlemen's agreement with John to the wind.

Meanwhile, Franklin's self-importance was showing itself more and more. In truth, Franklin had produced results, and most of that regal attitude was unnecessary. But his bragging and his public scorn for John Witherspoon's increasingly eccentric behavior were poorly received by some townspeople. The citizenry couldn't avoid the braggart as they watched Franklin lord it over everyone. Something like jealousy, disrespect, and lack of trust just set in. Increasingly, Franklin was viewed as a self-important, condescending, and imperial little czar.

He, and all the Cordells, for that matter, never seemed to grasp that real power need not be stated. It just reveals itself. Franklin died before all that public distain could play itself out. But he came close.

Simply put, Franklin was tarnishing his own trophy.

Money and power can corrupt. 'Whom the gods would destroy, they first make drunk with power.' Isn't that how it goes?"

"Yes, Owen, that is exactly as it goes," I said, impressed. Owen continued.

"Meanwhile, John was telling folks that his partner had stabbed him in the back. He referred to Franklin only as his 'former partner.' And so the bickering, 'love me, hate them' rhetoric had begun, on both sides.

It intensified as the children of both families met up at school. The town kids, like the Cordells, and the high-country kids, like the Witherspoons, were at odds from the time they were grade-schoolers.

They fought. One punched the other, one called the other names, one stole the other's lunch money, one tore up the other's homework. Bad blood was now family deep.

It boiled over when the kids were in high school. Merrilee Cordell was sexually assaulted one fall evening in the 1920s as she returned home from a piano lesson. Brutally so, actually. I won't go into detail, but the versions that got around town were horrific. Animalistic. Cutting, beating, vile sex, the whole enchilada. Poor thing crawled home without a stitch of clothing, save a bracelet. The whole town was abuzz with shock, outrage, insinuation, and rumor-mongering.

The Cordells were convinced the attacker was David Witherspoon, John's second son. While the rapist wore a ski mask and concealing clothing, he 'smelled like smoke, sawdust, and sweat,' Merrilee claimed. And, besides, David Witherspoon had just that week told her that someday she would get 'hers.' Plus, the trouble between the two families was common knowledge. This all made sense.

For sure, the Witherspoons denied any involvement. But David was a good and handy suspect. Different in every respect from his older brother Raymond, he was an eccentric loner. Traits of his father. He was in trouble with the law from age ten. He was a discipline problem in school, and he made no secret of his hatred for the Cordells. He also had no good alibi for the time of the attack. But then again, why should he?

The Witherspoons backed his innocence vehemently. He wasn't 'that kind of kid.' If he wanted sex, he wouldn't have chosen a Cordell girl, they argued. And, about two hundred men in Cordell smelled liked smoke, sawdust, and sweat. The Witherspoon family was as adamant in defense as the Cordells were in their charge.

There was no proof otherwise, and neither the authorities nor Franklin's lawyers could make a case against David. But the court of public opinion was against him.

Both families suffered. The Cordells in the obvious ways; bad things were not to happen to regal families. Merrilee was wounded and disgraced."

"Whatever happened to her, Owen?"

"As soon as she was old enough, Merrilee left town. We didn't see her for years. Her twin, Naomi, disappeared in her own way. She married an accountant, moved from The Wedge to a little Cape Cod on a side street, and sought a quiet, undistinguished life in marriage that didn't have the name Cordell attached to it. She simply melted into the community without identity. To this day, many residents don't know Naomi is a Cordell at all."

"And David Witherspoon?"

"Same thing. Left town as soon as he could." Owen rolled his eyes and then continued.

"Meanwhile, the Witherspoons had this cloud of guilt hanging over them. Both businesses lost customers. Being that there was now a second realtor in town, and wood was available up and down the Deschutes, the entire Cordell/Witherspoon alliance was now debunk.

Each family lost the glitter and sole-provider legacy enjoyed at the beginning of this undertaking. Instead, the 'for us or against us' attitude projected by both families simply made matters worse.

This was the beginning of the end of the dynasty the two men had begun. It became a 'pick a side and stay with it' situation that caused confusion, disinterest, or amusement among town folk.

But it wasn't amusing to either family. There were lots of incidents. Not quite Hatfield and McCoy stuff, with the gunfire and all, but lots of little things.

John moved the listings of all his properties over to Reddick Reality.

Franklin's realty business slowed enough after the initial boom that his son, Charles, added insurance sales when he took over the business. He had to tap the family fortune to support his existing lifestyle, not that there wasn't plenty of that.

But Franklin never let up on his relentless attack on John Witherspoon. Working now for his son, he told prospective buyers that Witherspoon's land was second-rate, in tax arrears, and that John was crazy and, therefore, a risk as a land provider.

He may have been correct, to some point. I believe that by the end of his life, in part caused by his Cordell afflictions, John did become borderline crazy.

Certainly his singular obsession of wood, wood, wood was part of that. But some of John's behaviors and business practices were weird, to say the least. He'd stomp about his cutting sites in the mountains, looking for slackers. He always believed someone, with or without reason, was somehow cheating him. Maybe a whip sawyer was working too slowly, maybe the skinners were too slow to bring the logs to mill. Somebody was stealing a log or some planed planks here and there for his own purposes. Any customer that took more than thirty days to pay a bill couldn't get another stick of fir from John until any bill, any size, was paid. Maybe not then, either.

If John Witherspoon put someone on the 'bad' list, the customer might as well find another mill. John would require cash-and-carry only, offering no loyalty or discounting.

John became overly defensive and paranoid about everyone. Any ripple in his business affairs, well, he figured it somehow involved Franklin Cordell and his son Charles. Probably wasn't true, at least most of the time but John could never get over the notion that Franklin was working against him in all instances. John's firm notion that the Cordells were always out to get him led him to suspect that any buyer might be a 'plant' from Cordell, there to trick or cheat him.

John seldom made appearances downtown, growing more and more reclusive. He went from his modest cottage home in the foothills straight to the mill and then back home. He had a wife and three children (town folk often wondered how that could ever have happened), but the entire family mostly stayed up in the forest. Every one of them was involved in the lumber business from about age seven on up. The oldest, Raymond, would take over the business.

John's wife June came into town for household errands and the business, collecting overdue bills. She did the banking and delivered small loads of lumber. John was seldom seen.

And when he was, the encounter could be a bit intimidating. John always looked like someone straight from the wilderness. He was perpetually dirty and greasy, layered in sawdust. His unkempt, untrimmed beard ran right up into his scraggly, white hair. He tucked the pant legs of his ragged coveralls into high-topped boots with split seams and holes in the toes, as if he were going to ride a bicycle and didn't want the chain to catch.

While John looked like a homeless person, everyone knew the Witherspoons were well off. So the operative notion was that he was just cheap. His zeal for collecting outstanding debts, his relentless obsession with the Cordell family, and his somewhat outdated logging equipment and operation supported this view.

He certainly didn't make his money through customer relations. Customers were often treated rather rudely. A friend of mine said he was once greeted in the mill office by John, cradling a shotgun.

Witherspoon swore a lot. Sometimes a customer had trouble distinguishing whether he was being sworn with or at. When someone would tell John what he wanted to build, John wouldn't offer any choice or selection of product. He would simply tell the customer what type of wood he needed, how much, and the price.

'What else is available?' the buyer might ask.

'Nothing,' John would reply. 'This is what you need. Are you paying cash, or do you need thirty days?'

Anti-social, frugal to a fault, stubborn, that was John Witherspoon."

"Wow, Owen," I interjected. "It's a wonder either man could stay in business."

"I'll say this. The overbearing Franklin Cordell got a bit too big for his britches, and people resented it. Meanwhile, John Witherspoon couldn't stand success. He had all the Cordell wood business and, like Peter, Peter, Pumpkin Eater, he couldn't keep her.

Luckily, both families made their money early on. If it weren't for insurance, Cordell would've been in trouble. If it weren't for some tract sales to the new timber wholesalers in the region, Witherspoon wouldn't have been making much money. They both left plenty, though, to their sons who took over both businesses: Charles Cordell and Raymond Witherspoon.

If his funeral is any measure of the man, this much is true. Franklin Cordell was buried on a sunny day, with more Cordells standing over his grave than anyone else. John Witherspoon was buried on a rainy day, and there were seven of us in attendance."

"So, what happened?" I asked. "Did the feud continue?"

"Oh, sure, bad feelings pass like flu. Each family spent way too much time trying to hurt the other. You know, resentment is like taking poison and hoping the other guy dies. That's how it was with the Cordells and Witherspoons. Both Charles and Raymond were apples falling close to the tree.

Charles Cordell didn't have his heart in real estate. With Franklin only around in an advisory capacity, Cordell Realty slowed to half speed. You hear about this now and then. A man builds his company from the ground up. He has his heart and soul in it. But the next generation takes over and either squanders the assets, or fails to further the tradition, growth, and reputation of his birthright. He runs the thing into the ground. Strong father, weak son."

Owen paused, framing his next thought.

Charles was a milquetoast kind of guy, meek, like his mother. He had the personality of a turtle, and he moved like one. He was a lousy salesman, of both real estate and insurance. Of course, the Depression was right around the corner, so you could say he had a tough road. But, Charles brought no spunk to his work. He'd sit in the office in his short-sleeve shirt, ugly tie, and baggy pants, waiting for someone to drop in. Or, he'd amble down to the café and sit at the counter, listening to the old men discuss past and pending perils. His insight to either was absent or inane. He lacked confidence and instilled none in others. For him, life was slow, business was slow, his get-up-and-go was slow.

Up in the foothills, Raymond Witherspoon's impact was much greater. His dad's eccentricities seemed to pass by Raymond okay, and he was a better businessman than John. But he was not nearly as passionate about wood. He'd watched his father's single focus on that and his slow descent into mental illness play out on a daily basis. Raymond wasn't going to be consumed by the heart and stomach problems that finally killed his father. He let his office staff, mostly leftovers from his father's day, run the milling operation. His job was management, planning, and finance.

Raymond recognized the need to expand the family business. It was Raymond who built a second Witherspoon mill, this one right here in town. It was Raymond who increased production and shipping, certainly made available by the railroad. It was Raymond's success that enticed a dozen other millers to town.

Raymond was a quiet, shy man. He knew no girl in town would ever have anything to do with him because of the Merrilee Cordell attack. When we all went to school together, Raymond never dated anyone. He eventually married the homely daughter of a lumberman in Oregon City.

In terms of 'grit for wood' his younger brother David had more heart than Raymond did. David could have run the milling operation himself, if it weren't for that troubled youth and the cloud of suspicion about a heinous act. He was also a bit unstable, traits of his father, but worse. As soon as he could quit school, he did, and left town. So David was never really in the picture, and Raymond took over the lumbering company.

Now Raymond did inherit from his father one passion. He hated the Cordells. He knew all about Franklin's betrayal of good faith with John. His brother had been publicly accused by the Cordells of rape. Only getting back at the Cordells seemed to bring any excitement to his life.

He was good at it, and he hurt the Cordells badly. One particular instance broke whatever spirit Charles Cordell ever possessed. It involved Patty Mayer, her baby, and the ranch she and her husband, Ronald, homesteaded north of town.

Turns out that Patty had a baby as a result of a year-long tryst with Franklin Cordell. This had gone undetected, as Patty told no one, certainly Franklin did not, and no one ever really asked. Ronald Mayer always had his personal doubts about the fatherhood, but these were not the times of airing one's laundry in public.

Now Mayer's ranch touched John Witherspoon's property on one side and The Acre on the other. It was there before the two entrepreneurs had staked their claim. The Mayers were trying to 'dry-farm' the land and were having a tough go of it when Patty and Franklin became involved.

Sometime before the 'great falling out,' as Franklin often referred to his relationship with John Witherspoon, he and Patty had this fling, resulting in that little girl. Franklin never acknowledged little Peggy nor offered any financial or other kind of support.

Before he fell deathly ill, Franklin told his son about the possibility of acquiring that ranch and developing it. He knew from pillow talk that the Mayers would sell in a heartbeat. All Charles had to do was obtain a right-of-way to it. He could improve the road up to it through The Acre, but who would be interested in getting to their new houses by that route? No, better to buy the property and go straight up from Witherspoon Avenue. This purchase would improve chances of developing that side of the tracks. The purchase would be devastating to the Witherspoons. That alone made the idea appealing to the listless Charles.

Charles, armed with his father's last creative idea, decided to pursue the acquisition of the Mayer ranch. This became the only sizable real estate deal Charles ever attempted.

He should have left it alone," Owen said, almost ruefully.

"Raymond Witherspoon got wind of that intent. He decided to buy the Mayer's ranch before Charles could. When he visited the Mayers to make an offer, he got more than he could've ever expected. Patty, it seems, had become increasingly guilty, ashamed, and bitter about Franklin's disregard for her. To an astonished Raymond and a crestfallen husband, she confessed to the affair and her despair in being further insulted by agreeing to a Cordell purchase of the ranch. Her teenage daughter deserved better than that. Besides that, she was tired of the hardscrabble rancher's life.

Raymond sat there, stunned. Then, gathering up his composure, he offered the Mayers a fair price for the ranch. Patty and the sullen Ronald agreed to his price on the spot. It would be the first and only land that the Witherspoons ever acquired that did not involve lumber. The Witherspoons now owned a site coveted by the Cordells. That in itself was a victory.

But Raymond wasn't finished. He made it very public that he now owned the Mayer ranch, and that Reddick Realty would be handling it. More brazen, he made innuendos about Franklin's affair.

Franklin's tendencies toward skirt-chasing made it all seem plausible, possible, probable. Wildfire never spread quicker. The Cordell reputation nose-dived.

Poor Charles never knew what hit him. His father had never told him about this indiscretion, and except for denial, Charles had no real response to this thunderbolt. The Mayers would leave town, but the Cordells were left with a scandal of illicit sex, conception, and failure of responsibility."

"I can't top that, Owen. Tale of a town, nicely done. You've told me how Cordell came to be, the two families and their problems, and about The Strip. You haven't told me how Ticket's comes to sit by itself.

Now it is late, and I don't want to overstay my welcome. When do I get to hear that?"

"You're coming back in a few weeks, right? I'll tell you that story then."

"Good enough."

We shook hands and exchanged telephone numbers.

Chapter Four

Stonekicker Bob

Forty-five days later, I was back in Cordell. I'd called Owen with my travel plan: arrive a day early for my presentation, and stay for a week afterward. My wife wasn't thrilled with the idea of my spending more time away and spending whatever income I made in the meantime, but I told her and Owen that this was simply an investment in what was becoming a minor obsession with me.

I slept in and had the free breakfast at the motel – different room, but on the same side of the building. I read a newspaper and drank coffee, watching the bar for signs of life. About mid-morning the non-confident neon sign flickered to life. I gave Owen a few minutes to settle in and get his tea, and then walked over.

"Good to see you again," Owen said, almost breaking a smile.

"Here, too. Am I too early?"

"No, I figured you for about this time. Never too early for company, though I am partial to visitors who actually buy something." He took any sting out of that shot with an actual smile. "I got some cold cuts and fresh bread – baked beans, too. That's a lot of lunch for Ticket's." Owen had gone out of his way for my second visit.

"Owen, as I told you on the phone, I want to change the deal. I'm stoked about your stories. I'm going to write a book about Cordell, this bar, and you. I need your help. I know you want to hear stories, and I'll do a few. But not one for one; maybe one for four. You'll need to trust me and just keep talking. I'll take it from there. You get to see the manuscript before publication. I hope that's acceptable."

"I got all that from our phone conversations. You want to make me an overnight sensation. Taken me an entire lifetime to do that. I'll tell you stories. You decide what goes into this book of yours."

This had gone easier than I expected. New game.

My coffee, his tea, the table beside the bullet holes, and we were off. Owen warned me that I still needed to tell the first tale. I objected, but he said something about giving before I could receive.

I was just finishing my tale about Herb Bierly saving my life in a mostly frozen creek when the door opened and in shuffled a peculiar old-timer. He had to be at least in his seventies, probably eighties.

Except for the little pointy cap, the fellow looked like one of those gnome statues that people put by their back doors. He wore a heavy, flannel, Irish-green shirt, and tan pants too large in all dimensions, with the bottoms dragging in tatters behind high-topped clodhoppers. Over all that was a black-and-silver plaid jacket with some serious stains and cuffs worn to the insulation. He wore an old railroader's cap, mattress blue and white, with an IH emblem on it. He was untidy.

His gray beard stretched from his drooping earlobes to the middle of his shirt, sticking out at odd angles. His red face was carved with age lines. He moved slowly but steadily, with no limp or lean. He looked down at the floor as he headed to the first bar stool by the bullnose.

"Morning, Bob," Owen said. The gnome murmured something, raising his head long enough to take note of a third party in the room. Bob immediately laid a smooth, radish-sized stone on the bar just in front of his right hand. He stared straight down at the bar.

Bob's world is a small one, I thought to myself.

"Be right back," Owen said, and made his way behind the bar.

Owen collected two draft glasses and filled one with water, no ice. He drew a beer from the middle tap and placed both in front of Bob. "Nice stone, Bob." Bob picked up the small rock and rolled it around his open palm so Owen could view it from all angles. Then he precisely positioned it back on the bar.

Bob finally spoke. "This is my grandfather's wood. He built this bar." Owen nodded and moved back down the bar. In two equal hauls Bob emptied the glass of water. Immediately he started to sip his beer.

"Finish your story," Owen said as he returned to his seat. I did, in about three minutes. We discussed it for about five more.

As if on cue, Bob polished off that glass of beer, dug in his pocket, and removed some change which he placed on the bar. He picked up the stone, got to his feet, and head down, strode out the door.

"Have a good day, Bob. See you later," Owen said to the only-slightly bent back.

"Who the hell was that?" I asked.

"Stonekicker Bob."

"Stonekicker Bob?"

"Yeah, he's Cordell's crazy guy. Every town has one, I guess. Most days you can find him on the streets, walking head-down and kicking a stone in front of him. Can't go anywhere without skittering a stone. Of course he's out of his mind, been so since he was a kid. Mostly he's harmless. Our meaner kids tease him, knowing they can get him riled. Bob gets all agitated and twitchy and starts hollering nonsense stuff. Sad, really."

"He seems odd," I offered. "A bit set in his ways."

"Oh, you noticed that, did you?" Owen's voice dripping sarcasm. "That is his major distinction. He's really compulsive about everything he does. Bob is all about routines. Everything has to be just so. Unless it's snowing hard or raining buckets, he'll be on the streets.

The time of his little sashays varies but little, but never the routine or route. He leaves his house and kicks his stone down the sidewalk to this place. He walks in, puts his rock of the day on the bar just above his right hand, and waits for his glass of water and his beer – always Bud.

You saw. Never orders a second beer, never chips, a pickled egg, or a sandwich. Then he puts two quarters on the bar, always face up and touching each other, like together they make a fifty-cent piece. Then he leaves. Go look at the quarters. You'll see."

I did. They were just as Owen said.

"Fifty cents? You are charging me $1.25; $1.75 for premiums. He only pays fifty cents?"

"Yep," Owen conceded. "Been paying fifty cents for years now. Years ago drafts were fifty cents. Somewhere back then Bob pretty much lost any sense of reality. He remembers paying fifty cents for a draft, and that's what he continues to pay, in quarters, always quarters. A new price would alter his routine, change his carefully controlled world. Bob doesn't like change."

"So what does he do next?"

"Right now? He is kicking his stone down The Boulevard, on the right side of the street. He'll kick it all the way to the river. He'll sit on a little perch down there and watch the water for about fifteen minutes. Then he'll get up and kick that stone up the other side of the street, making his way back to the house he shares with his sister. It's right up past your hotel. The blue Victorian clapboard at the top of the street."

"Does he keep the same stone forever?"

"He'd like to. From time to time, though, he loses one. Kicks it somewhere he can't find it or something. That ruins his day. Bob is in a foul mood, and very excitable, until he has a suitable replacement. Mostly, though, he guards a good stone with great care."

"Every day, the same routine?" I quizzed.

"Except for the exact hour or bad weather. Actually, there's a round two to this. Bob repeats one-half of his routine in the evening. He'll leave his house in just enough time to kick that stone down to the corner of The Boulevard. He's already seen the river for the day, I guess, so he turns around. He kicks the rock back to my bar, arriving exactly at eight forty five p.m. He's more careful about time in the evening. Wants to be in bed by ten o'clock. No water this time, but two beers. Four quarters on the bar. First time you came in, you missed him by five minutes. You come back tonight, and you will see him again."

"Stonekicker Bob, eh? Everyone call him that?"

"About everyone. I don't. Neither did Jimmy or Brush. About everyone else, though."

"Why not you guys?"

"History, I guess. One of Bob's set patterns is to tell me every day that his grandfather built this bar. He repeats it, both visits, every time he sits down. Always the same words, always the same emphasis on the words 'grandfather' and 'wood,' always to me or Brush, even though we've already heard it a thousand times.

Of course he's right about that. You see, Bob's last name is Witherspoon. Many folks around here don't know that, being at least two generations removed from the days of John Witherspoon.

But we Tickets know, and we remember." Owen's thoughtful look told me there was another piece to this.

"When my grandfather, Noah, had the financial resources to replace his wooden-plank bar with the real thing, he naturally went to John for a plan, the wood, and the craftsmen. John was a regular at Ticket's then, and he and my grandfather were on their way to becoming lifelong friends.

Witherspoon had already been thinking of how nice his wood would look in a more elegant bar and back-bar, so he and Noah planned it out quickly. During the construction, several other upgrades were undertaken as well. John installed this hardwood floor, added a hand-carved sign over the entrance that said 'Tickets,' and built that pretty staircase over there.

Noah didn't have the cash for all this, but Witherspoon convinced him now was the time. He offered to carry the cost while Noah made payments. That certainly wasn't John's regular way of doing business, and my grandfather was honored by that.

Noah simply moved his planks out to the center of the room and didn't lose a sale throughout the renovation. The bullnose bar you see today is made of differently stained and in-laid hard and soft woods. Old-world craftsmanship. Near the floor at the rear is etched 'Witherspoon Lumber Co., 1907.'

Noah paid off his debt as quickly as he could. The Witherspoons and the Tickets have gotten along wonderfully ever since.

Truly, the Witherspoons have helped our family the few times we really needed it. John helped Noah with the long-term lease, and later purchase, of this property.

John's son Raymond went to school with my dad, and they developed about the same level of relationship as that shared by their fathers. Raymond helped me years later when I was in a legal dispute with the Cordell family. His generosity in the debacle helped save Ticket's. It also cemented the connection between the two families."

Owen paused, ran his fingers across his chin, and looked over at his beautiful bar. "After he took over the lumber business, Raymond faced two family conundrums, both of which were continuing, embarrassing, and out of his control.

The first problem was his second child, Bob. Bob had inherited his grandfather's mental instability. Bob spent a lifetime becoming the 'Stonekicker Bob' you just saw. Even as a child and then a young man, Bob coped poorly with society, a misfit, really. He was petulant, distant, and obstinate, much more like his uncle, David, than his father. And insecure. Bob's personal guard was always up against anything or anyone who didn't follow patterns, protocols, or 'the way things got done.' Today they would call him 'obsessive-compulsive.' Back then they called it 'crazy.' He failed at any work his father tried on him when he was old enough.

Bob's life has been one downward spiral. He wasn't good at anything related to the wood business, and he knew it. People in town either liked the Cordells or the Witherspoons, and he knew it, even if he couldn't tell who was which. Raymond was watching his son sink slowly into madness.

Raymond's second problem was his daughter. From about age thirteen Charlotte was the wildest gal in town. She shared the Witherspoon passion, all right, but it wasn't for wood. Charlotte liked men. She was just plain promiscuous. She was available to all the men and boys in town, and she all but took out an ad in the *Gazette* to advertise that fact. A psychologist may say that her sexual proclivities were an obvious sign of resentment toward her family. I think that may be a stretch, psycho-babble, although she and her dad never bonded, that's for sure.

For my money, I think she just liked sex. She liked it better than she liked her reputation, her relationship with her father, and any other use of time. That she never ended up pregnant without the benefit of matrimony was a mystery to everyone.

So, here is Raymond, constantly dealing with Bob's mental instabilities and Charlotte's risqué lifestyle. When she was about twenty, Charlotte left the family residence and headed for town, closer the action you might say. Raymond was happy enough to see her go, so he bought her a place to live -- that Victorian. For several years it was a busy place. Incidentally, Raymond bought that house from me."

"What? You used to live where Charlotte and Stonekicker Bob Witherspoon now live?"

"Yep. That house was built for Noah by John Witherspoon with the same wood, same craftsmen as this bar. Noah bought the lot from John and moved out of the upstairs here after he married my grandmother. Noah raised George there. My dad moved his bride in later on, and that's where I was raised. My grandmother and my dad both died in that house. After my parents died, I stayed until 1987. I decided it was just too much space and work. Keeping up this bar was enough for me. So, I sold it to Raymond, and I moved upstairs here."

Owen shrugged again. "Weird, huh? I often think that the Tickets and Witherspoons just shared that place and space for about a hundred years. Raymond was just buying back what his father had once owned. That's mostly true about this place, too, 'cept that I still own this one.

I didn't get very far, did I? I ended up living in the same room my grandfather started out in."

"Owen, that's a curious piece of irony, isn't it? Life in a small town, eh?"

"I guess," Owen agreed.

"Anyway, back to Bob. He became such a problem that he needed daily oversight. Raymond already had his hands full with the lumber works and his tart of a daughter. Good it was, then, that Charlotte stepped up to the plate. For reasons apparent to no one, she moved Bob into her house and changed her ways virtually overnight. No more partying about town, no more men, no more Monday morning stories at the cafe. For the past twenty years, Charlotte has done Bob's laundry, has prepared him three meals a day, and has kept him in pocket change. All quarters.

Life is as good as it's going to get for Bob. He's fed and warm at night. He roams the town freely, kicking his stone out in front of him. He and his sister live a simple life, never really wanting for anything.

Raymond was ecstatic about this turn of events, the answer to both his prayers. He saw to it that his two children never lacked money. They lived off a sizable account Raymond opened for them, plus the monthly government checks each received.

When all that was in place, Raymond sold Witherspoon Lumber Company to a lumbering conglomerate. He and his wife promptly relocated to Arizona.

My dad watched after Bob as he wandered about town. If George saw kids teasing Bob, he stopped it. If it was really cold, snowy, rainy, or slippery outdoors, George saw to it that someone made sure Bob safely made his way up home.

Now I keep an eye out for him. It's about all anyone can do for old Bob. Who else will do it? Bob needs a little cushion here and there, and I can provide it. But honestly, such as Brush and Jimmy have always checked after Bob, too.

Given the ties between families, why am I going to tell Bob that he needs more quarters for a beer at Tickets?"

Owen showed me his two open palms, gesturing that it was my turn.

I told Owen my town had more than one strange character, and I offered a quick description and story of Paul the Pervert.

CHAPTER FIVE

Don't Mess With Jimmy

"**O**kay, Barkeep," I said, after we had restocked the table. "Let's hear about some of other fascinating denizens of Ticket's."

Sustained silence while Owen mulled the question.

"Many come to mind," he finally said, solemnly. "You know, a bar is all about its regulars. My whole life has involved those people. I'm not sure where to start."

"You've told some about Brush. And you mentioned someone named Jimmy," I reminded him. "Why not start with him?"

"Ah, Jimmy. Came to Cordell after WW II." Owen's face came to light just thinking about the man.

"Jimmy Delotti was a Sicilian; grew up in Chicago. He was young then, but he was already 'mobbed up,' as they say. An up-and-comer for them. At the time, though, he was just doing some of the heavy lifting. He and his two older brothers were doing street work, numbers running, that sort of stuff.

The Delottis were also in the 'redistribution' end of things. They provided their neighborhood with fridges, ovens, guns, fresh meat, whatever had 'fallen off' a truck somewhere. They didn't steal it, but they'd deliver it. Ends up that the two brothers went to jail, but not Jimmy — some technicality or squeeze that he never really discussed.

Jimmy was rough under a smooth skin, tough, loyal, and temperamental.

But then World War II happened. Jimmy was drafted and was in the army as soon as America entered the fight.

He was on the front in Europe, but that didn't last long. Through some lucky set of circumstances he got friendly with a colonel of some importance and became the guy's 'dog robber.' You know what a dog robber is?"

"No."

"A dog robber is a personal aide to a superior officer," Owen explained.

"Jimmy was the officer's 'gofer' – procuring anything the colonel wanted, legal or not. Sometimes it was stuff for the war effort. Sometimes it was scotch, women, steaks. If Jimmy was to get something – anything -- he did. Even if he had to rob a dog to do so. The job required everything Jimmy had already brought to the army: street savvy, cunning, smooth talk, movie-star looks, the whole deal. He was good at it.

As with most vets, Jimmy was a changed man after the war. Two things had come to him as certains. First, he wasn't going back to his old life in Chicago. His brothers were out of jail by then, but it was only a matter of time before they'd be going back. Jimmy knew that.

His dog-robbing days in the service had also shown him that his skills could be applied inside and outside the black market. The legitimacy with which he had operated in the army was altogether missing the drama, guns, violence, and rearview mirroring of his pre-war life. He was tired of looking over his shoulder. His were transferrable skills, and he decided he was going to make a clean break from both Chicago and the service.

It was less a matter of guilt than personal comfort and safety that appealed to Jimmy. Besides, Jimmy had all those Chicago — and therefore, Seattle — connections; they weren't going anywhere soon. So he had both sides of the legal fence working for him. He'd just keep a foot on each side.

Second, he had fallen in love with an army nurse he met at a soiree in Germany. Mary Coldiron was a beautiful, twenty-two-year-old brunette who had signed up directly out of nursing school. She was simple, shy, and quiet. She was genuinely smitten with Jimmy, although she worked hard for a while not to show it. She finally gave up all that reserve and allowed talk of life forever together. When the war was over, she was going home.

To Cordell, Oregon.

Jimmy said that he chased Mary Coldiron from the Rhine to the Deschutes. In truth, he did. Mary returned to Cordell first. Only months later, Jimmy arrived, having never been in Oregon or heard of Cordell. He came to claim his wife.

He passed through Chicago on the way, but never left the train station or called anyone. He bought a westbound ticket, rode the train, and thought about Mary. He was going to marry that girl. For his entire life, Mary was Jimmy's 'all in all.'

Unfortunately, he didn't marry her. Didn't, or couldn't.

Mary had returned to live with her parents and to help run their little clock, gift, and curio shop on The Boulevard. Her parents were God-fearing people, twenty years out of Eugene. Their shop and their only child constituted their world — those and the church. They were serious Baptists.

And Jimmy Delotti was a Catholic. When he first called on them, Mary's parents were cordial, even genial. They treated him with the deference of any guest, especially a veteran, in their home. Jimmy left thinking that he'd made a good impression. He knew they were already aware of his intentions for their daughter.

But in Cordell, and certainly in the Coldiron household, in the forties, Baptists didn't marry Catholics. The next day, at lunch at Prinder's Café, only a few doors down from Ticket's, Jimmy received Mary's heart-rending story about their star-crossed situation.

Through tears, Mary tried to explain her plight to Jimmy. She was trapped between her love for him and the wishes of her parents that she 'find a man of similar beliefs,' preferably Baptist, but certainly Protestant. Marrying a Catholic, her parents told Mary, would be almost as bad as her marrying a Jew or an Asian, or a Negro. All were pretty much in the same category: 'They aren't our kind.'

Jimmy was perplexed and unbelieving. 'What's wrong with Catholics? I can't be the only Catholic in town. Are we all a bad lot? What's the problem? Doesn't the fact that we are in love matter? Kids? We'll raise them Baptist if you want. Surely we can work this out.'

But young Mary knew how adamantly her parents held their beliefs. She could not defy her parents and whatever prejudices they carried. They were family. She was devoted to them. She remembered how upset they were when she enlisted. And their narrow acceptance of that was based strictly on patriotism.

Also, they needed her in the store. To go off with Jimmy was to exclude herself from her family. She couldn't imagine life in Cordell with parents who would disown her. Just when they needed her most.

And, she was ashamed to admit, there was fear of 'what would people say?' Probably things like, 'She married a Catholic. She turned her back on her parents. And good people they are, too. For what? Some fish-eater. After all they have done for her.'

She shared a tamed-down version of this with Jimmy.

'Then we'll move,' said Jimmy. But that was no option for Mary. It didn't really solve any of the turmoil in her head. Even knowing then that she was making a decision that she would regret for the rest of her life, Mary was just trapped in all those cords.

So there it was. The love of his life, the only one Jimmy would ever have, was unobtainable. With whatever mutual dignity each could muster, Jimmy and Mary parted. Neither ever married."

Owen paused. "So, Owen, I guess we have a Romeo and Juliet deal going here. Ended badly, neither ever happy again?"

Owen waved that off. "It worked out a bit better than that. After some awkward beginnings, they remained lifelong friends, and from the middle on, lifelong partners. For almost two decades they'd lived by her parents' edict. Some stolen hours, sure, but not what either really wished. After her parents were gone, Jimmy practically lived in Mary's apartment, making up for lost time, I suppose. They were recognized in the community as a couple; not married, but respected for who they were.

Before all this played out, however, Jimmy became a mostly legitimate dog robber, with no direct military or obvious mob affiliation. He rented an old warehouse down by the rail spur and opened Delotti Enterprises, registered as an import and consignment business. How's that for vague? Lived on the second floor, which he'd decked out to his taste.

He quickly became Cordell's go-to-guy. If anyone needed anything, legal or not, Jimmy Delotti could produce it. Maybe some special liquor – Ticket's was known for fancy brands – or a unique gun, or a diamond, Chicago steaks, or a truckload of fresh vegetables, high-end call girls, low-end strippers, tax-free cigarettes. Whatever, Jimmy could get it. Just never ask him where he got it.

Obviously, his Chicago connections were still in place. He cultivated personal and business relationships in Seattle, Portland, and Eugene, with people he'd met during the war, and western wise guys. He seemed to know everybody, everywhere."

"Interesting fellow, this Jimmy," I interjected, just to give Owen a rest.

"To say the least," Owen agreed. "Jimmy had sort of a beguiling fierceness, the presence of a lion with a short fuse. He was streetwise, and he could be moody. I once asked him why he always carried a weapon. 'What are you afraid of, Jimmy?'

'Nothing,' Jimmy grinned.

Now, remember, Jimmy was only about twenty-five years old in 1946. He sported thick, black hair, smoothed straight back over his head with lots of Trol, and light olive skin. Thin, muscular. But short, inches away from six feet. He looked great in quality clothes, and that's all he wore. He'd walk down the street in a natty camel-colored overcoat, suit and tie underneath, shiny shoes, the whole deal. Clothes were one of his few vices. Jimmy always looked like a million bucks. Dapper. Never a hat; I guess he didn't want to mess up that hair. He loved clothes and women, single women only, though. Jimmy never messed with someone else's wife. He always said that was alley cat stuff. He had no trouble with the young women from town, from Eugene or Portland. But he never really tried to find another Mary. Women were only sporadic pleasures to Jimmy.

Women wanted him, though. They flirted with him all the time. Ladies love outlaws, like little boys like stray dogs, you know. Some just wanted to be close to the heat; others thought they could change his basic nature. They all came up short."

Owen shook his head, as if in some disbelief. "Jimmy had that charismatic mix of confidence and charm about him. He was mannerly and engaging. Always the focus of any room he occupied. People liked him, but, in the early years, folks gave Jimmy a wide berth. Still, they would do just about anything for him; they followed whatever lead he took. They'd heard of his previous Chicago connections, but they didn't hear it from Jimmy.

The few who'd tried to give Jimmy the short end of a handshake agreement spoke with great respect, fear, really, about Jimmy's absolute, if subdued, ruthlessness. Crossing Jimmy was a fool's mission. Woe be it to the soul who tried to trick Jimmy. That was disrespectful, and the consequences weren't pretty. There were people in this town who could attest to that. There was a would-be dodger who spent most of his life with a limp of which he never spoke. A cagey fence salesman was short on his order. He was financially ruined and without a home in one week. We knew both had tried to jam Jimmy. Iron fist in a velvet glove and all that.

So, Jimmy always had this reputation. Still, you had to love him.

His warehouse held an amazing collection of all sorts of goods: furniture, alcohol, ammunition, canned goods, finished steel, you name it. If it wasn't there, Jimmy could get a truckload of it. He had a helper to run the everyday comings and goings. But if you wanted to find Jimmy, you were better off on The Boulevard. His office was really the street.

Day in and day out, he would amble about, chatting up the shoppers and shopkeepers. He'd be wearing that camel coat, looking like he was on his way to the bank. But he'd stop and talk to everyone. Someone would ask for something, a deal was made on the spot, and that was that. Slick, but fair.

Jimmy was a regular here. He'd come in two or four nights a week and have a couple beers, sometimes a bourbon on the rocks, still all dressed up – best-kept guy in the bar. Most folks had just come from the mills, fields, or factories; Jimmy looked he was at a sales convention. Jimmy became close friends of my father and me. And Brush too. He'd stop in the other places sometimes, but this was his haunt.

Everyone called him 'Jimmy The Was.' He probably caused that nickname himself. See, people already knew Jimmy was part of the mob before the war. The way his business operated, his ability to provide the most exotic goods, his reluctance to tell anyone just how he obtained them, well, all of that made folks think he was still 'connected.' Jimmy had to be a mobster, perhaps their mobster, but still a mobster. People would joke with him about it. 'Hey, Jimmy, how's the 'family?' 'Jimmy, you're not getting any dead fish in the mail, are you?' Sometimes, they just asked the direct question: 'Jimmy, are you part of the mob?'"

Owen laughed. "Jimmy never tried to laugh off the comments, never attempted earnest protestations. With a dismissive wave of his hand, he'd say, 'I worked for those guys once, no more. I'm legit.' End of conversation.

"Some believed him, some didn't. Jimmy simply said he 'was,' not 'is.'

"Jimmy The Was," Owen smiled. "I once tried to make a fisherman out of him, but that didn't work. I took him down to the Deschutes to catch some redsides, but he couldn't get it done. Mostly he caught his hook on the bottom, or the trees behind him when casting a line. Too much Chicago in him, and not enough country, I guess.

"They still tell stories about Jimmy The Was."

"Tell me one," I asked, with more request in my tone than demand.

"Easy. I told you that Jimmy had a temper. Usually, that wasn't a problem, but he had that hot Mediterranean blood, and if someone raised it, Jimmy's volatile side escaped.

"Case in point. One evening, Stonekicker Bob was on his personal barstool as usual, working on his two beers. Now this was somewhere around 1960, give or take a year or two. I know George was running the bar. Bob was no more than thirty years old or so, but that's right about the time his mind completely went around the bend. All his routines were in place by then. Bob had already quit cutting his hair and beard, neither as white, of course. He looked about the same as he does today, except for the whiter hair and deeper wrinkles.

Anyway, there were five or six other regulars sprinkled around the bar, in addition to a friendly, penny-ante poker game at the middle table.

In strode two young loggers, a curly redhead and a blonde fellow. Neither was far removed from legal age. They'd been drinking elsewhere.

I was a teenager then. Been working in the bar for years already. My dad was off that night, so Brush was behind the bar. I was washing barware and preparing a liquor order for Jimmy's monthly delivery.

Anyway, these two frisky characters came in with great show, slapping and head-locking each other, making enough racket so that everyone would be aware of their arrival. I sensed that these two were going to cause some commotion.

I was on my way to the basement to inventory the bottles of wine. I figured I'd be counting the same bottles I did the previous month. Ticket's was not a wine kind of establishment, but we kept some around for the ladies. I caught Brush's eye and nodded toward the two. Brush nodded back.

I was coming up from the basement while the two blowhards, particularly the red-headed one, were turning their appearance at the bar into a show. They ordered their beers and chasers loudly, so that everyone could see they were big drinkers. They quaffed off the first round and ordered a second in equally loud voices.

And they nestled down next to Stonekicker Bob, sitting there with his head and eyes down, as always, with his stone in front of his right hand.

They knew him and started right in on him. And they were lit up.

The redhead moved close to the deranged man and started to ridicule Bob's weird tendencies. 'Look who's here! Hey, Stonekicker, whatcha doin'? You don't need any more beer to make you crazy. Had a bath lately? That's some fancy coat you're wearing. Are you ever gonna cut that beard or start tripping over it? Come on, Bob, say something.'

Bob said nothing. He continued to look straight down at his glass. Bob seldom said anything to tormentors, or to anyone else, for that matter. He twisted himself around his barstool, trying to become invisible, hoping these two would go away.

Jimmy The Was watched this. He was in that poker game, but he noticed the humiliation at the bar. He was watching it so intently that he lost focus on a good hand. But he said not a word.

The redhead continued to heckle Bob. Those bullies just weren't going to let up. They were having fun. And Stonekicker Bob was squirming more and more on his barstool.

Then, the redhead made a bad mistake. He touched both Bob and his stone. 'Hey, Bob,' he said, 'where do you buy a jacket like this? I want one for my sister. This is the rock of the day, eh, Bob? Let me see it.' During his verbal attack, the redhead stood up and grabbed the sleeve of Bob's jacket and reached for the stone.

Bob grabbed his stone, clenching it in his fist. He looked up the redhead with bewilderment and despair.

'C'mon, Bob, let me see the rock. You crazy coot, I ought to teach you a lesson about sharing.' The redhead grabbed Bob's hand. Bob managed only a plaintive small cry and allowed the boy to peel back his fingers to expose the rock.

Without ceremony, Jimmy The Was excused himself from the poker game. He glided over to the bar. 'Hello, son,' he said almost in a whisper. The redhead turned to face him, dropping Bob's hand.

'What?' the boy asked.

Without a word Jimmy The Was gripped the flowing locks of the redhead's curly head. He slammed the boy's face straight down onto the bar. Immediately, there was blood. Jimmy repeated the process three more times.

It was a rudeful and thorough attack. There now was blood everywhere, even on Jimmy's collared shirt and silver tie. The boy's nose was broken, his forehead cracked open, his cheeks pulpy. His legs began to buckle as they lost a purchase on the floor, his eyes wide open in a blank stare. Shocked and battered, he could not utter one word. The only sounds of Jimmy's attack were the repeated thunks of face on bar top.

During all this, Brush had moved from behind the bar and stepped between the blonde boy and Jimmy's rampage. That probably wasn't necessary, because the kid was wild-eyed and scared into inaction. He actually stepped back from the fray, incredulous of the sudden turn of events, terrified, with no conviction to intervene. So, Brush just backed him off another step or so, with his own back to the beating behind him.

Mercifully, Jimmy stopped the facial assault. Jimmy pulled the kid upright and drove his fist into the boy's belly. The sounds of air propelled from both ends of the redhead's body were audible throughout the entire barroom, now silent as patrons watched.

The kid began to choke, and for a moment, seemed ready to expel his recently-imbibed alcohol. Jimmy let him loose for a second, apparently to see if he'd fall. He didn't.

So Jimmy took a half step back and punched the kid again in the stomach. The redhead slowly fell to his knees, his face expressionless. The kid seemed suspended, on his knees in motionless supplication. For three seconds, the only thing moving was the blood running down from his nose, cheeks, forehead, and lips. Bob sat, fidgeting on his stool, freaked out by the drama about him.

Jimmy grabbed the long hair in one hand and Red's waistband in the other. He turned his prey toward the door, which another regular dutifully opened. Jimmy propelled the redhead onto the sidewalk. With a final, violent shove, he pushed the kid across the pavement and onto the railroad tracks. The boy lay there, at right angles to the tracks and, by now, only semi-conscious.

Jimmy looked at the blonde companion, who, naturally, had followed the action outside.

'The nightliner comes through Cordell at eleven thirty-five,' Jimmy said to the blonde. 'Either have this moron on it, or under it.' Jimmy's first words since the attack. 'If I see either one of you in the next month, I'm going to beat you just like this.'

Jimmy turned back into Ticket's. He went directly to the toilet and washed the redhead's blood from his hands and face. He'd have a dry-cleaning bill, no doubt about that. He strolled over to the poker table, just as cool as the side of the pillow. The game resumed. No one had anything to say about the entire incident. Nobody had any question. Nobody was going to grade Jimmy's response. It was all done just that quickly.

Brush told my dad that it took an entire bottle of Lysol to clean all the blood from the bar.

The redhead must have been put on the train. Nobody ever saw him again. The blonde, Leroy McLoin, later became Jimmy's warehouse manager. Jimmy The Was."

CHAPTER SIX

Light My Fire

"**S**orry for the bar calls, but that's how I make a living," Owen apologized.

The few locals who imbibed their lunch had drifted out, and Owen and I were alone again.

"Sell all the beer you can," I told him. "I'll wait. Grover and I will be just fine. But now, keep going; pick any stories, any people. I'm having a great time with this."

"Actually, I'm starting to enjoy myself," Owen confessed. *A real move toward mutual goals*, I thought. "Few people want to hear old stories, and that's all I've got. You asked how Ticket's ended up standing here all by itself – what happened to the rest of The Strip. Time I tell you."

"Perfect," I responded.

Maybe not perfect, he cautioned.

"You have to know that Cordell, from about 1910 through at least the 1950s, was a lumber town. Wood, railroads, wheat, hops, cattle, sheep, and bootlegging. Those were the prime enterprises. But wood was king. Wood is what most people did, in some form or another. Lumber and the railroad went hand in hand, each dependent on the other.

Even before John Witherspoon started his large mill up on The White, there were small, often sporadic enterprises serving the homesteaders. The foothills of the eastern Cascades were the mother lode of soft wood. But these small, and sometimes single-product mills could not produce enough lumber to meet the demand of this part of Oregon. So Witherspoon's operation faced little real competition. He had location and size. He had a business sense for wood and real skill at timber selection. And, he had dibs on all the lumber needs of a brand-new town.

As Franklin Cordell had promised, the railroad came through. Timbering grew in Cordell, as in much of central Oregon, from those tiny sawmills of the late 1860s to a booming business. Cordell became a great location to get it, mill it, and ship it.

Everyone needed wood. Soon there were more than a dozen operating sawmills within a horseback ride of each other, maybe less. There were four or five within shouting distance of each other down by the Deschutes, right up against the rail spur.

Oregon became the soft-wood capital of the world. And why not? There was little regulation about harvesting and re-forestation, and the government was promoting growth and offering lenient logging permits. The supply seemed endless; acres and acres of wood to get out of the sky and onto a rail car.

There were the tiny 'stump jumpers,' who cut a few trees a year for income. There were Mom-and-Pop operations – family or independent foresters who mostly cut wood from their land holdings. There were small operations that specialized in certain woods, or rough-cut only, or planing mills, or laminating works. There were big, conglomerate operations – large, spreading affairs.

And technological advances had changed everything. Water power was replaced by steam, steam was replaced by electricity, mules were replaced by diesel tractors, and wagons were replaced by trucks. Meanwhile, the railroads made shipping it anywhere easy. All that meant that lumber mills no longer had to go to the wood; the wood could come to the mills.

The Hudson's Bay Company, the 'big' land operator early on, hired hundreds of lumbermen to work their new mills. From the twenties through the fifties, men from all over arrived, many of them Swedes from Minnesota, already mostly lumbered out. Lumber camps near logging areas ensured that the workers could be close to the forest.

Most camps offered pretty fair living conditions. Cabins and little houses, tiny schools, hearty food. But as soon as gas and diesel trucks and cars showed up, that proximity wasn't very important. Married men could now move their families to town, to a home of their own. So the population of Cordell grew. The bullwhackers, chokers, cat skinners, buckers, and such moved into The Acre, replacing most of those shanties and tents with sturdy, if small, frame houses. Actually, gave it a needed facelift. The fallers, sawyers, teamsters, and foremen built modest homes in the town proper, while the owners and supervisors erected monuments to themselves in The Wedge. All that called for more wood.

No matter that smoke, sawdust, and noise wafted over Cordell. No matter the influx of 'undesirables' who followed the woodmen. They were visible signs of prosperity.

Timbering helped this town survive the Depression better than many. Lumbering fed the post-war boom and provided Oregon wood products across the nation. It went that way in Cordell until the fifties. But kings live, and kings die. So it was with the forestry business.

All this time wood presented its own problems. Nothing is for nothing. One of the problems with wood is that it burns."

"Really, Owen? I don't think I knew that!"

"Yes, it does, he continued, ignoring my sarcasm. "Fire was the demon of the times. Many a mill ended up in ashes. They were simply tinderboxes waiting for a spark, easily enough produced.

Cordell was made of wood, stacked high with wood, milling more wood every day down in Franklin's 'industrial zone.' And outside of town. The rail yards were full of wood, ready to be loaded and shipped.

Yes, wood burns, and, where it can, it burns high, wide, and hot. Cordell has had two or three devastating fires since 1900. By devastating, I mean that entire mills, blocks of houses, anything, really, quickly leveled.

Nothing quite on the scale of the Chicago Fire, but they were bad enough. O'Leary's cow gets credit for that one. But here, in 1927, someone in our fanciest whorehouse got careless with a candle or a lantern. It being started in a house of ill repute made it difficult to determine exactly who that was.

The fire started on the second floor, near midnight. Several patrons exited the establishment in their long johns, clothes and hat in hand, headed for the river-bank. Anyway, our meager fire department and old equipment, even for those days, was no match for the ensuing inferno. By dawn, fourteen homes, three sawmills, several warehouses, two stables, other structures, and two rail cars were lost — massive destruction for a town this size, and untold amounts of lumber with it.

More than fifty years later, Geraldine Lustag sat right where you are now and quietly told a small group about the fire, which occurred when she was ten years old.

The Lustag family, father, mother, Gerry, and a younger brother, owned a small house in the middle of River Street, midway between where the street opened into the rail yard and the new bridge. That fateful spring night, she was awakened by her mother and told to dress quickly and throw whatever she could into her pillowcase. There was a fire down the street, and it was headed their way.

After her mother did the same for little Harry, they met on the front porch, smelling smoke immediately. To their left, a fire engulfed two buildings near the rail yard, and her father was running up the street to them. 'It's coming,' he hollered. 'It's already in the yard — on the wood — got Beemer's and James'. Out of control! Grab anything you can and go to the bluff. Get up high, farther than the hillside. Wait for me. I'll try to do something down here until we see just how bad it'll be.' He headed back to the flames, joining other men already scuttling about.

Gerry's mother shepherded the two children up the bluff, where other women and children were already gathering. Women were crying, children screaming, but there was little conversation. They simply watched in growing horror, trembling and wide-eyed.

Gerry described a fire that had taken a life of its own, a living, breathing monster. The wind was turning the huge flames into rolling hoops of fire, determined to arc from one building to another.

The rolling ball of fire on the roof of her neighbor's house was a perfect circle of flames. Then, in a heartbeat, the circle disengaged itself and shot a huge, red and yellow lance of fire into the air, curving itself as if it had a plan. It shot straight down, like a spear, and hit the Butler home with a sharp point. Immediately the little house became the leading edge of the devastation.

Sparks were lighting the sky. Smoke and soot were so thick that it was sticking to Gerry's wet face and sneaking up her nostrils. Those on the bluff watched men throwing up buckets of water, a futile effort for sure. Others were rushing in and out of buildings not yet involved, carrying out dogs, and sofas, and coats… anything else they could. A few neighbors formed little relay lines to pass valuables across the street. The fire equipment arrived, but the firemen didn't even know where to start.

The fire grew bigger and bigger. Gerry could feel the heat of the blaze from more than two hundred yards away.

Just a door away now, the flames were closing in on Gerry's house. There was that moment, Gerry remembered, when she conceded that her house was going to go. The moment when hope just vanishes, replaced by utter despair. She looked at her mother and saw the same awareness in her tear-streaked face. Through the thick, sooty haze, Gerry watched her neighbor's house succumb. *It won't be long now*, she thought.

It wasn't. But the rolling flame didn't ignite her house. A spark, or the pent-up heat, finally got it. Suddenly Gerry's home just immolated itself, a sort of internal combustion that just blew it outward. Clapboard and porch roof were expelled into the street, just missing several men. Flames shot skyward, as though a bomb had detonated. Her home gone in two minutes.

Almost the same thing happened to the first rail car over in the yard. Half full of two-by-fours, the metal box absorbed as much heat as it could. Then it just burst, from the inside out. Another rail car up behind it went next. Now there were huge fires bookending the line of terror.

The fire got two more houses on up the street, a few sheds, and a granary at the other end. Then, oddly, some say divinely, the strong breeze abruptly died. In fact, it shifted direction, suddenly pushing the fiery rampage back on itself, scrabbling for fallen fuel at the bottom of the leveled structures. And the worst was over.

The entire area had to be rebuilt. A different and better arrangement from then. Nicer homes, a few edging onto the receding rail yard. Two granaries now, each higher and larger than the first, steel-roofed railroad buildings, a new neighborhood bar, and a convenience store."

I wanted to give Owen a break from his narrative. "That would have been pretty traumatic. What happened to Gerry's family?"

"They used a miserly insurance settlement to build a new home, very near where their original one sat."

"Owen, I suppose this wasn't the only big fire, though."

"It was the biggest. But blazes broke out in The Acre over the years. During the Depression, several homes burned in a fire that took half a street. Some say it was the best thing that could've happened to that shabbiness, because no one died, and no one became homeless. I have to say that several millers stepped in and provided piles of free lumber and helped residents slap together some small cabins.

Sometime in the late forties, Jerome Fitner sat on his back porch and watched his upriver sawmill burn down before his eyes. His mill sat somewhat apart from other structures, so he just sat there and watched the fire burn itself out. Several stories just like that."

"So, fire and wood, one looking for the other," I thought out loud. "It was the fires that killed the Cordell wood business?"

"No, that would have been the spotted owl."

"What?"

"The northern spotted owl." Owen thought a second. "There is no official year of death, but the lumber business fell gravely ill somewhere in the late fifties. Only remnants left now. Several companies hung on for two decades or so, but the Wilderness Act of 1964 and the Endangered Species Act of 1979 were too much for local loggers. The spotted owl was the final straw."

"You want to tell me about that?" I urged.

"Sure. Environmentalists lobbied the government to protect the nation's resources, namely woodlands and the animals living there. In some crystallization of issues, the tree-huggers identified several species in danger of extinction because of man's attack on the American woods. The northern spotted owl was one of those species.

Now, understand that no one was killing spotted owls. They weren't worth a red cent to any forester. But the darned things lived high up in big trees, what's is known as old-growth timber. Old-growth timber is what foresters want. It's big, it's straight, and it's abundant. The Cordell economy was based on cutting it.

But because the spotted owl lived in old growth – they couldn't be bothered with the young trees of reforestation efforts – loggers couldn't take away the habitat of these endangered little buggers.

The owls weren't altogether wrong. Trees we called 'monarchs' could be 160 feet high and six feet wide. Great wood. New growth was short, twisted, knotty, and thin. The foresters didn't want that wood in the 1960s, either.

So began a controversy that ended mostly in the environmentalists' favor. The forests around here were off limits to loggers.

Not that the industry didn't fight back. Timber men maintained that the benefits of saving the spotted owl were negligible compared to the harm of such legislation. At the time, western forests accounted for about sixty-five percent of the country's wood demands. Jobs would be lost, maybe exceeding 30,000. Industry officials argued that towns like Cordell would suffer increased domestic disputes, divorce, violence, suicide, and alcoholism. Nationwide, consumer prices for wood products would rise substantially.

Woodsmen argued that cutting the old growth and large-dimension cuts were essential to present and future generations regarding wood and paper products. It was in society's best interest to replace these static forests with healthy, young trees that would provide an adequate supply of timber. The industry was already beginning reforestation programs. There was no real incentive to reforest, but they could do it.

The focus on the spotted owl was unnecessary, foresters argued. Half of Oregon's three million acres of old growth had already been set aside as national parks and wilderness areas. How much more had to be protected?"

Owen performed one his dismissive shrugs, then continued. "Of course, the environmentalists won. Old growth was off limits. That was the end of it for timbering, and most things connected to it.

But, in all fairness, it has to be said that a bird may have been the final focus, but the industry must take some blame, also. And so does the government."

"How's that, Owen?"

"In a nutshell, the industry overcut the forest. They did it knowingly, and the government allowed it, knowingly.

"You have to remember that western expansion, by plan and by action, was dependent on wood. The government made logging easy – promoted it, needed it. World War I made wood invaluable. World War II made it absolutely necessary, both during it and in the boom that followed. There was money to be made.

Loggers were coming in here to make that money. Some companies came here with the singular intent to cut as much lumber as they could, and then leave. These guys would get a permit from the government, or buy some forest rights outright, and 'cut and run.'

Meanwhile, local loggers were running out of woods and couldn't get rights to new sources. You know, the government knows how to do only two things with a faucet: turn it on, and turn it off. Adjusting the flow, well, that was just beyond them. Back and forth with the pendulum, never in the middle. So, when America needed wood, the government promoted timbering, full bore. When someone cried 'uncle,' lawmakers believed their only move was to stop the cutting.

Have you seen lawmakers do business that way?"

"Many a time, Owen,"

"By the time the National Forest Service started to impose allotments and seal off part of the mountain land, the whole thing was already out of control. The Service had trouble enforcing their own rules anyway, and many poachers continued to do what they'd always done.

Meanwhile, some forests were looking barren, while the lumber market was becoming saturated. The investment in mills and labor was huge, and most of the operators had already made their money. So, for twenty years or so, the industry wallowed about, doing whatever they could do. Timber men simply ran the string to the end of the line.

But all good things must end. That's what happened to wood. Throw in growing environmental concerns, several ugly scandals, bad business practices, some political posturing, and an owl, and you have the beginning of the end. All that started somewhere in the late forties. By the eighties, you had a depressed industry and a town of woodmen with no jobs."

Owen's shifted in his seat as he shifted focus of his narrative. "Around Cordell, more than twenty sawmills were shuttered – now big, wooden carcasses, slowly dry-rotting. Production stopped, sales stopped, lumbermen let go. Naturally, rail shipment plunged, so that industry went to half-mast. Many railroaders moved on, mainly to Canada, but to Washington, too.

Left behind were many jobless folks who suffered through times some compared to the Depression. The young people left, of course, being there were no jobs here. Some merchants dependent on lumber and railroad families hung on for ten years or so, their stores also going downhill. Some just moved to other towns. New construction was non-existent. King Wood was dead, taking many others along.

Two leading lumbermen closed their operations one day and committed suicide the next. Other company executives sold their homes in The Wedge and moved downtown. Downtown residents sold their homes and moved to the little bungalows in The Acre. Long-term residents of The Acre sat in front of their homes and drank."

Owen paused in reflection. "I've often thought that you could track the history of The Cascades simply by noting how people referred to them over the years. To the pioneers, the mountains were 'the woods.' During the lumbering era, they were called 'the timber.' Now they're referred to as 'the forest.' Tells you about all you need to know, eh?"

"Yeah, I see the connections, Owen. Proceed, please."

"Ticket's slid slowly south, just as everything else did. Not a good time to own a bar. And I had acquired this one in 1972."

"The end of the heyday George probably enjoyed," I guessed out loud."

"No guess about it," Owen said ruefully.

"During the demise of timbering, The Strip had become a no-man's-land, an island between the town and The Acre, now really on the wrong side of the tracks.

Slowly but surely, most businesses on The Strip closed. The first was Prinder's Café. Then the mercantile and clothing store. The post office was moved down to The Boulevard. Not long after that, the hotel closed. In the seventies, the motel chains built units not far from the new interstate highway. They took all of the hotel's business. That old building sat vacant and neglected – a teenager hangout for all the wrong things.

The Strip was dying. Even its name. With only our two bars remaining, sitting beside vacant buildings, we were looking seedy, downright dangerous, in fact. Locals started referring to us as The Barbary Coast. Of course, this term related to that section of San Francisco during the Forty-Niner days, rough bars, dance halls, lewdness, rowdy, bawdy behavior, dangerous, usually armed men, fueled by alcohol and lust, occasionally violent.

Locals who'd never entered our places had decided that we were hellholes. Why did anyone have to cross the tracks anymore? It was bad enough that they had to drive by our establishments just to get to the interstate or mountains.

But our godforsaken little strip acquired that reputation. Most of our patrons now came from The Acre, not the most highly regarded residents of the town. Other original patrons from the town proper had either died off or found new watering holes. The wood boom had brought with it several motel lounges, a few trendy cafes on The Boulevard, and a few sandwich-and-beer places down by the rail yard, near the river.

Ticket's survived all this decay, but never really recovered from the sixties and seventies. The easy way out for me is to blame the times, the loss of industry, the way the town developed. I could blame the environmentalists, or the greedy woodmen. I could even blame television, now bringing entertainment right into everyone's parlors. George's TV up there was no longer an attraction."

Another reflective pause from Owen. Then: "But I do ask myself from time to time if I should have done some things differently. I'm not sure that I know what those things would have been, but, truthfully, I simply stood behind that bar, hoping for more customers. I was just getting by on those regulars I still had.

My needs were simple, I had money in the bank, I owned the property, and I didn't owe anyone a dime. But I was young, and not very creative or knowledgeable about my business. Looking back on it, I think I was in relentless pursuit of the status quo. I assumed I was a victim of the bad times; nothing I could do about that.

Probably should've just closed up, like everyone else. When your horse dies, you ought to have the good sense to dismount. But not me. I just hung in, doing the same thing and expecting different results. That's the definition of insanity, you know."

Owen was warming to this self-flagellation. "I sometimes wonder how Noah or George would have handled the changing economy of this town. My sense has always been that they would've shown more initiative than I did. Proud of this place as I am, it's the years of Noah and George that I'm proud of. My only success may have been in just keeping it open."

"Owen, that may be no small accomplishment, given the times," I offered. Why did I feel this need to defend Owen to Owen?

"Maybe. But I have a difficult time getting to that. Too many memories of how it used to be.

"Part of my problem is that most of this town rebounded. Ticket's did not. The pleasant little town you see now – except for the abandoned mills – began to find its legs in the late eighties and early nineties.

Sheep ranching became a big business. One of our locals developed a strain known as 'Columbia,' and those wooly little buggers caught on around the world. Some small enterprises moved in, the shirt factory, bottling works, a local brewery. Oregon hops grew a national market, more ranchers moved in, more little shops downtown. Tourism increased because of the mountain and the river. Folks started finding work in new and different jobs. Even Ticket's started doing better then, too. But it wasn't because of anything I did."

"Owen, you must've done what needed to be done."

"Perhaps," he conceded. "But my conscience isn't straight about it. A clear conscience is the sign of a bad memory, you know, and my memory of those days is too clear to escape."

Finally, Owen attempted to skirt this little revelation of inadequacy. "Well, one thing I know for sure," he said. "You can't grind wheat with water that's already passed under the bridge. Ticket's is what it is. No use trying to undo the past."

Still, he couldn't quite let it go. One more reflection.

"You know, you reach my point in life, and you look back on things you should've, could've, would've done. My own regrets are not of what I have done, but what I didn't do. I didn't fight back.

Remember Shindler's agonizing self-assessment in *Shindler's List*? 'I could have done more.' That's Owen Ticket. Maybe we all live with that; I certainly do."

"So," I offered, trying to shift away from this mess, "You still haven't told me what finally happened to the rest of the buildings on The Strip."

"And I will. But first I want to tell a story from the old days – when The Strip and Ticket's were just picking up steam.

CHAPTER SEVEN

Pardon My French

"**H**is name was Anton Devereaux, but he was known as the Frenchman.'"

We were sitting again —I with a Coke and Owen with his tea, again. No chit-chat. Owen started right in. He had this story in mind, and my interest in The Strip's demise was just going to wait until he got this one told.

"The Frenchman was perhaps the last of the true and original frontiersmen in these parts. He was a legend. I, of course, never met him; he died sometime after World War I. Neither did my father, but Noah and his cronies talked about him often, so the stories were handed down. My grandfather believed that Anton Devereaux did as much for Ticket's success in about thirty days as Noah did from all his years running this place.

The Frenchman was a trapper, fisherman, and a hunter, too. He was born into a trapper's life. His dad, Basile Devereaux, was one of a thousand trappers who used to work the Columbia and the Deschutes. Until about 1840 they came in droves down from Canada to collect pelts from mink, beaver, muskrats, coyotes, bobcats, raccoons, fox, you name it.

They were so good at it that they almost made the beaver and the wolf extinct. Then the demands of easterners for animal pelts waned, as did any profitability, and the whole of the industry collapsed. By 1900, the Frenchman was one of only fifty or so trappers still plying his trade.

Well, up until that time, Basile worked the Deschutes, the valley, and the mountains for anything that had skin or fur. He and his young bride had a small cabin and big smoke-house just off the Barlow Road, up on the White River, about a dozen miles from Cordell. It wasn't far from where John Witherspoon later built his first sawmill.

Basile picked the spot because it was near water, edged the valley, and sat just at the base of the foothills. From there he could hunt, fish, and trap in all three. Until the trapping gave out, he taught his only son, Anton, how to survive and profit from the wilderness.

Let me tell you a quick story about Basile, and then come back to Anton.

Basile was known as 'Basile the Bear.' That was because of an old story he told years before his death. Now, remember, Ed, Basile, Anton's father, goes back into the previous century, so this is an old, and, perhaps, somewhat enhanced tale.

One day Basile was in the mountains tending his traps. Half-way up, he sees one of his traps had snared a mink. Mink were valuable. Basile, all happy, moved toward the trap to kill the mink and take it home.

Except that he encountered a huge brown bear with similar ideas. He and the bear had apparently arrived at the spot at the same time. Both realized, and wanted, the catch.

Basile had just killed the mink. He was extracting it from the trap when he heard the bear crashing through the woods and snarling behind him. He turned to face the bear, already on its hind legs, pawing the air, and intent on dragging off that mink.

Now Basile had two choices. Let the bear have the animal, or fight for it. Of course, the wise move would have been to throw the mink toward the bear and move away. But you have to know the mindset of the trapper. He captured the mink, and it was his. Bear or not, he was taking it home.

Basile decided he'd just shoot the bear and be done with it – a two-for-one, if you will. He positioned himself to do so. While Basile was considering these options, the bear charged. The trapper got off a rather wild shot that actually hit the bear, but only in the edge of a front shoulder.

The next thing he knew, Basile had been slapped up against a tree, the breath knocked out of him. Figuring that was enough time on Basile, the bear headed for the dead mink.

Basile watched the bear snatch up his quest, and looked for his rifle. Couldn't find it, so he jumped on the bear's back and started a wrestling match of epic proportion. His recounting of the incident – and the one Anton told for years – involved eyeball-to-eyeball contact, bear teeth-to- forearm, fist after fist to the bear's head, and kicks to its groin. Later, Basile said that was probably ineffective, because the bear turned out to be a female.

So, they tussled for what Basile considered to be hours. Probably about one minute. Basile couldn't find his fallen rifle, but he did have his pistol and big knife. He used both.

Very close up and personal, he shot that bear in the head. Stunned, the bear relaxed her grip and rip on Basile. Basile pulled his knife from his waist and slashed at the bear's throat. He must've hit something important, because the bear rolled off him, bleeding, and emitting the guttural sounds of death.

That'll earn you a nickname, eh?" Owen summarized.

I nodded agreement. Davy Crockett stuff.

Owen continued. "Basile took stock of his own wounds and ministered to them. He carried the mink home and went back later to retrieve the bear he'd killed at close quarters. Of the thousands of pelts and skins he sold over the years, he never parted with that one.

So, that was the family tradition in which Anton was raised. Anton spent his entire life in the mountains, the prairie, and the river, pursuing the same life as his father. He had the instincts of a cougar. He and the outdoors were one. He stayed on the small property when his parents were gone.

The Frenchman was an imposing figure. A big man, by all accounts, he was a gentle giant. He had the look of the uncouth wild all over him. Untrimmed beard and hair down his back, deerskin clothes, a raccoon hat, complete with hanging tail. Just unkempt, that's all. His horse-skin jacket was stained with the blood and bile of thousands of wild animals. He stank some, at least that's what Noah said. All his leather and fur, even his fringed, up-to-the-calf boots, collected that odor of gutted and scraped carcasses.

The Frenchman always had a muzzle-loader over his shoulder and a big knife at his hip. His English was delivered with a heavy French accent, the combination of both languages his parents used.

Anton lived and worked alone, except for the times each year that he came to town.

It wasn't that he didn't like people. He did. He told Noah that he liked society and solitude equally. But he didn't like to mix them. When he wanted the first, he came to town, to resupply, to drink at Ticket's, and to tell stories. When he wanted the second, he returned to the wilderness.

Owen smiled, warming to his topic. "But those visits to Ticket's helped Noah build a regular clientele, indeed, a cross-section of all Cordell social strata. The Frenchman provided free entertainment that Noah couldn't have paid enough to get.

The Frenchman was a great storyteller. And his stories were true – just like mine, incidentally."

I interrupted Owen. "I always fret, Owen, when someone has to tell me that what they are saying is true."

"A fair fret, I'd agree," Owen laughed. "But, in my case, you can trust it.

Anyway," he proceeded, "Ticket's would be wall-to-wall with beer-buying citizens, at the time when Noah's new enterprise needed the business the most. The Frenchman could pack the room and hold the crowd for hours."

"You're telling me that this mountain man would fill up Ticket's just by showing up?" I asked.

"Yep. The Frenchman had a fondness for Ticket's; he and Noah had become good friends. Everyone in the place addressed him as Annie, but referred to him as the Frenchman.

Once word got out of his arrival, men told their wives that they'd be late that night; the Frenchman was in town. They were going to Ticket's to hear some stories from the last of a dying breed. Nobody cared that he was a bit aromatic. They weren't here to make love to him, they came to listen.

Usually, it worked like this. The Frenchman would come into town every few months. He'd wander through town, filling the saddlebags on his horse and pack mule with the necessaries, and then come in here. Always, Noah said, always, Annie brought in a hunk of jerky of some kind. He'd smoke up a piece of deer shoulder or antelope flank and fasten it to a cord he'd hang from a ceiling hook, near the pot-bellied stove, right beside where the cracker barrel used to sit. Noah would bring him a beer and then a bottle of rye that Annie would pretty much empty by closing time. Soon drinkers were pulling over the few chairs and settling in.

Then a large semi-circle would develop, with some leaning against the wall, some leaning on each other. Someone would say something like, 'Tell us about the time you let that skunk bite you so he wouldn't spray you.' That's about all it took to get the Frenchman going. He'd dip into the open barrel, grab a cracker, and slice off a rash of jerky with that big knife of his, telling everyone to bring their knives up and cut their own slab.

Then the Frenchman would mesmerize folks with one yarn after another about the Devereaux' adventures in the high country. He would get all animated when he talked, whipping about the wolf fang that hung around his neck on a length of leather. He'd wave his arms, raise and lower his voice (you smart guys call it 'modulation) and make crazy-eyed facial distortions. Noah believed that Annie's French accent was more pronounced when the storytelling began.

Simply a spellbinding raconteur, taking his crowd back through the days of yore, along the streams and into the mountain, with enthralling, real-life stories about man and wilderness. Maybe the tale was about the time his father wrestled that bear, or his own long-running feud with a particular lone gray wolf. Maybe it was about some famous Indian battle his Canadian grandfather described. Once started, he didn't quit until Noah finally shooed everyone out.

Annie would sleep in the bar. The next day it would go on like that, all over again."

"Never ran out of stories?" I guessed.

"Are you kidding? The Frenchman had a million of them. Like I said, though, people often asked him to retell a used one. See, part of it was the story itself. But part of Annie's appeal was Annie himself. Being around him must have been like opening a time capsule. He was a throwback to an era and lifestyle that residents might've read about, but certainly never experienced.

Annie was free. Free of bosses, free of family obligations, free to hunt, to fish, and to trap. By the early 1900s, such indulgences had already become pastimes, not jobs. What you had here were railroad workers, business owners, sawmill hands, laborers, a group of people who were in the West, but not of the West, if you know what I mean. The Frenchman was of the West. This was Cordell's version of entertainment for a population that got little, otherwise."

"Owen, the Frenchman was the genuine article, eh?"

"He was the real deal." Owen thought for a moment. "You know how that old codger would end every night of storytelling? He'd say, 'Time to pee on the fire and call in the dogs.' Tickets always used that wrap-up to announce last call."

Owen stopped for several seconds. "Want more on the Frenchman?"

"Certainly," I responded.

"Okay. Annie wasn't just a story-teller. He was truly a gifted mountaineer.

His tracking skills were in great need on at least one occasion. I'll tell you about that.

Naturally, the Frenchman was a great tracker. It goes with any good hunter or trapper. They used to say that Annie could track a fly from tree to tree. I doubt that. But he had an amazing ability to find and follow tracks, through any terrain.

So, when Thomas Shelf and his son went missing up on Hood, the sheriff got Annie involved.

The Thomas Shelf family was a recent eastern transplant to The Dalles. With a new job in the lumber business, Tom Shelf was going to offer a new life to his wife and young son.

The boy was old enough to start hunting. Tom decided that his son should take his first deer in, or near, the snow up on Mt. Hood. So, the two of them took off one morning and chugged Tom's new 'gas buggy' up to the timberline, toward Government Camp.

Now you gotta know this about Hood. She's Oregon's monument, our highest mountain. More than 11,000 feet high – some say she was taller once. Her top 7000 feet are snowfields and volcanic rock.

As green and lush as she is on the bottom, she is stark and harsh up high. Weather conditions can change quickly up there. Might be sunny and clear, but clouds can roll in at the top, or around the tree line, in the length of time I need to take a leak. Visibility can be reduced to zero, the temperature drops, west winds and Chinooks blow, and rain or snow squalls crop up in a heartbeat. People have been disoriented, lost, or frozen up there.

Thomas Shelf might've availed himself of this information. He did not.

His noble intent on making a day for his son was absent of proper planning and caution. He had better odds of getting a deer in the forest than on the rocks, but he had this image of his son kneeling in the snow with a ten-pointer. With little knowledge of the mountain's mercurial nature, he had planned only for a day-long hunting trip, not a test of survival. Certainly he had no Plan B. He paid for those small errors of judgment.

His plan was for the two of them to hike up Hood until they got a panoramic view of the world beneath them, then descend slowly, rifles at the ready, hoping to snare a deer or mule deer on the way back down, and be home for dinner.

So, he and his son trekked up through the snowfields, beginning a glorious day of hiking and hunting.

Sometime around noon, with no deer in sight, clouds rolled in. It snowed. Within ten minutes Shelf couldn't see the bottom of the mountain, let alone the valley. Nothing green, no sun; just clouds and swirling snow that quickly added three new inches to the rock shelves.

Of course, they got lost. They had no compass, no survival instincts. Shelf immediately was disoriented, and his son was already frightened. Shelf thought only to walk downhill, toward the timberline. Conventional wisdom is to climb in such conditions, but the visibility and snow had the two bewildered.

Shelf was further confounded by the sense that he was going back up the mountain face whenever they encountered outcroppings, small knolls, and boulders in the blinding snow.

Somewhere during this endeavor, Shelf veered well west of his automobile. After stumbling about, this way and that, father and son finally reached the tall pines and slackening snow. They were in the middle of a crevasse, one that went both uphill and sideways. Shelf said later that his sense was to turn left, but, trying that, they ran into another three-sided swale. Now he was lost. Rain was falling at this altitude, and his terrorized son was crying.

Rather than compound his error, Shelf decided to hunker down right where they were. They built a fire and waited for the weather to change or to be rescued. He and his son were armed only with warm clothing, lunch, a flask of water, two rifles, and, luckily, some matches Tom needed for his pipe.

At dark, Shelf's wife called the sheriff's office to report that her two hadn't come home. The sheriff told her that he'd start a search at daybreak.

He loaded up two automobiles with searchers and drove up Barlow Road. He stopped first at John Witherspoon's home to borrow a few horses. Then he stopped at Annie's to enlist his tracking help.

The Frenchman's first response was, 'Has anyone been up there yet?'

'No,' answered the sheriff. 'We're headed there now. John is giving us some horses.'

Annie said he would help, as long as no one had trampled over whatever track he found. So, he told the lawman to stop the horse brigade at his place – one would be tempted to say 'hold your horses,' wouldn't one? –until he could have some time up there alone.

After animated conversation, the sheriff agreed that only he'd go with Annie. He promised to stay behind Annie all the way. The rest of the group could wait at the Frenchman's and come up five hours from the time the first two left. At that time they could do what they wanted."

Owen stopped long enough to get a fresh start. "So Annie and a young Clive Johnson rode horses into the timber, coming upon Shelf's car. They headed into the new-fallen snow on foot. The Frenchman took a straight path into the rocks, assuming the route the two hunters probably would have headed. It took him only an hour to find faint footprints in the new snow. These headed back down, but at that western angle. Turning south, Annie led Clive back down the mountain to the tree-line. Now it got tricky.

When the snow tracks faded into the wet trees, Annie changed strategies. He began to look about for disturbed leaves on the ground, freshly-broken sticks, or green needles on the ground. He told Clive to sit against a tree and rest for a while; this could take some time.

He disappeared into the woods, returned twice, and took different angles, disappearing again. Another hour passed. The sheriff was getting impatient.

When Annie appeared the third time, he was holding a smashed, muddy, fern plant in his hand. 'Sheriff,' he called out, 'get up and walk toward me in a straight line, but stay behind me. Let's go.' Off he headed back into the woods, pausing only to point to a fresh boot-sized skid mark in the soft soil. 'That's them.'

They had to change direction several times. Shelf had obviously not gone straight. The Frenchman suddenly stopped, looked about the surroundings, and said, 'Morgan's Ravine. If they stopped, they stopped at Morgan's Ravine. I would. Damn terrain is too steep on three sides to climb after the day they've had.'

He stopped and sniffed the air, actually sniffed about an entire circle. Clive thought Annie was nuts. He half expected Annie to get down on his knees and put his ear to the ground, but he didn't.

Confidently, Annie started on through the woods, down and a bit left. He kept stopping and sniffing the air. Thirty minutes later, he un-shouldered his rifle and fired a shot into the air, a small, muffled echo bouncing off the slopes above him. He reloaded and shot again. They walked for another ten minutes. Annie sniffed again. 'Green smoke. They're burning pine branches.' Again, The Frenchman fired off two shots.

And, then, Annie and Clive heard the echoes of a single shot, and then another.

Minutes later, Annie stepped into a small clearing wedged in the hills – Morgan's Ravine. Across the field, Shelf and his son were putting green pine branches on a small fire, smoke billowing up.

Shelf's son said later that when he first laid eyes on the Frenchman, he was terrified, not relieved. He saw him first, this huge man, dressed in skins, carrying a rifle, and squinting across at him. He thought it was Bigfoot, or some other mountain monster. After a terrible night, he thought he was now to be disemboweled by some unearthly being. But when Annie hollered out in his French twang, 'Are you two lost?' he grabbed his father and turned him toward salvation.

So the four of them gathered at the fire to hear each other's stories. Shelf could outdo the Frenchman in the tribulation department, for sure. He and his son had spent a sleepless night tending that fire. They couldn't really dry out, and both were miserable in a drizzly mist that lasted well into the night. Surely the fire kept the animals away, but they'd heard coyotes howling outside the dimly-lighted perimeter. Noises in the brush all night, impossible to say if they were large or small animals. Wet wood, cold air, no food, and very little water. Tired, cold, hungry, scared.

And Tom Shelf had hurt his back on the way down the mountain. He kept skidding downhill and had to reach back to brace his son. He was in real pain, and on the way out, Annie and Clive took turns providing another leg for him.

Annie set the direction to the car and horses, even though there were a few ups and downs involved. The car wouldn't start, for some reason, so the four of them climbed up on the horses.

A photograph was taken by the reporter from *The Gazette*, sent by the editor to Annie's cabin to cover the news. In it, the Frenchman is holding the boy in front of him on Annie's horse, and Clive is riding with Tom Shelf, behind the saddle of his mount.

And so legends are built."

"I wish I could've met the Frenchman," I said. "Unique fellow, eh?"

"Yep. Unique. Aren't many of those left." Owen paused for a moment.

"Hey, you know what? I just thought of someone you ought to meet. Can't rightfully compare him to the Frenchman, but he has story of his own."

"Who would that be?" I inquired.

"Kimo Leilani."

"Kimo Leilani? What kind of name is that?"

Hawaiian. Kimo and his son, Richard, run a water adventures operation on the river, just across the bridge and a half-mile to the left. Called 'Kimo Kayaks.' Kimo builds some of the finest kayaks and canoes in the world. Famous for them, he is. All painted in one-of-a-kind designs, every one personally signed by Kimo.

Kimo was one of the very first to open up the Deschutes to water sports and tourism. Came here just at the right time for that. Everything else was dying off. You'll like him. Want me to set that up for you?"

"Sure," I replied.

Owen made the call.

"You meet Kimo tomorrow morning, late. He knows you have to work first thing. Besides, Kimo is not too available in the mornings. He gets up early, takes his kayak out on the river for a couple of hours, and then opens the shop. In the afternoons, he just tinkers about, making someone a kayak.

Ask him about his family background and his stolen kayaks. That'll get him talking."

Owen and I ended the evening with me telling him two little stories. I was just trying to catch up, giving a little so I could get more of his stuff.

As I prepared to go, Bob stopped in for his scheduled second visit of the day. He actually managed a full nod this time. I sat down at the bar, with one stool between us, so as not to agitate him.

After his first beer, Bob showed me his rock. I made a big fuss over it.

Chapter Eight

Kimo The Kayak King

The next morning I performed my duties as the Speaker-of-the-Month. That all went well enough.

I returned to the motel, stripped off my "let's-make-a-living suit" and headed to Kimo Kayaks. Sitting right on the eastern shoreline, the smallish wooden building was painted in island pastels, pink, yellow, blue, and green, garish, actually. It looked as if it might glow in the dark.

I introduced myself to the fellow behind the counter. He turned out to be the son, Richard. He told me his father was expecting me, and that he was in the shop behind this office. I strolled back to the pole barn and found Kimo gently sanding the bow of an unpainted canoe.

"Yes, I know who you are," Kimo said, halfway through my introduction of myself. "Owen tells me you want to talk?"

Kimo was a handsome, wiry, craggy-faced gentleman in a bright, red and white Hawaiian shirt, loose over his Dockers and Hush Puppies. Slim, small, and relaxed, he looked as if he spent considerable time paddling a kayak. He featured the complexion of a man who'd been in the sun for a lifetime, augmented by a few black age spots. His hair was completely silver, long and combed straight back over his head. He smiled a broad grin, framing big, white teeth. He looked like a surfer – an old one, but a surfer nevertheless.

We progressed through the usual chat about the weather, me, my book, and whatnot. He showed me about the shop. About a dozen kayaks and canoes were in some stage of progress, a few being attended to by four other men. I was struck by the vivid and imaginative paint schemes, lacquered and polished. The ones near completion looked like NASCAR entries, without the advertising. Two, apparently ready for delivery, boasted "Kimo Leilani" in hand-painted script in large letters, creatively bedecking the craft.

"I personally paint my signature on every canoe and kayak built here. Our mark of distinction," Kimo said with hand-formed quotes.

We spent the next half hour touring the projects, Kimo showing me some of the artistic and quality features of the crafts for which he was known.

It was time to turn to the reason for my visit. We strolled to the office, filled two coffee mugs, and sat down on the low dock with our feet hanging very close to the Deschutes. There were about ten canoes and kayaks lying nearby, all typically-colored, solid blue or green or red.

"Owen tells me you're an interesting guy." Not a notable conversation-starter from me.

"He does, huh? Well, I don't know about that, but I'll try to give you what you came for. How do we do that? Do you ask me questions, or what?"

"Maybe I can get you started, but feel free to just keep talking," I offered. "I have a few areas of interest. Here's the first: how did a Hawaiian end up in Cordell, Oregon?"

Kimo laughed. "It may not be as odd as you'd think. I'm not the first or last islander to plop here. But there aren't many of us.

Islanders usually ended up in Central Oregon in one of two ways. The first group was really escaping the gallows. You see, a half dozen or so islanders killed a crimper and needed to get out of Portland quickly. They headed east along the big river and then down the Deschutes."

"A crimper?" I inquired.

Kimo laughed, his big, white teeth showing. "Yeah a crimper. Did you ever hear of the practice of shanghaiing sailors?"

"Now that you mention it, yes I have. Let's see. In the early days of naval and merchant shipping, owners lacked crewmen. So they started 'impressing' sailors, forcibly taking drunks, the un-employed, the poor, right off the streets. Made them sailors. They'd just knock them unconscious, get them drunk, or drug them, and drag them off. When they woke up, they were on a ship out at sea. Correct?"

"Mostly," Kimo affirmed. "Many countries actually allowed the practice. England, France, Spain, and the new Americas. Portland became known for this forced servitude, and lots of men, in this case, Hawaiians, found themselves on ships."

Kimo was warming to his story. "Now we come to crimpers. Crimpers were men paid by the shipping companies for every able-bodied man they could deliver to the docks. Madmen, some of these crimpers were, ruthless, mean, and heartless. They took advantage of any poor soul they could get to a ship.

Impressment in the U.S. was finally outlawed somewhere in the mid-1800s, but not before six particular Hawaiians returned to Portland after forced labor for several years. Throughout their voyage, they vowed to kill the crimper who'd dragged them to the high seas. In Portland, they found him and maimed him. He died an agonizing death. As he did, they headed east, far from town. They were never caught. Their descendants are still in the area. Most of them have never seen Hawaii.

Now the second batch of Polynesians arrived back in the twenties when lumbering started to be big business around here. The Hudson's Bay Company needed laborers. Of course, they already had long-standing fur and trading and shipping interests stretching from New York to Hawaii.

The company was heavily invested in the growing timber business. For that, they needed cheap labor, and the islands had plenty of that. So, the company signed up Hawaiians for three-year indentures. Islanders would come here to timber, get paid about $85 a year, live in free housing and eat all the fish, biscuits, and berries they wanted. After three years, those Hawaiians who wished were shipped home. A few stayed.

"And your dad was one of those?" I asked.

He shook his head. "No, my family landed here in a rather unique set of circumstances.

"My grandfather, Hiapo Leilani, is a story all by himself.

Hiapo Leilani was a Hawaiian soldier, back when the islands were a consolidated monarchy, the mid-1890s. Specially trained and educated, he was part of the palace guard for Hawaii's last ruler, Queen Liliuokalani. A decorated officer, Hiapo was part of the queen's tiny entourage, always nearby to protect her. He did so until 1895, when the United States overthrew the nation and made it an America protectorate.

Hiapo was with the queen when America ships trained their canons on the palace and demanded the surrender of the islands to U.S. control. He was in the room when Queen Liliuokalani decided she would surrender control rather than risk Hawaiian lives in a fight Hawaii could not win. (By the way, that little conquest doesn't get much play in American history classes, does it? Not America's finest hour.)

In the confusing aftermath of the takeover, Hiapo was told, as all ranking Hawaiian soldiers were told, that their futures were dependent on their allegiance to the United States. In other words, they were strongly encouraged to join the U.S. military, at some lower rank than they currently held in Hawaii.

As most, Hiapo agreed. Soon he found himself serving in the U.S. army, stationed at several non-distinguished posts in foreign lands. Upon his completion of twenty years of duty, he stopped at Portland to visit his indentured family members who were working the timber. He never left.

He married an Oregon Indian, a Paiute woman who was a cook in one of the lumber camps. My father was born from that union. He spent twenty-two years in the U.S. Navy, retiring and living in The Dalles, near his parents. I was born in 1927, after his marriage to Akahi Moi, my mother being another Hawaiian. So I am three-quarters Hawaiian and one-quarter American Indian.

I continued the family military tradition and signed up for the army during World War II. With humility, let me say that the three of us Leilanis remain as the single most decorated Hawaiian family in U.S. history.

So, I came back here after my military career, still a young man. I looked at the Deschutes and saw opportunity. I viewed the river not only as a source of fish, travel, and industry, but as a recreational site. I decided that people would enjoy floating down the river, riding its rapids, and enjoying its wonderment.

So I started building them rafts, canoes, and kayaks to do these things. I was good at it – opened my business and made stuff the way it was done in the islands.

My timing was perfect. The lumber business in Oregon had come to a halt, railroad traffic was decaying, things were going to hell in a hand basket. But we still had the Deschutes, and visitors who wanted to fish it and navigate it. So, I rented and sold canoes, regular ones, like those over there. Painted up my building so it looked like a French whorehouse or something. People like color. Soon, we were a tourist attraction. Several of us are in the business now, but Kimo's got the ball rolling in Cordell."

Kimo turned wistful. "Soon, I was selling more kayaks than I could build. I was making canoes and rafts for customers in Bend, Canada, Washington, Idaho. Kimo sort of became the Cadillac of kayaks, known for quality construction, creative paint jobs, and my signature splashed across them. Serious kayakers wanted everyone on the water to know that they were riding in the best. Tourists, of course, seldom care, so we rent slews of those single-colored canoes to them.

But I went after the new and growing numbers of serious adventurers. They want to enjoy the river and the rapids, and do it in style. The Hawaiian flair didn't hurt.

And here we are. It's a good thing Richard came back home to help me."

I thought I ought to give the gent a verbal rest. "Tell me about your son."

"Richard went straight to the military after high school, as all we Leilanis did, so now we have four generations of soldiers, spanning about one hundred years. Richard had tours on three continents, served in special ops, was decorated almost as much as his grandfather. He came home to manage the entire rental and adventure business. He has no interest in making kayaks; he wants to rent them, sell them, keep the books, and grow the business. A businessman, that one. Good enough.

So, now I am old. I spend my time on the river and building special-order kayaks, but fewer of them. I'm training Jake, my foreman, to take over the construction side. He's becoming a great builder."

"Owen tells me that you had a robbery, Kimo, I served up.

"Ah, yes. A thief named Bill Marchant thought he could make some quick money off my labors. He planned to sell my stock up on the Columbia. We soon caught that son of a bitch."

"Tell me about that," I asked.

One night Marchant and one of my employees, Sam Warner, broke into my shop and stole seven kayaks and four canoes. All but two were ready to go to buyers; it was the beginning of the spring season.

The two of them stuffed my inventory into a box truck and headed for Hood River, between Portland and The Dalles. The next day, these idiots sold several kayaks and a canoe to tourists who intended to paddle through the Great Gorge.

Trouble was that I knew all the water people up there. They'd bought stuff from me, they knew me, they recognized a Kimo Kayak when they saw one, and they wondered why folks had one they hadn't sold or rented.

So, in about forty-eight hours, I was getting calls from friends, asking about these new kayaks and canoes on the river. It was easy from there.

The sheriff and I went up there, and by noon had located Marchant's rented truck. We found him in a local diner, eating his profits. Caught red-handed. He 'fessed up quickly, implicating Sam Warner as his inside man.

We were able to retrieve a few of the pieces. I hated taking them away from the unsuspecting paddlers, but I had promised those craft to legitimate buyers. Some crafts were never recovered.

Funny thing, though. About two years later, I'm sitting on the river one morning and coming up-stream to me is this dandy little fellow in one of my lost kayaks. He stops to chat a minute. Of course, he had no idea who I was, that this was my kayak, or that he had done anything wrong in obtaining it. He just wanted to compare color designs."

"What did you do?" I asked.

"Nothing. I figured the man was happy. My insurance covered the loss of that kayak, and this man had paid something for it. Let him have it. Pretty thing it was, though."

A very cordial and well-met guy, this Kimo Leilani. For some reason I found myself envying his pluck, his peace of mind, his connection with the river, and his acceptance of his lot in life. I told him so as we parted.

He smiled. He knew.

CHAPTER NINE

Kings May Rise And Kings May Fall

"**H**ow'd you like Kimo?" Owen asked at the outset of our evening meeting.

"A pearl, and a good story. Thanks for sending me."

But I had another subject in mine. "You know, Owen, I still wait for the story of whatever happened to the rest of The Strip. Is it time yet?" I was growing impatient.

"Sure, sure. Kingsley Cordell is what happened, that's what.

Kingsley Cordell's giant ego and money lust leveled The Strip. This bar is all that remains, and that required going to court against that young, cocky, little twerp."

"Another Cordell? Who the hell is Kingsley Cordell?" I demanded.

Owen sighed. He gathered himself up to tell another story.

"Franklin's grandson. Kingsley grew up in the early forties, when Franklin Cordell was still the most powerful man in town. Franklin's lordly gene skipped over Charles, but his grandson certainly inherited it.

Of course, it was pre-ordained that Charles would take over the family empire. Long after his father brought him into the business, however, Charles was second fiddle. Franklin still ran the show, and Charles ran the errands. Charlie attempted to mimic his father's pomposity – probably to get old Franklin's favor as anything – but he just couldn't pull it off. No vision, no 'fire in the belly' for real estate. It was a job for him, not a calling. Straining to sound competent, he was in over his head.

Somewhere in the late thirties, Franklin slowly receded from good health and became homebound. He died just a year or two later. Now Charles faced some problems.

First, he was a lousy businessman. Second, his lack of passion for real estate development kept his eyes down, not up. He could handle normal land and home transfers. He knew how to create an advertisement. But, that 'vision thing,' made famous by the first George Bush? Charles just didn't have it. He simply lacked his father's strong business and personality traits. He couldn't grow the business; he could hardly maintain it. Look who's talking!" Owen spat through gritted teeth.

"Get off it, Owen, and get on with the story,"

"Yeah, yeah. Those two problems led to his third. By the 1940s, long-term residents were tiring of the Cordell family's command of town affairs. Newcomers didn't even know who Franklin Cordell was. The town history was lost on them.

A local named Elijah Reddick had given up on his dry farming experiment and opened a real estate business on The Boulevard. Now Cordell had a choice about land decisions. When people have a choice, they make it. Prospective buyers were no longer prisoners of the imperious Cordells, who'd never built a loyal or friendly client base. Besides, the Franklin and John Witherspoon feud was still a sore spot for those who identified more with the woodcutter than the mogul. There was all that Witherspoon land still for sale, and Reddick was handling it.

Franklin might have been up to these challenges; Charles was not. So, through the fifties the Cordell name, influence, and finances dwindled under Charles' reign.

But through all of this, the entire Cordell clan lived down in The Wedge in Franklin's big, three-story mansion. When Charles grew up and took a wife, he just moved up a floor in that monstrosity.

And then along comes the family hope: Kingsley Cordell. Franklin's grandson, Charles' only child.

Charles and his wife named their baby Kingsley, supposedly after some relative on her side. But, really, I think, the Cordells, both father and grandfather, had such regal plans for him that they bestowed on him a befitting name. The Cordells pampered the little prince and filled his head with both the achievements of his lineage and the assumed expectations they held for him. Unspoken was the devout hope that Kingsley would turn out to be more like his grandfather than his father."

Owen shook his head. "He did. Throughout his youth, Kingsley strutted about town, dressed like Little Lord Fauntleroy. Few of his classmates teased him about his wardrobe or his effeminate tendencies. After all, he was a Cordell, and little good could result by raising their ire. But behind his back, the children, shopkeepers, and the teachers would cluck about how he blustered about in that same way as his grandfather. Folks tolerated him much more than they liked him.

Anyway, King – he had early on become known as King – grew up in town as the 'chosen one.' By the time he entered junior high school, his parents had enrolled him in private school in Portland. We didn't hear much about him for years. Apparently, he went to college from that school and entered the Portland business world. Where he apparently had failed in several ventures. No real surprise there. Milk masquerading as cream, that was King Cordell. Oh, he always had grandiose ideas, but he owned nothing of his grandfather's skills at implementation. All that bluster must not have impressed Portland very much. All icing and no cake; that's how he must have been seen.

The king needed a smaller pond. Portland had treated him like the piker he was. Conveniently, King Cordell developed this romantic notion that he was just the person to resurrect Cordell. He fancied himself an entrepreneur who would make a triumphant return and re-establish his family's might. He'd return to Cordell to lift his dad's sagging business and return it to the glory days of his grandfather. With great fanfare, King exclaimed that he would cement not only the family enterprise, but its legacy in town lore.

King moved back to town and joined his father at Cordell Reality and Insurance Company.

With Franklin's swagger and brashness, King made it clear that he could heat up the sluggish economic stagnation of Cordell. The pompous little ass would introduce or re-introduce himself to townspeople with, 'I'm King Cordell of the Cordell Cordells,' with a big, sappy smile. 'I'm back to save this town.'

He thought that to be very clever. He told everyone that he was going to build things.

And he was going to start with the Barbary Coast.

He almost pulled it off.

Now, Ed, you have to remember that The Strip straddled both Cordell and Witherspoon land. That pretty much meant that King could do whatever he wanted with the Cordell properties, which Franklin had leased to the hotel, and to the Prinders, and a few others. However, two of us, Ticket's and The Golden Rail, had purchased our properties from John Witherspoon.

That fact was driving King to distraction. All of the buildings, except our two bars, were empty. King could raze everything else, but he'd have to get us out before he could move ahead with his big plan of building his strip mall – 'Gateway to Cordell' he termed it.

Lacking property rights to our holdings, here he sat with some private financing in place and a goodly number of residents agreeing with the concept, eyesore that we were."

Owen took on a hard look. "But I wasn't going to sell out to him. First and foremost, I not only ran a business here, I lived here. Truthfully, though, I simply didn't want to have anything to do with anything a Cordell wanted. The other owner was eager to sell, although he was a friend of mine who said he'd do what I'd do. The other two lots adjacent to Ticket's were still part of the Witherspoon holdings. Raymond still owned them, having never been able to get interested tenants.

The fulfillment of King's plan would require court action. He and the town lawyer, a squirrely wimp named Orvis Wagner, worked up a claim of eminent domain,' and on behalf of both King and the town of Cordell, filed suit, seeking our ouster so the mall could be built.

During this time, Tom Willis, folded, making a pre-trial deal with King regarding the Golden Rail. Apologetically, Tom told me that he just didn't have the heart for an agonizing fight over a property he was soon going to close anyway. So he sold the building and land to King for more than it was worth, receiving half the sum before the trial started, removing him as a defendant."

Some distain now on Owen's face. He continued the saga. "I was now alone in this battle. I knew I needed a lawyer, really for the first time in my life. I asked Jimmy for suggestions. He said he'd take care of it. Two days later, I heard from Nathan Bordman, a lawyer from Seattle. He told me not to worry, and that he'd come to see me.

One look and talk with Nathan Bordman and I felt better. Here was a knuckle-dragger in a fancy suit; a tough old bird who'd worked the Seattle legal scene on behalf of the mob for a quarter century. Orvis Wagner, the town counsel, was going to be out of his league with Mr. Bordman.

We contacted Raymond Witherspoon down in Arizona. As we'd assumed, he was not about to do business with a Cordell again. He had no interest in the fight, except that he did not want a Cordell to win it. So, he suggested he just deed his two lots to me for a dollar each. That ought to strengthen my hand, he thought. Nathan said it would, and we had that done in a week.

To make a long story short, we went to court. King walked in as if he were treading a red carpet with peacock feathers spread across his rear end. Orvis, who now knew that Nathan was representing me, timidly entered the courtroom with a sweaty brow.

It didn't take long. In one day, Nathan Bordman destroyed the legal basis of the complaint, King's stance as a bona fide petitioner, his reputation, his history as a reliable businessman, the town's interest and intent in the project, and poor Orvis's lawyering abilities.

Bordman argued that 'Gateway to Cordell' served no pressing public purpose. In fact, the municipality had no money or real involvement in King's plan. Eminent domain was a world of public government, and Kingsley Cordell and his financial backers were private entrepreneurs. Secondly, he filed suit on every member of town counsel for their sham involvement in King's plan. That did it. Bordman simply carved them up.

We left court with a judgment in our favor; the whole thing thrown out. The judge was moved, I believe, by the fact that I owned almost as much of the land as King did on The Strip. I should have some say in its use. I actually resided on the property to be razed.

Meanwhile, King's entire financial plan was beginning to unravel as several bank-rollers turned tail when they heard who my lawyer was. They knew better than to win a battle with me and lose a war with Bordman's main client.

Additionally, the judge recognized that King had placed money down for The Golden Rail. The judge said, 'Pay the rest of it, or walk away without refund of earnest money. Then continue to deal with Mr. Ticket in any way you wish, but privately, not under any finding of eminent domain.'

Trouble was for King that he no longer wanted that property if this deal went sideways. Without mine, he was going nowhere with his plan. Kingsley was fried in his own skillet.

King learned that at the end of the game, the king goes back into the same box as the pawn.

He left town about two weeks later, walking away from his one-half purchase of The Golden Rail. I bought it from Tom Willis for less than the other half. Now I own the entire Witherspoon half of the old strip. I knocked down The Golden Rail, so it wouldn't become an eyesore. Now I have parking for a hundred cars. I ought to hold a convention.

I never received a bill from Nathan Bordman," Owen added as an afterthought. "Jimmy The Was just smiled when I asked him about it."

Owen was finished. He stood up. "Gotta clean up the joint. You can stay or go, of course. I already know the first story for tomorrow."

"I'll go organize my notes," I said. "I'll come over a little later."

CHAPTER TEN

Out Of The Blue Of The Western Sky

"Ihave an odd one for you. I'll call it, 'Ticket's and D. B. Cooper.'" Seated with coffee, I looked over to Owen. He seemed ready to begin.

Oh yeah, I thought to myself. When they start putting titles on their stories, they are enjoying themselves.

"D. B. Cooper," I mused. "That name sounds familiar somehow."

Owen nodded. "I suspect so. D. B. Cooper jumped out of a passenger jet somewhere over Oregon or Washington in 1971. Parachuted out at 10,000 feet with a bag of money. Remember it now?"

"Vaguely, but I don't recall any details," I admitted.

"Here's all you need to know for my story.

D. B. Cooper – probably not his real name – hijacked a Northwest Airlines Boeing 727 after takeoff from Portland, claiming to be holding a bomb. His ticket was purchased under the alias Dan Cooper, but the news media soon dubbed him 'D. B. Cooper.' He demanded $200,000, to be delivered to the plane in Seattle, in exchange for the passengers. Northwest agreed to the ransom, and the FBI recorded all the serial numbers of the new twenties that Cooper had stipulated.

The exchange was made right on the aircraft, and then Cooper commanded the pilot to take off and maintain ten thousand feet. Somewhere along the way, he opened the hatch and parachuted to an uncertain fate. Despite an exhaustive federal manhunt and investigation, he has never been located or positively identified.

The FBI distributed lists of the ransom serial numbers to financial institutions, casinos, racetracks, retailers, and law enforcement agencies around the world. Northwest offered a reward of up to $25,000. It remains the only unsolved air piracy in American aviation history.

Most of the ransom money has never been recovered. While the authorities don't believe Cooper survived the jump, bits of the ransom have surfaced; maybe $20,000. A kid playing in an Oregon stream found two packets of 290 bills, arranged in the same order as given to Cooper. Other bills were located in strange places. Some counterfeit bills printed with Cooper serial numbers were used to swindle $30,000 from *Newsweek* for a bogus interview with the presumed hijacker.

Obviously, some of that money was passed, unnoticed, in trade or banking. This, even though many folks in all the surrounding states were checking serial numbers on $20 bills. Modern-day-gold-rushers still search the prairie and mountains for that money.

So, of all places, where do you think one of those twenties shows up?"

"Ticket's!" I exulted.

"Yep.

We had a young bartender named Vance Wright working for us at the time, mostly day shift, certainly on this day.

One afternoon, a vagabond gets off the train and wanders into the bar. He pays for his small order with a twenty. Now Vance, a supporter of the law, strident in his love for America, does what all the newspapers, government agencies, Interpol, and everyone else had instructed retailers to do: look for Cooper twenties. Vance was religiously engaged in that. Dad and I were not so diligent.

Anyway, this guy's twenty is on the list. Vance freaks out. Calls the sheriff, tells the guy he has to wait here in the bar, and calls me at home. I immediately show up and see the fellow trying nonchalantly to exit the environs, defying young Vance's insistence that he wait for the police.

I figured him instantly as some sort of gypsy. He just had 'the look.' Old World, baggy, travel-worn threads, head down, sly, furtive, swarthy, long, black, wavy hair, the whole package.

I told him that I owned this place and he'd better step back inside until we sorted this thing out. He muttered and attempted to slide away, but I put my hand on his chest and suggested he didn't want to try any escape. He looked me in the eye for the first time, seemed to weigh his options, and then decided I was probably right.

Back inside, I sat him down at the center table. Soon we have the sheriff and the state police roaring up with sirens blaring. They'd already called the appropriate federal agencies.

Well, I thought, *there goes today's business*. I was wrong about that. Once word of the incident got about town, scores of gawkers dropped in for a beer and the 'doings.' Only the first arrivals got to see the suspect, though, because the cops soon moved the interrogation up to the second floor.

The whole thing became a tangled mess of confusing details, provided by someone who wasn't exactly believable. Turns out the guy – I keep saying guy because he kept changing his name throughout the interrogation – wasn't travelling alone. Gypsies seldom do. He was with a lady, maybe a sister, a girlfriend, a cousin, an aunt. That was unclear also.

Where was she? the authorities wanted to know. He didn't have any idea, so that triggered a town-wide woman hunt that ended with her being taken into custody in Aisle Three of Burrill's Hardware Store."

Owen smirked and started in again. "Separated from her companion for questioning, she spun some tale about finding a wallet on the floor near her seat on the train. Obviously a man's wallet, stuffed with cash, she was tempted to keep it, but her conscience just wouldn't allow for that. She tried to find its rightful owner, but the train stopped in Cordell, and she and her companion exited.

Where was the wallet now? Well, she left it on a train seat after relieving it of the cash. She couldn't find the owner, she claimed, and why should someone else have the money? No real crime here, right?

That was a handy story. If not working with Cooper, these two were more likely to have 'lifted' the wallet in some close encounter with another traveler.

When the cops checked out the stash she was carrying, two more twenties were on the hit parade. They kept those, along with my twenty, which they did not replace.

I decided it was a good investment anyway, filling my bar, as it were, with curious drinkers. In fact, in a few hours, we had reporters and TV crews descending on Cordell. This was big news. Of course, they all started their coverage in Ticket's. Media folks can really drink. I sold more booze that day, especially the hard stuff, than I did all month.

So, were these two actually connected to D. B. Cooper? Clever as he was, that notion was a dog that wouldn't hunt. With the meandering lifestyle of these two, it would've been an unlikely partnership. The idea just didn't hang together, even though the feds pressed both of them hard on the possibility. They maintained that they neither knew Cooper, nor anything about the airplane thing. It seemed to be the only believable thing either said.

So, why did they stop in Cordell? Where were they from, and where were they going? Poor, convoluted, and conflicting answers to those questions. Just one-day tourists, they answered; passing through after enjoying a little local color. The better guess was that they stopped here to pull a scam or two on some small-town rubes. Gypsies work on the theory that sheep don't fleece themselves.

They probably were casing the joint, so they split up to target the pickings. They were interrupted by Vance's vigilance. In any event, the gypsies weren't looking like the smoking gun pointed back to Cooper.

It looked more and more as if the gal had simply pick pocketed a much more interesting suspect. These two had no idea whether the owner of the wallet had exited the train in Cordell. Didn't even have a description. So the cops launched another search of the town, a manhunt this time.

The only strangers they could uncover were either the media folks who were probing about for a story, or other cops. Perhaps the owner of the wallet stayed on the train. By this time, though, the train would've reached Portland, so the suspect would've disappeared into thin air.

With no real reason to hold them, the authorities strongly encouraged the couple to leave town if they had no further business here.

In fact, in one of the funnier moments, a state cop came down to the barroom and called up Jimmy to meet the pair. He introduced them to Jimmy The Was and told them that Jimmy kept an eye on all shenanigans in Cordell. He and 'his friends' were not people these two wanted to encounter.

Everyone in the room laughed but the gypsies, who jumped on the early-evening train, even though it was headed south, the same direction from which they'd arrived.

So, that's how it ended. The authorities had just lost their best shot at finding someone with some of Cooper's take. He was still in the wind, and apparently is to this day."

"Good story, Owen," I said, complimenting the effort. Then, this is Cordell's only claim to fame and famous people?" I sneered, a bit over the top.

Owen worked his memory.

"Well, yes, unless you count the visit of Annie Oakley and the attempted assassination of the governor."

"What! Sounds like two more stories, Owen."

"Which one do you want first?" Owen asked, looking as if he had just swallowed a bird.

"Annie Oakley, I think."

"Okay. This story goes back a bit – Noah's time in Ticket's, probably around 1920. I know that Annie was already in her sixties, and past performing. She was on her way back from the coast to Chicago, where she had business.

It seems that late in her career, she had legal problems related to her name and fame. She was gung-ho on clearing her name, and she was in court all the time.

Annie took a short detour to visit her aunt, who lived near Bakeoven. When she got off the train here, the town just went crazy over the sharpshooter. She came into Noah's bar only because her entourage wanted some drinks before moving into the hotel for the night. Noah said that he had the privilege of serving her a sarsaparilla.

Annie and Noah hit it off immediately. He was limping around with a bad knee, and she was wearing a leg brace, both of which each soon showed the other. Noah paraded out his modified shotgun for her review. She carved her initials into the stock and then dispatched her husband, Frank Butler, to her luggage to dig out her favorite guns. Folks in the bar watched all of that with great homage.

'Course her presence filled the bar in no time. Hundreds wanted to see the famous lady. Men were asking for her autograph, a picture taken with her, she in her full-length dress and boots. They pleaded with her to put on a shooting exhibition, pointing out the wide-open space directly behind the bar. She declined. She was retired. But she was gracious and engaging. Very down-to-earth. She told little stories about her travels with Buffalo Bill's Wild West Show and the several circuses she'd headlined.

Toward late afternoon, a spontaneous party broke out. There were more women present than ever before, or since. No surprise, given the suffrage movement of the times. Annie Oakley was a shining example of 'women can too.' Women everywhere were proud of her accomplishments in a 'man's field,' and were thrilled to be in her presence.

Nolan Wainwright, our local musician, brought in his accordion. Soon folks were dancing the polka, most with beer glasses held high. My dad, George, remembered that part. He was only eight or nine years old, but he was part of the bar service that day. He didn't know who Anne Oakley was, but he knew a party when he saw one. He and his father often talked of that grand event.

Even Franklin Cordell showed up, as did the mayor, Franklin's lackey. Not one to miss a political opportunity, old Fergy stopped the proceedings long enough to 'officially welcome the great Annie Oakley to our fair town.' He made some lame joke about not having a key to the town to present, but he was able to give her a ticket to return, a miserable play on Ticket's. He fouled it up so badly that many thought he was giving her the bar. Both Noah and Franklin cringed.

The party went well into the night. Things didn't settle down until Miss Oakley bid everyone adieu and left for the hotel. She saw her aunt the next day and left town without much hoopla that evening. But all that excitement helped cement Ticket's as the place it happens, if it happens in Cordell."

"An *Annie Get Your Gun* moment, huh?" I offered.

"Yeah. Given her popularity and status in those days, you have to appreciate her warm acceptance of all the fanfare. A fine lady, no doubt about it."

"So," I summarized, "we've got D. B. Cooper and Annie Oakley. Pretty good for a small town. Now, about the governor and some attempt on his life?"

"Sure. But this one didn't take place in Ticket's. This, too, is a story from Noah's time running the bar. Late 1930s. This one started and ended in the bar at the hotel.

"I'm all ears," I said. "Lay it on me."

"The governor, Paul Billings, was standing for re-election. It looked like a close call, so he went out stumping and chose Cordell as a likely spot to garner some votes. In a well-advertised event, the governor was to arrive in town on the three o'clock train. He'd check into the hotel and give a rousing speech to the collected multitudes about four o'clock. He'd stay overnight, giving the hotel the right to claim that Governor Billings slept here, and head on down to Bend in the morning.

Everyone in town knew about this, and many attended as it was to be the closest they were ever going to get to an important person.

Emmitt J. Sewell certainly planned on attending the governor's speech. He had no interest in the governor's stump speech. Emmitt was in town to kill the politician. He made little secret of the fact."

Owen interrupted himself with a sudden thought. "Ed, did you ever notice how assassins are referred to with middle initial? You often get referred to by your middle initial?"

"Not often. Only in fun, by family and friends," I responded.

"Me too. Of course, neither of us has ever tried to assassinate an important public figure, have we?"

"No." There was Owen, again, taking another measure of my volatility.

"What a relief," Owen smiled the same smile as he did earlier.

"So here's Emmitt J. Sewell, waiting on the governor's arrival.

Sewell owned a horse ranch northwest of town. He had dreams of becoming the owner of a large land tract that would make him the horse baron of the prairie. When he attempted to homestead some property contiguous to his, the paperwork got all mixed up with that of another rancher who also wanted that land. That neighbor was awarded the land on technicalities in an appeal that went the whole way to the governor's office.

Emmitt was miffed. More than that, he was really angry, felt cheated out of property that should have been his. In the process, he had lost money.

Someone was to blame, and Emmitt decided it was the governor, of the opposite party, who, in Emmitt's mind, had made a political decision. Emmitt could kill the governor for that. In fact, he planned to.

So he arrived at the hotel sometime after noon and started shoring up his commitment. He drank heavily and recounted his woes to the growing assemblage. He told his story, he drank more rye, and he hinted strongly of his plans.

Most of those in attendance laughed at Emmitt. He was a known hothead who knew a lot of stuff that wasn't correct. But surely he was incapable of such a daring and stupid effort.

But about three o'clock Emmitt pulled out the large revolver he was going to use, brandishing it about.

Less than an hour before the governor's speech, some of his friends started to take Emmitt a bit more seriously.

They began to plan some way of heading this off. Of course, they could load him in car and take him home. Emmitt was always a mouthy drunk, but certainly not out of his mind. Maybe this was all palaver. To cart him off would enrage Emmitt, who'd already shown a gun. They could attempt to disarm him. Dangerous that was, with Emmitt's current condition and temper. Someone could get hurt.

His friends could go with him to the speech and intervene, when and if he drew his weapon, but that was risky, too, what with all the other people.

They could inform the governor's entourage of the threat, but that was to condemn a man for his thoughts rather than his actions.

The only realistic ploy was to convince Emmitt that this was a bad idea. A few tried this, professing to be of one mind with him about the governor's ineptness and politics, and suggesting that Emmitt give it another go at the state house. But Emmitt wasn't much in the arena of compromise. Something should be done, and, by God, he was going to do it."

Owen paused to let all that sink in. "The appointed hour came; the governor descended the stairway from the second floor rooms and ascended the makeshift podium. He began his speech. In the crowd, a small group of men had completely surrounded Emmitt J. Sewell.

For a few minutes, Emmitt actually seemed to be cooling off. Maybe this thing wasn't going to transpire after all. But then the governor launched into some promise of continued fairness for everyone. Emmitt's head jerked up, and he regained his resolve. He drew his mighty pistol – well, mostly drew it.

Hands all around him grabbed for it. Some tried to pull Emmitt down. And then the gun went off.

Emmitt fell to the floor by himself.

Somehow, someone in the scuffle had pointed Sewell's gun inward on himself. The bullet Emmitt squeezed off ripped through his upper leg, by his groin.

It severed his femoral artery. Emmitt J. Sewell bled out in less than two minutes. End of the governor's speech, end of poor Emmitt."

"Well, I'll bet that made the national news," I guessed

"Yep, a big story for two days. Then the action moved to another town. I do know this, no Oregon governor, or anyone running for Oregon governor, has ever set foot in Cordell since that day. Let our votes fall where they may."

Chapter Eleven

Thou Shall Not Drink

Several customers came and went. Owen was right: Ticket's still had a clientele, albeit an early-to-bed one.

Maybe he should bring in a rock band and give this place some staying power, I thought. That thought made me laugh.

Later, Bob brought in his stone and finished off his day. He seemed a bit more at ease while I made short, one-sided conversation.

By now, Grover was leaving his landing to greet me, tail wagging. I decided I was well on my way to becoming a Ticket's regular. Maybe I have a way with misfits and canines.

By the time we ate and settled down, it was early evening. Owen's look across the room seemed colored by some sort of boredom, or disinterest, or resignation. I thought maybe I was overstaying my welcome, not only by hour, but by purpose.

"Owen, are you tired of story-telling?

"No, just tired, period. I'm ready to sit down for a spell."

We stopped at the center table, Owen with his tea, I with a Coke. I figured it would take a few minutes for the tea to kick in, so I started simply.

"Owen, I've noticed something about you. You don't swear. No matter what you are telling, you very seldom utter profanity. I'll bet I haven't heard you say three curse words in all the times we have talked."

"We Tickets don't swear much." He reflected for several moments. "You know what? Grandfather Noah instilled that in us. Noah was a

God-fearing man. He was no extremist about it; he didn't 'wear it on his sleeve,' as they say. But, he didn't like hearing the Lord's name taken in vain, and you could see it in his face when someone did.

From the time my father started working the bar, and when I started working the bar, we were instructed to keep our language respectful and bland.

In addition to his moral aversion to hard language, Noah also believed it was bad practice for saloon-keepers. He told my dad, then me, and everyone who ever tended bar for us, that taprooms already had lots of swearing. Customers brought bad days, bad thoughts, bad emotions, bad language to the bar every day. They provided more than enough vileness. We didn't need to add to it.

Noah told us all, one time only, and more than enough, 'I don't abide profanity coming from behind my bar. Cussing does nothing for us. Our customers come to Ticket's with all their troubles, searching for cures, usually from a bottle, or the man next to them.

But we don't cure; we sell salve, liquid salve. We can lament the miserableness of their marriages or the uncertainty of the world, but we don't cuss while doing so. Just not necessary to sell them the next drink. They're upset, not us.

Noah said, 'Good bartenders endure the misfortunes of others. Our job is to be agreeable, attentive, accepting. We don't have to fix their problems, but we certainly won't inflame them with ugly, inflammatory words. When you're behind Ticket's bar, you speak like you're speaking to my wife, the elegant Alice Owen. Now, nobody would swear in her presence, would they? Don't forget, we get more women in here than any other bar. We're not going to run 'em off with crude language.'

'No, sir!' we'd all agree. 'No strong language.' Like any other behavior, not cussing becomes a matter of habit.

By the way, we were similarly warned about discussing politics and religion. Can't win a battle in either of those arenas.

"That's a damn good idea," I responded, with a smile, of course. Owen caught it. Sipped his tea.

"Yeah, well, Noah probably had another idea in mind, as well. His son, George, named after George Fagan, of course, worked in this bar from the time he was seven years old. For that matter, so did I, about the same age, after my dad took over the works.

We both did the kinds of jobs the young kids get. During our time, my dad and I both emptied the spittoons fastened to that foot rail – pleasant. We cleaned both toilets – pleasant, also. We switched the kegs in the basement when we were both so small that the keg had the upper hand.

We kept the pickle jar filled, the cracker barrel and the hanging jerky strip supplied. We washed glasses, mopped the floor, and cleaned up vomit on Saturday nights. By the time we were about twelve or so, each of us would pull beers behind the bar, cook up burgers and dogs, and everything else about the place. We ran the errands for both the bar and any customer who needed something from downtown. My dad polished more than one boot. I did not.

The point is that Noah had a son in the place. In those days, all sons worked at the family enterprise, bar or farm. Well, Noah wasn't about to subject his son to harsh language behind the bar. Bad enough that the roughnecks brought it in.

My dad was the same way. It wasn't just a moral thing. Both my grandfather and my dad had to convince their respective wives that their dear little sons were not going down the road to perdition, what with all this drinking and cursing."

"So, Owen, you have worked in this place since you were seven! You went to school, played sports, dated girls, and all that, didn't you?"

"A little. I certainly went to school. My mother saw to that. I graduated from high school in a class of nine. Sports? Some basketball, but that's all. Girls? Scared of them. I seldom even went home after school. I came straight to the bar and helped my dad get ready for the evening crowd. I spent a lackluster semester at OU before Dad agreed that my place was behind this bar. We were Tickets, and we ran a bar.

Anyway, swearing wasn't that difficult to avoid. Sometimes, though, you have to work at it. There were times when a good swear word would've felt pretty good, even to Noah. I'm sure Prohibition was a word-selection challenge for him. Seems to me that would have made a priest look for a good curse word."

"Owen, I'm glad you brought that up," I brightened at the thought. "How did Ticket's survive that decade?"

"First off, it was more than a decade. Oregon actually outlawed alcohol sales in 1915, almost five years before the national ban. For us, it was more like eighteen years of silliness. I'll spare you a lecture on the idiocy of the law; I'll bother you with two things. First, it did nothing to reduce crime, illness, public safety, or improve our moral fiber. In fact, it organized the crime in this country. It expanded the criminal underworld and cemented what before had been disjointed gangland operations.

Second, in most parts of the country, especially places like Cordell, it was a tiger without teeth. The ban was unenforceable because of inadequate funding, insufficient enforcement, political corruption, and lack of public support. It was a law without real commitment. It was like the government set up a rodeo, but there were no cowboys.

But the Volstead Act complicated things. It was a tough time for most brewers and distillers, and many, many bars. Lots went under.

Ticket's survived, for a couple of reasons. First was Noah's singular resolve to stay in business. He regarded the 1915 ban as an unfair change in the game.

Noah sold alcohol. He figured he worked hard for that opportunity, and he appreciated the good fortune he'd experienced in America. His business was legal when he started it almost a decade earlier, and the government had had no quarrel with the taxes they had taken from him. Now they wanted him to cease and desist.

Second, Noah had little time for such do-gooders as the teetotalers, the temperance folks, or knee-jerk political hacks who couldn't wait to pass a law.

The dimwitted government plan was wrong on all fronts for him. Noah chose to recognize it only as a complication. He couldn't ignore it, but he was going to remain afloat, legally or illegally, period.

He knew this made him a scofflaw, for the first time in his life, but his family's livelihood trumped that easily enough. Those barkeeps who thought like Noah survived; those who didn't fell victim to the national stupidity.

The third reason this place persevered was related to product. Of course, the bigger U.S. brewers and distillers were put on hold, but alcohol was still available to any bar that wanted to serve it. Ticket's simply had to find different sources, mostly illegal.

Liquor was the easy part. We aren't that far from Canada, you know. As many bar owners did, we obtained Canadian whiskey, shipped down the Columbia River or over from Puget Sound, and then hauled into the countryside. In the middle of the night, smugglers would bring a truck down one side of the Deschutes or the other, floating crafts stacked to gunwales with whiskey to the other side. Those little crafts had all the fancy whiskey Noah wished. That included European scotch, champagne, and Irish whiskey. Big-name bootleggers had national networks, bringing in boatloads of the stuff to New York, Cincinnati, Chicago, Kansas City, Portland, and Seattle.

But moonshine became the house staple. 'Shine' was available from dozens of bootleggers, many of them out in the valley or up in the foothills. Some of that product was pretty rough; some of it dangerous rot-gut. I'm sure you've heard the stories of blindness from foul, and sometimes lethal, moonshine. That happened rarely, and never around Ticket's. Our regulars trusted Noah to keep any danger out of the equation. And he did. Noah dealt only with moonshiners he could trust; no 'extenders' of any kind.

Before Prohibition, the government permitted small-scale 'gallon houses' to produce liquor that could be sold in limits of one gallon per purchase. Some of our local gallon houses had learned to produce very good spirits, some aged, if only for a short time. When Prohibition kicked in, many of these distillers quietly continued their trade. Noah bought from these distillers because he knew the source and the quality."

Owen stopped just long enough to re-orient to the subject. "In fact, Noah used the 'shine' to add a new product to his shelf. He'd offer straight 'shin,' clear and really potent. He'd offer the brown from Canada. But he also mixed the two, stretching his Canadian supply, offering a hopped-up version of the smoother whiskey. His customers loved that. Noah called it 'Local Canadian.' Meanwhile, some Ticket regulars would bring in a few gallons of their own white lightening. Noah let them sell it right out of the bar. Everyone needed to make a living, Noah knew.

Beer was a little trickier. It was easy enough to make, but suds were bulkier and more difficult to disguise in transport. Still, illegal brewers kept finding ways to get it to the bars. There were a few guys, staying under the radar, brewing small batches of beer, and all that was snatched up by countryside bars like ours. These were amateurs, making beer in their garages, some better than others.

Some of our local farmers were growing both wheat and hops. For a while, the market for both was really bad. So they started making beer, and some got very good at it. When Noah's regular supplier in Portland switched his brewery to the production of soda pop, Ticket's didn't skip a heartbeat.

A farmer named Luther Jones wanted to get into brewing, but didn't know squat about it. He teamed up with Bruno Hauer, a German immigrant, who knew just what to do. Those two made good beer, and Noah bought and sold most of it.

After Prohibition ended, you know what happened? Luther, Bruno, and their sons continued growing wheat and making beer. Now they're a legitimate microbrewery. Their original brew is still the same, and goes by the same name: J&H. Pretty creative label, don't you think? It's still on tap here. Next trip around the bullnose, I'll draw you one. Pretty hoppy, though.

Anyway, Noah sold a lot of pop. Most bars were advertising both local and new national-brand sodas as the drink of choice. Noah actually changed the sign on top of the bar. Took the name Ticket's off altogether. Put up 'Best soda and sandwich in town.'

He served Coca Cola and 'near beer.' He offered a larger menu then, and had a cook, Connie, coming in part-time to prepare lunch and make some soup. Her chipped-beef-and-melted-cheese sandwiches, with bread browned on the grill, was a local favorite.

But once inside the bar, a patron could order a beer, a whiskey, or a glass of fermented grape juice.

Ticket's became almost a private club. It was a speakeasy without the peephole, with a sort of 'by identification only' admittance policy. Noah hired a doorman who would stand outside. If he recognized the visitor, in he could go. If not, the burly fellow would tell them that this was a private club and 'curb' them. That probably wasn't necessary, but it put Noah's mind at ease."

"So," I asked, "did Prohibition make business better or worse?"

"In some ways it made it better," Owen said, after a moment's thought. "It was certainly more difficult and sophisticated to operate on the sly. Here's the thing, though. When you can have a product, easily and legally obtainable, buyers tend to use it as they wish. When folks aren't supposed to have a thing, they tend to overdo it when given the opportunity. 'Forbidden fruit,' I guess. Prohibition caused drinkers to binge. When they found a source, they actually guzzled more than they might've if the product was legal.

Noah sold more alcohol in less time during Prohibition years than he did before the law, or after its repeal. I don't think there's such a thing as a 'glass-per-minute-ratio,' but if there were, Ticket's would've had a higher ratio than before the blight."

"Was Noah ever raided by the feds? Did he have barrels cracked open? Shut down? Fined?

"Not once," Owen laughed. "Cordell was just too far off the beaten path, just not worth the trouble. Fifteen hundred feds couldn't handle the outlets, the kingpins in any large city. How were they going to police illegal consumption in places like this?

The longer Prohibition went the more nonchalant Noah became. He finally just stopped worrying about detection."

During Owen's review, three or four patrons came, drank, and left. The first time back from the bar, he drew me a J&H. Good. Yes, hoppy.

"Owen, it must be the second cocktail hour in Cordell," I suggested.

"More like rush minute," he shrugged. "Be a few more soon. Factories and the rail yard changing shifts. A group of regulars on their way back to The Acre after a day."

"I'm glad to see that business is good for you."

"What, you think you're the only guy ever comes in here anymore? I still make a living here, you know."

So chastised, I said, "So, no gripping story about Noah's desperate times and measures during Prohibition?"

Owen thought. "Maybe one. Grandfather did tell me one little story about a whiskey runner. A 'skimmer' named Ben Tatum."

Without encouragement, Owen continued.

"There's always somebody looking to work an angle on someone else's enterprise. Ben Tatum was one of those, a ne'er-do-well who found a niche in bootlegging. Too stupid or lazy to make it himself.

Ben had a brother up in Vancouver who knew a guy who knew a guy, that sort of story. Ben had a car, and he'd go up to the Columia and load up as many cases as he could haul. He made good money. Bars paid well for the dangers of smuggling whiskey. But that wasn't enough for this thief.

Ben devised a sweet little scheme that shorted both the suppliers and buyers. He was skimming profits and product from both sides. Soon he built his own stash of liquor, bottle by bottle, case by case. Then he'd sell it to locals, at hundred per-cent profit.

That retailing part was his downfall. Ben should've stuck to cheating the system. But greed is an aphrodisiac. A drunken patron at a bar up the river told the owner where he was getting his syrup. That tore it for some of Ben's bar buyers, including Noah, who were already suspicious of Ben's accounting methods, made possible because there was no paper trail, delivery slips, or manifests of any kind. Until now, though, the barkeeps had to chalk it up to the cost of doing business.

Vengeance is a real motivator.

Four of the owners confronted Ben at one of his regular stops along the river. His protestations were lost on them. They beat him like a rented mule. They off-loaded the whiskey from his car, took all his cash, quite a bit, I understand, threw him in the vehicle, and headed north.

With a little prodding, they convinced Ben to lead them to his supplier's warehouse, an old barn deep in the woods. Like all the warehouses, this barn was guarded by thugs who were instructed to shoot first and ask questions later.

The barmen stripped Ben down to his long johns. 'Tell your story to those goons over there,' they told him. 'And, by the way, you now reside in the state of Washington, so find a way across the river. If we see you anywhere between The Dalles and Cordell, we'll have you shot, if these guys haven't already done it for us.' Then they pushed him out of the woods into the clearing, where he could deal with the whiskey runners."

Owen laughed out loud. "Noah said that when they left, Ben looked chagrined, maybe even a little scared."

"Why did they leave him in his underwear?" I wondered out loud.

"Couple reasons. They decided it would slow down any plan for escape or retribution. They thought it would force him to tell more of the real story to the bootleggers. And, they wanted to humiliate him without invoking physical harm."

"Physical harm? They already beat him. They told him they would kill him on sight."

"Oh, sure. With Noah and his ilk, you got one warning. The beating and promise was that warning. They weren't going to tell Ben twice how lucky he was to be alive."

Owen wanted to clarify the bar-keeps' position. "These were cutthroat times. Skimming in the liquor trade was akin to stealing a man's horse in the Old West. Noah would do what he had to do. Ben had to know that."

"Understood. It's getting late, Owen. I know you're tired. Want to stop here?"

Owen glanced at his watch. "I'll give you the time, but you're paying for your beer."

"Good. We'll sleep in tomorrow and start later. How's that? How about we end the night on a scandalous note. Tell about a town scandal. Have any of those?"

Silence from Noah, as he considered the question.

"I guess no community ever escapes scandal, does it? We've met our quota.

Sex, money, and drugs, that's the stuff of scandals. William Tanner provided all three. In 2000, he was the center of Cordell's most sordid scandal.

If Franklin Cordell was the most colorful man in town at the beginning of the century, Bill Tanner had that distinction by the end of it. (I guess you would have to give Jimmy The Was that title through the middle years.)

Bill Tanner made himself rich as a commodities trader, working out of both The Dalles and Cordell. He brokered wheat and sheep, cattle and produce, perlite for a while, anything our farmers, ranchers, and businesses needed to get to market.

Bill found the buyers, sometimes himself, and arranged for the transportation and sale to the highest-paying wholesalers and stock-yards from here to Chicago. He was known as honest and fair in the community. His commissions were reasonable, and he worked hard at what he did.

The only gripe you heard about Bill concerned his self-righteous-ness and a condescending attitude. He presented himself as the moral conscience of the community, wrapping his observations in billowy references to the Bible, the U S Constitution, ancient philosophers, and several Mid-Eastern religions. He was a regular at the café, where he'd rave on and on about 'the right thing to do,' and 'the higher calling of man.'

His squeaky-clean persona could sometimes be over the top. No matter the civic issue, the national politics, the morality of others, what have you, Bill always was the guy with the high ground. That left any dissenter with the low ground. That, and his ability to go on and on, stifled even the meekest of responses. He'd lecture the school board about tax increases, raises for teachers, and a focus on 'the children.' He'd write letters to the *Gazette* laced with lofty and noble principles he expected but wasn't seeing in our little town.

Of course, he headed the yearly United Way campaign. Certainly, he was president of the Rotary and the Friends of the Library. He was an elder in his church, his voice the loudest in choir. He was known to counsel —cajole actually — the new pastor about topics and activities he believed would most help the congregation. He provided the sermons when the preacher was unavailable. People say he would thump his Bible, recite scripture from heart, and dog the assemblage to live in peace, kindness, and love with one another. All his presentations seemed to end the same way: 'Go forth and sin no more!'

This sanctimonious attitude naturally spilled over to all his 'causes' and somewhat into his business. Somehow, he could make folks feel like not doing business with him was somehow against the American Way. If he were backing a local or national politician, if the Rotary was selling raffle tickets, he could squeeze money out of anyone. If he couldn't guilt someone into something, he'd badger them to death with one of his tirades.

But for all of that, most folks viewed him as earnest in his beliefs and reliable in his business. This 'holier-than-thou' demeanor grew old fast, but he did obtain producers the best prices sellers could expect. They accepted that an encounter with Bill would require some time.

He and his lovely wife built a huge house in the far corner of The Wedge. He owned about three lots back there, and trees, shrubs, and sloping hills provided him the privacy he sought when not instructing others.

But then his wife, Delores, died after a short bout with cancer. For the next dozen years, Bill lived alone. Or so we thought.

Turns out that Bill had cultivated a secret life that included male prostitutes and gay boyfriends. Stimulants, too, if you know what I mean. Bill had hit the trifecta: money, sex, and drugs. We came to find out that Bill Tanner was enjoying a somewhat 'alternative' life-style.

Most of us were taken aback to hear of booze-soaked weekend parties with these hired men and more than one gay lover. There were a few infractions of the law involved there.

As the story came out, it got more and more bizarre. You know what 'furries' are?"

"I think so, but I'm afraid to confess," I answered.

"Then you know. Furries enjoy a pretty extreme fetish. It's not illegal, but weird. These people, male and female, get their kicks role-playing and dressing like their favorite animal. They wear seriously-conceived costumes – bears, rabbits, mice, foxes, you name it – and pretend to be that animal. For some 'plushies,' as they're also called, there is sexual gratification in all this. Ed, can you imagine having sex with a bear? I guess after you start, you don't stop until the bear wants to. How about a swan then?

Well, Bill was a furry. Hosted parties for them. And filmed it all. Unbeknownst to anyone, Bill had rigged his house with hidden video cameras. He recorded these goings-on with his lover, furry friends, and prostitutes for his later viewing pleasure.

What finally brought Bill down were not the parties, the sex, or the prostitutes. It was Bill's recordings, shared with the police by his boyfriend, who discovered the tapes and jealously quarreled with Bill."

Owen shook his head in bewilderment. "For some warped reason, this fellow didn't mind male prostitutes around because he believed he was Bill's Number One. Suddenly, another guy seemed to challenge that, and Number One and Bill fought over that for about a week. Bill's fatal mistake was sharing with his guy one or more recordings. This was the first his lover knew he and others had been recorded.

In a snit, Number One went to the authorities, and the House of Tanner came tumbling down. Now the police blotter and the news media desktops were barraged daily with more details of this menagerie. Bill's whole life started to come apart, publicly.

Tanner tanked. He admitted early on to the taping. When that trove of recordings was seized, the magnitude and weirdness of the events were simply sick. Furry sex, orgies, drug use, all of it.

Do I have to tell you that the town was shocked? William Tanner? Epitome of rectitude? Director of morality and righteousness for Cordell? Scandalous!"

"So what happened to William Tanner?" I wanted to know.

"He pled to promoting prostitution, invasion of privacy, unlawful use of computer, or something like that. Paid a big fine, sentenced to home arrest, an electronic bracelet around his ankle, and public scorn. 'Feet of clay' as they say. Maybe Harry Truman cautioned us well. If a man sings too loudly on Saturday night, and prays too loudly on Sunday mornings, you'd best go home and lock the smokehouse."

"Does he still live here?" I asked.

"Still owns the house in The Wedge. But he owned a condo up on the Columbia, and I think he lives there now. Never see him."

"Sex, money, and drugs, eh, Owen?"

"Yes, and the greatest of these is sex."

"I suppose," I agreed. "We read about it all the time."

A nod. A silence.

"So, Owen, I'm assuming that Ticket's had to deal with the sex thing. How did you three deal with the hookers, the come-ons, the sexual tensions in a bar of men, women, money, and alcohol?"

"Well, there were always the hookers. They came even before the railroad. Certainly they followed the tracks in those Hell on Wheels encampments everywhere. Still available, I guess, not many, though. The few we have live up in The Acre. It's not nearly the business it was when Lady Pearl and Miss Veronica ran attractive parlors down by the river."

"Okay, then, Owen, let's talk whores. Did Ticket's aid and abet that business?"

"No, never," was Owen's emphatic response. "We were never known for sexual liaison, as they say. Noah wanted women in the bar. I think I told you that he offered tables for ladies with his sign in the window. But not for sex. Women were paying customers. Especially, he wanted escorted women, someone's wife, sister, or girlfriend. He wanted a strong, local, and decent clientele.

Noah sold suds, not sex. His focus was on stand-up drinkers, from all social strata. Ticket's was where the linen suit brushed shoulders with the plaid overcoat. Women? He couldn't make real money off someone else's business. He certainly knew the hookers, liked many of them. But he made it clear that they should do their business at the bar in the hotel or downtown.

In Noah's day, prostitutes were free to come in and buy a drink. They could use the toilet without buying a drink. But they couldn't loiter about Ticket's. One episode of that, and the lady was quietly told to leave.

The locals, the regulars, certainly, knew that Ticket's was no place to get their socks rolled. And they already knew where to go if that is what they wanted. Wasn't an issue, really. If a blitzed a stranger asked Noah about women, Noah would send him to the hotel, or up into the streets of The Acre.

That worked for Noah. Women about town were comfortable here. They could enjoy an evening in the company of large groups of men without being either propositioned or criticized for being here in the first place."

"And, your dad, George?" I asked. "Did he continue that tradition?"

"Sure. He and I were both trained by Noah. Maybe 'influenced' is a better word here. George didn't care as much as his father about building a female patronage. By the 1950s, Ticket's was a working man's bar. The linen-suit crowd was slowly moving to the new hotel on The Boulevard, which offered live entertainment.

My dad had to deal with the queries from the out-of-towners, but he simply chose not to play. Asked for some direction to girls, George would say that he knew of none, but perhaps the bartender at the hotel could help.

He told me once, 'By the time the guy gets up the nerve to ask, he only has room for one more beer anyway. Sell him that one and send him on his quest.'"

"And you, Owen?" I pursued.

"I handled the woman situation a bit differently, he smiled. "For all the years I've run this place, out-or-towners, drummers, company execs, or people like you would show up some evening and ask me where they could find some female companionship. I told them I didn't have any idea; this was a small town and women here were mostly otherwise engaged. But some of these modern-day travelers weren't buying that.

They figured a bartender like me would know of somebody. So, rather than disabuse them of that notion, I just went along with it.

I'd say, 'I know a gal that would probably take you on. Cost you $100."

"$100! God, she must be good!"

"Nah, she isn't good at all. She's fat, lazy, and dirty; lives with a jackal, but she'll do anything for $30."

"You said $100. Now you say $30! Which is it?"

"Well, she's worth the $30. I get the $70 just for hooking you up. She and I agree that it's a fair deal. Still interested?"

"Thirty dollars! She must be bad!"

"Yep, she is. If I were you, I'd go back to your hotel and order a pay-per-view."

Owen laughed.

"Did that work?" I asked.

"Always. Never had to tell 'em I was just kidding. Like my dad told me, I'd sell the guy one more beer and send him on his way." Owen laughed again at his own humor.

"But there were prostitutes in town, weren't there?"

"Oh, sure." Owen almost waved off my question. "Forever. Add it up. Railroad men, lumberjacks, mill workers, highway builders, mechanics and craftsmen of all kinds, tent-town laborers. That's a target-rich environment for hookers.

Many of the women moved on when the railroads throttled back. A few stayed. Some married, raised a family.

You have to remember something about prostitution in America. At the beginning of the century, the trade was – how shall we say – a recognizable, if a somewhat less-acceptable slice of society. Like the poor, we always had the oldest profession among us.

Prostitutes may have been low in the social order, but they were a recognized industry. A banker's wife might have sniffed at them in the grocery store, but the banker did his sniffing in The Acre, or by the Deschutes.

Remember, Franklin Cordell had actually planned for brothels down in his 'industrial zone'. That location was over-ridden by his establishment of The Acre. That's where the ladies ended up, and are to this day. Except for the ones that set up shop in or around the lumber camps some companies built near the wood. In fact, some of the sturdier housing over there was built by lumbermen for that express purpose. More than one mill owner or wood dealer erected homes for their girlfriends."

"Bedtime, Owen. Plan out a good 'platter.'

CHAPTER TWELVE

Christy And The Damn Depression

"I need another J&H, Owen." Thus supplied, I turned to a topic I had overlooked a day or so before.

"Owen, we've talked about Prohibition. Tell me about the Depression. How did Cordell and Ticket's fare with that?

Silence while the now-standard Owen rumination began. When he was ready, he leaned into the tabletop and began.

"The Depression. Bad times for folks here and everywhere. The thirties were tough. Noah kept the bar open, but it wasn't business as usual. He needed the same grit and business skills he used during Prohibition, but more so. Liquor was legal again, but few had money to buy it. Much bartering going on. Lumber traded for meat, vegetables for 'shine, milk for canned goods. Same in here.

Noah often traded drink for groceries, or fish, or clothing, or furnace wood. He'd trade labeled liquor for beer with several farmers who'd become very good brewers. One bottle of Jack for one keg of beer, that was the exchange rate.

Anyway, there were enough people in the bar, all right, but not much money changing hands. Noah didn't sell as much product through all of this, but, as he put it, 'A piddling is better than a zero.'

Men without jobs would come in to loaf or nurse a beer for an hour. These were good people, mind you, who sat only because there was no work. They congregated so they could commiserate, and Noah provided a warm, dry place to do so.

Ticket's actually became a handy place to be. If an employer wanted some short-term labor, Ticket's became the first stop, a sort of hiring hall. If a farmer needed help with his wheat, or hops, if a rancher needed some herders to get his sheep up into, or down from, the foothills, or a timber man needed strong backs to load rail cars, he did best to go to Ticket's. Men here would hire on immediately. Really, I think Noah was pleased enough to have people coming and going, and that his place played some role in people's attempt to 'get by.'

On the other hand, not every worker and employer match-up panned out. Noah loved to tell the story of old Grady Blanton, a muleskinner who thought he knew more than anybody about everything. Wanna hear about him?"

"Certainly."

"Grady was unemployed most of the time. It wasn't just the Depression that kept him unemployed. It was his lousy, self-aggrandizing, obnoxious personality. According to his own stories about himself, Grady was a specialist in about every field of endeavor. He knew lumber, he knew mining, he knew water, he knew farming, he knew government, he knew food, he knew women, everything. Grady was an expert at large. Said he could do anything and had done most.

The boastful little gnome would come into Ticket's and tell everyone how he once had done this or that dangerous thing, how tough and smart he was, and how stupid bosses were. By God, if he were in charge, things would be different.

That loudmouth braggart got tiresome, and soon people just quit questioning him, challenging him, or arguing about all these things he knew for sure. Everyone knew better, of course. Grady was all wax and no wick. But, here he was, and he bought beer, so Noah shrugged off his own irritation.

One morning, a small-time lumberman came in looking for help. 'I need to drag some logs out of the woods, to the prairie, so I can put them on wagons,' he announced 'I need someone who is good with mules.'

Before anyone could respond, Grady says, 'I'm good with mules. Probably the best muleskinner west of the Mississippi.'

'I hope so,' the cutter replied. 'I've got only one mule fit to work, and he's the meanest, most contrary mule've ever had. Won't take command, seldom abides being led or ridden, hates harness, and bites like a bitch. If you want this job, you have to be ready for 'Skikes.' He's just plain nasty. But I need to get that wood off the hill.'

'Ain't never been a mule I couldn't handle,' responds Grady. 'Trick with the contrary ones is to ride them, not to lead 'em. If I'm on his back, you can bet your own ass that those logs are coming out.'

'You'll be well paid if you can,' says the lumberman. 'But I warn you, Skikes has already hurt other men.'

'Well, Skikes has met his match. Let's go get those logs.'"

Owen laughed and shook his head. "Grady had nothing if not self-confidence, and his need to impress everyone."

"So, Owen?" I coaxed.

"Grady is taken up to the mountain, shown a small turn of logs, choker-chained to the infamous Skikes. Grady circled the mule, slapping his rump hard as he passed. He pulled the slack from the chain, violently, so Skikes knew he was tethered.

Grady walked up to the front of the arrangement, slapped the mule upside his jaw. Grady looked that mule in the eye and says something like, 'Now, you listen to me, you miserable big-eared bastard. We're going down this hill together. If we aren't together at the bottom of this hill, I'm going to put a .38 slug between your ears.'

With that, and a small group of buckers watching, Grady climbed up on Skikes and kicked him in the loins.

Skikes snorted, reared up off his front feet, and then kicked up his back legs. He did so with such ferocity that Grady wasn't simply thrown off. He was catapulted into the trunk of a large hemlock. Trouble was, Grady hit that hemlock with his face, and the force snapped his neck like a pea pod. The man was dead before he hit the ground. Three seconds, start to finish. One of the quickest accidental deaths in Oregon logging history.

The timber man felt badly about it, but he still had logs to move. He came back to Ticket's, told his story, and asked for volunteers. I have no idea how that wood ever got moved."

"I'll bet Grady's funeral was one of the smallest ones in Cordell, eh, Owen?"

"For sure, pompous little flea that he was.

But I digress. Back to the Depression.

The WPA and CCC programs helped Cordell weather the storm. When the government started building parks and roads and bridges to provide jobs, Cordell was fortunately located near a few of them. Men from town were hired for these projects and lived with later pride for their part. Loads of eastern men, some with families, followed the work to town. Most ended up in the government camps or The Acre. Most of them wanted a drink now and then. A man who wants to drink can usually find some way to pay or trade for it. And here we were.

Still, we three or four bars had to attempt creative strategies to survive. Noah's hiring hall was effective enough.

Now 'Goose' Singletary tried a novel approach in the hotel, on the end of The Strip. Old Goose took his best shot, and Noah always admired him for that, even if it was something Noah himself couldn't bring himself to do."

"What was that?" I prodded.

"William Singletary – 'Goose' to the locals – owned the hotel. Never mind how he acquired that handle. The point is that the hotel suffered greatly. Fewer travelers, less use of the passenger trains, fewer rooms rented, fewer meals sold, all reflected in bar sales, along with a local clientele with little money. Goose was going under, in a slow, agonizing spiral.

The lobby of the Cordell Hotel was large and connected directly to the sizable barroom. Goose figured that if he could open that space up a bit, he'd have enough room to operate a dance hall.

That's what he did. And then he went over to Portland and hired himself some taxi dancers."

"What's a taxi dancer?" I inquired, knowing Owen was expecting the question.

"A taxi dancer is a woman paid to waltz with patrons on a dance-by-dance basis. A 'hired hoofer,' you might say. The term 'taxi dancer' compares the lady's source of income to that of a taxi driver. She's paid for each dance. 'A dime-a-dance' was typical; the lady cleared five cents, the owner, the other five.

Taxi dancers were popular in San Francisco in the twenties, especially on the Barbary Coast. Ugly men; pretty ladies, lonely men with a dollar in their pockets, desperate women – a formula for success.

These dancers could make more money than their friends working in factories, sweatshops, or offices. But the work hinted of prostitution. That was fact for some of these gals. It was a job that required the relinquishment of reputation. The fad faded by the end of the Depression, but it was work for these women when they needed it.

When Goose opened his dance studio, there was quite a ruckus, at first, anyway. The godly were offended, the righteous outraged. Whores – that was what these big-city women were, plain and simple. And now Cordell was diving into sin. Married women locked their menfolk in at night. Men ran errands and had more 'business meetings' than ever.

Goose expected some reaction, but he was trapped. He had no choice but to persevere as he was going broke. Besides, business was good. Turned out, lots of men from the countryside did have a dollar or two in their pockets. Seemed to be a question of priority spending.

Still, Goose got a lucky break that helped him get past that early wrath and indignation. Christy Shoemaker showed up at the hotel, looking to make some money. Goose hired her in a New York minute. Christy Shoemaker was pert, shapely, and beautiful. She possessed a wonderful personality, all perky and friendly.

And, most of all, she was a Cordell girl.

That caused some comment about town. Here was this Shoemaker girl, a recent graduate of our local high school, in fact, the May queen, the girl voted most likely to succeed, the lithesome gal at the counter in the drugstore, dancing with men for money. Terrible! What was happening in this country, when a pretty, young virgin had to defile herself like that? Here's a home-grown lass, prostituting herself for money, in a sleazy, grimy, dance parlor. How could she?

Of course, the druggist fired her. Women about town sniffed at her when they encountered her on the street. Certainly the local boys created erotic dream sequences.

But for Christy, the choice was simple enough. There was a Depression in this country. Her parents operated a small ranch. Her mother was fighting cancer. They could raise enough food to keep body and soul together, but they had no money. Nobody was buying sheep; nobody was buying wheat. Portland wasn't the only town to have desperate women. Christy needed a job to help her family survive. Taxi dancing was it.

So, Christy started in at the hotel and was an immediate hit. Most attractive of the working women. The local men couldn't miss the opportunity to dance with the beauty who once cavorted around the maypole.

Good for Goose, also, is what happened next. Christy was certainly not the only local girl who took this opportunity. Following her groundbreaking choice, several other local girls showed up at the hotel, ready to dance with strangers. Several mothers, and a few young women who'd lost their factory jobs, needed cash. They certainly weren't whores; they were broke. A choice between reputation and food was not a difficult decision. So, several local girls joined the Portland women of questionable reputation in the dance hall. For a while there, Goose was able to hang on."

"Whatever happened to Christy?" I asked.

"Things turned out real well for her. Known as a trailblazer for women, she was an example of self-reliance, initiative, and personal sacrifice for her family.

In fact, in the western tradition of new starts, Christy Shoemaker rose above these scandalous beginnings to accomplish wonderful things.

During all the moral outrage at Christy's personal denigration, only one person offered a reclamation plan to her family. Most women of the town wrote off Christy as a shameless whore. But Stella Worthingham had an idea.

Stella was the wife of the local Chevy dealer, Thomas Worthingham. Stella was a substitute teacher in the high school. She knew Christy from that work. She went to see the Shoemakers with an improbable idea.

She made clear that she, personally, had no qualms with the decision Christy had made. Given the times and situation, she might've done the same thing. But all this talk about Christy was missing the point. For Stella, it wasn't about what Christy was doing, but what she might do with the rest of her life. After all, this Depression was going to end sometime.

Stella told the Shoemakers that their daughter was a gifted student. Stella had been in the school often enough to know this. Christy was good at math, she exhibited leadership qualities, and she was destined to do great things.

Stella told the parents that women like Christy were needed in our schools. Christy must become a teacher, right here in Cordell. She had to go to college for that. And if Stella and her husband Tom had to contribute something toward that expense, they would. Childless, as they were, she believed they ought to make some commitment to the future of some young person. Stella convinced the Shoemakers that Christy just had too many skills to waste."

"And?" I asked expectantly.

And, that's exactly what happened. Like all things, the Depression ended. Christy's family saved every nickel and dime they could, and they got some help from the successful car salesman. A thankful Christy went off to the state college and returned as a teacher.

Until she retired some years ago, Christy Shoemaker, now Christy Roman, has the reputation as the finest, most challenging teacher in this school district. No one remembers that she was a taxi dancer. No one ever mentions the shunning this town gave her. Christy Shoemaker Roman is now the respected math teacher who helped more students than any other, before or since.

The hotel didn't make it."

CHAPTER THIRTEEN

There Are Indians, And There Are Indians

I returned to Ticket's early in the cocktail hour. Owen was behind the bar, chatting with a few men on the stools. I sat down with Grover on the stairs with a draft.

In came a fisherman, his waders tied at the back of his waist. He was carrying a thirty-inch, shiny, gray and pink steelhead by its gaping mouth. Without comment he strode across the room and laid the big fish up on the bar.

"Owen, give me some wrapping paper and I'll stick this in the fridge for you. You have to gut it."

While he wrapped his catch, others asked him the perfunctory questions: Where did he catch it? Was he out all afternoon? Did he get anything else? None seemed as impressed as I was with the big fish.

Meanwhile, Owen drew him a beer. Finished, the man washed his hands and took a stool. Light chatter, and then the group slowly dissolved. The fisherman remained.

Owen damp-ragged the bar, motioned me over, and introduced me to Ross Wilson. "Ed's writing a book – stories of Cordell from the early days to now."

Ross and I shook hands, his mammoth paw swallowing up my hand. He looked me over closely, some form of face validity, I suspect. Perhaps I was doing the same.

Ross was a huge man, all of 270 pounds. He was wide-chested and slim-legged. His weathered face, a three-day beard, his not-so-clean jeans, a large knife sheaved on his belt, and unzipped hoodie all screamed outdoorsman. Yet, while he was obviously in his mid-fifties, he had an impishness in his twinkling eyes and wide, white-toothed smile.

Make a great Santa Claus, I thought to myself. *And, he'd be an imposing figure in a bar.*

Wait a second, I suddenly remembered, *I am in a bar.*

I hoped that this burly fellow was just a big teddy bear.

"Ross is someone you ought to talk to," Owen continued. "He might just be the smartest, most versed guy in this valley. His family has been here forever, and he owns the original homestead, touching Cordell, across the river. Also fixes cars and sells gas on the street behind The Boulevard. Knows the area, its history, the people. And he's a good story-teller.

Ross, it occurs to me that you could tell Ed some stories. Do you have some time to talk?"

"Whatever you say, Owen." To me, he said, "Don't listen to Owen. I'm a simple rancher and tinkerer. What are you looking for?"

"He wants stories about our town. He wants those big words you're famous for, and the richness of life around here. He wants to tie up our stories with one big bow, from 1900 to now. He wants the stuff of books."

The three of us chuckled. Ross looked at me hard and then said, "Big assignment. Everything is enmeshed, you know. One thing becomes the next. You want that?"

"I do." I was impressed by Ross. I was already expecting some big words.

"So, where to start?" It was a toss-up question Ross posed.

Owen thought about it for a moment and replied, "Tell him about the Indians."

"Which Indians? There are Indians and then there are Indians."

Owen nodded, seeing the point. "Start with the Native American Indians — something there, for sure."

"Yeah, something easy," Ross' voice dripped with sarcasm. A moment of reflection.

Then he began. "The story of the American Indian and the white man is very complex; damndest relationship you can imagine between two governments.

Actually, that depends, I guess, on what level you view it. My grandfather, Hobbs Wilson, arrived in the Tygh Valley in the 1890s. Warm Springs, the Indian reservation, was already there.

Hobbs' dad, however, had fought Indians during the 'uprisings,' and his stories are famous around here. But my dad also knew lots of Indians because of our garage. He loved to tell the story of a conversation he once had with an old, wizened chieftain. He asked the old warrior to tell him the Indian take on the past.

Here's the story the old Indian told my dad.

'The story of the Indian is simple. Once, many tribes roamed the plains. They hunted, they fished, and they trapped. They gathered food from the plants. Many tribes, many hunting grounds.

The younger men spent their days outfoxing the buffalo and the other animals of the prairie, mountains, and streams. They ate what they killed.

They wore as little clothing as necessary. They possessed little, only what they could move on horses.

The Indians made their own bows, arrows, and lances. They tamed their own ponies and horses. They built their own lodges. Problems were solved with powwows and peace pipes. The wisdom of the elders was the law.

The men of many nations taught their sons all these things.

With the setting sun, the young men returned to their camps. Here, their women tended warming fires and prepared food for them, some for now, some for later. Their women collected berries and roots, stitched hides into garments, created colorful jewelry and headdresses, wove blankets, washed clothes in the rivers, gathered water and wood, and dried hides in the sun.

In the evening, most of the settlement would come to the big fire, where the braves would sing and chant and dance and summon the spirits of the land.

Then all would return to their women for joyous lovemaking.

With the rising sun, they rose and did it all again.

They lived with purpose and pride. They were free.

And then the trappers came, and the soldiers, and later, the long lines of covered wagons. And then the Iron Horse.

'White people looked at the ways of our people and said, 'We can improve on that.'

That's the story. The rest is just history, written by the winners.'"

"Geez," I said, "you either have to laugh or cry."

Ross smiled. "Yep. Along our way to 'improving things,' we obliterated a culture of thousands of years. We killed them, we lied to them, we moved them, we ripped out their collective hearts. And they retaliated, in kind, best as they could. But we overwhelmed them. We made them wards of the state, but we gave them little to fight starvation, diseases they never knew, unhealthy living conditions, despair, and no genuine social integration. Indians, as a whole, are living down to the expectations we set for them. What the hell did we expect?

For sure, both sides deserve blame, if not in one place, then another. Communication difficulties, greed, stubbornness, governmental ineptitude – the whole damn effort was doomed from the start.

So what we're left with is the goddamn quagmire of the reservation system, cultural prisons, really, which has created generation after generation of poverty-struck, shiftless, non-engaged, alcoholic Native Americans. Shame on fricking everybody.

But you don't want history or opinion, do you? You want a story, right?"

Ross didn't wait for an answer; he was warming to the topic. Meanwhile, Owen dragged his new fish out of the refrigerator, hauled it up on the bar, and started to cut it apart.

"Back when I was a boy, not too many Indians came to town. When they did, they were usually here to barter for goods. They had no money to buy anything. We had one couple who made periodic jaunts through town on their horse-drawn wagon. Really, it was a surrey, just like the one in *Oklahoma,* except that this one was unpainted, wobbly, fringe-impaired, and creaky. Maybe it wasn't much like the one in the musical, now that I think about it. But it had a lid on it.

So Earnest Dunn, whose Indian name was Black Arrow, and his wife, I forget her name, would come through town or out to the ranches, bearing fish and Indian-made leather goods, squash and pumpkins, jewelry and Indian garb that they wanted to trade for food. Food only, mind you. Hell, they would trade two leather belts for a can of fruit salad, or a matched set of ring, earrings, and necklace for a package of hamburger. Sometimes Mom would throw in a cheap gemstone or trinket, or a second can of peas, just to square up a trade. They'd take it, but the mother always held onto the food until they left.

I say mother because they had a little boy who rode in the back with the cargo. His name was Jim, but I never knew that until we both grew up. Jim was just about my age. Always dirty and disheveled, he wouldn't say a word. He'd just sit there and stare at me, as if I were from another galaxy. I'd smile at him, but he just sat there. I always had some sort of flashback to those old western movies, where Our Hero had to look into just such a face. He moved only when his dad ordered him to produce the item under discussion. He would fish about for it, and then hold it out in front of him as if it were a prize. Deal completed, he would simply sit down again, with his back to the bench seat, and stare into the distance.

During my childhood, that was our major interaction with the Indians. Oh, we'd see them when we went fishing, us with rods, most of them with their dip nets on scaffolds on the Deschutes. There was no social talk.

I almost witnessed my first Indian-white man fight one day when I was a young man. I was walking across the bridge when I heard an awful tirade going on below me. I looked out over the railing and there were two men, one on each side of the river, hollering at each other.

One was an Indian, the other what had to be a tourist, because I didn't recognize him. Besides, a local would've known better.

'That's my goddam fish, you drunken Indian! I hooked him first! Cut your freakin' line and let him go!'

'My fish,' the Indian said more softly. 'Cut your line.'

Well, there it was. Two fishermen had snagged the same redside, and each was staking claim to it. A double hit. Rare, but it happens. If it had happened to me, I would've cut my line. Most around here would've. Lots of fish in the Deschutes. The Indian would've needed this one more than I.

But this gent wasn't about to give up his catch. The damn fool was arguing with an Indian for it. Meanwhile, the Indian was stoically defiant. In most dealings, that is not the case. Indians have become compliant, avoiding controversy. They put their heads down and shuffle away from confrontation. That is not quite so true where food, especially fish, is involved.

Indians have always believed they had first rights to anything related to the river. Indians, to this day, consider the Deschutes their rightful preserve. This Indian wasn't going to give in anytime soon; his adversary didn't seem to take proper note of that.

Reluctant though I've always been to hoe someone else's garden, I knew right then and there that, if left to their own devices, these two were headed to violence. So, summoning whatever community spirit I had, I shouted, 'Hold it, hold it. Wait 'till I get down there, and we'll reason this damn thing out.'

Diplomat that I was, I went to the east side of the river, where the Indian was. I didn't want him thinking the white men were stacked against him.

"When I reached him, the lines of both men were taut, meeting at the center of the river. *Why doesn't one of them just lose a hook?* I wished. But that wasn't happening. *Now what?* I thought of the redside at the center of the controversy. He was going to be a goner. But was he going to be fried, or dried?

'You need this fish?' I asked the young Indian.

'Wife and child do. I'll gut this man for it, just like I'll gut this fish.' With that, he reached to his waist and unsheathed his hunting knife. He waved it at his foe across the river.

The jerk misconstrued the message. 'Yeah, yeah, that's right! Just cut your line. Good.'

'Hey, mac,' I yelled over to him, 'this guy isn't going to cut his line. That knife is for you. Now let's think this through before you go home on a stringer line.'

A flinch, and probably a paling of the skin, if we could've seen him up close. Silence. Then, a lame, 'Bullshit. He won't kill me over whose catch it is.'

'Well, I'll tell you what. I'll hold his rod here and send him over. You two can discuss it and decide who gets the fish. How's that?'

'No, no. Any other ideas? It's my fish, you know. I can't just let some Indian take it.'

Meanwhile, the Indian stood stony-eyed beside me. His mind was made up. He either got the fish, or he was going to kill this guy, I could just tell.

'Yeah, I have an idea. How about this? Deepest hook gets the fish. One of you cuts his line, the other reels it in. All three of us look at the hooks. If it's close, I decide. I don't have a fish in this fight.'

Seconds pass. The Indian nods. The jerk says okay. 'Cut your line,' I call over to the other side.

'Let him cut his line. I don't trust the Indian bastard.'

'I'm on this side. I'll watch the fish come in; I'll watch the Indian. Do it now, or I send the Indian over.'

'Damn you.' But the fisherman cut his line. He scrambled up toward the bridge.

Now the three of us are standing over a flopping, double-hooked trout. We didn't even have to pick it up to see the first hook, looped through its lower lip. The Indian's line went far deeper in. 'His fish,' I say to the jerk.

'Screw you.' Without a look at the Indian, the fisherman spun away and headed for the bridge.

'Hey, Captain Ahab,' I said to his back, 'you still have a line, a rod, and a reel. Try again, and feel lucky for the chance.' No response, discounting the finger he held high above his head. The Indian nodded, picked up his fish, and headed upriver."

"Mighty Mouth to save the day," Owen said sarcastically.

"I would've said 'the voice of reason,'" I countered.

"Either way, I won the day," Ross maintained.

"Tell Ed more about Jim," Owen suggested.

"Well, Indian Jim grew up, just like I did. He sort of became the town Indian. Not in a particularly good way. He was really just a screw-up.

Everything he touched turned to crap. He wanted to work for me, said he remembered me and the ranch and the station. What could he do for me? Needed the money real bad and would work cheap.

I knew both of those were true. I thought I'd give him a try. Tried him first at the gas station. About all he was good for was pumping gas. Guys would come in here and, just to be ornery, ask Jim to fill it up and check the oil. They'd laugh when he couldn't locate the oil stick under the hood.

Forget having him do anything inside. He could take a wheel off a car, but it took him forever to get a tire off the wheel. Never could get a new one on. The poor son of a bitch was no mechanic, that was for sure.

So, when the garage thing didn't work, I thought I'd send him over to the ranch and have him tend the cattle. That didn't work either. If I gave him two jobs for the day, maybe get them up to the pasture and then wash the tractor or straighten up the tool shed, he might get one done, but never the other. One-step directions for Indian Jim; that's all he could handle at once.

'Worse, he wasn't reliable. Days would go by when he didn't show up at all. Everyone knew he was a big drinker, but that didn't quite explain it – we saw him do lots of things drunk. But he worked on Indian time, showing up when he felt like it. No sense of obligation.

So that was that. I told him I couldn't use him anymore. He offered neither apology nor promise to do better. Actually, he seemed a little surprised. But he just ambled off and shambled about town again.

For years, though, he'd stop by the ranch in the early evenings with something to trade, trinkets mostly. For a while there, Jim owned an old Dodge truck. It was originally green, you could tell that. But now it sported a replacement door of faded red, one old blue fender, and a yellow hood. When he came up the lane, the damn thing looked like some psychedelic hippie van, all rusted holes, scarred and peeling paint, and loose-fitting everywhere. Smoked and sputtered, back-fired when he shut it down. Screechy brakes. An accident going somewhere to happen.

Once he came by with a little pony; said it was broke and safe. He motioned to my youngest daughter. It was for her. 'Food, just some food for my parents and me.' My God, here it was, sometime in the 1970s, and Indian Jim was still bartering ponies for string beans, jelly, and spare ribs. Pathetic, really.

It is said that Indian Jim was one of the best dip netters on the reservation. Guys who saw him said he could always get more fish on one scoop than anyone. It's a matter of timing, and I guess he was really good at that.

He took more chances than others. Most Indians would tie themselves to their platforms so they'd be safe if they lost their balance. Jim seldom did. He was a freelancer. I guess he fell in more than once, but somehow survived the fall and current. Just a character. Sort of a damn stereotype of the American Indian, I guess, and that's too bad."

"Whatever happened to him?" I asked.

"Nothing. He's still around, but not as often. Older now. I don't think he leaves the reservation much. I don't know how he keeps body and soul together. I haven't seen the truck for years."

Again, I could tell that Ross thought he was finished. He drained his glass and made a move to rise. But Owen had other ideas.

"Now tell him about Rakesh Arun Baboor," Owen instructed Ross, chuckling even as he said it. "I'll get you another beer, but you're paying for this one."

"I'll cover it," I said. Both satisfied with that, Ross settled back.

"Ah yes, good old Rakesh. Damndest scammer ever," Ross laughed. "I don't know why I'm laughing, 'cause Rakesh's cult almost killed hundreds of people—and nearly took over the whole county."

I was already wild-eyed. "Get out!" I protested.

"No, I'm serious," he assured me. "Sometime in the early 1980s, Rakesh Arun Baboor moved about a thousand members of his religious sect into Antelope, northeast of Cordell. He and his evil wife and accomplice, Sheela, had gotten in enough trouble overseas that they moved their whole operation to Oregon… bought an old ranch there and made it into some sort of compound for these out-of-India fanatics.

He brought fabulous wealth with him, and he took all the money his followers had to give him. He lorded over fifty houses, a huge cafeteria, two big barns, five greenhouses, and 'science labs.' The group acquired a fleet of house trailers, cars, trucks, and earth-moving equipment. They were changing the landscape to fit their purposes.

It wasn't plain old Hindu or Buddhist, you understand. Baboor had created his own doctrines, which already had him in trouble in India. He was one of those charismatic leaders, like Jimmy Jones. People would drink Kool-Aid for him. I mean, they were 'true believers' in whatever mystic teachings Rakesh had concocted. End-of-the-world stuff, abject poverty of the faithful, all fortune to their leader, polygamy for himself, only sanctioned and very protected sex for others, euthanasia for children with birth defects—all that sort of weird, cultish nonsense. His maroon-robed followers prepared themselves for the nuclear reckoning, which Rakesh was predicting would occur in the next twenty years.

At first, locals were generally accepting of all this. 'Each to his own,' kind of acceptance. 'Didn't affect us' was the operative stance. An amusement, almost. Plus, these two thousand nut cases were spending cult money in Cordell.

But before long, the Neo-sannyas, as they were known, were making trouble. Conflict with locals became increasingly bitter, what with the commune's uncompromising, confrontational, and impatient stance. They were fighting for more water, better roads to the ranch, unmitigated land use, that kind of stuff. Rakesh's followers grew more and more threatening and deceptive. And they were so damn smug about it all.

Now here it gets weird. The Neo-sannyas realized that, with their numbers, they could capture political control of Antelope, population about seventy-nine. They could simply run the town through anyone they elected to public office.

So, they stood candidates in the local elections and won big, of course. Braced by that easy win, they gave the town a new name—some long Indian thing.

Next, they set their sights on a larger prize: the whole county. There were some circuit court and the sheriff's elections coming up, and Baboor's following wanted those seats. But here, their numbers weren't as competitive, so they devised a nutsy scheme to rig the election.

Believe it or not, they decided to poison enough voters in the county to incapacitate them—too sick to go to the polls. That would make their thousand or so votes matter."

"You're kidding me!" I blurted, thinking Ross was trying to lay a yarn on me. "No way!"

"Look it up," he insisted. "Baboor's followers actually cultured a large quantity of salmonella bacteria in their own labs. They spread the concoction on the salad bars of about ten restaurants in The Dalles, the county seat, where the most voters lived. More than 700 people fell ill. Many were hospitalized, though none died. Can you imagine? Poisoning the salsa bar at the Taco Bell?"

"Is he for real?" I appealed to Owen.

"He is," the bartender affirmed. "It was the first big-scale bioterror attack in American history. It was in all the papers and on TV. You must've been speaking somewhere in Africa to have missed it."

"I assume they got caught," I guessed.

"They did," Ross resumed, "but not right away. Within about a year, things started to unravel for them. Little facts leaked out, national leaders started pressing for an investigation. Evidence was found, and the leaders started playing 'he said, she said.'

In fact, Rakesh blamed the whole endeavor on Sheela, claiming he knew nothing of the plot. His dedicated followers believed that; none of us did."

"So, what happened to them?"

"Well, when things started going south, their candidates withdrew from the election and very few Neo-sannyas even voted. Later on, Rakesh, Sheela, and his first lieutenant, Poosar, were deported for all kinds of crimes: immigration, attempted murder, poisoning public officials, scores of things. I think they all served jail time in far-away countries. The group dissolved. Antelope became Antelope again."

"That's just wild," I said. "Did anybody see this coming?"

"Only in retrospect. They were a strange group, but religious people cause no problems, right? But that takeover of Antelope turned everybody. Strangely, though, Rakesh himself was better received than any of them.

He'd drive into town in one of his Rolls-Royces and stay for hours, chatting up the locals. On his way out of the compound, the faithful would line up along the road, heads bowed—probably in prayer that they'd see him and the car again. He was a lousy driver. He often wrecked; good thing he owned hundreds of Rolls.

"Hundreds? C'mon, Ross."

"Hundreds," he repeated firmly. "His followers were bound and determined to get him 365—one for every day of the year. Kept most of them back in India, I guess, but he had lots of them here. Had a couple of airplanes, too, and a helicopter, didn't he, Owen?

"Yep."

"Anyway, his driving was so erratic that everyone was scared to death of him. He rolled one Rolls in a creek. Then he hit a concrete truck in another. I guess he got better.

"So, how did his cult react to this?" he continued. "They built him a heated indoor swimming pool. Remember, this guy was rich, even before shaking down everyone who joined up. Called himself 'the rich man's guru.' Locals called him 'the Rolls guru;' some in India called him 'the sex guru.' A man for all reasons.

Odd-looking guy that he was—what with his straggly beard, pointy hat, white robe, and long fingernails—he was very engaging. He was personable, charismatic. The old boys in the café would get him talking and he would mix jokes while delivering spellbinding oratory. He'd offer fruitcake insights to the human condition in that funny accent of his, and people loved it. He spoke in paradox and contradiction. Easy to see why the insecure would see him as a savior.

I came to know him pretty well. If he needed work on that fleet of Rolls-Royces, like when he wrecked one, I'd get the parts and fix it. He'd hang around my station and chat with the loafers. He paid cash, and he always paid more than I charged him."

Ross stopped again.

"And… " Owen teased Ross onward.

"And, of course, I saved his life."

"What?"

"Just a matter of time and place," he insisted.

"So, tell him," Owen ordered.

"Rakesh loved the Deschutes. In fact, he saw it as a holy place; at least that's what the damn faker said.

He was particularly intrigued with three granite boulders sitting in the middle of the river. They were special to him, and he would park at my station and walk over to commune with them—meditation being a big part of his shtick. They gave him strength, he said.

One day, on his way to communion, he was bitten by a rattlesnake. Stepped right on its back, and it got him in his calf.

He comes limping and whimpering into the station like Walter Brennan, squawking about his leg, this snake, and is he going to die.

I tell him to lie down on the desk and keep his leg lower than his body. My mechanic, Shawn, was there, so I sent him to the back to fetch a filthy old turkey baster we used for engine fluids. I opened the big blade of my pocket knife. Shawn pulled out his flask and dribbled some whiskey over the baster and my blade. I tell Rakesh this is going to hurt. He's wild-eyed by this time, sweating, and hollering stuff in Sanskrit or something.

Shawn turned him over on his stomach and held him down. I trapped his ankle between my legs and found the two teeth punctures. I cut an X far beyond them, and in as deeply as I could without it being a certified stabbing.

Freakin' Rakesh screamed. I watched the blood flow. Then I stuck the end of the baster right into the slash, deep. Another scream, this one with a little terror in it. For good measure, I squeezed out the blood of the first plunge and did it again. Either that was good medicine, or I was acting out my tendencies toward sadism.

Well better, I thought, than sending him up to St. Mary's in The Dalles. Maybe he wouldn't have made that. There's no doctor here. How long do you get with a snake bite?"

"I guess he lived," I said.

"Yeah, he lived. Didn't engage in traditional medicine though, so he didn't get a tetanus shot. Rakesh had a miserable infection at the wound site, but not so much as a headache from the snakebite. I should've been a doctor."

"And he was appreciative?" I asked.

"Appreciative? Tried to give me cash. Later on, he'd show up with a harem of female members, a dozen Sannya virgins. Brought me produce from their farm, and new veal. He hadn't yet poisoned the salad bars, so I was too stupid to ask for anything.

Just as I get all proud of myself, his entire operation starts taking steps to take over the world. Bastard."

Ross was finished. "Tell you what. Let's meet for breakfast tomorrow. I'll have more stories for you then."

We set a plan.

CHAPTER FOURTEEN

The Erratics

"**I**t runs north, you know—aren't many American rivers do that— to the Columbia, of course."

Ross Wilson had invited me to his ranch for a pop-up breakfast. We sat three feet from the mild current passing by this corner of his property, on the eastern side of the Deschutes. It was a sun-dappled, glorious morning, and I was enjoying the slight breeze and tranquil water.

Ross had brought a folding card table and a picnic basket, from which he extracted a table covering, a large Thermos of coffee, a variety of McDonald's breakfast sandwiches, some biscuits and jelly, and two cans of orange juice. "Wife put this all together for us."

We chatted. But mostly we just ate, admired the Deschutes, and listened to its gentle breath.

"Delightful, Ross. I'm starting to love your river," I told him.

"Love is a strong word," he cautioned. "And it's not my river. To live with the Deschutes is not to love it—or hate it, for that matter. Our bond with the river is one of everydayness; we live with, at, on, and because of the river. The Deschutes is a member of our families, our way of life, our community. We're intertwined with it, sometimes for better, sometimes for worse. It's part of our DNA.

Little happens around here that the river doesn't figure in, one way or another. Psychologists would call it a 'symbiotic relationship.' Ours is a pragmatic, soulful intimacy with the water—transcending simple emotion.

For sure though, no one owns the Deschutes. People have fought over it for years—about water rights, irrigation rights, fishing rights, Indian rights, and property rights. No one ever really won any of that. The river just keeps carving its way north, as it always has, long before anyone tried to claim any part of it.

"Tell me more about that," I asked him. "The people and the river."

"Well, I suppose it's no more or less exciting than the lives of anyone anywhere who lives near a river or an ocean. I do know this—no one crosses that bridge without looking down at the river. No one goes more than a day without the river coming up in conversation.

Many livelihoods depend on it. A big part of that is tourism now, what with the fishing, the rafting, the scenery, and such. But for years, it has provided water for ranchers, salmon for Indians, sport for the courageous, solitude for the trout fishermen."

Ross fell silent, as if he were finished. He'd tried the same thing yesterday.

"Owen was right," I told him. "You're a man of big words and big thoughts, Ross."

"Never mind," he snorted.

"Ross, you can't get out easy here," I protested. "I want more." That moved him a bit deeper into the subject.

"Yeah, yeah. I don't want to wax poetic or lyrical. I don't ooze corny sentiment about the water. But think about it… our region has three major land features. We have Mount Hood, the high country, and the Deschutes, all defining life around here. But the Deschutes is the spine, the epicenter of the whole enchilada—and has been from the beginning.

The flora and fauna, the Indians, the trappers, the pioneers, the ranches, the towns, the railroad… the river is everything to our history and development. It's the connective tissue and sustenance for all who came here.

The Deschutes isn't majestic, like the Columbia. Hell, there are places you can almost jump across it. Some places it's silky, like this morning. Sometimes just a riffle, or beads of goose bumps from bank to bank. Hardly the Mighty Mississippi, but more predictable and stable.

The Deschutes seldom floods, and never dries up. It's a serrated knife blade, slowly cutting through the lava rock and sloping landscape. But it also rages, snarls, and froths. There are places where no swimmer would ever dare a crossing. Just upriver—well, both directions, actually—there are rapids and falls, steep canyon sides, and tricky bottoms. Its very name—Deschutes—is French for River of the Falls.

I'll tell you this: The Deschutes has a million stories."

"When you say that, you remind me of the old black-and-white TV show, *Naked City*. Do you remember that?" I interjected.

"No."

"In the introduction, the voiceover guy would deeply intone, 'There are a million stories in the naked city, and this is one of them.'"

Ross smiled. "Well, that would be the Deschutes, too, I guess."

"Stories, Ross," I reminded him. "Let's have one."

"Okay. Near here, downriver, is quiet water, wide banks. Easy to access. It's known as Baptist's Cry."

"Because… ?" I prompted him.

"Because that's the place of many religious ceremonies conducted by the largest church in town. Wednesday and Sunday evenings have always been big nights for the Baptists. They hold church down there, conduct weddings, baptisms, funerals—anything related to church doings. Baptists love water. They love tying water to any human event."

"I'm waiting for the 'Cry' part," I urged.

"Well, Baptists love water, and they love to make noise. If the breeze is right, people in town can sit on their porches and hear the Baptists down at the river. There might be shrieks attesting to God's power and presence, screams of sheer joy at being reborn, and chants of praise for all the Lord's blessing. All that's just for the weddings, baptisms, and Easter services. Funerals brought out the tears, and with them, the cries of agony over the departed, the mournful wailings of a widow. Some say they're handling snakes down there, and speaking in tongues. I don't know if any of that is true. But it is a noisy spot, and has been for years. That's how it got its name.

Here's a quick tale for you, now that you have me thinking about Baptist's Cry. It figured in a kidnapping some years ago."

Oh, do tell," I said to Ross, with genuine enthusiasm.

"Goes like this. Sometime back in the eighties—I know it was after Owen had taken over the bar—a baby girl was kidnapped up in The Dalles.

Andrew Victory was the successful and wealthy owner of a furniture store up there. He was instantly recognizable to everyone, because he appeared in most of the TV commercials he bought, selling sofas and love seats at bargain prices. Sometimes his buttery-blonde wife appeared with him, usually holding hands with their little boy, and later, with their baby daughter Charlene.

Andrew Victory was a pillar of the community—president of the school board, chairman of fundraisers, county head of the Democratic Party, grand poobah, or whatever, of the local Moose. A good enough guy, I'm told, although his TV ads were a bit over the top. Mostly, though, he had money.

And three crime-minded scalawags wanted it. One early evening, they overpowered Andrew's wife as she was packing her baby and groceries into her car outside a supermarket in The Dalles. They absconded with tiny Charlene.

They followed the typical drill: let the parents worry, call the parents, demand no contact with the police, set the ransom amount—$300,000—and promise to return the baby if Andrew followed their directions for the money exchange.

Of course, the distraught family did contact the authorities, and the FBI was in charge of everything throughout. So, this is in the papers for two or three days.

Against the better judgment of the FBI, Andrew Victory and his lovely wife agreed to pay the ransom. This in place, the kidnappers gave Andrew his first set of directions, which called for him to drive to a certain public phone booth after dark and wait for a call.

Directions there told him what to do next—mostly go somewhere else and take the subsequent call. They had Andrew driving from one phone booth to another and back again, all about The Dalles area.

He was finally instructed to throw the money bag into the driveway of an isolated house up in the Gorge, toward Portland. A 'drop' was successfully made.

The next morning, the parents were still waiting on Charlene's safe return. When that call came, it came to Owen Ticket."

"Owen!" I exclaimed. "How was he involved?"

"He wasn't.

Actually, that was a clever idea. The kidnappers wanted to move Charlene's release away from The Dalles, where all the police were. Notifying a totally uninvolved person in the exchange reduced the risk of capture or detection. So, they picked a town and called one of its local bars. I guess they figured someone was sure to answer the phone in such a public place. They picked Cordell. Probably from the Yellow Pages, they picked Ticket's."

Ross interrupted himself. "Did Owen tell you this story?"

"No," I replied.

"That figures."

"Owen was just opening his bar when the phone rang. A muffled voice tells him that Charlene Victory is waiting for pickup down at Baptist's Cry… he'd better hurry.

Owen calls the police and rushes over to the Deschutes. Before the police could arrive, Owen finds little Charlene—not a tall order, as she was crying her eyes out. He was holding her in his arms when the authorities arrived, guns drawn, pointed at him, ordering him to the ground. Spread-eagled, Owen told his story.

Obviously enough, Owen surrendered the child. He was the hero of the story without even being in it until the last fifteen minutes. "

"So," I asked, "did they get the kidnappers?"

"They always do. But Baptist's Cry was big news in Oregon for a few days. And about town, people said, 'Who else but Owen Ticket would get into such a story?'"

"Good story, Ross. I'll ask Owen about it. For now, just let me make a note or two."

That little task completed, I steered Ross back to the river. "Let's go back now to the Deschutes—the life it supports around here. Do you have any more on that?"

"You keep pushing for something esoteric, something mystical, something deep," he observed. "Look, the Deschutes is what it is. One thing we who live near it never forget is that the river gives and the river gets. It doesn't keep score, but it's unforgiving. It'll carry away any inattentive, disrespectful, or unlucky soul.

In fact, that's happened several times.

"Before the turn of the century Rennie Lennard drowned, about a mile downriver from here. Rennie was a French trapper who spent the first half of his life up north. As trapping bottomed out, he followed the old Indian trail down here to try fishing. He built a little place on the west side of the river—north of where Cordell is now.

There were several ferryboat operations during that time. One after another had washed out along the way. At this time, though, Jim Bukka was running a ferry, using a big flatboat fastened to a steel cable running across and above the Deschutes.

So, Rennie had a girlfriend on this side of the river—up in Bakeoven. One afternoon, Rennie and his horse showed up at the ferry to cross pretty high and rough water. Jim told him it would be a rough ride, and it was—but love above all, right?

Late that night Rennie left his dreamboat and headed for the ferryboat. At this point, it's all conjecture, of course, but the evidence points this way.

First, Jim had secured the ferry on the west side when he quit for the day. This was his habit. Second, it wasn't rare for a self-reliant, strong man to 'borrow' the ferry after hours. Third, neither the west bank moorings nor the rope used to secure the boat to them were damaged in any way. Rennie had obviously undone the arrangement. Fourth, some debris was stuck in the middle of the river.

Based on all of that, officials theorized that Rennie had climbed hand-over-hand on that steel cable and managed to get the ferry back to his horse. Somewhere on the return voyage, the torrent swamped the ferryboat. It flipped, and was later found in two inverted pieces.

The horse survived; Rennie didn't... should've held onto the saddle, I guess. The torrent must've just devoured him. Two weeks later, one or another little part of Rennie found its way to the riverbank. Mostly though, no real body. Not pretty—damn ugly, in fact."

"First one to drown then, Rennie Lennard?" I asked.

"First documented one, yes. There were probably some before—most likely Indians or foolish travelers. I'm sure some Indians drowned while they were dip-netting the fish from those platforms. They improved on that, however, when they started tying themselves to their perches over the river.

There were definitely some later drownings," Ross continued. "In 1954, a train went into the river. Lost some men then, and a rail car full of Campbell's Tomato Soup."

"What happened?" I inquired.

"Simple. A three-locomotive train came around a bend just south of here, on the western tracks. It hit some fallen rocks at a most inopportune spot—nasty rapids right below them. The strike derailed most of the thing.

An engine and thirteen boxcars plunged into white water. If several crewmen survived the tumble, they didn't survive the rapids. One boxcar spilled open, depositing thousands of soup cans into the river—a real mess. We now call that spot Boxcar Rapids."

"Terrible," I offered.

"Yeah," he agreed.

"The Deschutes claimed two young people in the mid-seventies. This one was really sad... really tragic... local families, popular kids, just about ready to graduate from high school.

Now you need to know something about some rocks sitting here and there in the middle of the river. The Deschutes, as the Columbia, was formed eons ago, from the Missoula Floods. Not far up that way, there are three huge, granite boulders, just about touching each other. All of them are least six feet wide and ten or more feet long.

Notice that I say these are granite. Granite is not the stuff of our dark gray-and-black volcanic cliffs and canyons. The stone in the mountains is lava rock, our prairie floor is lava rock and ash. Granite is foreign to this region.

So, granite boulders in the middle of the Deschutes? Geologists now know they were deposited here when the big flood, lava, and glacier flows came down from Montana, from a series of volcanic eruptions. They say that the floods caused four-hundred-foot waves barreling through here at sixty-five miles an hour. Can you imagine the power and size of those flows?

Anyway, these huge stones were actually ice-rafted all the way down here on glaciers, and finally dropped into the streambed. They're light gray or whitish, and hard.

Geologists call these glacial foreigners 'erratics.'

In fact, these were the rocks that Rakesh Arun Baboor visited for his meditations. Their difference from the other stone must've had significance for the damn shaman.

These particular three erratics are—or at least were—a popular hangout for young people. Rapids ran by the little island they formed, deep in the center, but more shallow by shoreline. If you're willing to get your feet wet, you can hopscotch across some small goonies out to the erratics.

Perfect lover's lane or party site… private, isolated, scenic.

That's what two teenage couples had in mind after the spring dance. Armed with two six-packs of Milwaukee's finest and a bag of Doritos, the four of them made their way to the boulders. They drank, ate, laughed, flirted, and talked.

The first couple wanted a bit more privacy, so they said their goodnights and made their way back to shore. The other two stayed out there for a while.

No one knows for sure what happened next. Perhaps one of them slipped on the damp stone and the other attempted a rescue. Maybe one or both of them made it only partway to shore and fell in the rapids. Who the hell knows?

What we do know is that they didn't return that night. A short search turned up their bodies in the shallows, a hundred yards downstream.

Swept away in the prime of their youth—two bright kids with promising futures; two kids who grew up around the Deschutes and knew its habits. Parents and an entire town in shock; a hard-to-shake sadness. A black cloud hanging over a desultory graduation ceremony for their classmates. And two other kids who were going to feel guilty for the rest of their lives. One damn bad thing; that's what that sad deal was."

"Sad, indeed," I agreed. We sat quiet for a few moments. "The river gets. It also gives, eh? Water for habitation and irrigation, recreation, trails for travelers and the railroads, electricity for homes, and fish, too."

"Ah, the fish. The Deschutes is teeming with fish. It's known around the world for the fishing.

We have trophy redsides—you might know them as rainbow trout—steelheads, large- and small-mouth bass, and salmon, of course. And a great fish called Dolly Varden—best-eating trout in the world.

But, of course, it's the salmon runs that get the attention. In the great circle of life—they're born here, swim down to the Columbia, and then out to sea. Two years later, they return to spawn, and the run is on.

A reporter once wrote that the salmon were so thick at the falls that one could walk across the river on fish skin—that's a lot of fish. There are Indians all along the way, dip netting, and shore fishermen reeling them in. For a couple of weeks, it's organized mayhem.

How much do the people love their fish? Well, I told you yesterday about an Indian who was prepared to kill for one. I have another story—about another Indian, coincidently.

Back in the 1860s, when there was still 'Indian trouble,' there was a ferocious chieftain named Paulina. He was a rogue Paiute, feared by white men and Indians alike. He raided farms and wagon trains, burned homes, and killed settlers. He stole crops and animals. He was the scourge of the entire area, and everyone wanted him dead.

But that proved to be very difficult. He was wily, skillful, and brazen. He and his band terrorized the people and escaped innumerable times. He was a ghost when he didn't want to be found.

You know what finally brought him down? A fish from the Deschutes.

One evening, after a particularly nasty barn-burning raid, Paulina and his warriors stopped by the river for a barbecue. While they roasted an ox they'd just liberated, Paulina went fishing. I guess he wanted surf and turf.

A settler named Howard Matter had been after Paulina for years… never could find him. Totally by accident, and without plan, Matter and his friend stumbled onto the Indian camp. Howard Matter shot Paulina right on the river's edge. Died with a fishing pole in his hand. Paulina's want of a fish cost him his life."

Ross went silent again. But this time he was thinking about the river. "Now, tourism is a big business around here. Whitewater rafting, kayaking, canoeing. That whole thing began as one or two little builders and guide shops, and fishing and bait stores, just when this town really needed an economic boost, after wood went the way of the kiwi. Now, there must be more than two dozen water adventure dealers within twenty miles of us.

I sometimes think that river use has come full circle. It's the spine and lifeblood of a new community, providing transportation, fish, and relaxation from the old Indian and trapper days. Then the economic base moved to the prairie and mountains. Now, here we are, the river providing all those things again, and the jobs that go with them.

Good people, these operators, but they can't take the danger out of the river, even with today's equipment. As you say, the Deschutes gives and it gets. We've had some nasty accidents with greenhorns and their inflatables and canoes."

Ross paused, organized his thoughts, and then continued, talking around a toothpick.

"Let me tell you one of the world's great myths: you're safe in whitewater as long as you're wearing a life vest. Ranks right up there with the peace of mind you're supposed to have in an airplane because your seat can also serve as a life preserver."

I laughed. Ross continued. "So these alcohol-stoked college kids or mid-age fathers load up a raft with their families and push off in some of the worst stretches of the rapids. The ones without guides are asking for it. Even if they have a guide steering the thing and giving orders to lean left or right, move to the front or back, paddle left—whatever—he's busy positioning the correct entry into the chutes or channels. Now and then, someone goes overboard. The next part of that person's 'adventure' is not very pleasant.

The water is cold, you swallow more of it than you wish, you panic, you hit something that hurts, you go into some form of shock. You need a plan quicker than you can manufacture one.

The life vest keeps you afloat, all right… face up. That way, you can see most of the things you're about to hit. Not all, though. There are rocks jutting off the bottom. A guy from Indianapolis lost his testicles that way.

The rapids gather power around the big stones sticking out of the water. When you hit one of them—several of them—your face takes on an entirely different look… broken legs, arms, shoulders, ribs. Gashes the length of sickle blades, black-and-blue bruises that last for months.

We've seen all that from our tourists. Two years ago, a petite college gal from down south was swept down the river for a half mile. Head up or not, she drowned. When they fished her body out, she looked like a hundred-pound skinned deer, only lumpier.

Another guy took a rented canoe into a chute after being clearly told to stay in the calm water only. Somehow he wedged that canoe up on an erratic, where it stuck. He didn't. He was propelled right over the bow. Luckily, he was pointed toward the shoreline, so he landed in shallow water. Unluckily, he landed in shallow water—five broken bones and a lacerated liver.

But, thank God, they still come. Thank God, those are exceptions. Most of them are caused by foolishness or the lack of respect for the river. For most, the Deschutes has been a source of wonderful adventure and world-class fishing."

I looked up from the river, over top of Cordell, just across the river, and toward Mount Hood. I fished out my camera and took a picture. Water, prairie, and mountains. "There's some calendar art right there," I said to Ross.

"Welcome to my world. Hood is beautiful, isn't she? Beautiful from any angle. Have you been over there yet?"

"Nope," I replied. "Too busy for sightseeing, I guess."

"You really ought to see the mountain up close and personal. How about we take a drive? You'll enjoy the scenery, and there are some stories that run from where we're sitting, across the valley, and into the hills that you might find 'of note.' You have another meeting this afternoon?"

"Nothing," I said. "But I don't have a heavy coat, or gloves, or hat, or boots with me. I can't be up in that snow."

"We're not going onto the snowfields. And we're not climbing any rock faces. We'll just drive through the forest, up to the timberline, do a little walking. You'll be fine; there's a jacket for you in the truck."

We packed up the breakfast remains and the table, and headed for the hills.

CHAPTER FIFTEEN

All The Gold

"**Y**ou can call this jaunt 'The Legends Tour,'" Ross announced. "We have legends and mysteries from the river to the snow. Most, as you might expect, involve money."

"Well, Ross, I guess that's the way of things, huh?" I remarked.

"Probably," he acknowledged. "Not too surprising, though. For a hundred years—the gold rush right into the 1950s—money was passing through northern Oregon like crap through a goose. Money to and from the east, money to and from California, money from everywhere, coming through on the stagecoaches, the wagon trains, and the railroads, the wood industry. Gold and silver bullion, nuggets, cash, coins, jewelry, heirlooms, even Spanish doubloons—most of it made the trip. Some of the lost or stolen usually became legendary.

Since the 1840s we've had lots of lost or hidden treasures, and lots of fortune hunters chasing this or that mystery. You and I are going to follow a money trail up to The Hood, with three stops—river, prairie, mountain.

We were in Ross's truck, tooling down the river road, after he'd shown me the erratics. Shortly, he parked in front of an old bridge.

This is Logan's Bridge. Before the bridge, there was a ferry here named—guess what?—Logan's Ferry.

Now the legend of Logan's Ferry really begins to our north, and probably east, somewhere between The Dalles and the Idaho border. Back in 1845, a large wagon train became lost, most likely because a guy named Meeks talked part of the group into taking a shortcut he said he'd previously used. The dissension caused by this divisive idea ended only when the big train split into two smaller ones.

Meek's splinter group didn't head back to the Columbia and the trail. They beat about the prairie for months, with the loss of scores of lives.

But they did find gold. When two boys scooped up some shiny pebbles and put them into their blue wooden buckets, the pioneers believed them to be copper. Remember, this was before the California gold rush, so it was a few years before a few of those nuggets were assayed. The problem was that no one knew where the group had been; they were lost at the time. As you might expect, treasure hunters and historians have been looking for the lost Blue Bucket Gold Mine ever since.

Legend holds that two of those lost pioneers left Meek's expedition and returned to the stream, knowing all along, but telling no one, that those pebbles were indeed gold.

Supposedly they filled three big wooden trunks with nuggets and headed southwest—probably hoping to find some route to California or Mexico… who knows?

They came upon the Deschutes and Logan's Ferry. As they loaded their two oxen, a packed, full wagon, and a mule onto the ferry, Wilfred Logan asked what was in the wagon—worried, as he might be, about weight. Apparently, Wilfred was nobody's fool, and the story told him just didn't add up.

Somewhere during that conversation, guns got involved. Wilfred won that shootout, leaving two dead deadbeats. Wilfred told the authorities that he'd acted in self-defense—the two customers had tried to rob him. He never mentioned the presence of gold.

Years later, Logan's family acknowledged that Wilfred had buried two of the three trunks. I guess the contents of the third eased any financial pressures Wilfred ever had. But where? Well, if they'd known that, the family would already have found it and turned it into cash.

"Now Wilfred's Ferry was, of course, adjacent to his property, so one could naturally assume that the fortune was somewhere near his home. Maybe, maybe not."

"Lost until this day, is it then?" I asked.

"Yep, but not for lack of effort. Generations of Logans have searched that property, and the banks and bluffs on both sides of the river. Fortune-hunters have tramped this ground for years, looking for both the mine and Logan's gold. Let's move on."

We headed west, across the prairie. Ross told me more of the story of the lost Blue Bucket Mine. After we collected some soft drinks, Ross turned on a gravel road that headed across the valley, putting Mount Hood in our windshield. He stopped near a small island of pines sitting by itself in the prairie grass.

"We call this Larch Island," he explained. "We're just off the Oregon Trail right now, you know. Early on, of course, this was the north-south stagecoach route. That meant people traveling with valuables, strongboxes of money for payrolls and banks, and shipment of various precious objects. Naturally, just like in the movies, the stagecoaches were vulnerable to robbery. There was lots of that going on in those days. Some were Indian attacks; most were just plain Hollywood cowboy crooks, though somewhat rougher.

There are probably ten or more legends growing out of some of the robberies. Some involve death or injury, but most have more to do with whatever happened to the money taken.

As you can see, there aren't too many places to hide treasures here on the high country—too flat, few landmarks, people can see for miles—all of that. If bushwhackers buried anything out here in the open, you can surmise that they came back for it real soon. Most likely, any booty too large to carry very far was stowed up in the timber… maybe even the snow country, although that would be stupid. Still, there are some hunters still marching about with instruments, crude maps, and drawings, operating on old information about treasure out here.

Not one dime of it has ever been found. Again, not because of lack of effort. Serious treasure hunters, crusty prospectors, nutsy fortune-seekers, government officials, university geologists, historians—all looking for the money, the diamonds, whatever.

I want to tell you about one of the nutsy fortune seekers."

I opened my notebook in anticipation. Ross immediately warmed to his story.

Frank Irwin showed up in Cordell one summer, about 1999 or 2000. He'd come to find the riches along the Deschutes and in the mountains. Frank was new to the fortune-hunting business—at least his gear said so.

He arrived all decked out in his store-creased Field and Stream gear—jungle hat, camouflage vest with all those pockets, stiff jeans with the legs rolled up to the top of brand-new hiking boots—the whole package. Honest to God, he looked like Howdy Doody.

Frank's first stop was the hardware for some tools, although his van was already packed with a metal detector, fancy new seismic devices—still in their boxes—and picks, shovels, a tent, everything he thought might come in handy.

His second stop was the grocery store, where he laid in some supplies for a few days in 'the outback.' His third stop was Ticket's, where he announced to the small crowd—of which I was one—his intention to solve two or three of our local money mysteries. He figured the task would require about two weeks—exactly the length of his annual vacation from a shoe factory in some little town near Boise.

While he didn't come across as arrogant, he was certainly upbeat and expectant about his success. Optimistic, excited, feeling good about his odds, full of his own abilities and specialized equipment.

He told the assemblage that he had some experience in treasure hunting up around some lakes in Idaho. With his trusty metal detector, he'd already unearthed several Native American relics, a pile of lost coins, and whatnot.

He was hoping that the results of this venture would allow him to quit making boots and wear them full-time in pursuit of his dream—treasure hunter extraordinaire. After all, he was armed with some maps of the old trails and paths of our forefathers. We residents have seen those maps dozens of times.

A fellow worker at the shoe place loaned him some hand-drawn sketches that an old relative had made from some sort of firsthand experiences out here. Frank had researched about five of the old tales on his computer, and was convinced that he knew where some of the booty from several stage robberies was likely hidden.

He had a plan. He was starting out first thing in the morning, to the mountain first, and then back to Logan's Ferry and the old perlite mines on the east shore.

Of course, we all knew how this was going to turn out. But we egged him on, showing great interest in his plans, as if he were the first guy to ever attempt this."

Ross stopped for a second. Then he said, "Now I wish you knew Pete Monroe, our local barber. You'd love Pete. Pete was born and raised in Cordell. He's a local character. He looks a bit like Floyd the Barber on that old *Andy Griffith Show*: little mustache, white barber shirt, gray-and-black short hair… same squirrely personality, but smarter. He'll prattle on about things, always anxious to please, on top of the beat of the town. He was a confirmed bachelor, yet always was on a love hunt. But he's one funny bastard.

His distinction lies in his love of the practical joke. Almost anyone in town can tell you how Pete pulled something over someone. He'll ask you questions all the time he's cutting your hair, and weeks later, something you told him will turn into some little drama of Pete's making. He's a great fibber and storyteller. He has this talent of reeling you into his joke. without you knowing that you helped him. You end up starring in some Pete creation that makes you look foolish. He's been doing it for years. Pete told me once that 'lambs go uncomplainingly forth.'

Everyone loves the guy. But you have to know not to trust anything he tells you. Crafty manipulator—that's Pete.

Now, back to our story. During the general conversation with Frank Irwin, Pete saw an opportunity for a shenanigan. Pete knew a gullible tenderfoot when he saw one.

"'I assume that the O'Day stagecoach attack is one you'll be pursuing?'" he asked Frank, as if he were stating the obvious.

"A look of bewilderment crossed Frank Irwin's face. 'O'Day stagecoach? I don't recognize that name,' he replied. 'I never heard of it. No, that isn't on my list.'

Oh, I'm surprised to hear that,' Pete said, with a mock sense of shock. 'That's one of the more famous, largest heists these parts have ever seen.'

All of us in the bar looked surprised, too. We'd never heard of the O'Day attack either. Before anyone could challenge him on it, Pete got off a quick wink. Now we understood. Pete was up to his well-known hobby, the practical joke.

Everyone just let him run with it. There was going to be fun in this somewhere.

Oh well, never mind,' Pete continued. 'Maybe you know it by another name, or it didn't make the eastern papers. It was just a regular Overland Stage, after all. Around here, though, it's known as the O'Day robbery, because Samuel O'Day and his wife were passengers.'

Who was Samuel O'Day?' Frank had just put his head in the noose. Pete said later that he knew he had his mark at that moment.

Samuel O'Day was a banker of some renown. Made his reputation in other people's banks in St. Louis, and then moved out here to start a couple of banks on his own. He set up shop in Maupin, opening a bank there with plans for a few more.

So in 1877, on a beautiful spring day, he and Moira—that was his wife's name—were riding back to Maupin on the stage with a strongbox full of gold, the asset money needed to back the transactions of his new bank.

Remember stagecoaches delivered the mail, carried travelers, and moved money well into the 1890s, until the north-south railroads got up and running.

Anyway, Sam had hired his own armed guard, riding inside the coach. The only other passenger was a young lady on her way home to Bend. Charley Purnell was the driver, with a guard riding shotgun for Charley. Samuel's metal trunk and the gold rode under their legs.

The long trip was going well enough until they neared this stand of larch off the trail by three hundred feet. Out of it poured about ten Indians. They quickly spread out in a straight line, straddling the trail to face the oncoming stage. They were so fast about it that the guard never even tried to raise his gun, let alone start shooting.

The stage pulled to a hasty stop. The Cayuse or Paiutes—Charley could never really tell the difference—rode in circles around the wagon, while Charley commanded everyone inside to remain calm and, definitely, not to show a weapon. He knew the jig was up. Charley's only real plan was to get everyone out of this alive.

The Indians ordered everyone to exit the coach and to stand away, weapons on the ground. Charley was in no position to barter, but he could still offer. With limited communication and a great deal of gestures, he conveyed to the raiders that they could take whatever they wanted. It wasn't his stuff, anyway.

What the Indians wanted were the weapons, the horses, all the jewelry Mrs. O'Day was wearing, and all the luggage and hat boxes on top. They didn't demand money—really, they had little use for it.

Things were progressing well enough, in Charley's mind. The attackers didn't seem particularly interested in killing anyone. Massacre seemed secondary to goods.

But then the lead Indian noticed the metal box under Charley's seat. That too, he motioned.

Well, Samuel O'Day was as scared as everyone else in the party. He was trying to comfort a simpering and terrified Moira and the other distraught young lady, who was fearful of what these bare-breasted savages might have in mind for her.

But when old Sam saw his money being taken, he went ballistic, jumping around the group, throwing his arms about, hollering at Charley to stop it, cursing at the Indians who were taking it, demanding a refund for everything lost.

Charley tried to calm him down, but to little avail. So, the lead Indian did it. He shot O'Day with his ancient rifle. Didn't really aim, just raised the barrel up and popped Sam. Hit him in the upper arm, knocking him to the ground. The bullet didn't kill Sam, but he was thereafter a one-armed banker. Think about that—a banker who could only get one hand in your pocket. That was a big joke around here for years.

So off went the Indians, with six Friesians, the guns, the travel trunks and, of course, the gold. They headed straight to the river. The travelers were left in front of what was probably the first horseless carriage in Oregon.'

During Pete's story, we beer-drinkers were cackling and nudging each other. One or two even added a clarification to Pete's telling. This was fun.

"The gold was never found?' Frank asked.

"Nope. Funny thing, though. When investigators searched along the Deschutes, they soon found remnants of the clothes and contents of the luggage left from the fire in which the Indians burned up anything they didn't want. Indians are like that, you know. They wouldn't litter the riverbank with junk; they believe the earth is sacred.'

"Not the trunk or the gold, though?'

"Course not. Both lost that day and never recovered, try as many have. Now my grandfather used to wander about out there—took my father with him a few times—looking for some sign. Several locals did that. Searched the riverbed, the stand of trees, some distinguishing landmarks on the prairie, even up in the timber. Nothing. Of course, none of them had modern metal detectors or any real scientific equipment, like you do.

'Meanwhile, no Indian ever spoke of gold or flashed any around here. So we can reasonably assume it's still out there—a mystery waiting for the right person to solve.'

"Maybe,' Frank's eyes were wide, and he was thinking. 'This spot is just up the road? Near the juncture with the mountain road? That's on my way to the mountain, then. I could take a look tomorrow; see if I want to try that area first. Hmm."

"Pete shrugged. 'I know I would, if I knew what I was doing and had the right equipment. I wouldn't tell you what to do, but I think it's worth a day or two to check. If you hit pay dirt, I'm sure that you'll remember me, won't you?

I can offer you this help. We all figure the area involved is pretty wide, but not so deep. Those Indians rode straight to the river—why not? Big country, shortest route. If they turned back later to the mountains, they would've used the only real trail there—again, a straight line. If I were looking, I'd go to that stand of larch and go in both directions.

I wouldn't bother with the trees, though. Lots of hunters have already done that, some with good equipment. Plus, I wouldn't look too far north. The reservation starts just up there, and no one really thinks the money ended up there. There'd be a rich Indian up there already, if that was the case. Besides, these Paiutes—I think they were Paiutes, from the sound of things—weren't from the reservation. That's pretty clear from previous investigation. They were renegades, that's for sure.

"Not south, either. That just headed to town; no good. Anyway, I don't think Indians would carry a metal box too far on horseback, so the narrow east-west route seems the best option.'

"Several other drinkers agreed with all that. More discussion, more beer.

"'Wow!' Frank Irwin said. 'I can't believe I never heard of this. You know what? I'm going to switch my plan; forget the old perlite mine. O'Day's is going to be my first stop instead. Then to the mountain and down to the river for my other two leads.'

"Pete said, 'Just drive up the road to the larches. Less than eight miles. Can't miss them, if you're looking for them. Here, let me draw you a little map,' he said, picking up a napkin.

Frank, all excited now, left. Everyone else stood chuckling and smacking Pete on the back for a great tale.

Tale, Ross?" I interjected. "The O'Day adventure wasn't true?

Hell, no. Well, this stand of trees is true enough, isn't it? Everything else in Pete's tale was fabricated from details of several other stage robberies. There was a Samuel O'Day, and he was a banker here. Never robbed though, in town or out on the prairie. A bushwhacker did shoot a guy who stupidly tried to draw down on him while he was robbing another stage—stuff like that. But Pete's story was only a piece of this and that. No wonder poor Frank never heard of it."

"Ross, whatever happened to Frank Irwin and his search?" I asked.

Ross started up the truck, and we headed for the mountains. "Old Pete Monroe was just getting started with the rhinestone treasure hunter. We still laugh about it. That's the great part of the story.

As the group broke up that night in Ticket's, Pete told everyone to check their basements and garages for any old Indian stuff, like feathers, headdresses, tools, arrowheads, bows, beads... anything they had that would fit into a metal box of his.

Pete gathered up these offerings the next day and packed them into an old, rusted container that his grandfather used to hold his wrenches. Pete called Bob Niven, who runs sheep on the Frenchman's old land. Pete asked Bob if he could bury some fake treasure in the foundation remains of the Frenchman's cabin. That being no problem, Pete told Bob to expect a digger in the next few days.

Well, you know what that damn Pete did? He drove his Indian-infested strongbox up to the farm, and artfully buried it near the back of the crumbled stone foundation. We'll be there soon."

Ross drove us up the Barlow Road. John Witherspoon's dilapidated sawmill sat beside the White River. We talked about that some.

On up, Ross pulled into the driveway of the Frenchman's old property.

"See the old foundation over there? That's where Pete buried the box."

"And then?"

"And then, about two days later a crestfallen Frank Irwin returned to town. He entered Ticket's and consoled himself with a few quick beers. Of course we were all waiting for him, and Pete was certainly there.

"'Judging from your look, I'm guessing you didn't find anything yet?' Pete asked, showing great interest.

"'No, nothing. It's discouraging,' Frank replied. 'I found some old pitchfork tines, and evidence of foreign objects under the grass. But nothing. I spent more than a day in the valley and worked my way over to the river. Uncovered some fishing lures, sinkers and whatnot, but couldn't find a good hiding place for the box.

"'I think I'm done with the O'Day matter. I'm going to head into the mountains and look at Franklin's Rock.'

"'Well, I don't blame you,' Pete said. 'This hidden treasure business can be frustrating. I'd quit too; everyone else has.'

Sympathy and then idle chatter ruled the bar for the next round or two. Then Pete started in again.

Frank, you know what? We were talking the other night, after you left, and Bert over there reminded me of something I hadn't mentioned when you were here.

Oh yeah? What was that?

Of the two plausible theories about that box—river or mountains—Bert reminded me that the second has an interesting twist in it. The trouble with the first—money buried at the river—is that the river isn't a great place to hide anything. Too much activity; too easily found. By the way, that holds for any tale you may have heard about buried treasure in the perlite mines. Just not a good place.

No, the better theory is that the Indians took the gold to the mountains. You're going up there, aren't you?'

A nod from Frank.

Well, anywhere in Cascades would be a better choice, in my mind. Problem with that is, there are lots of choices—big place. Still, you might try there, if you're still interested.

Silence. Frank looked hesitant. Then Pete started in again.

Here's the twist with the mountain: the Frenchman. That old trapper was a mountain man, hunter, and tracker. He knew the eastern side better than anyone.

'Bert's thought is this. If someone hid treasure in a mountain pass, he'd chose some unique feature as a marker... maybe a rock outcropping, a secluded woods or meadow, perhaps a fallen tree. The Frenchman would know this, too. He was certainly working the mountain in 1877, probably still with his dad. He also knew the habits of Indians. He'd know of the robbery, and my guess is that he figured where the Indians might bury the box. Probably, Annie would guess the obvious choices.

If the money was ever found, the Frenchman might be the one who did it. Of course, if he did, he wouldn't mention that fact to anybody. Now, after his death, years later, the whole escapade had been turned into legend, so few of us ever really thought about that box of gold anymore. But when Bert and I thought about it the other night, we agreed that we like that theory. I'll tell you that our best guess is that the Frenchman found the gold.

If he did, then he spent some—never seemed to lack for anything he wanted, after all—and buried the rest.'

"'Where?' Frank asked enthusiastically.

"'Well, that would be the great question, wouldn't it?' Pete responded dryly. 'I'll tell you what Bert and I think. Our bet is that he wouldn't take it into the mountains; he'd keep it very close to his home base. That means his house, near his well, beside some rock wall… who knows? That's where I'd look, though.'

"'Why hasn't anyone done that?' Frank asked.

Because, when he was alive, no one would've dared asking Annie. What would they do, tell him they wanted to search his land for his gold? After his death, a few people did search around the ground, until Ralph Niven bought it. On the chance that the treasure was there, he put an abrupt stop to that. Too busy trying to get his sheep ranch going to have folks traipsing about. And Ralph didn't believe the Frenchman's involvement anyway. He tore down the trapper's cabin and built a new home right beside it.

Now his son Bob owns the place, and the whole story has died down. But I'll tell you, I still believe the Frenchman is a good bet for this. I'd try that sheep ranch, if I were you. And I'd start with that old foundation. A guy like the Frenchman wouldn't put a fortune too far away from him. He probably sat on it, so he knew it was safe.'

Maybe I ought to check that out on my way up the mountain. Right at the bottom of the mountain, right?'

Pete said, 'Well, I would. If you want, I'll call Bob and tell him you want to take a pass at the place. He's a customer of mine, and I'm distantly related to his wife.'

"'Please, do that. It's worth a shot, I guess,' Frank's response showed renewed vigor."

Ross laughed out loud. "By the next afternoon, Frank had found the box. In a sweat, he pried it open and found it filled with Indian junk. He never made it to the mountain for the next quest. He went right to Ticket's to get drunk."

"Ross, did he ever figure out that he'd been had?" I inquired.

"I don't think so… certainly not by the time he left town. When he told his story in the bar, people were sympathetic, some feigning pride in the young man's accomplishment.

Pete offered him a possible explanation.

"'You know, Frank, Indians have many special rituals. Sometimes, in their ceremonial tributes to the spirits and the earth, they select items of importance and value to them and offer them up in tribute. Sometimes they burn valuables, sometimes they bury them. Perhaps, in this case, they emptied out the gold and used the box for such purposes.'

"'Why not the gold?' Frank agonized.

"'Because,' Pete responded, 'in 1877, gold wasn't important to them. That was white man's stuff. You make no sacrifice if you don't part with something of value to you.'

"'So, where did the gold go?' Frank wondered.

"'Hell, they probably threw it out, maybe into the river to attract fish. Maybe they slivered it off to make jewelry or decorate their clothes. Maybe they traded it to white men, piece by piece, for a rifle or canned fruit. Who knows? I'll bet the metal box had more value to them than the contents. Different culture, different times, you know.

Don't get discouraged, Frank. Look at the bright side. You actually found something. Few treasure hunters have done that. Yours is a valiant effort. You've added another chapter to our local legend. You enjoyed yourself. That's all good. You still have another week left. Are you going to pursue your other leads? I hope so.

Ross tied it all up and fired up the truck again. "And that's what Frank did. He spent a few days in the mountains and two along the

Deschutes. He returned to the shoe factory outside of Boise, tired, a bit frustrated, but with an old, rusty metal box and some feathers."

Fifteen minutes later, we were in the Cascades, Mount Hood looming over us at every curve.

"Now according to several legends, there's probably more than a million dollars' worth of treasure within a twenty-mile radius of us right now. It's all sitting on a volcano, you know." Ross said, resuming his tour guide's voice. "We're going right to the topmost point of the road, at the timberline. I want to show you a place that's said to be the major location marker of a bag of precious gems."

Ten more minutes, and we pulled off the road in front of a large stone outcropping. "Step out and look at the rock facing you. Do you see anything?"

"What am I looking for?"

Ross told me to look for a few more seconds. I did.

"Well?" he asked.

"I see rocks."

"Do you see a face formed in the rock?" he suggested.

"No."

"Look at an angle, toward the valley. Maybe looks like Ben Franklin, on the coin?"

"No."

"Well, then, the hell with it. Here's the deal. Back in horse-and-wagon days, travelers used this road, of course, to get to or from Portland, to the Tygh Valley, the river, or down south.

So, again, lots of valuables were coming up and over this road in both directions. If a wagon got swamped in the soft earth or heavy snow, if a horseman were ambushed by bushwhackers, these valuables could be lost, or stolen, or buried.

That brings us to Percival Ambruster. Percy Ambruster was a Portland jewelry store owner. Specialized in diamonds, but dealt in all sorts of stones and gold. He was wealthy, cunning, and astute.

Somewhere near the turn of the century—one side or the other—Percy was in the middle of his biggest sale ever. Some jeweler in eastern Oregon opened a store and needed inventory. Percy was delivering that. Alone. Now how astute is that? Did I say he was also a short-sighted, freaking tightwad?

So, here goes Percy, over Hood and down toward the valley. The last thing he remembered was a blow to his head, probably delivered by someone in a pine tree underneath which Percy had just passed. When he came to, Percy checked about. His total inventory was gone, of course. He followed some tracks in the thin snow as far as he could. The tracks gave out just yards from this outcropping.

Percy, so set in his mind that his jewels could be found, decided that the robber, or robbers, had buried the loot in, around, behind, in front of—you name it—this rock. The question has always been whether Percy knew that to be so, or was he just hoping to hell it was?

Percy looked for a while, but he had a bad headache, and an open wound; he knew he needed medical attention. So he finds his horse—his little buggy was gone—and rides down to Wamic. Sees the doctor there and tells his story, complete with his idea, and fondest wish, that the gems were still out there.

Well, that started a mini-gold rush. From all over, people descended on Franklin Rock—that's what it's called—scrabbling around for the stash.

At first, Percy welcomed these endeavors, assuming the locals wanted to get his stones back. Then he was struck with the obvious lightning bolt. What if someone found his jewelry and didn't return it to him? Percy was in a froth, wishing both for and against recovery.

The upshot of the entire thing was that the gems were never found. Percy mourned his loss till the end of his days. But others? Well, they're still at it. People come from everywhere to explore this or that theory. Some think the gems are near that rock. Others think the rock is nothing but a way maker, the first of a series of landmarks that the thief used to mark where he buried the goods. In fact, some years ago, some fool came through here with a little poem, supposedly a deathbed disclosure of the thief to a son or relative. Goes like this:

See old Ben's ear

And look through his hair.

Go left twenty paces

Turn left at the pair.

Find the rock

In a living tree.

Gleaming gold waits there for ye!

Wonderfully simple at first, it seems, but what does 'pair' mean? Through what part of hair? Is the rock-in-a-tree real, or an impression? Who knew?

Well, this guy couldn't figure it out. Neither could anyone else. So, the legend continues. Is Percival Ambruster's fortune still out there? Was it ever really stolen, buried, retrieved, lost, what? Who's to say? Just another mystery of the mountain.

So, here are three of your million stories of northern Oregon. Let's go to Ticket's and have us a beer." Ross was done—I could hear it in his tone. We got in the truck and headed back to Cordell.

"Ross, what do you think?" I asked. "All these stories, all these legends, all this history… what do you think about all that? Is there treasure out here?"

"You know what I think, Ed? These damn stories are one hundred years old or better. Been told, retold, changed, and enhanced by countless storytellers. I think Larry Gatlin is right."

"Larry Gatlin?"

"Larry Gatlin. Years ago, he sang a song that I think sums up everything I've shown you today:"

All the gold in California is in a bank in the middle of Beverly Hills in somebody else's name.

"Got it."

When Ross and I entered, Owen wanted the details of our day. I gave a quick review over two drafts. After another hand-smothering handshake, Ross left.

"Owen. I'm going to go back to the hotel and clean up," I announced.

"I'll pick up two steaks you can fry for us."

CHAPTER SIXTEEN

If You Go Down To The Woods Today

We took the evening off. I ambled about town, taking a few photos. I didn't go over to Ticket's the next day until I figured the lunch crowd—all six of them—would slowly meander out.

After the big rush, I told Owen two cute little tales about my friend Bierly. He laughed. *We've come a long way*, I thought to myself.

"Ed, let's take a little walk before we get going again. Grover needs to go out anyway."

Owen put the Closed sign in the window, but didn't lock the door. He wasn't expecting anyone else at this hour.

We headed up Witherspoon Avenue, so we could see the bar from most of our path up to Stonekicker Bob's house—Owen's old residence. Grover trailed behind us, no leash, stopping only long enough to relieve himself twice.

"So, Owen, this is your town, isn't it?"

"Used to be. Now I'm just an old guy, live above my bar. New faces; most of my friends have died."

"Did you get to travel much—ever get to any place exotic?"

"Very few. I haven't been too many other places. Running a saloon keeps you close to home, even if you have help. Got to a few other states over the years, but nothing very exotic."

"Did you ever get to another country? See any other part of the world?"

"Just one."

"And that was?"

A slight hitch in time; short, but noticeable.

"Vietnam." His voice had a hitch in it too. He glanced at me, looked across the street to Bob's house, and then turned us back toward the bar.

"Vietnam? You were in the military?" I asked.

"I was; the US Army. I spent a lifetime there during my seventeen-month tour."

"That's an odd stretch," I thought out loud.

Another pause.

"Well, I got out early—on a board."

"Will you tell me about that?"

"Let me think about it." In silence we strolled back to the bar, turned the sign around, and sat down at our table. Owen looked at me intently. I could see he was trying to make up his mind about the whole business—could he, would he, should he share what I already sensed was going to be a tough tell for him. Finally, he spoke.

"I'll tell you. Couple of things, though. First, you need to know that this is only the third time I've ever told this story. Second, we're about to get drunk. I'll be breaking my own rule here about daytime drinking, but I don't revisit 'Nam—especially these thirty-some hours—without alcohol. Third, don't ask me if I ever killed anyone over there. There's no good answer to that question, and I won't deal with it. Fourth, I have to call Phil and tell him to come in early for his evening shift."

Owen rose slowly, crossed behind the bar, and made his call to Phil. He took down a full bottle of Wild Turkey from the shelf and put it on a metal tray. He took two bourbon glasses from under the bar and filled them to the brim with ice. He then produced two shot glasses, placing them on the tray. He filled a tumbler with ice cubes. All of this he brought to our table.

"We'll drink a shooter first. Then we sip."

In silence, he poured and we drank, as Owen made up his mind how to organize this presentation. I waited.

"I was drafted in 1966—twenty years old. I went in with my best friend from high school, Joe Burrill, also drafted. I was working here for my dad, as was 'Birdy' for his dad at the hardware, so neither of us had a student deferment to exercise.

I wasn't too upset about it, but my parents were. I had this notion in my head that I was getting a chance to get away from Cordell for a while, and maybe even get to be a hero—you know, Audie Murphy and all that.

Did basic together, but got separated when we were assigned to different AITs—Advanced Individual Training. From there he went to Vietnam.

It was a circuitous route for me. Basic training at Fort Jackson in Columbia, South Carolina. I got orders for AIT at Fort Polk, Louisiana. I'll never forget that place… what a hellhole. Hot, snakes—I mean bad snakes, like cottonmouths, rattlers, copperheads, coral.

AIT had a singular focus: to kill, to kill, to kill. They called it Tiger Training.

I applied to, and was accepted into, Officers Candidate School at Fort Benning, Georgia, and the focus for us future leaders became more specific: to kill dinks, to kill dinks, to kill dinks. I guess I learned all that pretty well. I got high scores on the mental, physical, and soldiering tests. The army started to like me.

Soon, I was a Second Lieutenant. I arrived at Camp Alpha in Long Binh in December, 1968. I was assigned to Ca Mau. That quick I became a platoon leader, in charge of two dozen or more men. Immediately I was sent to Phu Bui, one of our bases south of Saigon, but north of the Mekong Delta.

For about six months I organized squads, almost always two at a time, and took them out on patrol. We looked for Cong; we found a few; we left some in the jungle. I had good guys; we worked well together, and we'd developed those bonds soldiers do when they look together into the eye of the tiger.

So this particular mission didn't seem to be anything special. It was a routine reconnaissance venture. All we were supposed to do was determine if recent intel about a POW camp for US soldiers in the forest was, in fact, true. Two squads from my platoon were to be inserted into the Hu Man forest to look for signs—Cong, supply trails, American debris—of the existence of such a camp.

As usual, we were to engage the enemy at our own discretion. We'd be in the jungle for less than twenty-four hours, typical for such missions. An extraction point was identified. I was given a map of that section, and we were set to go. We'd go in at midnight, move all night, spend the next day on recon, and meet our Huey well after dark.

For Bravo Team, that's just how it worked out. They took the northerly route, found no signs of the enemy, reached the designated LZ ahead of schedule, called in the Huey, and left the forest.

But I was leading Alpha Team. It didn't go so well for us. Let's have a shooter."

Another pause, a sigh of resignation, and then Owen forged on with it.

"Only hours after we crept into the southerly quadrant – still dark, maybe 0300 – we stumbled across Cong. They were unaware of us, even though we were almost on top of their tiny fire. Must've been a dozen or so of them, chatting and smoking. But we were surprised, too, as we were on them before anyone was ready.

You see a group like that, all in one place, you have to take your shot. Remember: kill dinks, kill dinks, kill dinks. We knew that engagement would give away our presence and location, but it was too good an opportunity, so we slid on our bellies to tighten our range – less than thirty yards. On my order the four of us unleashed a barrage into the camp. Several bodies shot backward, arms flailing, cries of pain. Most, though, grabbed their weapons and scurried back into the undergrowth, which provided immediate cover. We rolled off right to avoid what we knew would be next, a hail of rounds to our firing spot.

That occurred about three seconds later. We could see the gunpowder flashes at the ends of their muzzles. They began to spray the area in long sweeping movements, bullets whizzing by us. We were gripping the ground and thinking about better cover.

The darkness lit up with enemy gunfire. Muzzle flashes spangled the little clearing; powder smoke lay heavy in the air. I led the squad further right and told them we would take one more crack at these guys and then exit quickly, back and even further right. I moved the two specialists back toward our original strike position because the dinks had already hit it hard, with no returning fire.

This was a three-minute gunfight. Doesn't sound very long, does it?"

Well, these things seem to last hours. We fired, moved a bit, fired, moved a bit. They kept firing. I have no idea whether we anyone else or not. It was a maelstrom.

Then we fled. We slashed through the foliage and headed in the same general direction we'd started. We knew they'd follow if they could, so we moved fast, no gunfire, no talking.

We crossed a 'squiggly,' a little stream that I'd seen on the map during pre-mission planning. We called them 'squigglies' because these thin, filthy, algae-capped, shallow tributaries wound through the jungle to the rivers. They cut all over the jungle, snake-infested, tick-infested runs. They looked about the same from one spot to another. Of course, this one had to have a hole in the middle. Just deep enough that when the Buck and I ran into it, we were up to our armpits with leeches."

Owen paused long enough to make a point important to him. "I say leeches, and I know you're thinking of creepy, caterpillar-sized uglies about an inch or two long. These were not those. These were the mothers of all leeches. Some could be six or eight inches long. My God, they looked like small carp. And they wanted to suck your blood. They'd be on you in seconds, I mean, all over you. You needed to get them off your back, your arms, your neck. Once across we did that, helping each other in hard-to-reach places."

Owen's mood was intensifying as he remembered.

"We wanted to go north to the rendezvous LZ, but we figured the Cong had guessed that. There was no way we were going to outrun or outflank the numbers behind us. We were the rabbits in this chase. So we went to ground. We thrashed through the forest until we came to what we called a 'frond factory,' a stand of low-lying shoots of drooping green leaves so large they could conceal an entire body. We stopped right there and dug in.

We hunkered. Utter silence. When I look back on this thing, I think that this action was the first of a few things that saved our lives.

It was still pre-dawn, but we could hear the Cong—a lot of them—slashing through the foliage just north of us. Every few seconds, one would fire off a round or two to entice us into giving away our position by returning fire. Luckily, they simply took the wrong angle, and we were safe… for the time being. That's probably the second thing that saved us.

Then dawn, and heavy, heavy rain. Briefly, we thought that would discourage Cong movement. It didn't. They kept searching, kept yelling, kept firing off a shot now and then to assure us that they were still out there. We still had to hide hard. Constant tension, constant threat assessment, constant focus on concealment. That's hard enough on a good day.

But tropical rain—monsoon almost—gets at you. Dealing with it is another job. It cascades over you heavier and heavier, with a random, non-rhythmic white noise that drives you nuts. It's pervasive—no cover can keep it from seeping in everywhere. You can't keep it off your neck, down your shirt, out of your eyes, or from pulsating into your brain as it rattles off your helmet. Fronds or not, it's miserable. Wet—lousy wet—and constant. I can still hear that sound in my head.

And there were ticks. Our only movement was to remove those lousy ticks—hundreds of them.

You hope that this kind of rain will bother the enemy, too. Maybe they'll just hunker down, too… but they don't. You know they don't, because you can hear them out there, barking to either other, making their way closer to you, even if they don't know it. And you sit in a downpour, and you wait.

They looked for us for more than an hour, some passing within thirty feet of one or another of us. Finally, they gave it up and stopped to eat breakfast. They simply sat down in the jungle, not more than forty yards from us. In that heavy air, especially after the rain subsided a bit, we could hear them laughing and chanting.

My Specialist 4 told me later that he could hear the static and terse radio talk between our pursuers and their base. We could smell the smoke from their Salems, Newports, or Kools. Dinks loved American cigarettes, especially mentholated brands. I can tell you that none of us risked a smoke."

Owen stopped for a sip of Turkey. The alcohol was kicking in. For my part, I was simply riveted to my chair.

Owen's face was becoming a frozen mask as he unfolded this drama.

"They say that war is hell. Let me tell you what hell is. Hell is waiting. Hell is having no options. Hell is being wet and tick-infested. Hell is being scared and ignorant of what comes next. Hell is expecting a bullet from anywhere, but unable to swivel about to protect yourself. Hell is not having to piss, because you already did it; you just don't remember when. Hell is visualizing your own torture or death in surreal terms.

In mid-morning, the Cong headed northwest, up the far side of that brutal squiggly. With a little distance between us and them, we felt safe enough to huddle and eat C-rations. We inventoried our ammunition—we'd used a lot of it in that firefight—and risked our first radio call to base. Told them we were lost. My map was destroyed by the squiggly, we had a compass, but not coordinates, and we were being hounded by at least three squads. Low on rounds. What to do next?

Operations said they'd get back to us at 1200. In the meantime, stay alive, shut down the radio, and find a discriminating landmark. So far, I'd survived the first ten hours of the longest day of my life."

The fifth of Wild Turkey was starting to look as if it were under attack, defensive even. We put more ice in our glasses and topped them off. Fortified, Owen continued.

"A few details are important here. A platoon leader selects from his men the four or six he wants for any specific mission and reason. In addition to myself, I brought a Buck Private, a Specialist Four, and a Weapons Four Specialist—good men, all. You know the average age of our group? Twenty-one.

We were heavily armed, because that's the way I liked it. We probably carried more than 500 rounds among us. The Buck, the Specialist 4, and I carried M-16s with bandoliers holding eighteen or so rounds;

four or five more mags in our packs. My weapons guy had an M-79 and a 40-millimeter grenade launcher; he carried several magazines. We all had pistols… Colt .45s, loaded, with four additional clips.

I knew that the extraction point was still to our north. I had no idea how far, or whether we needed to go northeast or northwest to get there. I knew the squiggly split at the LZ, but that thing wound back and forth like a rattlesnake. And I knew that at least two dink squads had already headed that way. But that's where our Huey was setting down, and Cong or not, we had to get there, wherever that was. I decided we'd do details later and just head up.

That went well for an hour. We caught up with the Cong in front of us, as they were slowed by their search. That seemed fortuitous for a minute or two. But, wouldn't you know, just like that, the squads split east and west. The first—probably the one with the boss—headed up the west side of the squiggly, now in play again. The other crossed that muck and headed up the east side, after a leech detachment drill. We could actually see this from our distance, although we had no reasonable shot at them.

I stopped for a moment to reason this out. Now we had six or eight dinks to our left, six or eight behind us, and the same number to our right. I expect that each squad had been replenished for the ones we'd taken out the previous night. Worse, I was sure that they'd called in a few other squads to pinch us from three sides. That's what I would've done.

They weren't close yet; we didn't hear them or see them. They were fanning out in front of us. Good. Someone was probably behind us. Bad. One could deduce that the Charlies had no ammunition concerns, what with their supply line behind them. We could proceed up the middle—but that meant crossing, and maybe re-crossing, that mucky stream. We could hunker again, or engage the squad on our side of the water. Either way, we had to go north sometime.

"'Let's just kill them. We have enough ammo left for one more run,' my Buck said.

"And that's what we did. We moved quickly up the water's edge, staying in the forest, and attacked about noon. This second firefight was all ours, because we were hidden, and they weren't ready for a rear attack. Still, we used a precious amount of ammo. For the moment, that side of the water was ours.

The Cong on the east heard this battle and finally found us. More gunfire back and forth across the squiggly. Unwilling to cross the water again, they dropped back into the jungle. That move confirmed for us that other Charlies would soon be in our area, on our side of the stream.

The decision to engage that squad was our third life-saving grace. There were going to be too many of the enemy for us to poke out our heads when help finally came.

We dropped back a bit, so we weren't opposite the Charlies on the east."

Owen looked down at his watery bourbon glass and weaved over to Phil, who was now behind the bar, for some new ice.

Strange, I thought. *I didn't even see him come in.*

When Owen started again, his voice was whiskey thick, but he was focused deep now, into his own, vivid memories.

"At 1200 we called in. Operations told me that 2300 was extraction time. My squad needed to be at such-and-such coordinates by then—the little island in the squiggly. We should remain in the forest edge until the Huey pilot would call us on this same frequency with details.

"'Roger that. All good,' I said, 'but where's that from us?'

"'No idea,' the radioman said. 'Has to be north of your present location. Leave your radio on until we can triangulate you. Watch for Snakes overhead. When you have a visual, call it in.'

We spent the afternoon struggling our way north. We moved quietly—slowly—because of our depleted ammo. No more engagements for us.

Hours later, we saw two Cobras fly somewhat north of us. We called it in. 'Got ya. Head straight north —the island is less than three klicks. Get to its southern point, stay in the bush, and call in. Don't shoot anybody.'

'With what?' I asked. 'We're hiding like mice here, almost no ammo.' Fact is, on the way out, we had six rounds in my M-16. That's not even one burst, really. In other words, we'd fired almost everything we had.

"'Yeah, roger that. Look, I'm trying to find someone on station to get you. Hang in while I look.'

"'Roger.'

"Three klicks is a long way in the jungle," Owen said more to himself than to me, draining his bourbon glass, no longer sipping.

"We headed north, following the water; we found the island; we hunkered down again; we listened for Cong. Certainly they were both behind and in front of us, arcing across the water. Flanked, that's what we were. And then it rained again, about dusk. So we waited. Hell revisited. Hours passed.

Sometime after dark, we get the dreaded radio call from Operations. 'Can't go at 2300—no visibility, minimums less than fifty feet. Turn off radio until 0500. We'll give new time.'

Hell Squared now—six more hours tacked onto the soggy wait with the ticks.

CHAPTER SEVENTEEN

Johnny On The Spot

At 0500, up in the sky, Johnny 'Horse' Barrow thought his day was over. Horse was returning to Phu Bui with his crew of five, including himself. His Huey Iroquois had completed two brief missions fifty miles north of our problem. He and his low ship pilot, Bulls Eye, in his own UHIH, had ferried three squads over to the Laotian border. The soldiers were to fight their way back along one of the Cong's supply trails. Not according to record, but certainly by coordinates, Johnny knew his cargo was inserted in Laos, but that was all the same to him. Dinks were dinks. He, too, had been trained to 'kill, kill, kill.'

Then Horse received a radio call. What was his fuel supply and armament? Did he have enough of either to make a run down to Hu Man to extract four trapped US? Operations needed a UH1H because the B and C Hueys couldn't carry that many more souls, and Barrow's team was the only H already on station.

Johnny called over to Bulls Eye and found the same conditions as his own ship. One-half fuel, three-quarters armament. Tired crews. He radioed in an affirmative.

"'Roger, Nighthawk Six. Go down and take a look. These guys are glued down, out of ammo, and only fifty klicks from you. They got nothing to send from Ca Mau. Recon status when you reach area.'

Hard turn right, and the twin gunships flew south until they intercepted the squiggly. Then harder right, and straight down the waterbed. In the youngest dawn's light they could see the little island split the sluggish water into two trails. They circled it at 3,000 feet.

"'Bulls Eye, take a run down the stream. Stay on the deck and be fast. Expect engagement. I'll try to reach these guys.' Johnny's voice was calm as his battle focus ramped up. He explained the makeshift mission to the crews of both gunships, and they, too, attended to stations and preparations for an extraction.

The low ship went in fast and hard. As it reached the near edge of the pointy island, it took fire. Bulls Eye's gunners went to work. The chopper passed over the landing zone in several long seconds.

"Up and out, Bulls Eye radioed Horse. 'Well, there are at least thirty of them. Shooting up a storm, probably hopped up on dope—they see a bird, and jump up, and start shooting holes in the sky. Landing is going to be messy.'

Phu Bui was on the same frequency, so they heard this report to Johnny. 'Up to you, Nighthawk. If you can get in and out, go ahead. Or, turn for home. Your call.'

It was getting lighter—daylight extractions are risky. Bulls Eye hit his button. 'What do you want to do, Horse? I'll tell you this: those Cong are less than two hundred yards from the point of that island. If the US are jungled beside that point, they'll soon be under attack and dead in minutes. Still, we have ten souls up here. We'll be putting them in harm's way.'

Johnny had descended to a thousand feet, about a klick from the island. 'Two hundred yards and they die? We leave, and they might as well walk into the stream and take it in the chest. Bulls Eye?'

"'I'm in.'

"'Roger that. Here it is, then—I'll go in, put down on the point. You come in on the deck from the northeast with suppressive fire. Keep your nose south, though. Base, give me the Fox Mike frequency to the ground US. I'll tell him how to do this.'"

Owen topped off his glass and drank of the first third. "Seconds later, it was Johnny and I on the horn—neither base nor Bull's Eye said another word." Owen was in a kind of trance now, remembering words, conversation, and detail, as if everything were occurring in real time.

'US, this is Nighthawk Six. What's your call sign?'

"'Alpha Delta.'

"'Okay, Alpha Delta, still four of you?'

"'Roger.'

"'This is how we get you the hell out of there. Listen carefully; I'm not doing this twice, or you'll be gone before I put down.' Johnny's voice was quiet, deadpan, almost removed from its producer. Steady, battle-leader mode. He sounded more like he was planning an elegant arrival to someone's office party than into the maw in front of him. I latched onto that strong confidence and felt some hope for the first time in the last thirty hours.

"'You're near the point?'

"'Thirty yards south.'

"'Can you see me?'

"'No.'

"'Good. My low ship is coming in first—from the east, behind you. When he arrives and starts shooting, count to five. Then, one at a time, send your men, you last with radio, straight to LZ. I'll come in from northeast—low, and fast, and crossways to the stream. Don't wait for me to land—I'll put it on the point, all right, but real light on the skids, so don't worry about the knives. You and I get there at same time.'

"'Affirmative.'

"'Don't linger. I'm not staying long. One minute from now my low ship comes in. Be ready.'

"'Affirmative.'

"I relayed the plan to the guys and named the first man, second man, third man out. 'Leave your backpacks here. Carry your weapons. Zigzag your way to the chopper on that point. We either do this right, or somebody isn't going home tonight.'

A minute later, I saw and heard the first gunship. Seconds later, he came in over our heads. His gunners opened up on the jungle. Then the second gunship was coming in at an angle. I gave a push to Boyer, the first to leave. 'Go!' Five seconds later, 'Go,' and then again, 'Go.'

I could feel the air thump and the roar of the low ship above us, laying suppressive fire. I still had those six rounds. I planned on using them. That was probably stupid. The Huey was providing the real firepower. Like carrying beer to Milwaukee, I guess. But I wasn't going to leave this hellhole with any rounds in my pocket.

So, I jumped into the clearing, fired them off, and ran for it.

My three guys were already in or across the squiggly, moving at sharp angles.

The dinks? They were firing. Funny way of fighting, those guys. As soon as Boyer ran into the clearing, those guys reared up from the foliage on both sides of the water. They made no effort to conceal themselves. Rose up and unloaded a barrage of gunfire at him. They did this even though the gunship was beading right in on them—and hitting some of them. All that was in my peripheral vision as I chased my squad to the chopper. There were more Cong than we'd thought.

The game was out in the open now. Charlie knew we were headed toward the Huey getting ready to light on the island. They shot at us, but now at the chopper, too. It was a big deal to shoot down a helicopter. They were running up the embankment, trying to get a shot at more of the craft than just the nose that Barrow was showing them.

Some of them were hitting the Huey. Ping, ping, ping—the metallic sounds of bullets piercing the shell of the gunship. They shot at Boyer too, because he was first, and overshots might hit the chopper. They were right about that.

So I'm running. I see Boyer make it. He leaped up to the door and arms reached out to pull him in. Then the other two. I was getting there.

I made it two yards from the open door—there really wasn't any door, actually. Both side doors were removed to lessen the weight and to give the gunners more range.

Then I collected a round. I was thrust forward, with my chest crunched against the door sill. My feet were dragging behind me, and I couldn't seem to get them under me. Arms reached out and pulled me up straight so they could drag me into the craft.

And I got hit again. Turns out, the second wound was only a half inch from the first. As I was being heaved aboard, I could hear ping, ping, ping. I remember thinking that I might be entering a tin coffin. Later, I was told that the mechanics counted eighty-eight bullet holes in that Huey—so there were at least forty-four hits. I remember seeing and smelling oily black smoke—the power plant had been hit somewhere.

I was sprawled across the floor, my face behind Barrow's seat. I could hear soldiers yelling, 'Got 'em, go, go, go!'

"'Right over their heads,' I heard Johnny say to his crew. 'I don't want to give these bastards a shot at the rotor. Gunners, targets are front and low. Bulls Eye, left, out, 3,000 and hold.' All of this with that disembodied, almost serene voice.

I felt us dipping forward, and then up. I was wet, and began to feel the nausea. I could smell my own coppery-scented blood, and when the medic started to roll me around to see the details, I heard that sticky, almost sucking sound of my chest being removed from pooled blood.

"'We've got blood,' he announced, confirming my own opinion of the situation.

"'We'll go to Long Binh,' I heard Captain Barrow say above the roar of the engine. More ping, ping, ping.

"I turned my head sideways; I vomited. The Huey was ascending; I was going south.

"Before I passed out, I heard Barrow's even voice, 'Smitty, take the controls. I've been hit. Legs. This isn't goo…'

"The last thing I saw in that Huey was a hole in the greenhouse, the Plexiglas hood on the top of the craft. Well, somebody would just have to fix that."

Owen sighed, reaching for the last three fingers of the Turkey.

"I woke up in a hospital bed in Long Binh. Spent several days there, recovering from those two through-and-throughs. They'd ripped through three ribs, which were pretty much shattered. One of them caught my left lung, collapsing it. I'd lost a lot of blood, and I needed a small procedure or two to clean up the general area. The lung healed itself.

"But there was pain… pain for about a year, actually. I tried to keep the painkillers to a minimum, but after a while, pain simply wears you out—every move you make must involve the ribs—and I slept in a chair for eight months.

I saw Johnny Barrow in the hospital. He was in much worse shape. The flesh of both legs was shredded up to his crotch. Severed bones in different places in each leg. He needed three operations. They soon moved him to the air base in Yakota, Japan, for advanced care.

I got to talk with him first, though. I said my thanks, in probably the only six or eight ways I knew how to, and we promised to stay in touch. I never saw him again. We did talk on the phone and exchange mail for a while.

I recovered pretty much completely. Johnny Barrow now lives with constant pain. So, the army discharged us both. I came back to Oregon, and he went back to Pennsylvania. Purple Hearts all around.

"Damn, Owen." Mired in alcohol myself, and in the reality of war, I searched for something appropriate. *What the hell would that be?* I wondered. "Rough stuff, Owen. Must be tough to tell. You've only told this two other times?"

"Yeah. I told the counselor they assigned me at the Portland VA hospital. He thought it'd do me good to 'get it all out there.'"

"Did it?"

"No." Pause. "I also told my dad. My behavior back here was—umm—'erratic' for a while. Drinking too much, moping about. I was quiet, moody, and sullen. Angry all the time. A pain in the ass. A pain in my side, too."

"Ah, yes, your weather-predicting ribs," I chimed in. "If I recall, they don't work very well."

"Better than you think," he snapped. "Anyway, I told George the saga because I sensed that he was getting ready to tell me to shape up, buck up, get on with your life… that sort of thing. I figured him knowing what had happened would help me get a free pass."

"Did it?"

"No. He told me to shape up, buck up, get on with your life, that sort of thing." Owen smiled faintly. "You know the line—war is hell. Now get on with it."

"You and John are American heroes," I offered.

"No, John is an American hero. I was a soldier, doing what they sent me there to do. I got shot; I recovered. Lots of guys did that. Fifty thousand died trying to do just that.

When I left the service, I flew home in government-issued army fatigues. No one noticed me. By the time John could come home, they dressed him like a hippie and flew him to Newark on a 707 that had no other passengers... only John and the flight service crew. Landed him in middle of the night, so no protesters would spit on him.

John spent months in physical therapy and medication; never got any recognition for the lives he saved, except his Purple Heart. He never really recovered. He lives with physical pain every day. On the ten-point pain scale, his best days are a five. Gets to nine often. He's been maxed out on pain pills, NSAIDS, since 1970. Needs a stick to walk. He has nightmares.

When I was processed out, I came back to this bar. Worked with my father like before. I just drank all day. Then my father and I had that little talk. I worked it out. Still here.

But John... John came back with that constant pain, the inability to do anything for eight hours straight, and the humiliation of long-term assistance from others. He tried alcohol too, but he wasn't cut out to be a drunk. He had to face all that with a sober mind. His wife stayed right there for him, and that might've saved him.

John led dozens of guys and flew scores of missions. He saved lives, and did so mostly under enemy fire. Not easy to forget that. I know this: he saved four lives the night I met him. Not easy to forget that either, even though it makes me feel guilty. He's a hero in my book... that's always going to be for sure."

"But you don't stay in touch with him?"

"Not anymore. We traded 'How are you doing' phone calls and Christmas cards for a while. But we're two guys from two backgrounds, in two states far apart. What do you do after you say you're grateful? He had to face his demons, and I mine. All we were really doing was keeping that wretched night alive. Like scratching a scab... it just made it worse. No real need for that.

"And that, my friend, in a nutshell, is why most veterans talk so little about their combat experiences."

"How about your friend Birdy? How did he make out?"

"Birdy returned to Cordell with a flag over him. He didn't survive the Tet Offensive. He got here before I did—1968, in fact. I heard it was a nice funeral, full military honors—the flag, the honor guard, and the guns. Mostly family, though. Townspeople were scarce. It was the beginning of the end of support for the war. Many didn't quite know how to deal with Vietnam soldiering deaths."

"No hero stuff?"

"Hero or villain, no one knew for sure. Whatever—Birdy was a case in point. Cordell finally got to honoring him during the centennial celebration in 2005. His name and contribution to freedom were etched into a slab of marble and placed in a little tanbark garden with flowers around it. It sits right at the end of The Boulevard, where it meets the Deschutes. Spruced up the town a bit for the big doings."

"How about you? A hero's welcome?"

"'He also served'—that was about it."

"So, Vietnam in a nutshell, as you say. What do you think about it now?"

"What do you think I think? Bunch of twenty-year-olds, dying with quivering lips for God and Country. Thousands of mistreated and maligned vets. A waste of a full generation of American men and women, for a war from which we got nothing. And a wall for all the dead."

Owen had finished. There was little either of us had to say. Both drunk, both spent.

"Owen, I'm going to leave now. Go to my room and take a nap. Get some dinner. Maybe I'll come over later."

Owen nodded, said a word to Phil behind the bar, and slowly steered himself to the stairs. Grover got out of the way, and then followed Owen.

I napped for two hours, had dinner at the cafe, wandered about town, and went over to Ticket's. Bob entered as he finished his daily ritual. We both drank two beers. He showed me his stone. Both of us were in our beds before 10:00. I didn't see Owen.

CHAPTER EIGHTEEN

By George, You've Got It!

Islept until I heard a muted rap on the door and a tiny voice say, "Maid service."

I ate brunch at a restaurant downtown. Good food, bad spelling. The sign outside proclaimed this as a family "resturant."

I poked about town, chatting up some local shopkeepers. The druggist actually took me out to the sidewalk to point out the three tiers upon which the burg sat—from the valley, over to the bluffs, and down to the river.

We chatted there long enough for him to describe his family connection to Pennsylvania, somehow making us important new acquaintances.

Late in the morning, I entered Ticket's. I knew I had to wait through the lunch bunch's feeding, so I volunteered to take Grover for a walk. That made all three of us happy. Upon our return, Grover headed to the landing, and Owen and I to the bullet-hole table.

"Owen, tell me more about George, your father. You've mentioned him only in a few stories."

"I don't much like sentiment, and no one can talk about his father without sentiment, either positive or negative… not my style."

"George surely figures importantly in this bar and town," I pointed out.

"That he did," Owen acknowledged.

"Okay, George Ticket… probably the finest man ever to live in Cordell. Respected businessman, influential citizen, an ear for all, trusted. Tried to live by strong principles. He failed rarely.

If Noah Ticket represented the Old West, George was the embodiment of the new. Noah could be tough, ruthless, single-minded, and aggressive… all traits required of an America saloonkeeper at the turn of the century. George inherited all those genes, but, by necessity, he was gentler, less violent, and more astute. He was perfectly prepared to be part of the postwar boom.

My dad was a handsome man, born in 1913. My grandmother raised him by the book. George learned to read, went through school, attended Sunday school, and married his high-school sweetheart, my mother, Greta Sealander.

Still, he worked in Noah's bar, at the old man's insistence, from age seven or so on. Early evenings and Saturdays he'd be in here, washing glasses, swabbing floors, running errands, whatever. On busy nights, he'd work the grill or pull drafts and slide them up and down the bar to Grandpa or Brush. Preordained it was that George would someday take over the place, and he did. By 1938, his dad worked for him part-time, until Noah's death.

George ran Ticket's during the golden years of Cordell. From about 1940 through the late sixties, this was a vibrant town, and Ticket's profited from the wood industry boom, and the railroads, road-building, wheat, sheep, hops, and perlite mining as well. People were having more and more babies. The Strip and The Boulevard were humming, and so was Ticket's.

George needed more barkeeps and another cook to assist Connie. He remodeled both toilets, added those barstools, removed the spittoons, mounted a TV in the corner up there, and added the take-out cooler. He dominated the market in wine and champagne sales, targeted to the growing number of female patrons, with a more impressive wine cellar than the hotel. I still have some of his upper-shelf stuff.

Ticket's was busy every day and night. George made more money than Noah and I combined. Naturally, I was here for the second half of this boom, being in this place since age seven. I did the same things George had done as a lad.

George knew everybody. He supported every fund-raiser and worthy cause going. Ticket's sponsored both a Little League baseball team and our sandlot team, what we called 'the town team.' That group won the county championship two years in a row, and Ticket's threw huge parties for both, the second better than the first—still legendary.

While it struck us all as a bit puzzling, this quiet family man loved a good party. Baseball championship? 'Let's party!' Salmon running? 'Let's grill 'em outside and invite everyone! Free fish—just bring the fixings! All alcohol one-half off!' A freight manager going to get married? 'Let's do it here!' We must've done a dozen weddings here over the years. One couple had George perform the nuptials himself. They figured if the captain of a ship could do it, why not a bar owner?

There'd be music and dancing till dawn. George loved a great party, especially ones fueled from his taps.

All of that made Ticket's 'the' bar in Cordell. That may be a bit unfair to my grandfather. Noah probably had that distinction, too, but he had less to work with, and less competition.

If Noah was a legend, George was an icon. There was a certain fullness and authenticity to the man—reasonable and compassionate, but given to good times. My dad had many friends, of course, none greater than Brush Washington and Jimmy Delotti.

They were the three musketeers—in fact, many called them just that. Immediately bonded, fiercely loyal to each other. After World War II, Jimmy, my dad, and Brush, for different reasons, were viewed as the most influential men in town—not the banker, the baker, or candlestick maker—these three. Not the mayor, nor the lawyer, nor the realtor. These three.

Their opinions not only mattered; they were usually the operative position of the population at large—certainly Ticket Associates on anything big or small. 'Well, George says… ' was often the introduction one took when getting ready to take a stance on something.

Ask one for a favor, some help, or backing on an issue, and you got the efforts of all three. No politics, no muscle, no power or authority or title, mind you. Just the three men in town who could get it done, whose assistance was given simply because they had it to give. They were like that right up until Jimmy, then Brush, then George died."

Owen suddenly stopped. He thought a second or two.

"Ed, I want to say this before I forget it. The four biggest funerals ever in Cordell, Oregon, weren't those of any Cordell, or a Witherspoon, or war veteran, or hero. The four largest funerals were in this order: George Ticket, Noah Ticket, Brush Washington, and Jimmy Delotti. What else can I say?"

"That pretty much tells it, Owen," I remarked. "Go on."

"My dad had those mostly indefinable skills that make the great bartenders… well… great. You know, most of those skills are listening skills, not talking skills. George was no 'Chatty Patty,' you understand. The great ones aren't. Quality bartenders will tell you that conversation with a man with a drink in his hand isn't difficult to start. Some patrons come in to be alone, but most belly up to talk with the tap operator.

Great bartenders don't probe, chitchat, or run their mouths about politics or social issues Their job is to release, to receive, to accept the topic of the day. Usually the customer takes care of that. They want to talk about the toils and snares in their lives. The bartender's role is to listen, to extend the conversation without agitation, and to sell another drink. Noah taught us all that.

George was the master. He had the knack of getting people to talk. More than that, he was perceptive, and took more from the conversation than the drinker thought he was giving.

Without confrontation or prying, George's receptive skills prompted people to reveal much more about themselves than they'd intended. And yet, they did so willingly.

Ed, you know what? I think you might've made a good bartender."

"Get on with it, Owen," I retorted.

"Anyway, George's approachability is why so many came to George with their problems, conflicts, or questions. My dad's strengths were his common sense and ability to influence others. Over time, these qualities led town folk to seek his judgment in myriad matters.

Even that started innocently enough. One evening, two of our drunks became engaged in an argument that George feared might turn violent. By necessity, he intervened. He ended up settling the issue such that each man thought he had prevailed. Each mentioned 'good ol' George' to others, and suddenly, George was the recognized arbiter in Cordell. Sort of like Judge Judy, without the robe and lace collar.

He used to laugh that he settled more marriage difficulties, financial disputes, fence line placements, and who-shot-the-sheriff conflicts than all the judges and lawyers in town. In fact, he was so practiced at it that his lawyer friend and customer, Tom Paisley, told him to stop it; George was costing him business.

He did the painful stuff, too. When the young child of a local pastor died of leukemia, it was George who provided the solace, the succor, the shoulder for someone's pain. Who ministers to the minister? Well, a barkeep.

George helped more than one person accept that it was time to put down an Angora cat or a prized hunting dog. It was George who convinced an embezzler to turn herself in. In for a dime, in for a dollar, I guess.

Folks once tried to convince him to run for town mayor, but George begged off, telling them that he was just a country boy, and a busy one who owned a bar.

Well, George's psychologist's-couch demeanor once placed him in a dilemma regarding our town's biggest unsolved mystery—who raped Merrilee Cordell back in 1918? He solved the case all right, but he didn't know what to do about his discovery.

"Owen, you're saying your dad knew who attacked her?" I broke in. "How and when did he determine that?"

"To be precise, a full forty-three years after the assault. Only two other people knew he knew, though."

"How'd he come to this little discovery?" I urged.

"It was 1961; I know this because that was when Charles Cordell dropped dead on the street, right outside the café. Brush happened to be there, picking up some Danish pastries for George, my mother, and him. They were going to do some spring housecleaning in the bar that morning.

Charles rose to leave, passing Brush on his way out the door, chatting with Banker Bill as they exited. Charles stepped outside, looked at Bill and said, 'You know what? I don't feel so good.'

Bill said Charles gave him an odd look, put his hand to his chest, and fell straight on his face, dead—deader than hay. It was instant.

That brought Merrilee Cordell back to town—for all anybody knew, for the first time ever. Maybe she'd come back, unnoticed, for a few holiday celebrations at the big home in The Wedge, but townsfolk never saw her. She certainly hadn't attended her father's funeral. When Franklin died, her sister, mother, and Charles were the only family members present. But Charles was her brother, and, I guess, she figured enough water had passed under the bridge. Whatever, Merrilee returned for her brother's funeral.

Of course, Merrilee was in her late fifties or early sixties by then. When Dad told me the story, he took great pains to say she looked good, prosperous, and demure.

During the church basement meal after the service, Dad and Merrilee stumbled into each other at the coffee urn. He identified himself and offered his condolences. She responded that she remembered him as Noah's young child, and that she'd known Noah Ticket, as everyone had. They chatted.

And George's charisma somehow manifested itself. Either that, or Merrilee had returned to Cordell to bury her brother and to rid herself of a monkey she'd carried on her back for all this time.

For whatever reason, Merrilee broached the subject. 'You know, Mr. Ticket, I left Cordell under awful circumstances. I can't say that I've missed the town, but I knew when I was sent to private school in Portland that I was to turn my back on a travesty. There was some injustice surrounding that night. It's burned in my heart and mind for more than forty years.'

Out came the George Detector. But he went slowly.

Injustice? You mean the injustice to you and the ordeal you suffered? I think most of us understand the trauma you must've endured. On top of that, your attacker was never identified, never convicted. I'm sure you've often wished for some form of closure over the years.'

There's more to it than that, I'm afraid. Mr. Ticket… my experience involves much more than anyone, except my sister, would ever know. It has hung over my entire life.'

George knew, at that moment, that there was much more to the Merrilee Cordell story than had ever been made public. He looked about the church room and decided this wasn't the proper time or place to get, or expect, more revelation.

Merrilee, I can see that you have something on your mind. Let's do this—today, you bury your brother Charles and mourn your loss. If you want to talk to somebody about the rest of it, I'm at your disposal. Perhaps you'll call on me tomorrow—are you staying over tonight?—if you want to talk more."

A slight nod from Merrilee. 'I'll think about it,' she said.

The next morning, George was refilling the beer cooler when Merrilee Cordell entered.

"'Can you listen to me? Do you have time for me to tell the real story about my attack? Can I trust you, Mr. Ticket?' she asked.

"'The answer to the first two questions is certainly yes. Only you can decide about the third. I have to tell you, though, Miss Cordell, I'm pretty good at holding my own counsel.'

"'I want to tell someone,' she said. 'I have to tell the real story. I'm ashamed to say that I've waited all these years to do it. Could you make me some tea?'

Tea. A full pot.

"Merrilee breathed deeply and dove right in. 'David Witherspoon didn't rape me—Jeremy Lansome did. I knew it that night; I've known it all these years. Only my twin sister Naomi, Jeremy, and I ever knew that… until now.'

"'And you came in here this morning to tell me?' George asked.

"'Yes.

"'Jeremy Lansome hated me—and he had good reason. My sister and I were very mean to him. We played rotten tricks on him, we led him on, and we made a fool of him. I was deceitful and dishonest to him.' Merrilee, again, gathered herself and plowed forward.

Jeremy lived in The Acre. He was a good-looking kid, but poor, unkempt, and dull. My sister and I started playing games with him.

I mean, we, being identical twins, would pretend to be the other one when we were all in school together.

We agreed to come on to him, as if we were actually romantically interested in him… of course we weren't. Naomi and I decided to tease him into some sort of love fantasy in which he'd come to believe that I, or my sister in my identity—Merrilee to him—wanted him desperately.

Sometimes one or the other of us would meet him in isolated places and allow him to get to first base. We wanted to determine whether he could tell any difference, either in personality or physical attributes—if you get my meaning. He couldn't, and we took great delight in that.

That was about as far as we wanted the game to go. We got bored, and there was only so far that Naomi and I were willing to go. So, we ended the charade.

But Jeremy didn't. By this time, he was all caught up in his affection for the girl he knew as Merrilee Cordell. Here he was, this poor kid from The Acre, making time with a Cordell girl. He was in the big leagues, big time.

Now we had a problem. We'd started this ruse, but we were unable to shut it down. First, Naomi and I tried subtle hints and waning interest. That didn't work.

So we switched tactics. We got just plain mean. We took turns insulting him in public. We told our school friends that Jeremy actually thought he had a chance with me. We made him a joke about school. All our townie friends joined in the bullying.

We stood him up on the meeting dates upon which he insisted. We questioned his manhood, his predictable future, his lack of class. We reminded him that Merrilee Cordell was, after all, a Cordell, and would have no business with someone from across the tracks. We sent him hateful notes. We were despicable in our attitude and actions toward Jeremy Lansome.'

"'And he snapped, as they say,' George interjected.

"'Yes. You know how.'

"'But you never told this to the authorities? Jeremy was never a suspect. David Witherspoon was, and you didn't challenge that?'

"'No. And I live with that. At the time, I was facing several issues. First, of course, was the humiliation of rape. Second, I was afraid of Jeremy Lansome. He'd shown me how violent he could be.

Third, I felt the guilt of contributing to his rage. I was—and am—embarrassed by what Naomi and I did. My parents would never approve of such behavior. Cordells just don't do such things. Facing my father was just impossibility for me. I knew that I'd be creating an embarrassment for the entire family. My sister and I didn't want to face the music for our foolishness.

Fourth, I had a plausible suspect—a way out. The spat between the Cordells and the Witherspoons was growing and growing, and everyone knew about it. David was a convenient red herring, as it were. I took the easy way out. I remained vague on the details. I said nothing when attention turned to David Witherspoon.

Allowing everyone to suspect David was, for me, a matter of convenience and dumb luck. I wasn't proud of it then, and I certainly am not proud of it now.

But, Mr. Ticket, and I say this as honestly as I can, I never, in my wildest dreams, imagined that my failure to speak up would have the impact on the two families, or this town, that they did. I have no defense, certainly, except that I was young and terrified. My sister and I were all wrapped up in being Cordells, in dealing with boys, in our own little games.

'Poor Naomi went along with the whole thing; she was my twin sister, after all. But it really affected her, too. She just kind of dropped out of life, attempting to smother the sin of omission. She married the first man available, even though she, a Cordell, certainly could have had many choices. She lost her spirit, I think. You know the isolated, uninvolved life she's lived… a waste, really.'

"'I understand,' said George. 'You and David both left town, him with this cloud of guilt, his family with a questionable reputation. There were consequences all around, weren't there?'

"'Certainly,' she agreed. 'I know David has paid dearly for my failure to name Jeremy. So have all the Witherspoons. I've paid dearly, too.'

"'You had no one to go to?' George asked. 'No one to help you, then?'

"'Who?' she retorted. 'Our preacher? Tell him, tell my father. A schoolteacher? They all feared my dad; probably bought land from him. Actually, what business owner or rancher didn't do business with Franklin Cordell? Avoiding my father's involvement was my major concern.

Strangely, I kept coming back to only one real choice… your father. I truly wanted to talk to Noah Ticket about my plight. But I knew that the Tickets were more bound to the Witherspoons than the Cordells. Perhaps your father would use this knowledge to help the other family bring shame to mine. Looking back, I wish I'd done that anyway. I think I could have trusted Noah Ticket, just as I'm now trusting his son.'

"'Merrilee, where does that leave us with Jeremy Lansome? I don't know him, even though I know most families in The Acre. Whatever happened to him?'

"'He left. Right after the attack, he cornered me in the grocery store. He told me that, if I ever mentioned his name, he'd kill me. He also told me he was moving to Illinois. If I ever mentioned his name before he left, I was a goner. I believed him.'

"'Is he still out there? Still alive? Ever contact you?'

"'No. I have no idea about any of that. For me, his absence is a blessing. If there's one person I never want to see again, it's Jeremy Lansome. Yet, he's not my source of misery… my own silence is.'"

Owen sat back in his chair. "My dad told me that story in the midst of getting me ready to take over this establishment. He was making the point that a little knowledge is a dangerous thing. Big knowledge is worse."

"What did George do with that knowledge, Owen?" I asked. "Did he make it public? Did he clear David Witherspoon's name? Did he tell the cops to go after the elusive Jeremy Lancome?"

"Dad said he thought long and hard about it. In the end, he did nothing, and that was the point of the story to me.

He did nothing, because he could envision little result. David Witherspoon's good name could never be resurrected. He no longer resided near Cordell, and current-day residents had never heard of him anyway. They really wouldn't care. Franklin Cordell was dead, Charles Cordell was dead, and no Cordell or Witherspoon, Kingsley, Bob or Charlotte, could benefit from the truth.

Merrilee Cordell wasn't seeking justice against Jeremy Lancome, who was gone, or perhaps dead, by then. Naomi Cordell was in as deep as her sister with the deception, and was living her life with that knowledge. She didn't suffer Merrilee's indignities, and though she stayed in town, she'd lived her life in an unloving marriage, except for a family inheritance that had kept her comfortable.

So who was to gain, what was to be won, by the truth? In the end, George chose to let it ride, hoping only that the confession he'd taken from Merrilee was some help to her, a Cordell or not."

"And your dad told you all of this?" I asked.

"Yes. He told me so I would know how a bartender gets involved with nothing of his making. I also think it was his way of coming to grips with a decision he made years ago."

"And perhaps warning you of dilemmas facing a barkeep, you think, Owen?"

"Probably," he agreed.

CHAPTER NINETEEN

He Started Out As A Child

Time to change topics.

"Owen, your childhood must have been interesting. You did have a childhood, right? Are there any stories about Owen Ticket, the little boy back in—what, the 1950s?"

"Probably not."

"C'mon," I pressed. "You were young once. Tell me something from that."

"Remember, I was tied to the bar even in my early years. But I had a childhood, much like anyone else. I have to reach, though, for stories."

Owen sat back again, stood up, stretched his legs, thought for a minute.

"Okay, okay… yes, I grew up in the fifties and sixties, in a small town. We kids back then could roam this town from sunup to sunset without the parental supervision required today. We made up our own games and excitement.

Joey Burrill and I—well, lots of kids, actually—would meet up in the summer mornings and do as we wished all day… play pick-up baseball, build little stone dams along the edge of the Cry, stocking them with crayfish or salamanders we freed from under the rocks. We fished, from the bridge and from the shore, shaded by some rimrock near the bluffs. Sometimes we waded out to the erratics and told each other stories; smoked cigarettes, and told dirty jokes.

Now and again we'd pack up peanut butter sandwiches and snacks and a big jug of water, and ride our bikes up to Larch Island—Ross had you up there, didn't he? We'd pretend it was a real island, surrounded, not by high country, but ocean. The general theme was that we were marooned on this ground, and under constant attack by pirates who wanted the booty we'd salvaged from our shipwreck. We could while away the middle of the day fighting off intruders with intrepid acts of derring-do and personal sacrifice. Or, we'd change the game to capture the flag, teaming up and outsmarting our friends for the prized Hershey bar.

Then, we'd ride back to town and report to the bar, or the hardware, or whatever, to help our fathers.

If we were loafing on The Boulevard, we could entertain each other with fantasies and suppositions which somehow just grew and grew into bigger and bigger tales, which we came to believe were probably true. Our imaginations were certainly far ahead of what we knew for sure. For sure that was true regarding Miss Leber, the witch."

"The witch?" I broke in. "Cordell had its own witch?"

"That's what we decided," he affirmed. "She looked like a witch, she acted like a witch, and she sold stuff she mixed up—brews, potions, and lotions that sounded very witch-like to us. More than that, we decided that she entertained men for nefarious goings-on, and that other witches from far away visited her combination home and store for witch activities. For a while, we decided she might just be a vampire, too.

"Let's hear about that," I demanded.

"Miss Leber—I didn't know her first name, Theresa, until I was much older—was an attractive young lady, less than thirty years old at the time. Again, I was about ten, but I could appreciate pretty faces and fine figures by that age.

Miss Leber had white, white skin and long, loose, jet-black hair hanging down to her waist. She was full-figured, shall we say, with a small waist and long legs. If Miss Leber had a physical flaw, it was her nose. Just a bit too long, a bit too sharp at the end, and a little bit distracting.

And she dressed only in black... always black: Black dresses, black gloves, black stockings, black coat and hat, if needed. She wore those old-style black, low, boot-like shoes—black, of course, and reaching to the hem of her button-up dress. That was all we boys needed to declare her a witch. We all had seen *The Wizard of Oz*, so we knew what witches looked like. Miss Leber just happened to be better-looking and younger than that one…no greenish skin or pointy hat…no cackle, either.

Those differences didn't matter. Miss Leber's behaviors fleshed out the title. From our vantage point, she acted like a witch, too. She lived alone in a quaint purple house at the very edge of town, just north of Baptist's Cry, actually. A hand-painted sign out front announced 'Miss Leber's Herb and Potion Shoppe.' A picket fence separated her property from vacant lots on both sides. It also helped keep varmints out of her back yard, which was taken up almost exclusively by an herb garden, complete with several close-to-the-ground greenhouses, a small algae-rimmed pond sprouting water plants, and several berry-bearing shrubs and vines.

We knew all this because we frequently spied on her—from a distance, of course. Once we got our suspicions revved up, we studied her the way motorists rubberneck as they pass a car wreck.

Miss Leber fascinated us in a terrifying way. We were too scared of her to get too close. What if she hexed us? What if we made eye contact with her and she put us in a trance? What if she lured us into her home so she could test out some of her concoctions on us?

All those boyish fears kept growing in our heads, mostly because we ourselves kept adding to them as we created what-if scenarios that always ended with us under Miss Leber's satanic powers. Our fascination with her and the whole concept of demonic activity fueled both an increased fear of encountering her, and an increased desire to do just that.

Of our group, only Mason Pettis ever saw the inside of that house. His father swore by the cough syrup Miss Leber blended from her rich inventory of honey, herbs, and spices. So one morning, Mr. Pettis took a reluctant Mason to Miss Leber's for a refill.

Mason was terrified, of course. He doubted that he or his father would ever escape the plans this evil sorceress might have for them. He entered, shaking in his Keds, he said later.

Mason said the front room of the house was dedicated to everything witchcraft. That parlor had become a combination witch's showroom and laboratory. In the middle was a marble-topped table outfitted with mixing bowls, Bunsen burners, and all the tools of a pharmacist.

Shelving lined three walls, jammed with little brown bottles with one-word labels. Long and short stalks of strange plants were pinned to the wall, along with a few leather harnesses, eye patches, and bracelets and necklaces featuring turquoise and crystal stones. There were tubes of creams and poultices behind the counter and various exotic tea leaves in glass containers.

The overriding, sweet smell of the occult pervaded the place, what with all the scented candles, open vials, and burning incense sticks, and an Ouija board hanging for sale from the back shelf.

Mason stood there in terror as his father made a matter-of-fact transaction for the cough medicine. Mason waited, fully expecting Miss Leber to conjure up the dead in some mystical invocation.

Mason survived the ordeal and stretched the facts into his notion that he and his father were very fortunate indeed.

So, we spied on Miss Leber. We set up a lookout station across from her house. When we felt brave enough, we ambled by her picket fence, sometimes as she worked in the front yard. She always acknowledged our presence, saying a pleasant hello, and often, some nice words. Yet there was an almost imperceptible hiss in her voice, sort of a 'Come hither, my pretty little boys,' that did nothing to allay our fears.

We carefully replied in kind, but we avoided direct eye contact, instead mumbling some response. Once she asked us if we'd like a glass of sun-brewed tea. We ran.

But we knew her routines. People would drop by, mostly women, and they'd be inside that den for some time. Often they'd carry in some strange flower arrangement or pan of leaves. They'd emerge with something else—devil's stuff, we were sure. Had to be an entire coven of witches, we decided. (Mason taught us that witches came in 'covens.')

And men came, too. For whatever reason, they seemed to stay longer. We figured they were getting their socks rolled, but we never had any proof of that, or even how long it should take. They'd enter a bit more slyly than the women, looking about to see if anyone was watching. We were. We'd time their visits. They seemed more relaxed when they left. Could it be? Well, our pre-pubescent minds had this all figured out. She was seducing the willing. Miss Leber's house was a strange and mysterious place.

Ah, youth! We had no fact onto which we connected these assumptions. Maybe that was how the herb business operated. Who knew? In the meantime, Miss Leber was supplying us kids with a scintillating view of adulthood."

"Kids will do what they must to scare themselves, Owen. Can't allow reality to get in the way of a good fantasy."

"I guess," he agreed. "In truth, I now believe that Theresa Leber was completely on the up-and-up. Her lifestyle was different, that's all. Adults in town used to snicker about her, but never about witchcraft or servicing men. Mostly, it was just that she was weird. Still, we kids had a great time with our views of Miss Leber."

Owen paused. His eyes brightened suddenly, and I knew he'd thought of something else. Good.

"Sometimes it wasn't our imaginations, but our real experiences, that got to us. I remember one of those.

When Joey and I were about ten, we had one of those scarred-for-life moments. It all started when we were out in the woods above town, looking for a lost dog.

Joey's family was dog-sitting Pixie, a little terrier that belonged to the local druggist, who was going on vacation. The only problem the dog posed for the Burrills was a tendency to run off if left outside without a tether. The Burrills could handle that, they thought.

I couldn't. One summer day, I entered the Burrill house to meet up with Joey. I left the screen door open for only a second or two, but Pixie took the opportunity to exit the environs. Joey and I chased after her for some time, with her eventually leading us into the woods.

We were just closing in on her when we came upon the preacher of the biggest church in Cordell. He was standing among some trees, with his pants down at his ankles. Mrs. Adams, the secretary at our elementary school, lay on a blanket, totally naked.

Sort of an awkward moment," he observed.

"I guess. What did you say, Owen?" I asked.

"What do you say to a naked lady? Or to an abruptly compromised preacher? I think Joey managed something like, 'Have you seen a dog around here?' Something not at all capturing the moment."

"What did the other two say?" I was laughing now.

"Well, Mrs. Adams quickly got some feet under her and snatched her discarded clothing to use as a shield. She said nothing coherent, just some strange babbling, mixed in with a low, shrieking noise."

"And the preacher?"

"Joey and I laughed about that for years. When someone is caught *in flagrante*—that's the technical term for it, you know—they generally have to say two things. The first is easy; the second very difficult." Owen had a sly look about him.

"I'll bite, Owen," I laughed. "What's the first?"

"They say, 'This isn't what you think.' That's the easy part."

"And the hard part?"

"What they say next." We both laughed.

"So, how does it end?" I asked.

"Luckily, Pixie provided an out for everyone. She suddenly appeared, off to our side, amongst the trees. I hollered, 'There she is,' and Joey and I took off in chase."

"And the sight of a naked lady and her pastor scarred you for life?" I asked.

"Well, I suppose Joey and I could've risen above that scene, all right, but think about it—two kids see two respected people consorting naked in the wild. All of a sudden, sex—illicit, forbidden sex—is up close and personal. When did you see your first naked lady? Then, there's all that business about respect for your elders—a preacher, no less—and a woman who once helped you unstick the zipper on your corduroy pants.

These weren't strangers. Cordell is a small town. We still had to go to school and see Mrs. Adams every day. One or the other of us encountered the preacher in stores or on the street. It took awkward to a whole new arena."

"Did either of them ever say anything else about the incident?" I inquired.

"Not Mrs. Adams," Owen chuckled. "She'd never look directly at me when I had to go into the school office. For my part, I acted as if the whole thing never happened.

Now the preacher was a different story. I didn't go to his church, so that was no issue. But, of course, I'd run into him about town. He did stop me once and started one of those adult-to-child lectures about secrets. He was embarrassingly poor at it, and condescending. I cut him off at the kneecaps—which I'd already seen. Told him that his little secret was probably safe with me... I was sure to use 'probably'. I said I didn't want to talk about it, so let me alone. We left it at that. Joey told me of a similar experience.

"And the tryst was never exposed, so to speak?"

"Nope. But the preacher was long gone about five years later. Seems he had a real fondness for other men's wives. One of those little dalliances cost him his job as a Bible thumper. Resigned from the church one day, left the next."

It still was early afternoon, but I had a sense Owen was packing in the storytelling for the day. I shuffled about, getting ready to take my leave, when a pickup truck dragging an open trailer with a little Bobcat strapped up top pulled into the gravel. A minute later, a small, mud-caked, whiskery old codger entered.

"Hello, Moses," Owen said from our table. "You did the Weldon funeral today?"

"Hey." The old-timer took a stool at the bar. "I just put Claudia tits-up an hour ago."

Owen rose and passed behind the bar. "Want a beer, huh?"

"Yep." Owen drew a draft for Moses.

"I heard she passed," Owen said matter-of-factly. "Nice funeral?"

"Nice enough, I guess," Moses replied. "Most of Claudia's friends are already waiting for her, so the crowd was small. The preacher said Bible things; no mention of her big tits."

Owen looked over at me and grinned. "Moses here—that is, Moses Doyle—is our local gravedigger." Moses and I nodded at each other. "Comes from a long line of gravediggers, don't you, Moses?"

"Yep. My grandfather and father dug graves—with shovels. I use my backhoe now. Still the same thing. Dig a hole, wait for the prayer, fill the hole. Me and my forefathers have done it forever."

Moses had one of those distinctive, musical voices. There was an amusing Irish lilt in there, but it was muttered through tight lips and a mouth that was missing at least four front teeth. An Irish brogue, for sure, but a singsong rasp with a hiss… the kind of utterances that make you laugh, serious topic or not.

Moses looked at me. "We're Irish, you see. We take death very seriously. We're a sorry and sorrowful group, we Irish. 'Twas us who brought the American Way of Death to this land. 'Twas us who invented the wake; 'twas us that learned to drink our way through it. 'Twas us who knew how to mourn our departed. Oh, yeah, we Irish know how to deal with the dead."

Moses knocked off his first draft in three easy gulps. Asked for a second, sipped it a bit. He and Owen reviewed the deceased and her family. Finished, Moses said goodbye on his way out. No money had changed hands.

Owen came back to what had become our storytelling table. "Owen, you didn't charge Moses for his beer. Do you give away most of your inventory?"

"No, 'course not. I give away a beer now and then. Lucky for you, huh?

Some guys deserve a beer. How'd you like to be the town gravedigger? Not real rewarding, uplifting work—no pun intended. Surrounded by death and weeping relatives. Putting people you know in the ground, but not really part of the ceremony. Dealing with death as a living. Ah, Moses deserves a free beer now and again.

He usually comes in here after he fills in someone's resting spot. I guess he needs a drink afterward… some sort of coping thing. Besides, we honor the dead here. Often happens to be one of our customers. 'So, here's a glass to you.'

Moses is kind of the flip side to Stonekicker Bob. Bob says little, has all these odd tendencies and paranoid behaviors. Moses, on the other hand, speaks right up, says things in creative, colorful ways. As Irish as the potato. Sure, he's a bit weird—unique, like Bob. Just does his thing differently. Unlike Bob, Moses is a participant in the life around him; unfortunately he has the ugly, sad, black side of it.

I think his offbeat reflections disassociate him from the job. If you're as near death and grieving as often as Moses is, it helps to trivialize a serious deal. Moses' musings seem to toss off death and loss, almost as a clever remark, but I think he's just protecting himself from feeling. I get that.

Moses always has some really novel, strange description of what he does. He never 'buries' people. He 'started a worm farm today,' 'he put someone on the other side of the grass,' 'he made someone a root inspector,' 'he made a boxed lunch out of someone.' Brand new, every time.

Most often, Moses' comment applies to some personality trait or behavior of the deceased. That makes the whole thing funnier. That, and his funny voice.

I think that, and a beer or two, keeps him at it. For my part, not much to give."

"Sounds about right, Owen," I assented. "A lousy job. Wonder what those guys who empty septic tanks or slaughter cattle say?"

"Same kind of stuff, I'd bet. Now this might strike you as odd. But, after a while, after you hear Moses referring to his role in funerals in such crazy ways, the whole thing becomes a local joke. One night—I'll bet it was twenty years ago—a room full of Ticket's Associates started laughing about Old Moses' references to the burial process.

Now Pete Monroe, our town barber, spends a lot of time in here. That night, he established himself as the official Moses imitator."

"Yes, I know the name," I told him. "Ross told me about the practical joker."

"Well, Pete started quoting some of Moses' greatest lines. Not only that, Pete can mimic Moses' morbid manner of delivery and quirky voice so well that my regulars just love to hear him do it. Been doing it ever since.

"Pete has Moses down to a tee. Many a night, our crowd eggs on Pete. 'Tell about your day, Moses.' 'Hey, Pete, tell Bill what Moses said the other day.' Pete, on command, would assume center stage.

"Later on, someone started a list of Moses' pronouncements, so Pete could do a dozen in a row. I keep that list under the bar for him. In fact, I ought to add that tits-up thing to it."

"Owen, I'd love to see that."

Owen retrieved the greasy old legal stock and slid it under my nose. I laughed out loud, and I didn't even know the departed.

> *Elsie Stambach will need a stepladder to pick her turnips this year.*
>
> *I just put gabby old Iris Links in a horizontal phone booth.*
>
> *Old Harry will be having his mail delivered by moles from now on.*
>
> *If ever there was a dead beet, it is Allen Merrow.*
>
> *Claire Huffman is in a grave situation.*
>
> *Well, Owen, you won't have to run Ken Kinlaw out of here anymore. He just answered last call.*
>
> *I checked Mrs. Orner, our world traveler, into the Wooden Waldorf today.*
>
> *Old man Star is the meat of the day at the coffinteria.*
>
> *I had to hurry Harry Winston into the ground today—get him there before the Devil finds out he's dead.*
>
> *Blanche Traini no longer works at the café. She'll be cooking for the Kennedys now.*

If there are no such things as zombies, we won't see Ward Jenkins again.

I gave Stella Douglas a suite with no view today.

I moved Matt McCarty into his bone home this morning.

Louis Debeer bought a pine condo this morning.

Well, O'Shura finally kicked his oxygen habit today.

I laid "One More Wilber" down for a dirt nap this morning.

Score another one for the Grim Reaper; I sent him a package today.

The gossip Frieda Hammaker has a mouthful of dirt she can't spread now

I planted Teddy Felts in Fertilization Square this morning.

Wanda Fairchild is now fully committed to pushing daisies.

Owen cackled. "If you could hear Pete say these the way Moses does, you'd be on the floor."

"I've gotta have this, Owen," I begged.

"I'll make you a copy. Now, you done for a while?"

"Done."

I left.

I napped for two hours, had dinner at the cafe, wandered about town, and went over to Ticket's. Bob entered as he finished his daily ritual. We both drank two beers. He showed me his stone. Both of us were in our beds before 10:00. I didn't see Owen.

CHAPTER TWENTY

Amazing Grace

I arrived at Ticket's the next morning so late that Bob was already shuffling out. Owen got me coffee and poured tea for himself.

I wasn't going to mention Vietnam unless he did.

He didn't. Maybe three's the charm.

"Owen, let's do another famous Ticketonian," I suggested, adding. "I just made up that word."

"Catchy," he remarked. Then, "Brush," he said. "We should talk more about Brush."

"Go."

"Of course 'Brush' was not his given name. His real name was Abraham Q. Washington. His mother was on a patriotic high when Brush was born in 1908. Bess was a black woman of infinite optimism in America. She'd married the son of a former slave, and the two of them moved out here from South Carolina. She'd grown up a free woman, but she knew about the pre-war days. As a young lady, she believed racial equity was just around the corner. She already had the name Washington to offer her new son. She added Abraham for the obvious reason, but the Q. is kind of quirky.

She knew of only one Q in American history, but he was a founding father. Good enough. So poor Brush got stuck with an elevated moniker.

It didn't matter, though. When the Washingtons settled in Cordell, Brush was born in The Acre. After school, he started to paint houses, indoors and out. He was good at it. His friends took to calling him 'Brush.' The name just stuck, is all.

Brush spent many of his evenings in here, not that he was a big drinker. He was a family man, but said that his little wood shanty in The Acre was crowded, what with the wife and three kids. So, after he got everyone settled down, he'd walk in, sip a beer or two, and talk with Noah. They became enduring friends.

Over the next fifty years, he worked for all of us—Noah, George, and me. Brush Washington just became part of the family business.

Brush was the perfect employee. Never tried to be special, but was always around any important happening. Never the center of anything, but always helping it form. You know, there's no center if there isn't something around it. Well, Brush was around it.

He liked the background. When he started working here, sometime in the thirties, he naturally became the bar back. Noah tended the customers, while Brush refilled the ice bin, replaced beer kegs, cut garnishes, washed glasses, all that stuff. On really busy nights, Brush would take care of the people at the far end, but only a few. He did the same for my dad and me.

I think he liked the backbar duties better… not because he was shy, or ever at a loss for words. Brush could shoot the breeze with about anybody, and on most topics. He was clever, and witty, and up on current events, but never haughty or arrogant or loud about it. He was subtle, with a quiet, steady voice… humble.

One night he said to Noah, 'This place needs a paint job. Look at this beautiful bar, and this wonderful floor, but then at those walls. Look at that ceiling. Pretty lights hanging down from patched plaster that's never been painted.'

'Hmm,' Noah said. 'Never got to it. Never wanted to spring for it.'

You know what happened next. Brush talked Noah into painting the whole place. They agreed on green… a calming hue, I'm told. For the most part it, must've worked.

Anyway, Brush painted, top to bottom. But you know what? When he came to those bullet holes over there, he couldn't bring himself to cover them. 'Too much history there,' he said. Painted right around them, so that bullet and jagged edge still show.

Over the years, we've had many bartenders in here. My dad, during his heyday, had about four guys at any one time. But Brush was the first lieutenant. He came to take over the scheduling of barkeeps, the cleaning schedule, the management of supplies, the chores. Learned it all from Noah. Did it for me, too."

"So, whatever happened to him?" I asked.

"He died, just like everyone else did, or will. July 4, 1976—can you imagine? His mother would've been ecstatic with his timing, super patriot that she was.

I have to tell you, I think of Brush about every day, one way or another."

"Like the shooting of Gus Driver—Brush and the trusty shotgun, huh?" I suggested.

Yeah, that, but more," Owen replied. "Around 1972 or '73, Brush was working for me, the third Ticket. In fact, he usually called me Three. He comes in one day and says it's time to repaint the place. Hadn't been done since Noah's time. Gave me the same story he gave Noah, about the unique bar and the wonderful floor.

This time, he used that lighter shade on the door trims and baseboard. Painted the wall behind the mirrors in a slightly darker shade. Looked great when it was new. But when he got to the bullet holes, he did the same thing he did the first time—painted around them.

"Do you have any stories about Brush?"

"Sure, but typical of Brush, he was never the main character—always appeared in someone else's story. Never the center attraction, understand? Except that night when he was holding the chambered shotgun and everyone was looking at him. Still, he could make things happen; his influence in Cordell was significant. He was always in on the bigger thing.

Our Ticket Associates—that's what our regulars came to call themselves, not Ticketonians—included shopkeepers and working stiffs, many from The Acre. Of course, most of them were poor; maybe mill workers, timber beasts, old trappers, and railroad hands, unemployed. Mostly Irish, but immigrants from everywhere... white, black, Asian, Mexican. A rather rough-cut crowd, although their behavior in here was generally good.

At the time, folks from both sides of the tracks mingled comfortably at Ticket's… always been that way. While no bar in Cordell was ever blatant about prejudice to Acre residents, there was a certain, unmentioned tone that the desired client base did not include Acre folks, especially blacks.

But Noah, and the next two of us, always welcomed everyone. Ticket's had no social, racial, or economic client base. Brush's presence in the bar certainly was a signal to everyone about that. We sold spirits to anyone of age.

Brush was an invisible link among our mixed crowd. White town folk knew Brush, liked him, had him painting in their homes, and chatted with him in Ticket's. Meanwhile, Brush's roots were so deep in The Acre that no one dared call him an Uncle Tom.

I was in George's bar one day when the town council president observed that Brush was smart, and really up on important current events. 'A knowledgeable fellow, that one,' Harold declared. Dad heard in Harold's tone and insinuation that Harold didn't provide the real ending to his pronouncement: 'for a black man.'

"'Don't get it wrong, Harold.' My dad replied. 'Don't confuse knowledge with wisdom. Knowledge is realizing that the tomato is really a fruit, not a vegetable. Wisdom is knowing not to put it in a fruit salad. Lots of us are knowledgeable. Brush is wise. Our town is better served by wise men.'

"Brush did plenty for our sizable black community—well, all minorities, really. Did it all from 'stage left,' as they say in the theatre business.

In the early fifties, the high-school kids were still performing minstrel shows—in blackface, of course—for the community's entertainment. Without making a big fuss about it, Brush mentioned to George that this nasty mimicry was hurtful to blacks, insulting, and disrespectful. It was time for Cordell to realize the racial implications of minstrel shows. It wouldn't be long before there'd be reason enough to halt the practice. Something ought to be reconsidered here.

Brush had just posted an early warning flag.

George got the point. Perhaps, as so many whites, he'd never even thought about the racial inanity of the shows. It was just American humor, nothing pointedly racist. But then, of course, he wasn't black. Dad had no sensitivities toward race, positive or negative. But, after his enlightenment through Brush, a bulb went on in Dad's head.

Forthwith, he met with the school principal and, without mentioning Brush, shared his concerns about the shows. He offered at least three other choices for showcasing student artistry.

To his everlasting credit, the principal agreed, right there and then. George was known for wisdom, too. I guess the light bulb in the schoolman's head also went on. The principal said he'd take this advice and his personal and professional support to the next school board meeting. He did, and he must've done it well. Without fanfare or comment, the last minstrel show in Cordell had already been performed.

Brush certainly influenced the actions of Acre residents when racial issues were breaking out across the nation in the sixties. Older by this time, Brush's dignity, reserve, and leadership were respected in The Acre.

He spoke against violence and public disruption. He asked his neighbors what they'd gain from burning their own streets or The Boulevard, marauding about as if there was real personal or racial gain from such action. Brush wanted racial equality as much as any. His mother had thought she already had it. But violence would only inflame the town, not move it toward the needs of the minority community.

Sure, Brush agreed with his neighbors that things needed to be changed. Certainly a pretense played in Cordell. Cordell residents pretended there weren't any problems, because we didn't openly exhibit any. There were no separate water fountains, inadequate voter registration, limited employment opportunities, and social separateness.

But both blacks and whites harbored deep-seated prejudice not shown in daily activity; there was still a great divide in our town, subtle though it was. Brush's take was that whites certainly 'didn't get it,' but their views were the stuff of ignorance, not malice. And that's what needed to be addressed.

Brush believed lasting change could only be built on awareness, not violence. Brush advocated a sense of relationship, not confrontation.

His word was taken to heart by most Acre folks. While other American cities burned, Cordell residents met in Ticket's, and local churches, and the town hall to discuss racial issues without conflict. In the background were always Abraham Q. Washington and George Ticket. Both deserve statues in the town park."

"The voice of reason, not the hammer of justice," I summarized.

"Yeah, I guess that's one way of putting it." Owen thought a moment.

"Without credit, Brush did as much for this community regarding race and socio-economic relations as anyone, except maybe for Grace Campbell. But that's the other story, even though Brush figures in that one as well."

"I'd like to hear it. Give me a second to get my notes straight."

"Grace Campbell, a slightly swollen-bellied lass, warily entered my dad's saloon, brimming with tears. It had to be 1948, because I was almost four years old at the time, and I know the age difference between Grace and me. So I know only what I've been told. The night of Grace's appearance, Ticket's was very busy—three-deep at the bar, tables full, and people about the middle.

The circus was in town, by accident. The caravan was on its way to Portland from the south, but the locomotive developed engine problems, and the train limped into Cordell sounding like a John Deere tractor.

When it was determined that the train was going nowhere for two days or more, awaiting repairs, Cordell suddenly had a full-blown circus on its hands. The town was filled with high-wire walkers, clowns, animal trainers, and all the other carnies.

The owners—maybe the Sells Brothers, but I'm not sure—decided the show must go on. Cordell had all that land right behind The Strip here, and the circus owner offered to put on two shows in one day if he were charged only the smallest of fee. Within a few hours, they'd organized their pre-show parade of stilt-walkers, elephants, and scantily-clad lion trainers. Word passed quickly up and down the Deschutes, and the next day, Cordell hosted its circus

It was an economic boon for both the stranded circus and local businesses. Lots of people in town, lots of excitement, lots of money floating across all the bars and store counters. My dad and Brush worked triple shifts. Even Noah came in to draw beers. Ticket's made a lot of money that day. Actually ran out of scotch and birch beer. Not beer, though. Dad would never let that happen.

Anyway, the matinee and evening shows went off well. The Strip was jumping. Late that evening, just as things were starting to slow down, in walked meek Grace Campbell.

Unkempt and grimy from circus work, she stopped at the bullnose. Disheveled hair, tattered old shirt, and men's pants, she smelled of animals and holding pens. But she was a pretty little waif, with auburn hair, freckles that were going to last forever, and street-smart, penetrating eyes... a miserable version of Little Orphan Annie, my dad told me. She looked older and wiser that her eighteen years, even though a naive decision currently had her in dire straits.

George saw her first—barkeeps know how to watch a door. He motioned to Brush to stay behind the bar. George walked over and asked if he could provide her any service.

It all just poured out of her. She worked in the circus; she was tending the livestock, or some grunt job like that. And she was pregnant. Pregnant to a magician who'd beguiled her with fantasies of marriage and money, a great future built on his enormous talent. Except that when she found herself with child, he immediately denied all responsibility. In fact, he told her that he had no reason to believe he was the only possible father. Then he exited the train, and the circus, down in Bend. And here she was, alone and penniless. She also knew that when her condition became an impediment to her job, the circus would cut her loose. Could anybody help her?

Gentle George Ticket responded with hope, if not idea. He told her that Cordell would find a place for her She needed to trust him to work out some details, although at the time he didn't have a clue how that might be accomplished.

An unwed mother carried a social stigma in the forties, especially in small towns like Cordell. Helping Grace get along wasn't going to be easy. But George couldn't just turn her out, either. She'd come to Ticket's for help, and he was going to provide it.

Beyond that, George later said that he was struck with an odd sense from the moment he laid eyes on her. He often played the prophet in the bar; it was a standing joke. His notion was, once solved, Grace's crisis was going to be Cordell's gain. 'Weird,' Dad said, 'but I just had this feeling. True or not, somebody needed to help this girl.'

George put Grace at a table with a ginger ale and huddled with Brush. What to do with her? Where could she go for bed and breakfast? He couldn't take her home—he had a young son there, with a problem or two. His small house wasn't going to accommodate two women with babies born, or almost so. Besides, in Cordell, that would cause a stir, another taproom scandal.

Certainly the little gal couldn't afford a boarding-house room. George Ticket couldn't cover that, and have tongues wagging over it. Not fair to his wife or his business.

Brush solved the problem in one stroke. 'I'll take her to my place,' he said. 'No one cares what happens in The Acre. My wife will care for her. She can sleep in the living room for a night or two. Give us some time to work this out.'

A bit guilty, but grateful, George agreed.

And that's how the love affair between Grace and the town of Cordell started. Grace took up residence in The Acre. She ended up staying with the Washingtons for months, her pregnancy monitored by Mrs. Washington. They burned her vile work clothes and cobbled together a wardrobe of hand-me-downs and home-sewn dresses that allowed for her condition.

Amelia Cortez took her to her front-room beauty shop and re-styled her hair. A midwife, Bente Bishop, oversaw her prenatal care, and later delivered the baby.

By this time, Grace had pretty much been adopted by the populace of The Acre. People treated her well, with no signs of prejudice, malice, or moral judgment. The new baby, a girl named Rebecca, gathered a crowd when Grace rolled her through The Acre in a wobbly, battered baby carriage.

At first, of course, Grace was the topic of gossip and sniping downtown. Heads and tongues wagged about this young, obviously immoral girl moving into a black household. 'What must be going on there? Why do all those drunks over at Ticket's take such an interest in her? Have you seen her? She's as big around as she is tall. It's just wrong.'

But George was right on the money with his premonition about Grace. She was going to be good for Cordell, and slowly, people started to realize it, begrudgingly or not.

After Rebecca's birth, Grace never again showed weakness, misery, shame, or guilt. She'd push that carriage down The Boulevard with her head held high, smiling at everyone she met. As they do, women wanted to admire the baby. But soon they found themselves talking with Grace and telling her about their own lives. She had this way of making people think their lives were much more important than anyone else's. People often said that, after talking with Grace, they always felt better about themselves.

You couldn't help but like her. She had this... well... this grace about her. Maybe part of that was Grace's open acknowledgement of how this town had saved her and her Rebecca.

She started by doing any work she could find. She cleaned homes in The Wedge. She worked in the shirt factory, and afterward, watched three or four children, so their second-shift moms could go to work there or the bottling works.

Not long after Rebecca's birth, Grace got a lucky break. As you know, lucky breaks often come at someone else's expense. In this case, it came at Prinder's Café. Owned by Nevin Prinder and his wife, Susan, Prinder's was a going concern here on The Strip. Prinder had been here from the beginning. In fact, Ticket's had a natural relationship with them. People would go into Prinder's for a late breakfast or lunch, and then amble down The Strip to Ticket's for a few beers. They just moved their conversations down The Strip with them, and continued arguing most of the day away.

Well, about the time of Grace's arrival, Nevin Prinder developed cancer. He was dead ten months later. That put Susan Prinder in a real bad spot. She needed help in her café. She could do the cooking, all right, but she needed help to run the counter.

It turned out about the way you think. Susan hired Grace. More than that, she moved Grace out of The Acre, into the second floor of the café. That needed some remodeling, but Brush and his friends did all of that in about a week. With Witherspoon wood they turned the storage area into a two-bedroom apartment, with a small kitchen and living room. Brush painted the apartment and organized a furniture and appliance drive, right here in the bar.

Rebecca Campbell was a beautiful baby, a delightful child, and the object of affection of everyone in town. From the time she was seven years old, she worked in the café alongside her mother—just like George and I did with our fathers. Everyone in town knew her. Rebecca sort of became the town's child. People loved her warmth, charm, and work ethic. Leaf from a tree, I guess.

In high school, Rebecca was an A student and a fine athlete. She led our regional high school to the state championship title in field hockey—the only one ever won by our school in any sport, male or female. Of course, she was the homecoming queen, and boys about town pursued her relentlessly.

Rebecca received an academic scholarship to OU. Lives now in Portland, with a husband and three children. When she comes back to visit her mother, everyone still makes a fuss over her. Grace did a fine job.

All this time, Grace worked to repay the kindnesses once extended to her.

She faithfully attended a church, her little girl in tow. Served on various committees there, got involved in community projects, collected money for local fund-raisers and national charities. Any civic venture, Grace had a hand in it. She worked the concession stand at the Little League ball field and cajoled George into sponsoring a team. She continued to clean the homes of others, even while she kept long hours at the café. Her friendship with Susan and Mary Coldiron grew. Find one, find three. Grace was like the youngest sister. Those three were the most refined, the most respected ladies in town. Grace's standing in the community escalated.

No men, though. That was Grace's decision. Always pretty, she grew into statuesque woman who, commonly dressed and modestly made up, turned male heads about town. What can I say? Quietly feminine, exquisitely modest, fiercely devoted to Rebecca, reliable in the cafe and community involvements. Took classes at night school, a few college-level correspondence courses, read good books. She was living a second-chance life without a man about, and she was just fine with that.

So Grace never married. In fact, she never intended to marry—probably some deep-seated mistrust of men, although she never said that. She would go out with some of the locals to dances at the fire hall, or the movies, or dinner at the hotel. But clearly, she wasn't looking for some long-term commitment, and I'm sure that even the best of our young bucks couldn't really think otherwise.

So, Grace wandered in here and made a life for herself and her daughter. Then, in 1957, she made a life for some others that this town has never forgotten.

I know it was 1957, because that was the year of the Asian flu. That epidemic killed almost 100,000 Americans—not as many as the 1917 flu, but more than the later Hong Kong flu."

"I've noticed something, Owen," I broke in. "You have a great memory for dates and details, don't you?"

"I do," he agreed. "Some people remember one kind of thing or another—who was somewhere, what was said, how someone talked, acted, or dressed… history, science, trivia, what have you. Me, I remember times—when, the year or decade, sometimes the month, or the hour of the day… no big deal. I know a guy who can tell you who won the '86 Sugar Bowl, the score, and the big play."

"True. Still, what with our jumping around the century, putting a year on things is helpful," I pointed out.

"I'm so glad you like my storytelling style," Owen said sarcastically.

Let's move along. While this is really Grace's story, Brush, from the background, figured in that little drama.

The Asian flu hit Cordell hard. Actually it hit The Acre hard. The poor always get the first wave of anything bad, don't they? First and worst. Everybody over there seemed to get it. Sickness in every house. Men couldn't work; women couldn't prepare food for their children, kids not in school, no money coming in, no medical care, and no help at all.

During that season, no one wanted anything to do with anybody else. People pretty much avoided each other. People changed sides of the street if they saw someone from The Acre on The Boulevard. Factories wouldn't allow workers to come in. Shops closed. Schools closed. It was a tough time.

Enter Grace. She still worked at the café. Grace, just as anyone might expect, decided to help her longtime friends in The Acre. They'd once saved her, hadn't they?

So, with Susan's approval, Grace started making chicken and tomato soup in the café kitchen and driving it through The Acre, giving a quart or two to the afflicted. Walked right into the homes, fed the soup to some, straightened up the kitchens or changed the sheets—whatever she could. She moved about The Acre as if she were impervious to the flu. She was a godsend.

But alone, she couldn't do enough. The flu was spreading like wildfire. Brush quickly got wind of the story. He told Dad that he was going to help Grace's mission of mercy.

He was going to need some time off work. George agreed to that. 'We'll take care of the place,' he said. 'Flu has thinned out our crowd, anyway. I'll get Ralph to take more hours, and I'll cover the rest. I'll pay you as if you were here. Take the time you need to do what you have to do,' he said.

Around town, housewives heard of Grace's mission, and they started contributing to it. Grace would open the café in the morning to find a fresh loaf of homemade bread or more soup, or some cookies, or a fruit salad, or some canned meat. No names… just the donations.

Grace and Brush spent the next week distributing food in The Acre.

But then Jimmy the Was got involved. Of course, he knew what those two were doing. He talked with Brush about how much more was really needed. Remember, we're talking epidemic here. The Acre was just one large disaster area of sickness. Grace and Brush were meeting only a slice of The Acre's needs.

About two weeks into the siege, a huge, green box truck pulled up in front of Ticket's. No name on it... just a Washington license plate. Two men crawled out and threw up the rear door. I happened to be washing tabletops that morning, while my dad was prepping for the lunch crowd, and I went out to the walk to see what unexpected delivery we were receiving.

That truck was stacked with food, blankets, medicines, toilet paper, towels, cleaners, soaps, and whatnot.

But the food—frozen chickens, hot dogs, and beef roasts, canned soups and vegetables, sacks of flour, potatoes, onions, and carrots. Crates of eggs and boxes of cereal, bags of noodles, packages of spaghetti, sticks of cheese, sugar, mustard... you name it.

It finally hit me. This was Jimmy's work. This stuff was going to The Acre.

And it did.

In a few minutes, Jimmy arrived. He explained nothing to my dad; he just started telling the men what to unload to our back wall and what to leave on the truck. Then he asked George if I was available for the afternoon. It was a rhetorical question. I got in Jimmy's car, and the truck followed us down most streets in town.

When we turned into a neighborhood, Jimmy parked the car and went to the back of the truck. The four of us would grab some flour, a chicken or two, some noodles, or whatever Jimmy had in mind.

We just walked up to every home and knocked. When the lady of the house appeared, she'd immediately recognize Jimmy. Everybody knew him by name, reputation, or previous dealings. Without introduction, Jimmy would say, 'We're taking food up to The Acre. We need your help. Please take this flour and make us some bread for those sick people—or roast this chicken, or make this soup, or bake these potatoes'—whatever he wanted. Then he'd say, 'We need this on Tuesday by eleven a.m. Not Wednesday, not Monday, not whenever. We need it Tuesday, so it's fresh, and goes with what else goes over there on Tuesday. Just take it to Prinder's; no need for you to go into The Acre. Grace and Brush will get it there.' He wasn't asking, he was telling.

The two guys and I would hand over the raw ingredients. Not one lady had a question. Each just said it would be done. We weren't waiting for any response, anyway. It was all pretty much matter-of-fact. We went from house to house like that for hours. Jimmy would tell one lady Tuesday, the next Wednesday, the next Monday. He had all these meals planned in his head, so he ordered the bread, the meat, the soup, the pie, whatever, for when he wanted it.

Do I have to tell you that the thing went like clockwork? Food all over the café sidewalk before noon. Brush would pull up in his old blue Ford pickup, and he and Grace would load up all the day's offerings, sometimes making three or four trips a day. They'd roll through The Acre like strawberry vendors, stopping long enough that each could run food into the homes. Sometimes Grace would duck inside to help someone with a chore or two. Brush would stop long enough to gather up debris or toys left in the yard, or mow the small patches of grass between two homes. Total disregard for their own exposure to the Asian flu. Amazingly, neither ever contracted it. And not one Cordell resident died of it.

They spent every afternoon like that for three weeks, till some folks there were well enough to help themselves and each other.

While she kept the café going, Susan Prinder was mostly packaging up food into family-sized servings. Carved out roasts, ladled soup, bagged paper products. And Jimmy and several volunteers helped, too. Mary Coldiron simply closed her shop for about two hours a day to organize deliveries from Prinder's.

This all may sound like just another heartwarming story, but I assure you that it went far beyond that. For the first time ever, scores of town people were engaged in an organized endeavor to do a good deed for the less fortunate. Many downtown citizens contracted the flu, just as anyone else. But the impact was just less, and they knew it. The Acre was certainly the worst in terms of size, numbers, and proportions.

In some ironic way, the Asian flu was the best thing to happen to this town. As people pulled together, the cultural separation of Cordell proper from the folk in The Acre just seemed to disappear. The railroad tracks just didn't divide the two so much. For a while, at least, The Acre lost its stigma as the wrong side of town. Oh, yes, it still was home to the poorest among us, but its residents were no longer second-class citizens who did the grunt work of this town as the social underbelly. Beyond being just the help, the impoverished, the low-life, residents of The Acre were now imperiled families, prone to sickness beyond their control, too, and thankful, too, for help provided in desperate times.

There was a connection forged from these dark days that improved the community relationships across all of Cordell.

Grace Campbell became a Cordell hero, or, what—heroine? For that matter, so did Susan, Mary, Brush, and Jimmy, too. But each of these were on their way, anyway. Their behavior was just what most of us might've expected.

But Grace… Grace became a goddess in this town. The sanctimonious who had fed off her early, outcast life couldn't say enough good about her—her willingness to step up, her perilous persistence, and her compassion simply led to sainthood status in the high plains.

Grace Campbell is still revered in this town. Jimmy once said something about her that I've never forgotten: 'Grace doesn't just belong, she participates. She doesn't just care, she helps. She doesn't just believe, she practices.' I think that pretty much sums her up.

And in The Acre! Most of those sick folks may have long forgotten the kindnesses that they and Brush's family had shown Grace. But none are likely to forget her personal repayment of that debt. When Grace goes over to The Acre now, she's treated as the second coming.

About twenty years ago, when The Acre was growing itself onto a new street, guess what they named it? 'Grace.' Not Grace Street, not Grace Avenue, not Grace Boulevard, not Grace Way—'Grace.' It starts at the corner where Brush's little house sits, and angles toward the foothills. When it grows southeast, it'll cut right through the old strip, across the tracks, and end up at the Deschutes. I'll be dead by then, but I wish I could see that."

"Whatever happened to Grace?" I inquired.

"She's still alive. Lives now in the small house she shared with Mary Coldiron, who inherited it from her parents. After Prinder's Café was razed and Mary sold her shop to a pizza chain, the two ladies lived together for years. Mary died several years ago. Grace is about ninety or so. There are no more sumptuous Christmas or Easter dinners than Grace and Rebecca prepare. That's where I spend both holidays—with several residents from The Acre."

"I'd like to meet Grace," I said.

"I'll set it up. Like with Kimo."

Owen made the call.

"I trust you like crumpets," he said. "You're invited to afternoon tea."

CHAPTER TWENTY-ONE

Tea For Two

With minimal directions from Owen, I found the indomitable Grace Campbell's tidy home off The Boulevard.

I was expecting to meet an octogenarian in frumpy clothes, hair in a bun, wan skin, wearing a house dress with polyester sweater, sensible shoes, maybe even rolled-up stockings. I guess I expected a frail old woman who might have difficulty thinking of words or staying on topic.

I wasn't even close.

Grace Campbell was stylish, without glitz. She sported a contemporary hairstyle, nuanced with just a bit of coloring in her gray hair. She wore a trendy, hazy-blue dress with a scarf about her neck, sapphire nail polish with silver cuticles, a huge ring with a matching aquamarine bracelet, and low-heeled pumps. There was an understated elegance about her.

With a warm welcome and some questions about my time in Cordell, she ushered me into a pleasant front-window parlor. No small talk about the weather or "forgive the mess." We both knew there was no mess; I could see that from the foyer.

The house was clean and tastefully decorated. No crowding of overstuffed furniture… there was a sense of openness, though the house was small.

We chatted. There was vim in her projection: animated conversation, bright eyes, quick movements. I was struck by her genuine charm. As she brought forth the silver tea service, we settled in easily.

"Owen tells me I might figure in a book you're planning. Please tell me about it," she invited.

I related my chance meeting with Owen, how one thing had led to another, and how fascinated I now was with Cordell. I listed some of Owen's stories, from Franklin Cordell and John Witherspoon forward.

"And all of that has brought Owen and me to your arrival and impact on this town."

"Impact on this town!" she protested. "I didn't impact this town; it impacted me—saved me, really."

"Yes, I know that part," I assured her. "Owen says the people of Cordell think highly of you—especially regarding your efforts during the famous flu."

"Oh, that Owen... he flatters me," she chuckled. "He had a boyhood crush on me."

"A crush, you say? He hasn't mentioned that to me."

"Oh, he wouldn't," she assured me. "I'm sixteen or seventeen years older than Owen, but from the time he was a little boy, he was over the moon about me. His dad, George, would've certainly spoken kindly of me, and Owen picked up on that and more, I suppose. For my part, I viewed Owen as my younger brother. After all, his father always treated me as a daughter. We were all very close that way.

"Owen always had that puppy love for me that I could never return—nor would I have ever led him on. I was older, and his family had been good to me. At the time, I thought that any encouragement to Owen's feelings for me would've been wrong."

Grace studied me for a moment. She apparently decided she could trust me.

"I'll tell you this, Ed, in confidence. Were things different then, if it weren't for that age difference, if Owen's life had turned outward instead of inward, if his father hadn't been such a father figure to me, I would've considered Owen. He's one of the finest men I know. For that matter, everyone at Ticket's was. I owe them so much."

Surprised, I asked, "Does Owen know you know about his crush? 'If things were different?' Does he know about that?"

"He must know I know," she said. "Kids don't hide feelings too well. I never did or said anything about my own feelings... no use going down a road that leads nowhere. It would've just made him more miserable. At the time, he was miserable enough."

"I'll say nothing about it," I agreed. "But I'm here for your stories."

"Perhaps about Owen himself? I'll bet this tea set that he hasn't told you much about himself, has he?"

"Well, he told me about Vietnam, and his dogs, and his lineage—that's something."

"The Vietnam thing is a surprise to me," Grace said, raising an eyebrow. "He's never said much about that. He must trust you. I know of his terrible experience, because his dad told me when Owen was going through his rough patch."

Grace stopped for a few moments. Then, "I'll bet he didn't tell you about Rita, though."

"Rita?" My ears perked up. *There's a story here,* I thought. *Is she going to tell it?*

"Rita Norwood. The only romance in his life, discounting that halo he put above my head."

"Owen never married," I pointed out. "What happened with Rita Norwood?"

"A sad story with two terrible endings. Rita was the bank manager's daughter. She was an attractive—voluptuous, actually—high-spirited young thing. She was devilish, bright, and active. Young men swoon over such nubile delights, and she was constantly pursued.

Somehow though, the quiet and tame Owen became her choice, so that by the end of high school, they were a couple. I suppose she was impressed by his basketball skills and rugged good looks, but still, I found it an odd match. But slow-and-steady Owen wasn't quite ready to commit to something as big as marriage, and he kept forward progress at bay longer than she was willing to wait. Besides, she liked to socialize and carouse, and Owen just wasn't into that, as the kids say. While Owen was making haste slowly, Rita started seeing other lads behind his back.

Not behind the backs of others in town. Several of us knew she was sneaking around with other young bucks. When Owen went off to war, she didn't exactly sit at home waiting for the mail to arrive. She was out amongst the partying set. When he returned, wounded and somewhat at sea, she continued to slide off to the other side of the county.

Owen was stuck behind his father's bar, and suspected nothing. Everybody's somebody's fool, I guess. He was living in a much smaller world in those days, wrestling his own demons.

And then one night, Rita and her newest fling were up at The Dalles, nightclubbing and whatnot. On the way back to Cordell, that kid drove his Buick right off a bluff into the Deschutes. Both were killed.

Poor Owen. In one fell swoop he learned his girlfriend was dead and that she'd been cheating on him."

"Oh, man," I said, "all this right after Vietnam. Can you imagine what Owen was going through?"

"You had to imagine it, because Owen simply didn't talk about it," she said. "Any of it. If someone asked him about Rita's death, or the circumstances, or how he was doing, Owen responded with almost nothing—a shrugged shoulder, maybe. If asked about Vietnam, he'd say only, 'I was there, and now I'm back.'

"Even I couldn't penetrate his thinking, feelings, or anguish. I say 'Even I,' because George asked me to help in any way I could. George certainly knew of Owen's thing for me, and we both believed Owen might open up to me. But I got nowhere in several attempts. I guess cowboys only cry in the rain.

"Owen just cocooned himself. No one has the key to his own prison, or he wouldn't be there. That's how he dealt with Vietnam, and that's how he approached this tragedy… just wallowing around in some nether world. That he emerged as well as he did from the war and Rita, on the heels of one another, is a testament to Ticket resiliency.

"Still, of course, those two traumas changed Owen. He managed to escape bitterness, a descent into drugs or alcohol, or bad behavior. But he never tried love again, and he devoted whatever energies he had left into running the bar—being there all the time, he and his dogs. He'd act like those mongrels were just pets, but they really became his best friends… especially after Jimmy and Brush died.

Fortunately, the blackest cloud can only block the sun for so long. Owen hauled himself up. He's made his own way, and I respect him for it.

Now I wish to say this—the strongest steel is tempered at the highest heat. Dusk before dawn, and all that. Owen, locked in his bar, has experienced the joys of happy people and the throes of personal loss. His years behind that bar have provided extraordinary insight of human nature and the human condition. He's not a philosopher—too homespun, too practical, too taciturn for that. But he's blunt, keen-minded, wise, and instinctive.

But Owen has always flown close to the ground. I mean here that the Tickets have a wonderful history in this town, and Owen has borne his lineage very well. Quietly, he simply goes about his business, help-ing untold numbers of people, with no real recognition for his efforts.

Not that he expects any, of course. But it saddens me to know that most people don't even know who he is. If they do, they think of him as the old barkeep at that bar near The Acre. I regret to say that Cordell hasn't given Owen Ticket the recognition he deserves."

"Grace, I have a question," I interjected. "Did Owen ever have any interest in your daughter? He was only a few years older than she, and obviously, Rebecca would've had it all over the likes of this Rita. Why was there no spark there?"

Grace paused.

"Incest, I suspect… at least, in Owen's mind. Here's the thing: they grew up almost as sister and brother. Our families were—are—very close. George always watched out for me, as I've said… almost like a daughter. Then Owen had this crush on me. A turn toward Rebecca would've been too weird for him.

"We were all trapped in a mid-generational, interfamilial maze… too much baggage. At least, that's how I see it. It's a simplification to say that things are the way they are because they got that way. But the twisted-up, mixed-up, complicated relationship between the Camp-bells and the Tickets resulted in something we can't be surprised to see."

Another pause, another decision, and then Grace moved ahead.

"I have to tell you that you are correct about Rebecca. She was simply 'it' in Cordell. Everyone just adored her. Girls wanted to be like her; boys wanted to be with her. She's still the All-American girl. That's her college yearbook picture there, on the side table."

I'd already noticed it. Now I rose and regarded it more closely. A stunning, remarkable, blonde beauty. I said so.

"Yes, but this is my favorite picture of her." She went to the piano in the dining room and returned with a smaller picture of a little tyke on a little trike.

"This is the Rebecca I remember the most. And my granddaughter, Sydney, looks just like Rebecca did in this picture. Did I tell you that I'm a grandmother? Sydney is the brightest little child, and best softball pitcher in her age group. A special child, with her mother's spunky personality."

Grace returned to our previous topic. "I look back on that loss of spark, as you so aptly put it, as a real shame. Mighta, coulda, shoulda. Rebecca and Owen would've been a fine couple. But Owen's reluctance—well, Rebecca's, too, I guess—to abandon that almost filial relationship got in the way. Of course, I figured in that, too.

I'll bet Owen would say now that he and Rebecca should've given it a go. I see a forlorn and hopeless intimacy between them when we all gather for holidays.

You know, the most bitter tears we shed are those of regret… Owen and Rebecca and me."

"Well, I guess Rebecca turned out fine enough," I observed. "Nice family, great mom, a rich, full life."

"She did," Grace replied. "I think she's happy, except for this underlying tension with Owen, and the miserable experience she had with her father."

"The magician?" I asked. "She knows her father?"

"Since she was eighteen, a new, high-school graduate."

"I'm guessing that didn't work out well," I commented.

"Horribly, actually. But it was her choice, and she knows it."

Grace looked out the living room window, at Mount Hood. "Rebecca got this notion that she ought to meet her birth father. In her senior year, her history teacher got going on family trees—you know, genealogy. Why the schools do that kind of thing these days, with all the kids of split families, I don't know.

Anyway, her class was asked to see how far back they could go with their family trees. Of course, Rebecca was stopped after her grandparents on my side. Nothing on her dad's side except his name, Marvin Melchoir, stage name Marvelous Marv, the Greatest Magician of Our Time.

The assignment was embarrassing for her, but it also was intriguing. She became infatuated with the notion of finding Marv and meeting him.

She spent the summer after graduation, before she went off to OU, searching for her father. Hell-bent as she was, she didn't ask me if she could, she simply told me that she was going to find him. I was cool to the notion, but I realized there was no good that could come from impeding her quest. She's a stubborn girl, I promise you that.

She used the means available to her at the time. No internet, no name registry, no real clues upon which to build, except that she knew the circus had folded. She also knew that Marvin had departed the outfit in Bend.

She figured that he didn't follow his former employer north. She ruled out east, because it was just all prairie, no real place to ply his trade. South wasn't much better. So, Rebecca set her sights on western Oregon and northern California. Pretty good deduction, don't you think?"

"Excellent, I'd say," I replied. "I guess she found him?"

Grace nodded. "She did. Probably just luck, but Rebecca is the kind of person who would get lucky like that. Somehow, she got a list of performers created by entertainment bureaus, checked the magician category, found a guy named Marvin. She called several booking agencies as if she wanted to book him.

Sacramento. Rebecca found Marvelous Marv in Sacramento. She obtained a phone number, an apartment address, and his long-standing booking at a local revue.

And that's where she went to meet her father. She took the train, arrived in town, went to the club, and saw her father perform. Tired, typical magic tricks offered by an unmotivated old-timer, probably more drunk than sober." Grace stopped, studied the mountain again.

"And?" I nudged.

"And he hit on her. After the show, Rebecca sat down beside the wormy old fart—excuse me—and steeled herself to present her carefully prepared little introduction.

Before she could get a word out, Marv decided she was some groupie or had sexual designs on him, him being the legend in his mind that he was. He started in on her right away. Offered her the magic of a lifetime—a turn in his bed."

"No, no," I moaned.

"Yes. Rebecca looked at the son-of-a-bitch—excuse me again—and walked out without identifying herself. To this day, Marv doesn't know he was looking his daughter in the eye.

For her part, Rebecca was crushed. The dream of reuniting turned into a traumatic nightmare. She came home still shaking. I ached for her. We talked about it once or twice. But we haven't mentioned him since. Experience is what you get when you don't get what you want."

I used the brief lull to switch topics.

"Grace, I have an awkward question. Please don't take offense at this. But here's what I see. You came to this town in your own personal dilemma, young, pregnant, no man, uneducated, from the bowels of the circus—not a glamorous start. Yet here you are today, an accomplished lady and mother. People in this town adore you—you of flawless character and reputation. My heavens, they named a street after you. So here's the question: How did you overcome such a rough beginning to such an exalted standing?"

She blushed, humbled by the recognition. Someone once said that beauty without grace is a hook without bait. "That street naming thing," she protested, "I know who was behind all that: Abraham Q. Washington.

Ed, you are kind, but too generous. I've come a long way from that circus. What one makes of her life is determined by how she seizes the opportunities upon which she stumbles. Cordell provided me a life-saving opportunity. Let me restate that: George Ticket and Brush Washington provided me the opportunity to make something of my life.

"Owen speaks of your compassion for others."

"Ah, that Owen," she countered. "Let me tell you about compassion. Compassion is what I saw in George Ticket's eyes that night I was at the end of the line. Compassion is how I was treated in The Acre.

While I lived in The Acre, I'd hold my sweet Rebecca and realize my huge responsibility for her. Our survival was in my hands, and that meant getting a job and working hard at it. I owed Rebecca a quality life, and I owed this town—two debts I was going to make right.

I also decided that I was going to educate myself. The circus wasn't a great environment for formal learning. I was ignorant, barely could read, I had no social skills. I knew nothing about money, business, politics, sports, or entertainment.

The work part was easy. I cleaned houses. I was in the homes of people in this town whom I admired. I waitressed at the café. I was serving coffee to the most important people in town. I watched and listened to how they talked, and acted, and explained themselves. During my time in the circus, I was always taken by the ways of our ticket-holders. I envisioned myself in their lives, even as we were taking their money in our fake freak shows. But the circus had taught me hard and dirty work, and insight into human behavior. I could use all that, I thought. I scrabbled by.

For some kind reason, Mary Coldiron took me under her wing. She and I became close friends, really more like older and younger sisters. She invited my daughter and me to move into the small apartment above her shop after her parents died. She ran the shop and lived here, her family home. When she retired and closed the shop, Rebecca and I both moved into this house with her... a good arrangement for everyone. When she fell ill, she willed the property to me. And here I am. I've enjoyed some good luck."

"Maybe, Grace," I interjected. "My mother often told us children that the harder she worked, the luckier she got."

"I'm with her on that," she smiled. "I read once that luck is where preparation meets opportunity. It's certainly true in my own life. I worked hard. But I also tried to educate myself. I took adult education courses in the evenings at the high school. I read. Our local theatre has a tiny library off the anteroom, and Rebecca and I read the best of its meager collection. I studied the newspapers as if they were textbooks.

I spent time with Mary and Susan Prinder, two great modern women. I imitated people I liked. Believe it or not, I learned much from smooth-talking, self-made Jimmy Delotti. He was around a lot because of Mary.

When Rebecca was old enough, we four gals would go on little excursions to Portland. We would go to the movies to watch the stars, and to the tea rooms to observe the manners and ways of refined people. Sometimes we'd attend a play and any free concert.

And I got involved in every civic venture that would have me. I really became interested in causes.

Then I got an opportunity—more good luck, if you will. Raymond Witherspoon sold me—practically made me buy—a small ranch, for pennies on the dollar. He knew I didn't have much money, but he liked me. I'd cleaned for his wife, and he thought I was a good influence on his troublesome brother and sister, Bob and Charlotte. So, when he wanted to leave town, he fixed up Bob and Charlotte with a house and made me a crazy and low offer on the ranch. I sold that ranch two years later at considerable profit, and invested the money when one could still make money in the market.

And here we are today."

Grace was finished talking about Grace. Abruptly, she clapped her hands on her lap and said, "But enough about me. Let's get back to Owen."

"Fine," I agreed. "An interesting guy, Owen is. You've helped me understand some of his somberness and reserve. He's struggled, too, hasn't he, like the rest of us?"

"Certainly he has," she said. "And you are correct—'like the rest of us.' But I also think Owen has expected the very best from himself, and when he fails, it takes a greater toll on him than many of us deem necessary."

"You have an example of this, don't you, Grace?" I guessed.

"I do. And, as with the Rita affair, I don't think he'd share this with you. Again, I ask that you don't share my telling of it with him."

I won't." I was more and more surprised at how quickly Grace and I had developed this bond of disclosure. She certainly wasn't a busybody or a gossipmonger, I knew that. Yet, insightfully knowing the kind of things I was looking for, she was decidedly forthcoming, about both herself and one of her dearest friends. It was an impressive distinction.

"Here's the bottom line: Owen has always felt that his inaction cost a woman her life. To this day, he struggles with the notion that, given the opportunity to do the right thing, he didn't. It happened back to the 1970s.

"The 1970s. Please tell," I prodded.

Grace didn't need prodding. She was ready to tell the story.

"Walter Conroy was a wife-beater. He finally beat her to death, but that took several years, so Anita Conroy really died of a thousand cuts.

The Conroys lived in The Acre, but in one of the better homes up there. Walt came to Cordell to work in the wood mills, first as a saw man and then up from there. By the seventies, he'd become a foreman in one of the smaller mills here in town.

This Welshman was a lush. He was a regular at Ticket's, usually drinking until Owen shut him off and sent him home to Anita and their three children. Apparently, once he got there, he would abuse Anita in what became more and more violent ways. He punched her around so much that she wouldn't emerge from their home for days, helping this bum hide his little secret.

There were rumors of this—maybe suspicions, more than rumors—throughout The Acre. But Acre folks went public with very little. They had no political clout, no important ear to fill, very little involvement with the town proper. The Acre was its own little community. Residents shared with each other, but dirty linen was not hung about town.

Walt, being a foreman and all, had a foot in both labor and management camps. His job was slightly above the norm for The Acre. In fact, he supervised some of his neighbors. His job required him to deal with the bosses—the town heavyweights—on a face-to-face basis. Few in The Acre were going to accuse Walt of wife-beating and be subjected to reprisal from either Walt or their superiors. Anita Conroy was nobody's cause.

"Therefore, she suffered, in pained and isolated silence.

"Except for Owen.

"He knew the Conroys. Of course, Walt was in the bar all the time. Walt was always an angry man, quick to take offense, easy to get into an argument with. But Owen never had any real problem with him. He drank, he shot off his mouth, Owen red-flagged him, he obeyed Owen's direction to head on home, and he paid his bill.

"But Owen knew Anita, too. The Conroys lived near Brush Washington, who, incidentally, was sure of what was going on down the street. Anita was part of every worthy cause in the community—much better liked than her loud-mouthed husband. Owen worried about her when Brush, now sick and working only part-time at the bar, hinted that there was violence in that family.

"So, one day in the mid-seventies, Anita came into Ticket's in mid-morning, soon after Owen had opened. He told me later that she was such a sight that he hardly recognized her. Her face was a pulpous mass of red. Both arms had bandages, and she couldn't climb up on a stool. He led her over to a table, where she cried for five minutes before she could speak.

"'Is this what I think?' Owen asked.

"'He beats me,' she sobbed. 'All the time. After the kids go to bed. He leaves here, he comes home, ranting about something at work. Then he gets going about something I did or didn't do, and hollers about that. Then he starts throwing me against the wall, hitting me, cutting me with scissors, or his straightedge, or a broken plate. I'm going to die there.'

Here was the defining moment. What should Owen do? Does he get involved or not? Does he call the authorities, does he talk to Walt? Does he tell Anita to run? Whatever his thinking at the time, he curses himself for the choice he made.

I'll talk to Walt.' he offered. 'Is that what you want me to do? If you won't go to the police, how can I?' Owen was feeling guilty about his role in all this—he allowed Walt to stupefy himself at Ticket's, didn't he? His judgment of what might be best for Anita was clouded.

Owen told me this later: 'When the choice was between me and Anita—what was best for each—I chose me. I really didn't want to get involved. An ear and shoulder were all I really gave her. I told her how sorry I was, and that she ought to see a doctor. I let her leave the same way she came in… with no hope.'

Two days later, Owen spoke to Walt when he came into the bar.

Three days later, Anita was dead.

Walt simply went too far this time—the thousandth cut, I guess. Anita was dead before her neighbors could get her up to The Dalles. Walt remains in jail. Owen testified, guilt-stricken. It was the only time ever that he came to me to tell me something, rather than waiting to be asked. 'I knew,' he said. 'I talked to Walt. I didn't do enough. I didn't do anything. If I did, I only made it worse. And I sold Walt all that beer.'

He lives with that self-reprisal to this day. My poor Owen."

Grace was starting to wear down. It was time for me to take my leave.

A warm embrace, a promise to sign her copy of the book. I left. I already feared the look in Owen's eye when he read the book. He wasn't going to be happy about parts of it.

But Grace had shown me something. Truly, flowers leave some of their fragrance on the hands that bestow them.

CHAPTER TWENTY-TWO

The Courting Of Constanze Osterhagen

"**H**ow'd that go?" Owen asked when I returned to Ticket's after the dinner hour.

"What a lady," "everything you said, and more. A lovely time; a story or two."

"Did you talk about me?" Owen looked at me suspiciously.

I'd just finished a tale about unrequited love. I needed to offer up a story for Owen. He'd been a good sport about not trading stories one-for-one. He seemed to like this one. In fact, I briefly thought I might've nudged him into a story about Rita Norwood—or Grace Campbell, for that matter. If he was thinking about them, he chose not to be forthcoming.

Instead, "Ah, love," he sighed theatrically. "That was my grandfather's generalized explanation for the otherwise uncharacteristic behaviors of the love-smitten.

So, love is our topic, then. Luckily, I have a love story for you. My father particularly liked to tell it, coming in on the tail end of it, as he did. You see, it actually began during the Noah reign."

"Owen, please warm this coffee, and let's sail into the Sea of Love," I requested.

This story involves one woman and two men—a love triangle, maybe, maybe not—you decide.

The woman was Constanze Osterhagen, Ticket's cook… she called herself chef… for about thirty years. Now this story goes nowhere unless you know something about Constanze—Connie.

Noah hired Connie as Ticket's first cook not too long after he opened. Noah soon realized that drinkers got hungry. Ranchers and Acreites—I just made that word up, Smart Boy—often came in for their only real meal of the day. They wanted food, and if Ticket's didn't serve it, they were going to go somewhere else to get it. So Noah acquired the necessary equipment and stuck it in that corner there. He looked about and found Connie to use it.

Constanze Osterhagen was a young gal of German extraction. Lived with her parents two blocks away, her dad being an engineer on the railroad. Her mother taught Connie, at an early age, how to cook, knowing that it was a skill valued by men shopping for a wife.

Cooking was Connie's allure. She wasn't of great pulchritude. She was very plain-looking, and was pretty rough around the edges, if you know what I mean. Connie was big-boned and fleshy. Not fat, mind you, but bulky, sturdy, fifteen degrees north of 'voluptuous.' She was physically larger than many a man in town. Ratty brown hair, brushed straight back, revealing a flat face, wide cheeks, pug nose, and sallow complexion.

Throughout her early life, no one would've considered her a catch. Her teen years ended without dating. She worked in Prinder's for a while, hidden in the kitchen, making strudels for the dinner crowd. Wherever she went, she went unnoticed.

But she could cook. Noah observed that fact and hired her away from Prinder's with three promises: One, he'd pay her more. Two, she'd run the entire food service. And three, she'd have the opportunity to meet a man.

Connie liked all three ideas, but had no illusions about the third. Now in her early twenties, she'd come to grips with her lot in life. She didn't appeal to men. She knew she looked nothing like those girls in the Montgomery Ward catalog. She knew she lacked social grace and charm.

But self-pity was not her style. Beauty and charm were overrated, she conveniently decided. Her natural compensation for lacking both was an assertive, in-your-face, tough-edged personality.

She could handle her end of any conversation. That appealed to Noah, likely as it was that she'd be the only female in the bar at any given time. Noah didn't want to worry about how his cook could handle flirtations, hard language, unseemly behavior, and complaints.

Clearly, Connie could hold her own in a room full of high testosterone and alcohol. In fact, Connie necessarily received the Noah presentation on swearing. Took her awhile to master such restraint.

Connie became a crowd favorite for these very reasons. Few could best her in social banter or barbed responses. Old Sean O'Brian used to say that Connie was the type of gal who'd pour water on a drowning man. She was spirited, and she ruled her corner of the bar with an iron fist. Even Noah didn't attempt to tell her what to do, or when.

So, from early on, until about 1940, Connie prepared lunch and dinner in Ticket's. Only a few choices a day, but good, hearty food. Connie's rotating menu offered stick-to-ribs platters—as you'd call them—to Ticket drinkers.

Of course, her specialties were German: beef stew, pork and sauerkraut, hash, and casseroles heavy on the noodles. But she'd churn up liver and onions, meat loaf, vegetable soup… always vegetable soup… pot pie, spaghetti, too. Fish, if someone brought in some fresh catch. Mostly two-scoop affairs that were served easily, garnished with a half of tomato or a wedge of lettuce, a slice of carrot or celery. She kept a few steaks in the place, but would only fry one up for a customer if she wasn't busy, or if she felt like it. She boiled up eggs, and pickled some, for two big glass bottles on the bar top.

She'd come in to cook a few burgers or cube steaks for the lunch crowd, and then mix up the big pot for the evening's offering. She'd usually go home in the afternoon, returning for the dinner group.

Her custom was to make two pies at home, twice a week, the same thing—shoo-fly, apple, huckleberry, or other seasonal fruit. When they were gone, they were gone; four pies a week was her limit. She'd often make up a sheet cake, usually white or chocolate, with the opposite icing, and serve that until it expired.

This all worked really well for both Noah and Connie until she fell in love. With Ken Jackson or Billy Bechtel? Well, one or both, really—only God knows. What we do know is that Kenneth Jackson and William Bechtel stopped into Ticket's for a beer one day, and things weren't same for the next decade, maybe longer.

The whole thing started harmlessly enough. These two would come into the bar for a beer and dinner. As many in the bar did, they'd tease Connie—Billy naturally leading the assault—about her food, her good looks, and her charming demeanor.

Connie would respond in kind, throwing back one surly insult after another. A stranger would think they all despised each other, but it was all in good fun.

While both men were seeking female companionship, they agreed that no other girl in town had Connie's spunk, Connie's wife-worthy skills, or her genuine, raw nature.

One thing always leads to another. Noah watched as the two ranchers showed up more and more often. He noticed the verbal games increasingly turn into outright flirting, and that Connie was softening her usual gritty responses. And Noah knew Connie was, for the first time, struggling with the attention and the odd sensation of romance. He thought about offering some fatherly advice, but, he said later, he had no dog in the fight.

Ken and Billy had met during the Spanish-American War in 1898. Helped push Gattling guns horse carts with up San Juan Hill, with Teddy Roosevelt. Each always claimed that he'd saved the other man's life. Their different and varied versions of the story made it impossible to know.

Whichever way it really went, a permanent friendship was formed. Joined at the hip, they were. It was, to everyone else, a strange relationship, because they couldn't have been more different.

Ken was a bit older than Billy, maybe by five years. Shoot, Billy had just been a kid in Cuba; maybe seventeen or eighteen. After the war, Ken came back home to homestead a one-hundred-acre sheep ranch, near where his parents lived. Billy, having no particular place to go for any particular reason, decided he'd come to Cordell and help Ken get started.

Ken Jackson was the son of a rancher. He knew ranching. His future was ranching. He was a country boy, born and bred. Ken was rugged, single-minded, and hard-working. He was reliable and at ease with himself. He was good-looking, even with his short and getting-ready-to-thin hair. My father, years after Ken's death, said that the Marlboro Man in those cigarette commercials was cut from Ken Jackson cloth. He was robust, muscular, and manly in his plaid wool shirts, canvas coat, and boots.

Quiet for sure, Ken was measured in all things. He was a conservative, but with an air of masculinity and confidence… except when it came to the ladies. Ken was shy—reserved, you might say—around women. Very laid-back, not particularly engaging. Even with that, though, he had a sly, perceptive humor which elevated any conversation. People liked Ken Jackson.

Billy was none of that. He had no roots. Raised by parents we'd now call hippies, he was a footloose, fancy-free rogue with no commitments, no sense of responsibility, and no restraint. More youthful than his friend, Billy sought excitement, adventure, and immediate gratification. Life was a lark to him.

He was irresponsible. He had no interest in shaping a future, he was simply looking forward to it. He was fascinated by airplanes and had flown several, recklessly barnstorming the high country. This after pulling fish on the commercial ships of the Great Lakes, and mining silver in Nevada before the war. He was a young lad for all this, but thrill-seeking always appealed to his free spirit. Drank to excess, given any opportunity to do so.

Much smaller of build than his friend, Billy tossed about his thick, black hair, which fell over his face and neck. Billy was a pretty boy. He was loud and brash, engaging everyone with easy humor and animated gestures. Loved to laugh and joke. Ken often referred to Billy as 'Little Teddy.' That boy, he said, could talk paint off a park bench.

The men offered totally different futures. Ken was stable. He was of safety. He owned land, he had a business, he was making money, and he was kind and clever. Quiet, though… uninspiring, and a bit close with a dollar. A future with him would be predictable, but secure… loving, but not exciting… comfortable, if not adventurous.

Billy was everything else. He offered a future of uncertainty. He exuded danger. Obviously, he would go where the wind blew. He owned little, and he cared little about things. Money was for spending. Billy was spur-of-the-moment. For Billy, life was an adventure, his next landing being wherever and whatever. Stability was a joke to him. Women loved him, and that would always be a problem.

Knowing all this didn't help poor Connie. There was one thing for certain: Constanze Osterhagen loved them both. Of this, there can be no question. These opposites, taken as a pair, were perfect. But one? During the next year or so, Connie faced a paralyzing conundrum.

But Connie brought no experience to the sweet agony of love. Heretofore, love was found only in dime novels. Men had never attempted to impress her or to openly court her. She didn't know how to be coy, or how to be pursued by a man, or how to choose a life partner. Suddenly, not one, but two men, at the same time, were clearly interested in her. Two men, opposites for sure, offered her vying futures. For a gal who never had one man paying attention to her, two were just overwhelming.

She decided on a first and easy step… she began some self-renewal. She visited what passed for a beauty shop in The Acre, allowing Agnes Strange to coif her hair. She started a diet, giving up the draft or two she usually enjoyed before heading home for the day. She experimented with rouge and eye makeup… all with good results.

Billy began making more and more comments about her appearance, with Ken murmuring assent. She was beginning to feel, if not beautiful, at least attractive.

She was becoming more of a prize, but her personal improvements were not helping her select a front-runner. Truly, Connie was equally attracted to both men, for obviously different reasons.

Her plight changed Connie's demeanor. She kept up the lively banter with Noah's regulars; she was the same old Connie, exchanging insults, ladling out food and sarcasm, tending to the business of Ticket's.

But when Ken and Billy seated themselves across from the food nook, she turned from Wicked Witch of the West to the fairy princess. Connie's strident repartee shifted to feminine, more bashful responses. The blushing role of poor-little-pretty-ol' me.

Now the brittle German cook was demure, timid, vulnerable. Just that quick, the bawdy, witty chef turned enchanting—enchanting as a rookie at the role can be.

Meanwhile, Ken and Billy were fawning over her with appreciation or praise. The insults about the stew of the day were replaced with praise. All three were playacting in unaccustomed roles, foreign to themselves and everyone else in the place. You know, Ed, I think the line between friendship and romance is not a line at all. It's a chasm."

"A gaping one, Owen." I was trying to open that door again, to the Grace-Rebecca-Owen relationships, but Owen didn't bite. He looked away for a second, then resumed his story.

"So it began. Ken would supply an awkwardly-worded compliment; Billy a poem. One agreed to replace the front porch on her parent's house, the other would start before his rival could get organized.

Valentine's Day was a study of one-upmanship. One would bestow a dozen roses, the other, dinner at the hotel. Christmas was just over the top—bracelets, rings, a new dress, tickets to the theatre in Portland—all of that. It was fun to watch. Noah used to laugh out loud about it. 'Ah, love,' he'd intone. 'I should be selling tickets to Ticket's Opera House.'

As this run for the roses became increasingly apparent to everyone in Ticket's, other regulars actually started placing bets on which man Connie would finally choose. They'd joke about the two Connies they now watched, the witch and the waif. 'Connie, here come your heroes… better shape up.' 'Hey, Ken, tell Connie to settle down and get me some stew.' Hey, Billy, Connie's been waiting for you all afternoon.' 'Connie, get out your girly face… Ken and Billy are here.' 'Hey, Connie, which one of them gets that last piece of pie?'

Unbeknownst to Connie, the two men confronted the situation, which had started out in good fun. Neither was stupid. Both knew Connie was getting serious, in one or the other's direction.

While draining a bottle of rye whiskey at the ranch one night, each admitted to strong feelings for Connie. The marriage card was laid. What had begun as a game—a friendly rivalry—was now on the table. Certainly, Connie liked them both, but it was unfair to her to force her hand. It was, apparently, a moment of truth.

It was Billy who gave way. 'You'd make Connie a better husband than I, Ken,' he said. 'You're marrying material; I'm not; too wild and too self-centered for all that. I'm going to back off. I won't compete with my best friend for the love of a woman. I'll do whatever I can to help you win Connie's affection. You big, clumsy oaf, you get that girl to marry you.'

Compared to Billy's charm, Ken felt inadequate to the task. 'I'd appreciate that, long as she wants me, and not you.'

So, the two had reached an agreement. Connie was to be Ken's, if he could close the deal. But Connie was never to be told… Billy insisted on that. 'Let's never let her think that I didn't want her. We won't do that to her; no need to pain her with rejection by anyone.'

Both men agreed that it would be difficult. The damage had already been done. Connie was attracted to both men. Both men knew Connie's mental anguish of picking a winner, believing, as she did, that both were in play. Billy promised to handle it.

To the graves of all, Connie never knew of this agreement.

So, Billy toned down his flirtations and abandoned the compliments and come-ons. In fact, he tried to make himself look like a bad catch for any woman, especially one as virginal and conservative as Connie.

He attacked his own character: 'You know, Connie, I spent most of my money on girls and alcohol; I wasted the rest.' His contributions to most interchanges now included Ken. Clever Ken. 'Ken's correct when he…' 'This Ken, he'd be quite the catch.'

Billy thought he was conceding the match very tactfully, so well-disguised that Connie would never notice.

But, naïve as she might have been in matters of love, Connie was perceptive. Her heart was on her sleeve. Nary a word, intended thought, or body language slipped by her. If experience is a great teacher, love is a quick one. While she knew nothing of the whiskey pact, she sensed Billy's retreat, the subtle differences in his behavior.

She noticed that it was Billy who arranged the first date for Ken and Connie. When the Valentine's Dance down at the fire hall approached, Billy suggested that Ken take Connie. Lovable Ken couldn't seem to get up the nerve to ask her himself. It was at Billy's urging that Connie and Ken went to the annual Cordell town picnic.

At first, she wondered if she'd angered or hurt him in some way. Typical, isn't it, that she'd initially blame herself? But she saw clues that led her in another direction.

Billy's decreasing fervor and ardor toward her was more abrupt than either man might've thought. She found Billy's buttressing of Ken's virtues too convenient, too sudden, and too obvious.

But you can't un-ring a bell. Connie had strong feelings for Billy, and the increasingly apparent waning of Billy's affection saddened her. Surely, it would make her decision easier, but the fact remained that she loved Billy.

Whether he was giving way to his closest friend or had become disenchanted with her didn't really matter. As a lover or potential husband, Billy was exiting the picture. That was the bad news. The good news was that Ken Jackson was a great admirer in his own right. She loved him, no question. Too shy, yes… not as exciting as Billy… but considerate, steady, and honest.

Connie spent weeks building some acceptance of this change. She battled her own emotions to shape a new view of the three-way friendship. She slowly came to accept that her love must be directed to Ken. She needed to love Billy as only the closest of friends or siblings. Without a word about her own turmoil, she attempted to play her role in the new boundaries.

Difficult. Forced is forced. Force undermines real commitment.

Meanwhile, Billy kept harping on Ken to pull the trigger, if you will. 'You know what, you idiot? If it weren't for me, you'd never have a date with that girl. Ken, you need to step up if you expect to win Connie. I think she'd have you, but you have to make a move. Thank God I'm around. I plan everything for you two.

You know what? Without me, no you and Connie. You know what? You know what my job is? You know how when you solder something, you use flux to make a successful union of the metals? I'm like flux for you two—that's me. I have to do everything to get you two together. Get with it, my man. Start taking control.'

Not an easy task for the reserved and reticent Ken Jackson. But he kept trying, following the kid's leads as best he could.

And here's Noah, watching all this unfold. He was, at first, pleased that Connie was developing a love life, never mind with whom. Then he, too, observed the change in all three, as the game went from rivalry to Billy's letting loose.

He tried to talk with Connie throughout these unravelings, but Connie, for all her bluster, was hesitant to discuss her love life with anyone. Noah also realized he was running a bar here, not a match-making business. Finally, he decided his only role could be that of support for his cook. I think he did his best at that."

"And so, Owen, which did she select?" I inquired.

"As it turned out, she didn't have to select."

"Why?"

"World War I—then called the Great War."

"Let me guess," I broke in. "The two friends went off to the military again?"

Owen shrugged. "You're half right. Billy joined up; Ken didn't. Ken had had enough war for one lifetime… disinclined, he'd say. And he was old for army enlistment. He wouldn't be included in any conscription plan. The country didn't need him anymore.

Besides, his attention was focused on the gal behind the counter. Then there was his sheep ranch, and all those obligations.

Billy was a bit old for the service, too. The US wasn't officially in the war yet, but everyone knew we'd soon do more than simply support our European friends. Billy couldn't resist the pending adventure, and wanted to be in the thick of it when it began. He was struck less by patriotism than by excitement.

He had a plan. He'd sign up with the army, get himself over the water, and get assigned to the RAF, which was already using aeroplanes. That's what they called them in those days—aeroplanes.

Of course, it would mean leaving his best friend, and a woman for whom he had deep feelings. But he also realized that his departure would clear the way for Ken. Billy could only hope that his buddy was up to closing the deal.

"They talked about it for a week or two, at the ranch and in Ticket's. But, really, Billy's mind was made up. If he could get in, he was going.

Connie was distraught, naturally. From the beginning conversations, she argued against the idea, cried for Billy, and entered an extended period of silence, half anger and half fear.

All this had Billy feeling badly, but he'd made his decision about the pursuit of Miss Osterhagen. He hoped she'd come to terms with his leaving and fall into Ken's slightly-open arms. If Ken could come out of his slow dance and offer marriage, things would work out just fine. They'd be happy together, and Billy would return to be the best man.

A change would also release him from the current charade he'd been conducting with Constanze. Simply better for everyone.

"Getting back in the army was easy for Billy. Charmer that he was, he simply talked his way through his own plan. Remember, Billy could've sold ice to Eskimos. He told the army that he was a Rough Rider with battle experience, said he'd already flown aeroplanes, and that he could teach others. No family obligations, he said—the army needed a man just like him.

However he did it, he not only was permitted to enlist, he was soon a pilot, assigned to the RAF, just as he'd planned. Off he went to Europe.

Billy made quite a name for himself over on the Continent. Early on, he was known as one of the most vicious and risk-taking pilots in the air. He showed the same brashness and self-confidence… he was fearless. He had many kills. The German fliers in those nasty Fokkers knew him as a threat. He flew beside ace pilot Roland Garros, the flying Frenchman, and, later, Eddie Rickenbacker, the most famous American pilot of the war.

The Brits loved him. When America entered the fray, Billy was reassigned to one of our units, bringing along both skill and reputation.

He was really happy. He loved flying and, apparently, the thrill of aerial combat. In one note home, he wrote that he wanted fly for the rest of his life.

"Did he come back to Cordell after the war?" I asked.

"Couldn't. One day over France, he became one of the Red Baron's eighty kills. Billy had written his own prophecy: he flew aeroplanes for the rest of his life. The young von Richthofen finally got Billy's measure. Billy's name is the first of fallen Cordell soldiers on a big plaque hanging in the municipal building."

"Oh no!" I exclaimed. "That must have been devastating to Connie! And Ken, too."

"Certainly. They suffered the same agony as any family who lost someone. Deep mourning, no smiles, listless at the grill and the ranch. But time heals things, and life goes on."

"So, did Connie and Ken ever get together?" I asked.

"Yeah, sometime after Billy left. Ken finally asserted himself enough to ask Connie for her hand in marriage. I'm sure she had to encourage him, but they got it done.

Connie joined Ken on the ranch, but kept her job here in the bar. Their sheep business was good, but they needed the ready cash, especially during the Depression. They had two sons, both college boys. They lived the American Dream, as the times allowed for it, but with a hole in it. A deep hole with a heavy, black, but unspoken, question lying at the bottom. If Connie'd had to choose, if Billy had returned and forsaken the whiskey agreement, which man, which life would she have chosen?

The question gnawed at Ken for the rest of his life. It wasn't about whether or not Connie loved him—of that, he was sure. But what if Billy were still in the picture? Worse—and what bothered him most— was that he was also sure that Connie could never answer those questions. He never asked them.

Connie carried the same questions. If things had been different, what would she have done? Loving both men, she knew only how fate had made her decision for her. Not knowing about the whiskey agreement, she often thought about what life might've been with the adventurous Billy. But she had no answer to that, and while she knew it bothered Ken, she never broached the subject with him.

But, again, even with that nagging proposition, Ken and Connie forged a loving, if subdued and predictable union. Number Two or not, Ken got his girl. Connie had found love in her life—two, actually—and considered herself lucky for that.

Years later, my dad heard Noah tell this story often. It was really George who kept the tale alive. Easy enough to do, because Connie was Ticket's cook for several years after he took over the place.

George and Connie had a great friendship. She continued to chef for him when the bar was at its peak. Only George could tell the story in Connie's presence (never in Ken's.) He loved reminding the lady that she, too, had had a love life. And, I think, he helped her keep Billy's spirit alive in her. Connie seemed good about that.

I met Connie when I was a kid, starting to work in the bar. Now gray-haired, Connie ran the place as if she were the queen. Right back to the gritty, self-confident, hard-nose she originally was.

I remember her as Connie Jackson, a kindly lady who cooked good food."

CHAPTER TWENTY-THREE

Naomi Uses Her One-Way Ticket

It was my last day in Cordell. I had a ticket for an afternoon flight.

We were about finished with storytelling. It was time to start writing. I am sure that was more on my than Owen's, but when he slumped down in the booth of Friendly's for a goodbye breakfast, I knew something was really off.

He's sorry to see my go, I thought.

He dashed that flight of fancy right away. "I got a call last night. Naomi Griser died yesterday."

"Who?"

"Naomi Griser. I've mentioned her before—Naomi Cordell, the twin sister of Merrilee, the rape victim. Married Alvin Griser way back when. Well, she died... been sickly for some time. I mean, she was ninety-three, or something like that... no big surprise. Still, her demise ends an era. There are no more Cordells. Franklin, Charles, Kingsley, Merrilee, and now Naomi. Everyone else on the nameplate of this town is now gone."

Owen was exhibiting more reaction than I expected. After all, the Cordells and Tickets had never been close.

We ordered, and Owen began to fill in the blanks.

"Remember that Naomi was one of four people who knew the rapist. That number includes my father, who found out years later. Well, and me, so that's really five. Both the twins could reasonably guess that my dad told me. Naomi certainly assumed that when she visited me. She assumed that I knew.

Merrilee's rapist disappeared, so who knows if Jeremy Lansome is still kicking? George is dead. Merrilee left town and died some years ago. So, until yesterday, just Naomi and me.

Naomi stayed in Cordell… lived with the truth, and was truly trapped by it. Her knowledge of what really happened was a burden to her. She regretted her own role in the sham seduction of Jeremy Lansome, her failure to tell the truth at the time, and her support of her sister's version of the event that raised everyone's suspicion of David Witherspoon.

She dealt with that by marrying beneath her station and living a middle-class lifestyle that buried her in a modest, single-story home downtown. Hers was a loveless, childless—probably sexless—marriage to Alvin Griser, an accountant at the largest granary in town. Alvin was a small, timid fellow in a short-sleeved shirt and a tie, with a pencil in his pocket protector and horned-rimmed glasses. A perfect provider, but a wimp of a guy. Naomi married him, some of us think, to forsake her storied family ties."

Owen paused. He gazed out the window. "And now I have to do something for the Cordells… an illogical predicament, since neither family had much truck with the other. I'm feeling a bit odd about it."

"What the hell are you talking about, Owen?" I demanded. "Naomi's death affects you how?"

Coffee arrived. Omelets soon after. Owen reached in his pocket and pulled out an envelope. "Naomi came to visit me, back in 1985— that's the date on the letter. Read it."

I took the proffered letter. It, and the copy I received later from Owen, read:

> *November 14, 1985*
>
> *Mr. Ticket,*
>
> *Thank you for your willingness to hold this authorization until the first of our deaths, and for your agreement to see that our wishes herein are fulfilled.*
>
> *I, Naomi Cordell Griser, and I, Charlotte S. Witherspoon, hereby name Owen Ticket as the executor of the estates of both of us, and that of Robert Witherspoon, a brother, for whom Charlotte holds power of attorney.*

As provided for in both our wills, Mr. Ticket, named here and in our three wills as the executor of our estates, is singularly charged with the distribution of our joined assets in line with the appropriate clauses in the Cordell-Witherspoon Foundation, as set forth in each will.

The mission of the Foundation will be to serve the community of Cordell in any way that Mr. Ticket agrees is of direct benefit to a sizable portion of the community residents.

These funds are provided by the only existing members of both families.

It is our wish that both the establishment of this foundation and the dedicated expenditure of these two estates remind the current Cordell population of the significant and founding roles of both families in our community by the Deschutes.

Several administrative details of the Cordell-Witherspoon Foundation are found in codicils in all three wills. Anything uncovered will be at the discretion of Mr. Owen Ticket.

Signed: Naomi Cordell Griser

Charlotte S. Witherspoon

Date: November 3, 1985

Witnessed by, attested to, and cc on file: Milo J. Borgan,

Attorney at Law, Date: 11-3-85

"Owen, your stock just went up in this town. People are going to politic you for the money," I said sarcastically. "Did you know about this when Naomi came to see you?"

"Guessed most of it, given her comments."

"Tell me about that meeting," I requested.

"Naomi came to my bar back then and gave me this sealed envelope. She asked me for the only favor a Cordell ever asked a Ticket. In fact, that's exactly how she said it.

"'I ask that you keep this until I die, Mr. Ticket. Or Charlotte Witherspoon, if she goes first. Please see our request through. We both have wills with the attorney Borgan, and this special request is referenced in them. Borgan knows our plans, but I want you to be aware of, and agree to, our wishes."

"'Might I ask what you're thinking, Naomi?' I asked.

"'I'm thinking, Mr. Ticket, that I want to use my death to square a couple of things. First, I want to put to rest the long-term animosity between my family and the Witherspoons. Now, Charlotte Witherspoon, and Bob—God help him—and I are the only ones left. Charlotte and I agree that neither of us wants to go to our graves thinking that the age-old feud between the families was never settled. I know that few people in town these days even know of those cantankerous days. But we do, and you do.

Second, I want my family to give back to the community the profits that made us rich. Third, I want to make as right as I can some decisions I made as a teenager, which I've regretted all of my life.

Basically, this document charges you with establishing a foundation—Borgan has it listed as the Cordell-Witherspoon Trust—naming you as the executor. All my assets, and those of Charlotte and Bob, upon their deaths, go into the trust, minus last expenses.

Charlotte, who also signed the paper you're holding, and I make clear the intended use of our funds. However, both our wills also stipulate that Owen Ticket, our executor, must agree to every expense town council makes regarding this money—before one red cent is spent.'

"'Why me, Naomi?' I asked. 'The Tickets and Cordells have never been close.'

"'Because everyone in Cordell knows the Ticket family. The reputation of the Tickets crosses three generations. People have more respect for the Tickets than they do the Cordells or the Witherspoons.

My daddy always envied the sway that you Tickets had in Cordell. Franklin used to say, "Those damned Tickets. They lead public opinion in this town. People think what the Tickets think. You need a Ticket if you want to get something done around here. Why is that?"'

"I smiled. 'Too much credit,' I responded.

"'Please, Mr. Ticket. Don't be humble. Your bar was the crossroads of Cordell. Public opinion about my family and the Witherspoons started here, and everyone knew it. How Ticket's went dictated how The Acre went, how the downtown neighborhood went, how the people went. No Tickets, no deal. Let's not argue this.

"'So why not the only Ticket left to handle the conclusion of all those early years? Charlotte and I would be proud to have you represent us when we can't do it ourselves.'

"'How much money are we talking about here, Naomi?' I asked.

"'Combined with the Witherspoons', maybe a million dollars.

"'Let me explain. I received a one-third share of inheritance, with Charles and Merrilee, after my father's death. I also had a special fund that my daddy set up for me when I married Alvin.

"'Franklin was not at all pleased with my choice of mate. He believed I was marrying down, just to spite the Cordell name, and to slide into anonymity. At the time, remember, Mr. Ticket, the Cordells and Witherspoons were caught up in all that feuding… and there was the Merrilee scandal, and the waning Cordell influence about town. He thought all of that was why I'd settle for Alvin Griser.

"'He may have been mostly correct. I told him I loved Alvin, but I wasn't that sure when I said it, or that I believe it now. I think I just wanted to get away from the shame, the bickering, and the lying over the Merrilee mess.

My support of Merrilee's damning story about her attacker probably being David Witherspoon was a load for me. I knew better—she told me herself—and I was actually part of the torment of Jeremy Lansome. Of course my parents jumped all over the David Witherspoon probability, and we girls let them. The Witherspoons suffered from our insinuations; David especially.

I wanted out. Merrilee took her own route; she left. And there was sweet, gentle Alvin for me.

Daddy was angry, and he was fearful for my future happiness as a common Cordellian, not a powerful member of the royal family.

There might've been some favoritism there, also. I was Franklin's only unsullied child. Merrilee was stained by the rape, and Charles the Meek was destined to make a mockery of Cordell Real Estate and Insurance.

So, as he later told me, Daddy hedged his bet. He set up an account for me in The Dalles First National Bank. He deposited $200,000 in my name—in case. He told me not to tell Merrilee or Charles about the money. 'Just save it,' he said, 'in case of a rainy day.'

I've never used that money, so that money is added to my inheritance share from Franklin, and to whatever the Witherspoon estate is finally worth, and you have a sizable sum.

Who knows when the three of us will pass? Between now and then, the whole thing is earning interest. To whom should Charlotte and I give it? Neither of us has any heirs.

Surely very few townspeople have any knowledge of the old falling out between our families. So, this isn't about clearing family names… names that have long lost their importance. But I, as a Cordell, and Charlotte Witherspoon have not forgotten. And you, the last of the damned Tickets, too.

Let's put it all to rest,' she concluded. 'Let's do something good for a town that bears my father's name, represents the very best of both families, and provides a community service along the way. So, Mr. Ticket, will you help us with this?'

"No one can say no to a lady of clear mind and resolve. And I, as she said, knew her family history better than most. A Cordell or not, Naomi deserved some fulfillment of last wishes. We were talking last chapters here. So, I've kept this letter in my safe upstairs for twenty-some years."

We ate our omelets, Patty the waitress warmed our coffee cups, and in doing so, patted Owen on the shoulder. Both smiled. Owen leaned against the booth back and looked over at me.

"So, Owen, the two families made their separate peace," I observed.

Owen was coaxing a square of omelet onto a piece of toast.

"Yep. And I guess I'm the only one left who gives a rat's kneecaps. A feud that died out years ago is officially defused by the remaining combatants. No one else in town will care until we start flashing about a million dollars."

We sat in silence for a minute or two.

Then Owen spoke, with a faraway voice, "You know what? I've been thinking about this all night. I probably ought to do the same thing as Naomi and Charlotte did—just add the Ticket balance to the town's coffers when I'm gone… put it all in the Cordell-Witherspoon Trust."

"Owen, that sounds good," I told him. "But I'd think it ought to become the Cordell-Witherspoon-Ticket Trust. Your family deserves that."

"Maybe. I'll think about it—maybe see the attorney Borgan.

"So, what happens now for you and me?" Owen asked.

"I write the book," I replied. "You execute the will of Naomi Cordell, as you agreed to. Good thing I'm leaving; you're going to be busy. Later on, I share a galley proof with you. We make a few changes. I publish it. I get rich; you get to read the stories you told me. Sound fair to you?"

"Nothing less than I expected.

"Ed, let me say that I've enjoyed our time together," Owen said. "Felt good to tell some stories. Even better to hear yours."

"I'll be in touch, Owen," I responded. "Thank you. Let's have you there when we do the big launch. You'll be a hero by then… the man in charge of spending all that Cordell and Witherspoon money.

"Now I must leave. I want to take a few pictures about town, and on the way up through the high country.

"It's been a pleasure," I told him.

"Likewise," Owen said.

We parted.

ABOUT THE AUTHOR

Ed Frye has been writing all his adult life. Ticket To Oregon is his second novel, following his 2011 autobiographically-based, Fools and Children. Ed has also authored three textbooks used in colleges and high schools and more than two dozen articles published in numerous educational journals and popular magazines.

Dr. Edward T. Frye is a nationally known writer and speaker. For the last two decades he has worked in 36 states, addressing more than 77,000 program participants.

Prior to this work, Ed served as a school administrator in three Pennsylvania school districts for most of his 32 years in public education. His career titles include Executive Director, Assistant Superintendent, Coordinator of English and Federal Programs, and Director of Community Relations. Dr. Frye has been a part-time professor in two universities.

A native Pennsylvanian, Ed resides in Mechanicsburg, PA with his wife of fifty-five years, near his two daughters, and three grandchildren.

Ed is an avid racquetball player and a licensed pilot, flying a Cessna Cardinal for years.

Dr. Frye holds degrees from Lock Haven University, Temple University, and Penn State. His professional website offers a complete resume, a listing of his publications, photos, and client responses: www.fryedock.org.

www.ingramcontent.com/pod-product-compliance
Lightning Source LLC
Chambersburg PA
CBHW021145310726
48971CB00002B/485